COLLECTION

VOLUME
—2—

THE
Regency
COLLECTION

VOLUME
—2—

The Last Enchantment
by
Meg Alexander

Serena
by
Sylvia Andrew

*MILLS & BOON and MILLS & BOON with the Rose Device
are registered trademarks of the publisher.*

*First published in Great Britain 1999 by
Harlequin Mills & Boon Limited,
Eton House, 18–24 Paradise Road,
Richmond, Surrey, TW9 1SR.*

The Regency Collection © by Harlequin Enterprises II B.V. 1999

The publisher acknowledges the copyright holders of the
individual work as follows:

The Last Enchantment © Meg Alexander 1995
Serena © Sylvia Andrew 1994

ISBN 0 263 81708 3
106-9906

*Printed and bound in Spain
by Litografia Rosés S.A., Barcelona*

THE LAST ENCHANTMENT

by

Meg Alexander

Dear Reader

I hope you'll enjoy *The Last Enchantment*. This was the first of my Regency novels, written because I'd always been fascinated by the period. It was truly the age of elegance, in costume, furniture, learning, musical appreciation and a love of English life. Women had few rights, but this did not deter the stronger-minded.

Aurelia Carrington, the heroine of this book, is determined to save Caroline, her niece, from an enforced marriage to the terrifying Duke of Salterne. Aurelia and the Duke detest each other on sight, but he is not her only enemy. She has also to outwit her repellent brother-in-law, Caroline's father, who is set upon the marriage. Aurelia's efforts lead the female members of her family into mortal danger, but her strength of character helps her to win through, aided by the Duke. By this time she herself has fallen in love with him and he with her. Against the glittering background of the Prince Regent's court at Brighton they come to realise that each has misjudged the other's feelings. Their long battle of wills is resolved in mutual happiness.

Enjoy your reading.

Meg Alexander

After living in southern Spain for many years, **Meg Alexander** now lives in Kent, although having been born in Lancashire, she feels that her roots are in the north of England. Meg's career has encompassed a wide variety of roles, from professional cook to assistant director of a conference centre. She has always been a voracious reader, and loves to write. Other loves include history, cats, gardening, cooking and travel. She has a son and two grandchildren.

Other titles by the same author:

The Sweet Cheat
Farewell the Heart
His Lordship's Dilemma
Miranda's Masquerade
The Love Child*
The Merry Gentleman*
The Passionate Friends*

* linked

CHAPTER ONE

AURELIA was about to ring for candles when she heard the sound of carriage wheels. She looked up in surprise. Only the most foolhardy of travellers would venture on to the marshes in growing darkness. Whoever it was must have an urgent reason for their visit.

An emergency in the village? No, it could not be that. The messenger would have come on horseback, or on foot. It was doubtless a case of lost direction. Jacob would deal with it. She hesitated for only a moment. Then, with a sigh, she replaced the stoppers on the bottles in the still-room. Courtesy dictated that she should offer hospitality in that isolated spot. The batch of simples must wait. She rinsed her hands, smoothed her hair, and made her way to the Great Hall.

Her eyes widened as a small figure hurried towards her.

'Caro...my dear! I had not expected you...of all people.' Aurelia looked into a pair of swimming eyes.

Caroline launched herself into her aunt's arms. 'I've run away,' she sobbed. 'Please let me stay. I've nowhere else to go.'

Aurelia laid a soothing hand on the blonde head.

'You are chilled to the bone, my love.' She led the trembling girl towards the fire. 'Now, Caro, do compose yourself. Tell me what has happened.'

'They shall not drag me back. I'd rather die.' The

dramatic announcement preceded a fresh outburst of tears.

'Few things are worth dying for,' Aurelia observed drily. 'Suppose you begin at the beginning. . .'

Caroline was beyond such reasonable advice.

'I won't marry him! I won't! I don't care how deep Frederick is in debt. They shall not make me. . .'

'And who is it that you have refused to marry?' Aurelia realised that she would come at the gist of it only by a series of questions.

'Salterne, of course. He's old, and ugly, and I cannot bear him.'

Aurelia tried to hide her surprise. The Duke of Salterne was well-known, at least by reputation. Since he was a friend of the Prince Regent, and one of the wealthiest peers in England, it seemed unlikely, to say the least, that he had offered for a penniless and unsophisticated child like Caroline.

'Perhaps you are mistaken,' she suggested cautiously. 'Has he made his intentions clear?'

'It's all arranged.' The girl's voice was bitter. 'Father was only too happy to agree.'

'And your mother?' Aurelia spoke without much hope. If Ransome had made the bargain her sister would not dispute his wishes.

'She says. . .she says that I have no choice. Father's pockets are to let, and Frederick is in the hands of the money-lenders. If I don't marry Salterne he'll go to a debtor's prison.'

Caroline sank into a chair and began to sob as if her heart would break.

Aurelia flushed with anger. She had never liked her nephew, or his worthless father. She had never understood why her brilliant elder sister had married such a wastrel. Ransome was as handsome as Lucifer, but his wife had paid a heavy price for her infatuation. Her fortune had disappeared before her son was ten.

Aurelia had come to the rescue on more than one occasion, but last time she'd vowed that it must stop before her own inheritance went the way of Cassie's.

She turned her attention to the wilting figure of her niece.

'How did you come here, Caro? You did not drive alone from Surrey?'

'Richard brought me.' Caroline turned as a young man moved out of the shadows. His bow was graceful, but he was obviously ill at ease.

'What is the meaning of this?' Aurelia said stiffly. 'Do you make a habit of escorting young ladies about the countryside without the knowledge of their parents?'

The young man coloured, but he stood his ground. Before he could speak Caroline rushed towards him and took his hand.

'Richard loves me,' she cried. 'We hoped to marry but Father won't hear of it. Richard is a younger son . . .and his people. . .'

'Hush, Caro!' The words were gentle, but Caroline was silent as her companion spoke. 'I had not intended to intrude, ma'am, but Caroline would have me stay in case you refused to help her.'

'And if I do. . .?'

'I won't go back!' Caroline was on the verge of hysteria. She threw her arms about Richard's neck. 'Why would you not listen to me? I begged you to take me to London. We might have been married there tonight.'

Richard disengaged her gently. Then he looked at

Aurelia. 'It is true, Miss Carrington. We do love each other, but I thought it best to bring Caroline to you. She would not stay at home, you see. It seemed to be the only solution.'

Aurelia eyed him with sudden respect. 'Possibly,' she observed quietly. 'Yet you have taken a serious risk, young man. You realise that you might well be charged with abduction?'

'I wasn't abducted.' Caroline's face grew sullen. 'I should have run away whether Richard came with me or not. I told him so.'

'That was ill done of you, my dear. You have placed your friend in a dangerous position, though he has shown good sense in bringing you to me.' Aurelia turned to Richard. 'I suggest, sir, that you return home at once, before your absence is remarked.'

'No, no! Richard, you cannot leave me!' It was a wail of despair, which died away at the sight of Aurelia's expression.

'Caroline, you impress neither of us with your grasp of the situation. Please try not to make matters worse. Would you prefer to see your friend in the hands of the magistrates. . .?'

'No one knows we are here,' came the sulky reply.

'Someone does. . .or so it would appear. . .' Aurelia's quick ear had caught the sound of a horseman riding at full gallop. She walked over to the window. 'Our visitor has been travelling hard.'

Caroline ran to her side and gave a shriek of terror.

'It is Salterne! Richard, we must leave at once!'

'You will do no such thing! I will see the Duke. Now quickly, go upstairs to my sitting-room. You must stay out of sight until the Duke has gone. . .both of you.'

'You will not—you will not make me speak to him?' Caroline quavered. 'I do not wish to see him; indeed I could not bear it.'

'There will be no need for you to do so. Now please obey me.' Aurelia walked swiftly across the hall. 'I will see His Lordship in the library, Jacob.'

Richard Collinge hesitated, a mutinous look upon his face.

'I should prefer to face him, Miss Carrington.'

'And I prefer that you should not. Where is your common sense, young man? Think of Caroline's reputation.' She paused only to watch them hurry up the stairs, then she entered the library and closed the door behind her.

A moment later it was thrown open with a crash. Jacob was thrust aside as a giant of a man strode into the room. He was bespattered to the thighs in mud, and his face was dark with rage.

Aurelia's courage almost failed her. As the Duke towered above her chair his presence seemed to fill the room. The well-cut riding coat and breeches served only to emphasise his massive chest and heavily muscled limbs, but it was his face which held her.

A long scar bisected his forehead, only partially hidden by a mass of black hair, trained in the fashionable 'Brutus' cut. It curved along his cheek, only faintly paler than the deeply tanned skin, and almost reached the corner of his mouth. As a pair of cold grey eyes stared into her own she made a conscious effort not to show her repugnance.

'A shock to you, ma'am? Don't trouble to deny it.' The full lips twisted in a sneer.

Aurelia coloured. 'I beg your pardon. I did not mean to. . .'

'To show your disgust? Spare me your apologies. I'm used to the effect of this pretty sight on impressionable females.'

Aurelia's temper flared. 'It might be less unpleasant, sir, if it were accompanied by good manners. I do not know you, yet you enter my home unannounced, treat my servant roughly, and use me with scant courtesy. You will try for some conduct, if you please.'

'Don't trifle with me, ma'am.' He took a step towards her. 'You know who I am. That chit must have left you in no doubt——'

'You cannot be referring to my niece.' Aurelia's tone was icy. 'I see now why your suit has prospered. Such charm, Your Grace! It cannot fail to win all hearts.'

He stared at her. The sharp set-down appeared to have robbed him of speech. His brows came together in a frown.

'Since you will have it, then, let us preserve the amenities. Allow me to introduce myself. My name is Salterne. I take it that I am addressing Miss Carrington?'

Aurelia inclined her head.

'Your servant, ma'am!'

'Now that I should never have guessed,' Aurelia murmured.

In spite of herself her lips twitched, and he looked at her suspiciously.

'You will not insult my intelligence by attempting to deny that your niece is here,' he continued. 'I must see her at once.'

Aurelia gave him her sweetest smile. 'That will not be possible, Your Grace. My niece is exhausted and has retired to her room.'

A muscle twitched in his jaw.

'Yet I will see her.' His voice was soft with menace. 'Together with her paramour.'

Aurelia stiffened. 'You will not attempt to browbeat me, if you please. You have had your answer, sir. I think you had best leave.'

'Really?' He bent down until his face was close to hers. 'Madam, I have been on the road all day. I have not come so far to find myself denied.'

Aurelia yawned and reached out for the bell. 'I find your energy fatiguing, my lord. Will you sit down? Some refreshment, perhaps?'

He laughed then, and it was not a pleasant sound

'This is not a social call, Miss Carrington.' He did, however, spare a glance for his muddy boots and breeches.

'Then we shall not stand on ceremony. Pray do not trouble yourself about the mud. My nephews were used to romp about with no care for the furniture.'

His eyes glinted. 'A set-down, ma'am? You would seem to be mistress of the art.' He strolled over to the fire and rested an arm on the mantelshelf. Aurelia raised an eyebrow in pointed disapproval of his lack of courtesy, but she did not speak until Jacob entered the room.

'Canary wine, Your Grace, or a glass of orgeat?' She ignored Jacob's startled glance as she waited for the reply.

'Nothing, I thank you.' The Duke was well aware that he had been offered refreshment more suitable to feminine tastes, but his face was impassive.

'You know my errand, Miss Carrington. Your niece disappeared early this morning. I undertook to come in search of her.'

'That surely must be her father's part.'

'Ransome was—er—not available, ma'am.' For the first time His Lordship appeared to be nonplussed. 'I understand him to be in London. As Lady Ransome was so distressed, I undertook to come in search of Caroline.'

'Very noble of you,' Aurelia murmured smoothly.

The Duke's face darkened with anger. 'Her Ladyship felt that time was of the essence. It was—ah—necessary that she be found before nightfall.'

'I agree.' Aurelia gave him a limpid look. 'So dangerous for a young girl to travel in the dark. Thieves. . .footpads. . .so many hazards. . .'

'And one above all, Miss Carrington.'

'What can you mean?'

He gave her a mirthless smile. 'A good try, ma'am, but it will not serve. Your niece was not alone. She was without the means to pay for a seat on the stage, or to find lodgings. She must have had help. Her mother suspects——'

'My sister had always a vivid imagination,' Aurelia assured him. 'You may set your mind at rest, Your Grace. Caroline is quite unharmed. She arrived here not an hour ago. It was wrong of her to run off in a pet, but her mother had promised that she should visit me, and the young are so hasty. . .you must recall. . .'

'In the distant past, naturally.' Salterne glared at her. He was quieter now, and infinitely more dangerous. 'Would you care to explain how she found it possible to come so far alone?'

'Perhaps she is more resourceful than we suspected.'

'A family trait, no doubt.' He did not believe her

for a moment, but he could hardly accuse her of lying. 'May I see her?'

'I think not. I prefer that she should rest.'

'Then I will wait.' Salterne had recovered his self-possession, but his face was grim.

'I believe I asked you to leave, my lord.'

For answer he threw himself into a chair and looked into her eyes.

'Will you ask your servant to put me out?' he enquired.

In spite of her annoyance Aurelia found it hard to keep her countenance. The thought of frail old Jacob attempting to manhandle this provoking brute had its comic side. She strove for a severe expression, but her dancing eyes gave her away.

'Quite!' His Lordship murmured. 'You know, of course, that I have asked Caroline's father for her hand, and that he has agreed to the match?'

'And Caroline herself? What has she to say?'

'She is young.' The lines on the sombre face might have been etched in stone. 'She has not yet had time to weigh the advantages. I can give her all that a woman could want.'

'Then she is fortunate indeed.' The sarcasm was unmistakable, and a dark flush stained the Duke's face.

'Forgive me, ma'am, if I am at pains to point out that the matter is no concern of yours. Caroline must be guided by her parents.'

'You are mistaken, Your Grace. The welfare of my niece concerns me deeply. I intend to speak to my sister and her husband. . .'

'I see. May I know your objections?'

'Need you ask?' Aurelia was incensed by his peremptory warning not to interfere. 'Your age, your reputation. . . Do you wish me to go on?'

His Grace swung a booted leg in contemplation. 'Your brother-in-law sees no obstacle to our marriage.'

'He would not!' The hot blood rushed to Aurelia's cheeks. 'His own reputation is such that. . .' She caught herself up and averted her head. A long silence fell between them.

'Then if you will summon your niece, ma'am,' he said at last, 'I will take her home.'

'I have already told you——'

'I know what you told me, Miss Carrington, but I must insist. I was charged by your sister to bring Caroline back. Please don't try to gammon me further. I was not born yesterday.'

Aurelia was tempted to retort that so much was evident, but she controlled her temper with an effort.

'I could not permit it,' she announced. 'I have only your word on this betrothal, and it would be quite unseemly for my niece to travel unchaperoned with a . . .*gentleman*.' She stressed the word deliberately and was happy to see his lips tighten. 'It is out of the question. You came on horseback, did you not? How do you propose to convey her back again?'

'Perhaps by the carriage in which she arrived?' The hard grey eyes held her own, and the Duke gave an ironic laugh. 'I followed them, you see. They were not difficult to trace.'

Aurelia eyed him with acute dislike. She opened her mouth to speak, but there seemed little point in arguing further. He had known her to be lying from the first. Her face flamed.

She was saved from further humiliation by a disturbance in the hall. Then the door opened and her sister swept into the room.

'Caro is here?' Cassandra Ransome's face was ashen, and her eyes were bright with unshed tears.

'Of course she's here, Cass. Where else would she go?' Aurelia vented her irritation sharply.

'Thank heavens!' Cassie sank into a chair. 'Then we've found her in time.' She looked at her prospective son-in-law. 'Salterne, what can I say?'

'The less said the better, I should think!' Aurelia's voice was tart. 'You seem to have some wild idea that Caro was eloping. If so, why would she come to me? You didn't really believe it, did you, Cass? Otherwise you would have made for London.'

Cassandra looked bewildered.

'This was the first place I thought of. . .'

'Of course it was. You had promised her a visit. I am surprised at you.' Aurelia was careful to avoid the Duke's penetrating glance.

'We appear to have drawn the wrong conclusions, madam.' His ironic tone caught Aurelia on the raw. 'I beg your pardon for this intrusion. Now that I know my bride-to-be is safe I will take my leave of you. Your servant, ladies.' He bowed and strode towards the door.

'Salterne, I beg of you. . .do not attempt the marshes in darkness. It is suicide. Aurelia will tell you. . .' Cassie's face puckered in dismay. 'You must stay. . .at least until morning.'

Aurelia gave her sister a speaking look. Of all things to suggest! She prayed he would refuse. The thought of dining in a country mansion with two women who were scarely known to him would doubtless promise intolerable boredom. She gave him a limpid smile.

'Much as I should wish to offer hospitality, I fear that it is not possible. It would not be correct. Three women alone in the house but for the servants. . .'

'Oh, Lia, what a goose you are! You could not believe that I travelled here alone. Frederick will act as host.'

Aurelia's spirits sank. Her nephew was no favourite of hers. On his last visit he had been ordered from the house after an unfortunate incident with one of the maids.

His Grace was enjoying her discomfiture.

'We. . .we are not prepared for guests,' she said with resolution. If she could suggest that the beds were damp, and that he must dine on bread and cheese, he might prefer to risk the marshes in favour of the local inn.

The grey eyes held her own, and in them she saw determination to repay her with interest for her folly in defying him. He was under no misapprehension. He knew as well as she that she longed to see him go.

'Your concern is touching, Miss Carrington, but as a soldier I assure you that I am no stranger to—er— trying conditions, and since your invitation is so pressing I must accept it.'

'Then as a soldier we must hope that you do not find the conditions impossible,' Aurelia said sweetly. If this overbearing creature intended to indulge in a bout of verbal sparring he would find that he had met his match. Behind her she heard Cassie gasp.

'My sister likes to tease, Your Grace.' The words were accompanied by a nervous laugh. 'She keeps Marram as it was when Father was alive. . .though why I cannot imagine.'

'I do not care for mouldering ruins.' The tart reply

brought a glint to the Duke's eyes, but Aurelia was undismayed. If he chose to regard the remark as a personal gibe she had not the least objection.

'Present company not excepted?' he murmured.

Cassie had turned away and was searching for a handkerchief in her reticule, so she did not see the flush which rose to her sister's cheek. Aurelia was already ashamed of her lack of hospitality, and Cassie had said nothing which was not true. The marshes were dangerous at night for all but the local men, and not only because of the nature of the land. They were a favourite haunt of smugglers, carrying goods from the coast, and strangers were seen as enemies. They might be revenue men.

But tonight of all nights. . .with Richard still in the house? She had no wish for a confrontation between the two men. She must keep them apart at all costs.

'Jacob will show you to your rooms,' she said calmly. 'If you'll excuse me I must speak to Cook.'

Cassie gave her a troubled look, but Aurelia's face was impassive as she closed the door, leaving her guests to what she was sure would be an uncomfortable conversation.

There was no time to lose. She hurried upstairs to her sitting-room, to be greeted with a barrage of questions from Caroline. Aurelia held up a hand for silence.

'The Duke is still here,' she announced. 'At your mother's request he is to stay overnight.'

'Mother is here too?' Caroline's lips quivered. 'Oh. . .! She will make me speak to him, and I cannot—I shall not. . . Aunt Lia, you promised. . .'

'Do not distress yourself,' Aurelia soothed. 'You need not come downstairs tonight. Mr Collinge, it is much too late for you to leave the house now.' She smiled at the two young people. 'If you and Caroline will dine up here. . .?'

The young man's face flushed with a mixture of pleasure and embarrassment.

'That is most kind,' he said. 'But I do not wish to be a trouble to you.'

'Then you will serve me best by doing as I say, and keeping out of sight. Jacob will put you in the west wing for the night. It is far enough away from the other rooms. Tomorrow you must leave at first light. You may take the bay mare. I have no need of her at present.'

Richard Collinge took a step towards her and bowed his thanks.

'What can I say, Miss Carrington, except to apologise for causing you this worry? I can only thank you for your patience.'

Aurelia gave him a brilliant smile.

'It is I who should thank you for your excellent good sense. I wonder if my niece has any idea how lucky she is to have such a friend? Matters might have been very different.'

She glanced at Caroline, who had the grace to blush.

'I. . . I'm sorry, Aunt,' she said uncomfortably.

'Very well. Now do not leave this room until the coast is clear. I will see you a little later.' Leaving them together, Aurelia made her way down to the kitchens.

'But what can we give them, Miss Lia?' Cook asked. 'Five extra. . .and three of them men?'

'They must take us as they find us, Bessie. There is the cold pigeon pie, which we were to have tomorrow, and the remains of yesterday's beef. And did you not make some of your excellent broth for the villagers?'

'Aye, ma'am. 'Tis as well you're always so generous to the poor. . .but for His Grace? I doubt it's fitting.'

'The Duke may think himself fortunate to be fed at all,' Aurelia said sharply. The knowledge of her own grudging invitation and Salterne's clear determination to infuriate her still rankled. Common sense returned as she saw the scandalised expression on Bessie's face.

'Do your best,' she encouraged. 'Look out the preserved goose, and the vegetables which were salted down. There is a ham, I believe, and afterwards perhaps a syllabub?'

Having given Jacob instructions as to which wines to serve, she made her way to Cassie's room, closing the door firmly behind her.

'Cassie, how could you?' she reproached. 'That hateful creature! Caro cannot possibly marry him. She's right—he's a boor.'

'He's also very rich.'

'So you will sell her to the highest bidder?' Aurelia's eyes flashed. 'You disgust me! I wish now that I had not agreed. . .'

'To give her a season? That was generous of you, Lia. Ransome could not afford it.'

'What can he afford? If he would but stop gambling, and attempted to control Frederick. . .'

'Ransome will not change. Gambling is his life, and he takes a positive pride in Frederick's debts.' Cassie patted her blonde curls as she gazed into the mirror. 'In this world, Lia, men do as they choose. Had you ever married you would know the truth of it.'

'Whom should I have chosen from that crowd of

popinjays at Almack's?' Aurelia demanded. 'Better to live alone than to submit to a life of misery.'

'Your season was not a success, I know. I could not understand it. You were always a beauty, Sister, and even now, at twenty-five. . .well, it is not too late. You are thinner, which is not so becoming to you, but your eyes and your hair are still so fine. . .'

'My appearance is not the point at issue here,' Aurelia cried impatiently. 'What are you going to do about Caroline?'

'I shall take her home, naturally. Ransome must not learn of this escapade. He would thrash her soundly.'

'A bully too?' Aurelia raised her eyebrows. 'You have had more to suffer than I thought.'

Cassie flushed. 'It's easy for you to criticise. You have all the money you are ever like to need, but since Father died you have become so hard.'

Aurelia looked at her steadily and Cassie's eyes fell.

'I'm sorry, Lia. That was ill said.' She put out a placatory hand. 'You have been more than generous to us. If you could but see your way. . .?'

'Not another penny,' Aurelia said firmly. 'My fortune shall not go the way of yours.'

'Then Caroline must marry Salterne. His pockets are deep enough. The duns will hold off when the betrothal is announced.'

Aurelia shuddered. 'When I think of him. . .his manner. . .and that scarred face. . .'

'That is unfair. The scar is not the result of a duel. He was wounded at Talavera. You of all people should sympathise. Was not our own brother killed there, and that friend of yours, Tom Elliott?'

Aurelia turned away. The pain of Tom's death was with her always, though she knew that the living must go on. Even four years later she could not bear to speak of it.

'And Salterne is not so very old,' Cassie continued. 'He is but in his late thirties. . .'

'You do not consider a man of your own age too old for Caro? I am sorry to have spoken of the scar. He cannot help his appearance, but think of his reputation, Cass, and his manner is so arrogant.'

'You saw him at his worst. He was well out of temper, and who could blame him? Do try to understand. He has had a sad time of it in recent years. His son was stillborn, and the mother died in childbed. I believe he was devoted to her. There is an older child . . .a girl. . .who is about six. . .'

'That is sad, and I feel for him, but why Caroline, Sister? With his wealth he might have chosen anyone . . .and she is but eighteen.'

'She has the family looks,' Cassie said complacently. 'It puzzled me, though, I will admit, but I could scarce ask him outright. And Ransome was so pleased that she had caught his fancy. The truth of the matter is that Salterne needs an heir, and a mother for his child. She lives with the Dowager Duchess at present, but the old lady is failing. He may have thought that Caro would be biddable, and kind to both of them.'

'Possibly. But will she be happy with him?'

'He is no worse than many another.' Cassandra walked over to the mirror. 'What a wreck I look! This gown is crushed beyond anything.' She made an ineffectual attempt to smooth her skirt. 'Will you send Hannah to me? I cannot dine in this.'

'Hannah is too busy,' came the uncompromising reply. 'Cass, promise me that you won't force Caro into marriage.'

'What can I do? Caroline must marry him, and that is an end of it.'

'She doesn't love him,' Aurelia said in a low voice.

'What has that to say to anything? I married for love, and much good it has done me.' Her voice trembled. 'I have seen what poverty can do.'

On an impulse Aurelia kissed her sister's cheek.

'Forgive me,' she said. 'You'll stay, of course? Ransome can spare you for a few days, I'm sure.'

'I doubt if he'll know we're gone.' Cassie looked uncomfortable. 'I haven't seen him for weeks.' She sighed. 'I had best see Caro, I suppose, though how she is to explain her behaviour to Salterne I cannot imagine.'

'She is distraught,' Aurelia said quickly. 'Caro is in no fit state for company. Would you have Salterne see her as she is? I should not blame him if he had second thoughts. . . I have promised that she need not join us this evening. She may dine in my sitting-room.'

Cassie looked doubtful.

'The Duke will think it odd.'

'He may speak to her tomorrow,' Aurelia cried impatiently. 'And you may scold her later if you will. Now, Cass, we must make haste. Come help me change my gown. In any case you will wish to attend to your hair. It is sadly disarranged.'

The remark was enough to divert Cassie's attention, and by the time they joined the Duke and Frederick in the Great Hall she had recovered some of her composure.

CHAPTER TWO

With punctilious courtesy the Duke advanced towards them, briefly raising Cassandra's hand to his lips. Then he turned to Aurelia. She had perforce to allow him to do the same, though she felt a curious reluctance to submit to what was, after all, the merest civility.

She glanced down at the dark head bent low before her, realising, to her annoyance, that the gesture was prolonged far beyond common politeness. Unobtrusively, she tried to draw her hand away, resenting the disturbing sensation of his lips upon her skin, and at last he released her.

As he straightened she saw the mocking amusement in his eyes. She gave him an indignant look, and the look of amusement deepened. It was a deliberate attempt to discomfit her. Aurelia looked at him coldly.

'You are quite recovered from your journey, I trust?'

Salterne bowed. 'A trying experience for a man of my advancing years, Miss Carrington, but your kind offer of hospitality has done much to restore my spirits.'

Aurelia saw the gleam in his eye, and she stiffened. If he intended to amuse himself at her expense she would teach him that two could play at that game.

She turned to her nephew.

'Well, Frederick, how do you go on? It has been some time since your last visit.' It was as clear a

27

warning as she could give that Frederick's previous misdeeds were not forgotten, and that he was to behave himself.

'So unexpected, Aunty, dear.' The young man's smile was calculating. 'My sister is not to join us?'

'Caroline is resting. You will excuse her, Your Grace.'

It was a statement rather than a question, and Salterne was aware of it.

'We must trust to your judgement, for this evening at least,' he told her smoothly.

Aurelia's look would have frozen a lesser man, but the Duke appeared to be unaware of it.

It promised to be a difficult evening, but a quick glance at the serving tables assured Aurelia that, whatever else, her guests would dine well. She was prepared to find that Salterne, accustomed to the Regent's lavish fare, might find the meal beneath his attention. She had not allowed for the appetite of a large and hungry man who had spent the day in the saddle.

He ate heartily, and with evident relish, though he drank but sparingly of the vintage wines which Jacob had produced from the cellar.

The same could not be said of Frederick. His glass needed constant replenishment, and long before the meal was ended his speech was becoming slurred. Aurelia eyed him with distaste. Unusually subdued in the Duke's presence, he had added little to the general conversation.

His Grace had all the address of a man of breeding. With the ease of an accomplished raconteur he chatted throughout the meal, ignoring Cassie's anxious glances at her son.

Aurelia's anger was growing. She signalled to Jacob with a barely perceptible shake of her head, but when he moved away from Frederick's chair the young man stayed him and seized the bottle.

Perhaps it was all for the best, she told herself. If Salterne saw this young puppy in his cups he might think twice about the proposed betrothal. Frederick as a relative was not a pleasant prospect.

It was as Cassie was speaking of a mutual acquaintance that he interrupted his mother's conversation.

'You've some fine horseflesh in your stables, Aunt.' He gave her a knowing look. 'I can get you an offer for the mare.'

'The mare is not for sale.'

'Only trying to do you a favour,' he muttered. 'I know a fellow...'

'I'm sure you do, but I repeat, the mare is not for sale.'

Frederick was an expert judge of horseflesh. It was his only talent. Aurelia repressed an acid comment.

'Lia...you can't be keeping bloodstock?' Cassie was appalled.

'I had considered breeding. It is profitable...as Frederick will assure you.'

'But for a woman to do so...?'

'Haven't you heard of Letty Lade?' Frederick sniggered.

'I have indeed.' Cassie looked down her nose, but she made no further comment. Her son had no such reservations.

'Did you hear of her latest wager, Aunty, dear? She offered five hundred guineas to any female who would drive a four-in-hand across Newmarket Heath.'

'She had no takers, so I understand,' the Duke murmured quietly.

'I should hope not. I wonder that she lays claim to the name of female,' Cassie asserted.

Frederick gave a shout of laughter.

'She's that all right. You know where Lade found her, I suppose?'

It was common knowledge that the redoubtable Letty had enjoyed the protection of the Regent's brother, the Duke of York. Earlier she had been the mistress of Sixteen-String Jack, the highwayman. Letty had seen him hanged at Tyburn. Sir John Lade, it was rumoured, had met his future bride at her place of business, a bordello.

Aurelia attempted to change the subject, but Frederick was not to be diverted.

'When the Prince wishes to describe a particularly foul-mouthed acquaintance he says that the man can swear like Letty Lade,' he announced. As the Duke's eye rested upon him he fell silent. Salterne turned to Aurelia.

'Sir John, you must know, is a close friend of the Regent,' he said carelessly. 'Not only is he the Prince's riding tutor, he is also Master of the Royal Stables.'

Cassie was scarlet with mortification. Sir John might be as uncouth as the lowest of his grooms, but it was not for Frederick to criticise the Prince's friends, especially before a member of his inner circle.

'Sir John, I am told, is the finest whip in the country,' Aurelia said quickly.

'Indeed, ma'am. That is beyond question.' To her relief the Duke accepted the proffered olive-branch. He went on to speak of the forthcoming races at Brighton.

'Shall you attend, Miss Carrington? I think I have not seen you in the town before.'

'I was there some years ago, but recently I have had no opportunity to go.'

'Nor the desire, Your Grace, I assure you.' Cassie frowned at her sister. 'Aurelia has elected to bury herself in the country in spite of all our efforts to persuade her otherwise. I cannot understand her.'

'I have my books. . .and the garden.' Even to herself the reason for her self-imposed isolation sounded thin, but Aurelia treasured her quiet life. She could not explain this to a member of the *haut ton*, for whom the pleasures of gambling and womanising were likely to be all. And why should she attempt to justify herself to him, or to Cassie either, for that matter?

Salterne gave her a strange look.

'You find it enough, Miss Carrington? You do not yearn for balls, cards, and the pleasures of society?'

Aurelia's answer was already on her lips when Cassie gave her a warning look. His Grace would find it difficult to appreciate Aurelia's views on what he regarded as the pleasures of society.

'Life here has its benefits,' she murmured quietly.

'Your cook would appear to be one of them, ma'am. Will you give him my compliments?'

'Bessie will be happy to have pleased you, sir.' She gave him a demure look, gratified by his evident surprise.

She signalled to her sister. 'We will leave you to your wine, Your Grace.'

'Unnecessary, ladies, I assure you. May I take a turn about the grounds, Miss Carrington? I am used to walk a little before I retire.'

Aurelia bowed her assent, and bade him goodnight.

She saw Cassie to her room, looked in on the sleeping figure of her niece, and hurried back to the dining-room. As she had expected Frederick was slumped across the table, the remains of a bottle at his elbow. As she approached him he raised his head.

'This is damned fine claret, Aunt. You keep a good cellar, I'll say that for you.' His face was flushed and the slurred words came with difficulty. 'Now, about the mare. . .'

'How many times must I explain? The mare is not for sale.'

'The chestnut, then? You've some useful horseflesh there.'

'Not in any circumstances.'

'Only trying to do you a favour,' he muttered.

'Spare me your lies. The only favours you are like to do are for yourself.'

He shot her a venomous glance. 'Clever Aunty,' he jeered. 'You may have gulled Salterne with your story, but I am not so easily persuaded. I know what happened today. Father will give Caro the thrashing she deserves, and she won't have a shred of reputation left when I——'

'You will hold your tongue.' Her voice was like the crack of a whip.

Frederick staggered to his feet and stumbled towards her, but Aurelia stood her ground. She was almost as tall as he.

'I should advise you to be very careful,' she said softly. 'What will you gain by spreading rumours? I do not ask you to lie to your father, but you would do well not to indulge in speculation without proof.'

'And we don't have that, do we, thanks to you?'

'What a very unpleasant creature you are.' Aurelia's

voice was chilling. 'Shall I make myself clear? Salterne may own to a tarnished reputation, but he will not have it in his bride.'

Frederick was breathing heavily. He shook his head as if to clear the fumes of wine.

Aurelia pressed home her advantage. 'What will happen to you then?' she asked.

Her nephew wavered, still befuddled.

'I... I wasn't thinking. Excuse me, Aunt. I am somewhat disguised tonight. It is the wine. I am not used to take so much.'

'When your head is clearer, think about my words.' Aurelia rang for Jacob. 'You will see the sense of keeping silent.' She looked at Frederick for a long moment. 'It is a pity that we cannot offer you in the marriage market,' she observed. 'That would solve all your problems.'

'I ain't unwilling, Aunt.' The sly smile reappeared. 'A warm little wife would suit me well enough, if she had plenty of blunt... But who would take me?'

'Your name is an ancient one.' For a moment Aurelia felt a pang of pity. 'And you are a handsome boy. If you would but try...'

'Don't preach at me,' he snarled. 'God knows I've chased wenches enough, but their families will have none of me. Money is all that counts...'

Aurelia gave up a further attempt at conversation. She signed to Jacob to assist her nephew. As they left the room she sank into a chair. Her mind was deeply troubled. In just a few hours her pleasantly ordered life had been thrown into chaos. More distressing were her worries about her own part in the affair. The Duke had made it clear that she was interfering in matters which were none of her concern and there was some truth in his words, yet she had acted in good faith. Her few evasions and straight words to Frederick might prevent a scandal which would be of benefit to no one.

Absently, she filled her glass. The wine might help her to sleep.

'May I join you, Miss Carrington?'

To her horror the Duke uncoiled himself from a long settle by the window and moved towards her.

'Oh!' she cried. 'How could you? You should have discovered yourself, Your Grace. Eavesdropping is not the act of a gentleman.'

'But one learns so much,' he protested. 'Some of it may be a trifle mortifying, but it is doubtless good for the soul.'

Aurelia rose from the table and made as if to leave him.

'No!' A firm hand closed about her wrist. 'Allow me to explain. Your nephew promised to need assistance; that is why I stayed.'

'I see.' Aurelia felt wretched as she searched her mind to recall the gist of her conversation with Frederick. 'Then you. . .you must have heard everything.'

'Your words came as no surprise,' he shrugged. 'Did you imagine that they would?'

'No, I did not,' Aurelia admitted. 'Yet had I known you were in the room I might not have been so. . . so. . .'

'Forthright?' He smiled at her then, and the harsh planes of his face were transformed. She could see something of the man he used to be. 'You are direct, at least. I do not take it amiss. I should have handled the matter much the same myself.'

'If you understand, then why. . .?' She caught herself before she committed a further indiscretion. 'I beg your pardon,' she said stiffly. 'I have no right to question your motives.'

'That is true, but I doubt if it will stop you.' He was very close and Aurelia felt unaccountably breathless. A lean forefinger slid beneath her chin, and tilted her face to his. 'Beneath that cool exterior, ma'am, I fear you are a firebrand. Take care! You may get burned. . .'

Aurelia gave him what she hoped was a downing stare.

'Threats, my lord? May I remind you that you are a guest in my home. . .?'

'I am well aware of it, and I thank you. I have much enjoyed this evening. So—er—instructive to be drawn into the bosom of my family-to-be. I shall find it difficult to tear myself away.'

Aurelia was tempted to strike him. Her face paled, and her deep blue eyes flashed fury.

'That was unworthy of you,' she cried fiercely. 'No doubt your words are justified, but they might have been left unsaid.'

'Piqued, Miss Carrington?' He was much too close, and her heart gave a curious flutter as the dark eyes continued to gaze into her own. Impatiently she struck his hand away.

'I find your manner offensive,' she said coldly. 'Your rank does not give you the right to treat me as . . .as. . .'

'As a woman?' She heard the laughter in his voice. 'But you are a woman, my dear. . .beautiful, high-spirited, and altogether irresistible.'

Aurelia sat down suddenly. For a second his sheer

effrontery robbed her of all speech. This. . .this roué was to marry her niece? She began to tremble with rage. No woman would be safe with him. With an effort she forced herself to look up at him, but that glance did nothing to reassure her. A trick of the light had thrown the scarred side of his face into shadow and for the first time she was aware of the clean lines of his jaw, the strong column of his throat, and the beautifully moulded lips.

Her eyes lingered on his mouth, and colour flooded her cheeks as she recalled the warmth of those lips against her hand. She could well believe the stories of his sexual prowess. This was a man who would take women and enjoy them as he willed.

She gave a small *moue* of distaste and rose to her feet. He should not have Caroline if she could prevent it.

'It is late, Your Grace. You must excuse me.' It was said with all the dignity at her command.

'Running away, Miss Carrington? Surely a compliment cannot frighten you?'

'"Fright" is not the word which springs to mind, my lord. "Disgust" would be more accurate.'

'Come now, you shall not be so hard on me. Am I not to be allowed to express my admiration?'

She stood in front of him then, her blonde head barely reaching to his shoulder. It was difficult to retain her self-control before this powerful figure. There was something about him. For a second she wondered what it could be. Then she had it. It was sheer physical grace. He moved like an athlete, perfectly in command of his body, and incapable of an awkward gesture.

Impatiently she thrust the troubling thoughts aside.

'Let us understand each other,' she said quietly. 'You have been much provoked, but so have I. If we are to deal together at all you will forgo this childish nonsense. Pay court to my niece if you will, but pray do not insult me by treating me as a fool. You will not find me easy to intimidate, Your Grace.'

To her astonishment he gave her a smile of singular sweetness, totally devoid of mockery.

'Forgive me,' he said quietly. 'Shall we call a truce?'

Aurelia nodded, and gave him her hand. He raised it to his lips, but he did not prolong the courtesy, and Aurelia was quick to excuse herself.

As she climbed the stairs she wondered if she had done enough to disarm his suspicion of her. He would be a formidable adversary, and she was in no doubt as to his ruthlessness. Yet she would find a way to save her niece no matter what steps she might be forced to take.

For some hours sleep eluded her. She tossed uneasily throughout the hours of darkness, turning her pillow, and finding herself first too hot and then too cold.

From the hall below she heard the clock strike first the quarters, then the hours, and it was after two before she drifted into oblivion.

As the sky paled, heralding the dawn, she awakened with a start. Something had alerted her. Then she heard a creak as someone descended the staircase. Swiftly, she slid out of bed and opened her door the merest crack.

Below her she saw the massive figure of the Duke, fully dressed in riding coat and breeches. As he strode across the hall she hesitated. He might be a law unto himself, but even he would scarce leave Marram without making his farewells. She guessed that he intended to take an early morning stroll about the grounds. She shrugged, and then stood frozen to the spot as memory flooded back.

Had she not insisted that Richard Collinge should leave the house at first light? The Duke could not fail to see him. With a muttered exclamation of annoyance she snatched at the gown in which she had been making simples and dragged it over her head. Her house shoes were too thin and would at once be drenched with dew, but she dared not wait to button up her fine kid boots. She tied a scarf about her hair and ran downstairs.

To her relief the Duke had paused to examine the inscription over the entrance door. He looked up and smiled and she hurried towards him.

'Love conquers All,' he translated easily. 'That strikes a fitting note, Miss Carrington. Don't you agree?'

Aurelia nodded hastily. This was no time for argument. At any moment Richard might appear.

'If. . .if you are interested in Latin tags there is another in the study,' she said quickly. 'I have forgot its meaning. Perhaps you could help me.'

He gave her a long look and then he bowed.

'I had intended to take a stroll. Shall we strike a bargain? If I am able to translate your mysterious inscription you will show me about the grounds?'

'Of course,' Aurelia agreed. At all costs she must draw him back indoors, and the study was at the back of the house, with no view of the drive.

Crossing her fingers, she prayed that Richard would take his departure within the next few moments. Even as she closed the study door she heard the sound of a horseman, but if the Duke was aware of it he gave no sign.

Hastily she drew him to the window embrasure. High on the wall was a carving in the stone. The lettering was almost worn away.

'This part of the house was built from the ruins of a monastery,' she chattered nervously. Even to herself her voice sounded too loud.

'Fascinating! But I fear that the insciption is too worn for me to distinguish more than a word or two. May I take a guess at the meaning? Does it now warn against deception?'

'I. . . I have forgot. . .as I explained.' In her confusion Aurelia backed away, overturning a small table. The bowl of flowers on it fell to the ground with a crash, shattering into fragments.

'Allow me,' the Duke said smoothly.

Aurelia looked at the black-haired giant kneeling at her feet. At least he did not use pomade, she thought absently. The dark hair gleamed with vitality and a lock or two had fallen across his brow. Without thinking she put out a hand to touch it, and then drew back as if she had been stung. What was she thinking of?

'Please do not trouble yourself, Your Grace. I will do it.' With shaking fingers she began to gather up the pieces.

'You will hurt yourself.' Imperturbably he moved her aside, collected the shattered fragments, and reached down to draw her to her feet. He did not release her hands at once.

'May I give you a word of advice, Miss Carrington?' The fine grey eyes shone with mockery as they gazed into her own. 'You should not attempt to dissemble.

You have not the talent for it. Your face is the mirror of your thoughts.'

'You speak in riddles, my lord. I do not understand you. Do you care to look around the grounds before we breakfast?'

'Now that the coast is clear, you mean?'

Scarlet with mortification, Aurelia did not reply. She lifted her chin and marched ahead of him to the side-door of the house.

'You will find it chill outside,' the Duke observed smoothly. 'Is this yours?' He reached for a cloak which was hanging by the door and placed it about her shoulders. Then he looked at her thin slippers.

'I cannot allow you to put yourself at risk in those. The grass is still wet.'

'I will wear my pattens,' Aurelia announced through gritted teeth. He was treating her like a child. So much for his promise of a truce. With every look and word he was attempting to annoy her, and he seemed to have a supreme gift for putting her in the wrong.

'A sensible idea,' he approved. 'May I help you?'

'Certainly not.' Aurelia picked up her pattens and sat down on the staircase to the servants' quarters, praying that the awkward fastenings would give her no trouble.

She was to be disappointed. Though His Lordship averted his eyes with studied indifference and strolled to and fro with no appearance of impatience, in the end she was forced to admit defeat.

'They are too stiff,' she said at last. 'If you will excuse me I will change into my outdoor boots.'

'Nonsense! We are wasting time.' He seated himself by her on the stairs, reached down and gripped her ankle. Next moment her foot was resting on his knee and the patten was fixed in place.

'Give me the other one,' he ordered.

Aurelia was too bemused than to do other than obey him. No man had ever presumed to take such liberties with her. Stiff with annoyance, she raised her other foot, glaring at him as she did so.

The Duke hummed softly to himself. He might have been shoeing a horse, she thought in fury. The task accomplished, he gazed down at her feet.

'A sure sign of a thoroughbred,' he announced.

'Pattens?' Aurelia gave him a freezing look.

'No, my dear…a pair of slender, well-shaped ankles.'

Aurelia did not deign to answer him. She stalked out through the open door and made her way to the herb garden.

She had hoped to spend as little time as possible in his company, but once out of doors his manner changed. In spite of herself she was impressed by his interest in local farming practices and his pertinent questions.

The sun was high in the sky before she bethought herself of the time.

'You will wish to breakfast before you leave, Your Grace,' she said at last. 'Do you travel far today?'

'I have some acquaintances in the neighbourhood.' He did not elaborate, and she dreaded to ask. If he intended to stay within a mile or two of Marram he could visit at will, and that she must make every effort to avoid.

They found the dining-room deserted. Cassie was not an early riser, and Caro, she knew, would stay out of sight until the Duke had gone. As for Frederick, she guessed that he would be nursing an aching head.

The Duke made an excellent breakfast, and to Aurelia's relief he confined his remarks to the running of her estate. At length he rose to his feet.

'I must not trespass further on your hospitality, Miss Carrington, but, believe me, I am happy to make your acquaintance.'

'Will you. . .will you not wait to see my sister? She would wish. . . I mean, she would not care to think that you had left without bidding her farewell.'

'Will you make my apologies to her and also to Caro? I shall not be far away. With your permission I shall call within a day or so. They remain here for the present, I believe?'

'Yes—er—of course.' Aurelia was mystified to find that Salterne intended to leave without speaking to his betrothed. She did not trust him in the least, but she too had plans.

With a sigh of relief she stood in the doorway to watch him ride away.

CHAPTER THREE

'CASS, what do you say to a trip to Brighton. . .just the three of us?' Aurelia perched herself on the end of her sister's bed.

Cassie almost overset her cup of chocolate.

'You wish to go to Brighton? Why on earth. . .? You never go into society.'

'May I not change my mind? Life can be dull at Marram, as you are never tired of telling me.'

Cassie eyed her narrowly. 'Have you come to your senses at last? Or are you up to some mischief, Lia?'

'Possibly.' Aurelia gave her a demure look. 'I am no longer in my first youth. If I am to settle myself I cannot afford to waste more time.'

'Marriage at last? No. . .you are making game of me!'

'Cassie, I mean to go, but I shall need a chaperon. You have offered in the past. . .and Caro may come too. It may serve to divert her attention.'

'That's true.' Cassie frowned. Then she shook her head. 'No. . .it would be impossible. Ransome would not agree. He could not afford our lodgings, and we have no suitable clothes. . .'

'It need cost him nothing,' Aurelia said curtly.

'He would not allow it, even so.'

'Cassie, he knows that the Duke will come to Brighton in the Regent's company. In such a setting Caroline may be more amenable.'

'I thought you were against the match?'

'It was a shock at first. I had not time to think. Now I believe that if Caroline is not pressed too hard she will find happiness.'

That much, at least, was true, Aurelia thought wryly. Though that happiness might not be what Cassie had in mind. In Brighton Caroline might receive a more acceptable offer.

Aurelia looked up as her niece sidled nervously into the room. Cassie's face hardened.

'Well, miss! What is the meaning of this disgraceful escapade? I have half a mind to send you home at once and let your father deal with you.'

Aurelia saw the look of terror in the girl's eyes.

'Nonsense!' she said briskly. 'Cassie, pray do not scold. No harm has been done. Let us look on this as a visit which was long overdue. I am so happy to see you both, and to have you to myself.'

'Lia, you may make light of Caroline's behaviour, but what of Salterne? He was in a rare taking yesterday.'

'He seemed pleasant enough this morning,' Aurelia murmured mildly. 'He sent you his apologies when he left.'

'He has gone?' Caroline's face cleared at once.

'But I do not understand. He did not ask to see Caro, or myself? Now see what you have done, you wicked girl! Salterne has changed his mind. He will withdraw his offer.'

'Calm yourself, Cass. He did not give me that impression. The Duke appeared to accept my explanation.'

'Are you sure?' Cassie eyed her suspiciously. 'You must be cleverer than I thought.'

'Oh, Cassie, do not worry so! Now, what do you say to my idea?'

'To go to Brighton? Well, I cannot deny that I should enjoy it above anything, and it is high time that you found yourself a husband, if that is truly what you want.'

'Caro?'

'Do you mean it, Aunt? Am I to go as well?' Caroline's face shone with pleasure.

'Of course. Jacob may leave today, to take a house for us. Meantime I must make arrangements for my absence.'

'This is all very sudden,' Cassie demurred. 'I do not know... But then, Frederick is here. He may escort us.'

'You are mistaken. Frederick will not escort us. I draw the line at that.'

They were still arguing as they sat down to a light luncheon. Then Frederick lurched into the room, blue-jowled, and in the worst of humours.

'Taking my name in vain? I don't doubt that you were speaking kindly of me, Aunt.' He gave Aurelia an ugly look.

'Your mother and Caro are to accompany me to Brighton,' Aurelia said coldly. 'You will please to find your father and give him a letter explaining our intentions.'

'A sudden decision, ain't it? Mother did not mention it to me. I thought we came to fetch my stupid sister.'

'Don't be tiresome, Frederick. Caro has been under a strain, due largely to your own behaviour. It ill becomes you to criticise.'

Her nephew shrugged. 'Have it your way, Aunt.

I've no objection to a trip to Brighton. It's damned dull here, saving your presence.'

'You misunderstood me. You will not accompany us.'

'But you will need an escort, ma'am. You cannot travel without protection.'

'I shall take the servants.' Her eyes met his. He knew that look of old. Further argument would be useless. The last trace of his self-control vanished, and he swung round on his mother.

'Father ain't going to like this above half,' he snarled. 'You had best ask him first. . .'

'Be quiet, you insolent puppy! Since when do you advise your mother? You will do as you are bid.'

Frederick's face was flushed with rage, but as Aurelia faced him his eyes fell.

'You have not forgot my advice, I trust,' she said softly. 'You would do well to heed it. Do you understand me?'

He nodded a surly assent and flung out of the room.

'You are so hard on him,' Cassie reproached.

'Not nearly hard enough, my dear. Now, if you will write your letter Caro shall help pack my things.

As they turned out drawers and cupboards Aurelia affected not to notice her niece's swollen eyes, though it was clear that the girl had spent the night in tears.

'Come,' she said. 'We have not much time. . .'

A silence greeted her words, and then she heard a sob. Turning, she gathered the desolate figure in her arms.

'Do not distress yourself so,' she comforted. 'We may yet find a way. . .'

'You do not know Father,' Caroline choked out.

'But I cannot marry Salterne. He frightens me. Aunt, you have met him. Is he not hateful beyond anything?'

'We could scarce expect him to be in the best of moods.' Aurelia chose her words with care.

'But...but how did you explain to him? What did you say?'

'I assured him that you were safe. It was no more than the truth.'

'Did he believe that I came alone? I was so afraid. I thought he might call Richard out.'

'He showed great forbearance. He followed you, you see.'

'Then he will not wish to marry me now.' Caroline brightened.

'He did not give me that impression,' Aurelia told her grimly.

'Then what is to be done?' The girl's voice was little above a whisper.

'For the moment, nothing. We shall go to Brighton, and there perhaps——'

She stopped as Cassie entered the room with no pleasant expression on her face. Aurelia guessed correctly that her sister had been treated to the rough side of Frederick's tongue.

'Children!' Cassie slumped into a chair. 'Lia, do you not find it strange that Salterne did not request an interview with Caroline?'

'He did—er—suggest it yesterday, but I explained that she was resting. He wished to take her away at once, but I could not permit it.'

'Have you run mad? They are betrothed.'

'I am not aware of it. No announcement has been made. I had only his word for it, as I told him.'

'You questioned his word? Aurelia, how could you? He is a close friend of the Prince.'

'And that makes him perfect? I did not find him so.' Aurelia stopped, suddenly aware of the expression on her niece's face. 'Caro, my dear, will you ask Hannah for a dish of tea?' She waited until the door had closed, then, 'The Duke must learn that the world does not jump when he raises a finger,' she continued. 'I found him insolent in the extreme.'

'Oh, Lia, you did not get upon your high ropes with him?'

'No more than he did with me. But do not distress yourself. I have not ruined your plans. His Grace, I believe, has every intention of proceeding with his suit.'

She was surprised to see that Cassies lips began to tremble. Then her sister turned her face away.

'I am so unhappy,' she whispered. 'This betrothal is none of my doing, Lia. You are right about Salterne. I cannot sleep for thinking of Caro at his mercy. I know it is the way of the world. . .but it is like offering a lamb to some ravening beast.'

'Now, Cass, that is too dramatic. Did you not tell me that he loved his first wife dearly?'

'He is too old for Caro, and too. . .too experienced. There have been so many women, if the stories about him are to be believed.'

Aurelia did not doubt it. From her own experience she knew that the Duke had little regard for the proprieties. He appeared to believe that a compliment or two would bring women fawning at his feet, and she could not deny that he had a certain animal attraction.

Her cheeks grew warm as she remembered the way

he had kissed her hand for much too long. She had felt that his lips must burn her skin. . .and that caressing grasp upon her ankle as he'd fixed her pattens. . . The man richly deserved his reputation as a roué. To him, any woman was fair game.

'Gossip loses nothing in the telling,' she said carefully. 'The stories may not all be true.' There was no point in upsetting Cassie further.

Her sister would not be comforted.

'Caro is terrified of him,' she continued. 'It was pitiful to see her when Ransome forced her to listen to his suit.'

'That was brutal!'

'You see, she fancies herself in love with Richard Collinge. He, at least, was kind to her. It is more than I can say for myself.'

'He knew that he was with her?'

'Of course. That is why I followed Salterne. He is capable of violence. . .'

'I don't doubt it, but he did not see either of them. Now dry your eyes, my dearest. All will be well. We shall find some way to make things right.'

Aurelia spoke with a confidence she was far from feeling. She had no idea as to how she might achieve such a desirable state of affairs. For the moment her main objective must be to leave Marram before the Duke returned. She had not mentioned to Cassie that he might be staying in the neighbourhood, and for the next few days she prayed fervently that she might be spared the sight of that tall figure riding towards the house. He did not appear, but it was with some relief that she greeted Jacob on his return from Brighton. He had found suitable lodgings on the Steyne, the servants had been engaged, and now there was nothing to delay their departure.

They left on a perfect summer morning, and Aurelia's spirits lifted as they bowled through the leafy lanes of Sussex. Though the marshes had a beauty of their own it was pleasant to find herself in rolling countryside. A week ago she'd had no thought of leaving Marram. Now she looked forward with keen anticipation to a change of scene.

How green it was in this rich farmland. An overnight shower had cleared the air and freshened the new growth on trees and hedgerows. Overhead the branches curved to form a tunnel, their foliage blocking out the strong rays of the sun. The half-light had a mysterious quality, as if they were travelling beneath the sea.

Her reverie was broken when Jacob stopped the coach.

She leaned out of the window. 'Something is wrong?'

'Two horsemen behind us, Miss Lia. They have been following for some time.'

'Footpads!' Cassie paled with fright.

'That is unlikely,' Aurelia told her. 'They are more probably gentlemen riding about their business. The lane is narrow. They could scarce pass us here.'

She signalled to Jacob to drive on, but she could not repress a slight feeling of anxiety. She was carrying jewels and a large amount of gold, but both Jacob and Matthew were armed. She settled back in her seat.

It was some time before Cassie recovered from her fright, but as Aurelia appeared to be untroubled she slipped into a doze, lulled by the rocking of the coach. Caroline had brightened at the mention of the horsemen, but Aurelia dismissed the notion that Richard might be following them. Even on short acquaintance she had become convinced of his good sense. By now, she imagined, he would have returned home, anxious to protect Caroline's reputation.

Unwillingly her thoughts returned to Salterne. What an enigma he was. She would never understand him. half dreaming, she wondered what it would be like to be loved by such a man. There had been moments when the sardonic mask had slipped and his smile had been free of mockery. Then his face had been transformed as the fine lines at the corners of his eyes had crinkled. They too could change, from the forbidding grey of a winter sea to a disturbing warmth.

Sternly she took herself to task. The man exuded a powerful sexuality, and honesty demanded that she must admit it, but her own reaction troubled her. She frowned. It was high time that she got away from Marram and took her rightful place in society. If casual contact with a well-known rake could cause such turmoil in her mind. . . She was behaving like an embittered spinster who had been starved of affection for too long.

She pushed the unwelcome idea to the back of her mind and gazed once more upon the passing countryside. There were no further alarms and Jacob drove on steadily, making for Hailsham, where they would rest the horses and refresh themselves.

She was roused by a violent jolt. Then, to her horror, the coach began to tilt. She heard a shout of panic and then they were over, amid the sound of splintering wood and breaking glass.

As the vehicle came to rest Aurelia found herself on top of Cassie and Hannah, with Caroline beneath the three of them. She realised that the coach was on its side in a ditch.

There was a long silence. Then Cassie began to scream.

'Stop that,' Aurelia ordered briefly. 'Help me climb out.' She tucked up her skirts and secured them with her scarf. Then she reached for the door above her head.

'Lia, please!' Cassie stopped screaming and caught at her sister's arm.

'What is it? Are you hurt?'

'No...but you cannot climb out like that. Your... your limbs are visible.'

Aurelia gave a shout of laughter.

'Really, Cass! We are overturned and you must think of the proprieties?'

'But Matthew and Jacob are out there.'

'I do not hear them. They may be hurt.'

She gave another hitch to her skirts and resumed her climb. It was difficult to open the door from below, but by exerting all her strength she forced it aside at last.

'Hannah, will you give me a push? Brace yourself lest I slip.'

She had set herself no easy task, but eventually she managed to inch through the open doorway. She found herself high above the lane, and in imminent danger of sliding down the polished side of the coach. Before she could decide on her next move a strong arm closed about her waist.

'Keep perfectly still, Miss Carrington. You are quite safe.'

Aurelia turned her head to find that she was gazing into the Duke's eyes. She was plucked from her dangerous perch as if she weighed no more than a feather, and then was lifted easily on to the saddle of Salterne's horse.

For a moment she allowed herself to rest against his broad chest as a surge of relief swept over her. Then she attempted to struggle free of the comforting safety of his arms.

'My sister...and Caro...they are inside. Can you get them out?'

'You are unhurt?'

She nodded, and he allowed her to dismount. Then he rose in the stirrups and gripped the sill of the carriage door. With barely an effort he lifted himself clear of his horse and, spread-eagled against the side of the coach, he reached inside.

'Give me your hands, Lady Ransome,' he ordered.

Aurelia could only marvel at his strength as he drew her sister through the opening, and slid with her to the ground.

'Thrust her head between her knees,' he ordered. 'She is faint, but she appears to be unharmed. Then you had best see to your servants.'

Aurelia did as she was bidden. Then she hurried to where a groom, resplendent in the Duke's livery, stood at the horses' heads.

'Over there, ma'am.' He gestured to where Matthew bent over Jacob's unconscious form.

'Is he badly hurt?' Aurelia fell to her knees beside the old man.

'He's taken a nasty fall, Miss Lia. There's a lump the size of an egg on the back of his head.'

'And you?'

'Just winded, ma'am. It was the rut in the road. Jacob didn't see it.'

With shaking fingers Aurelia ripped off a length of petticoat and dipped it in the shallow stream which ran along the bottom of the ditch. As she laid it on Jacob's head he stirred.

'Lie still,' a stern voice ordered. 'You will serve your mistress best by resting until we right the carriage. John, mount up and fetch some help. Miss Carrington's man will hold the horses.'

The Duke knelt down, ignoring the effect of the muddy ground upon his immaculate buckskins. He examined Jacob's head with surprisingly gentle fingers.

'He is badly shocked,' he told Aurelia quietly. 'I will stay with him. Do you attend your sister.'

Aurelia did not argue. She rose to her feet at once and returned to the others.

'What happened? I thought we should all be killed. . .' Cassie was perilously close to hysteria.

Aurelia caught her by the shoulders.

'Pull yourself together,' she said sharply. 'Caro has need of you.'

'My poor child! Are you hurt, my dearest?' Cassie forgot her own distress as she turned to the slight figure of her daughter.

'Naught but a cut, Mama. It must have been the broken glass. I put out my hand, you see.' Caroline was pale and shaken but she managed a faint smile.

'Well done, Caro! Are you able to stand unaided?' The Duke loomed over the little group, and Caroline allowed him to draw her to her feet. 'We shall not have long to wait for help.'

He walked over to his horse and reached into the saddlebag for a flask of brandy, offering a measure of the spirit to each of the ladies in turn. Then he turned his attentions to Hannah, advising her to walk up and down with the others to avoid a chill. His manner to her was as courteous as it had been towards the other ladies, much to Aurelia's surprise. She had thought him too high in the instep to trouble himself about a servant. Her eyes rested on his powerful figure. He had lost no time in taking command of the situation, she thought ruefully. And help would most certainly arrive. She might be sure of it.

As Salterne had predicted John returned within minutes. With him was a group of farmhands. Under the Duke's direction the coach was swiftly righted, and other than a broken window and splintered panelling in the door it was found to be in reasonable order.

After a generous distribution of largesse the Duke turned to Aurelia.

'Your coachman must go inside,' he announced. 'Your other man, I take it, is able to handle the team?'

'My lord, I cannot. . . I am but a groom.' Matthew's face was pale with fright.

'Then I will drive, and John shall ride my horse. Think you that you can manage his?' A quelling glance dared Matthew to disagree. 'Miss Carrington, you will ride with me. You are more warmly clad than the other ladies.'

Aurelia admitted the truth of his remark. Her travelling dress might not be the height of fashion, but the cloth was proof against the elements.

'Lia!' Cassie tugged her arm and looked pointedly at the bronze redingote, now sadly muddied and torn.

'Oh, yes. I had forgot.' Unruffled, Aurelia began to untie the scarf which held her skirt above her ankles.

'Leave it,' the Duke commanded briefly. 'Now

ladies, I suggest that we waste no more time.' A quick word to John ensured that Jacob was carried to the coach with Matthew's help.

'Now, Miss Carrington, up you go.' Before Aurelia knew what was happening she was seated beside him on the box and the Duke had whipped up the horses. It was clear at once that the management of a four-in-hand presented him with no problems. Aurelia could only admire the skill with which he guided the badly shaken team along the narrow country lanes.

'I must thank you for your help, my lord. Had you not come to our aid I am afraid. . .'

'That is your trouble, ma'am. You seem to be a stranger to fear. What in the name of heaven persuaded you to entrust a team of thoroughbreds to a feeble ancient?'

'Jacob has always driven for my family,' Aurelia said stiffly.

'That may be so, but the years take their toll. He no longer has the strength. . .'

'Please. . . I beg of you. . .do not go on. Nothing you might say can make me feel worse than I do at present. I blame myself entirely for this mishap.'

'Well, that is something,' he admitted grudgingly. 'At least you did not give way to a fit of the vapours.'

Aurelia was silent. With bent head she studied her hands. Then her eye fell on a long rent in her skirt. It reached almost to her waist and beneath it a shapely leg was fully visible to her companion. She made a stealthy effort to draw the edges of the cloth together, but to no avail.

'Keep still!' The Duke frowned down at her. 'You will not shock me, Miss Carrington. I have seen women's limbs before.'

'I do not doubt it.' Aurelia was stung into an incautious reply.

'Dear me!' The Duke kept his eyes on the road. 'Did I not know you better I might ascribe that remark to jealousy or pique.'

'Why, you. . .you egotist!'

Salterne ignored the insult.

'You need have no cause for concern,' he resumed in a conversational tone. 'Your—er—limbs compare favourably with the best.'

'And as a connoisseur you would know, of course?'

'Of course!' His lips twitched as he looked at her flushed face. Then, satisfied that the set white look had vanished from about her mouth, he flung the skirt of his riding coat across her knees.

'Thank you,' she said shortly.

'I do not care to be distracted,' came the cool reply.

'If you will take us to the nearest inn, Your Grace, we need trouble you no longer. Perhaps in a day or two we may resume our journey.'

'With Jacob at the reins? Don't be a fool, Miss Carrington. I will take you to your destination. It is Brighton, is it not?'

Aurelia stiffened. How could he know? Her plan had not been thought of when he'd left Marram. Now another question troubled her.

'Your appearance was most opportune,' she murmured. 'I had not thought to find you still in Sussex.'

'No?' His smile was ironic.

'Two horsemen followed us,' she persisted. 'Yourself and your groom, was it not?'

'It was.'

'What a coincidence!' she cried hotly. 'I understood you to be staying with your friends.'

'Circumstances made it necessary for me to take my leave of them.'

'To follow us? My lord, I do not care to be spied upon.'

'But you made it necessary,' he said in mock-bewilderment. 'I guess that it would not be too long before your fertile brain thought of some means to attain your ends.'

'And they are. . .?'

'Come, my dear lady, you are transparent. You will stop at nothing to prevent this marriage, is that not so?'

Aurelia did not trouble to reply. 'Yet you are in a difficult situation,' the Duke continued. 'Your adversary is in an almost impregnable position. It would appear that he holds the high ground. You may chance a few guerrilla skirmishes, but they can have no effect on the final outcome.'

'This is not a war, Your Grace.'

'No? I thought it was. I have seen eyes like yours above a loaded pistol.'

'And that is your excuse for setting your man to spy on us?' Aurelia had no doubt that the groom had been ordered to stay close to Marram, to learn what he could. 'What a very excellent Bow Street Runner you might have made, my lord.'

'I like to be appraised of the enemy's plans in advance,' he assured her. 'I put myself in your place when I considered your possible strategy.'

'Indeed!'

'You had not many options open to you. Either you stayed at Marram and awaited the arrival of Ransome, come to remove his wife and daughter from your care, or you left for an unknown destination.'

'A remarkable deduction!'

'In London or Brighton some reason might be found to sanction the visit. Brighton, I felt, was more likely to be your choice, but I had to be sure.'

Aurelia was too angry to reply. How well he had divined her intentions.

'The estimable Frederick will doubtless lose no time in informing his father of your whereabouts. His Lordship, I understand, is still in the stews of the capital.'

'You are well-informed by your network of spies.'

'Ransome makes no secret of his pursuits.'

'As you appear to think so highly of my family, sir, I wonder that you care to contemplate an alliance with my niece.' Two bright spots of colour appeared on Aurelia's cheeks.

'I have my reasons, Miss Carrington. Shall we leave it at that?'

CHAPTER FOUR

THE Duke drove on in silence, with an occasional look at the sky. A bank of cloud had obscured the sun, and the wind was chill. Aurelia began to shiver. For all the protection offered by her redingote she might have been naked.

Salterne stopped the horses and shrugged out of his riding coat. He threw it about her shoulders. Then he reached out and drew her close to his side.

'Put your arms about my waist,' he said. 'You are suffering from delayed shock.'

Thankful for the promise of warmth offered by his body, Aurelia did as he suggested. He might be the most obnoxious creature she had met in the course of her experience, but there was something of comfort in being able to rest her head against his shoulder, and to feel the steady pounding of his heart beneath the fine cambric shirt.

He was her enemy, that was true, but the rules of war allowed one to make use of an enemy. She smiled at the thought. Was he not playing into her hands?

Slowly she relaxed and nestled closer to him as her eyelids began to droop. The Duke looked down at her and a slight smile curved his lips.

'You must take care, my general. Even the great Napoleon is not at his best when he is weary.'

'You would compare me with that. . .that monster?'

'A genius, ma'am! I venture to think that he would not be too proud to take advantage of a little warmth as you are doing now. It would, after all, give him the chance to fight another day.'

He tightened his grip and Aurelia was tempted to pull away from him. Then her sense of humour came to her rescue. Her shoulders began to shake with laughter.

'You are still cold?' His voice held concern.

'N—no, my lord, but it occurred to me... I doubt if Napoleon has ever found himself in this position.'

Making light of the situation was the only way she could think of to drive away the disturbing sensations which possessed her. By turning her head only slightly she could see a small pulse beating in the base of his throat. She clenched her fingers into a fist, to prevent herself from touching the tanned skin.

How dark he was...almost gypsy-like in colouring. She could understand why Caroline found him such a threatening figure.

Great heavens! Caroline! And she, Aurelia, was the aunt of the bride-to-be. What could she have been thinking of to allow herself to get into this ridiculous position, embracing—actually embracing—the Duke of Salterne?

She stiffened, dropped her arms, and tried to pull away, but the Duke tightened his grip.

'I should advise you not to struggle, my dear. The horses are still nervous.'

Not only the horses, Aurelia thought uneasily. The rent in her skirt had opened wide, and her leg was pressed against the Duke's thigh. She was intensely aware of the sinewy strength of his muscles against her own soft flesh. The male scent of his body filled her nostrils, combined with the smell of newly washed linen, and her heart gave an odd little jump.

She could not but compare him with the perfumed dandies of her London season. However she might criticise Salterne's arrogance and regret his ugly reputation, this, at least, was a man. If only he did not have such an infuriating urge to put her at a disadvantage every time they met she might learn to tolerate his company, though she was determined that her niece should not be forced to marry him.

A small frown creased her brow. She would fight him, but he had pointed out her difficulties only too clearly.

'Something is troubling you?' The heavy-lidded grey eyes were regarding her intently.

'We had planned to rest the horses at Hailsham, Your Grace.'

'They will do well enough. I have not pushed them hard, and there is still some way to go. Your man will need attention. I had best send John ahead to find the surgeon. Will you give me your direction?'

Aurelia had hoped to keep their whereabouts a secret, but she did not hesitate. Jacob must be her first consideration. As the team continued to cover the miles she began to doze.

'Asleep on duty, General?' The teasing voice roused her with a start. 'You must remember that the enemy will always take advantage of a lack of vigilance.' The Duke bent towards her and Aurelia looked at him with startled eyes.

'No. . . I did not intend to kiss you.' A large hand reached out and brushed a strand of hair from her cheek. 'Though the thought is tempting.'

Aurelia was tempted to strike him and he laughed.

'I should not advise it,' he warned. 'I have sparred with the professionals.'

'Then I wonder that you should care to spar with me, even verbally,' Aurelia answered coldly. 'Since our first meeting you have done your best to annoy me.'

'With compliments?'

'With a manner which I find over-familiar.'

He gave a shout of laughter.

'We cannot stand upon ceremony on this box,' he said drily. 'However, your trials are almost at an end. There is your destination.'

He pointed ahead and minutes later he turned off the Brighton road into a stable-yard. Along one side the lights of a small house gleamed softly in the dusk.

'A good choice,' he approved. 'Stabling is hard to come by in the town.' He dismounted from the box and held up his arms. Aurelia was tempted to announce that she would descend to the ground unaided, but common sense prevailed. She was tired and the drop to the ground was steep. She had no wish to end up prone at his feet. Without more ado she gave him her hand and allowed him to lift her down.

To her annoyance he showed no disposition to release her, holding her against his breast until she was forced to protest.

'My lord,' she said with dignity, 'if you are determined to convince me that your reputation is justified you have succeeded. Must you continue to insult me?'

He grinned down at her and tightened his grip until she thought her ribs must crack. Then he shook her slightly to and fro.

'You are not some schoolroom miss, but a full-blooded woman,' he said softly. 'Is it an insult to be found desirable?'

'As you are planning to wed my niece the answer must be yes.' If she stamped hard on his instep perhaps he would let her go, though she suspected that her small kid boots would make no impression on his Hessians.

He dropped a kiss upon her head as she began to struggle.

'There,' he said. 'Now I have confirmed your worst fears. I am beyond redemption.'

Aurelia felt strangely breathless. For the first time her resolution wavered. This infuriating creature was too...too...well, he was too much of everything. She did not doubt the size of the task before her. In some odd way he seemed to have the ability to read her mind. He would be a formidable adversary.

She broke his hold upon her abruptly and hurried round to the door of the couch.

'What a journey! I vow I am more dead than alive.' Cassie climbed down stiffly, followed by the others.

The Duke paid them no attention. He reached inside, lifted Jacob in his arms, and strode across the courtyard to the house.

'Ah, Lessing. I'm glad to see you here.' He nodded briefly to a middle-aged man who stood in the doorway holding a lamp aloft.

'This way.' The surgeon led him up the stairs, and waited as he laid Jacob carefully on the bed. 'Now let me see my patient.'

Salterne took Aurelia's arm and led her from the room.

'Lessing is the best. You must try not to worry.' His voice was oddly gentle.

'I cannot forgive myself...' Aurelia was close to tears.

'Now, General, you must not give way. The troops rely on you. You have been a Trojan up to this.' A strong hand rested on her shoulder. 'Will you forgive me if I leave you now? You will all wish to rest. . .'

'Of course, and. . .thank you for everything.'

'For everything?' She heard the laughter in his voice, but she did not draw her hand away when the Duke raised it to his lips.

'Take care to redeploy your forces, ma'am,' he murmured softly. Then he looked up as the surgeon joined them.

'How is he, Lessing?'

'Shocked and badly bruised, Your Grace. His head will be tender for a day or two, but I doubt if there will be lasting damage. He wishes to speak to you, Miss Carrington.'

Aurelia slipped into the sick man's room.

'What is it, Jacob?'

'You have not forgot the Frenchie, ma'am. . .the mantua-maker. She is to come tomorrow. You asked me to arrange. . .'

'I have not forgot,' she soothed. She was tempted to assure him that the visit of the dressmaker was the last thing on her mind. Instead she patted his hand. 'You must try to get some sleep,' she told him quietly.

When the Frenchwoman arrived next day Aurelia detected a certain reserve in her manner. It surprised her. Cassie knew the woman well, and the introduction of a new client might have guaranteed some expressions of pleasure.

Madame Claudine looked sharply at Cassie. 'Shall you wish the total, my lady? It is for several seasons.'

Cassie flushed, but before she could speak Aurelia intervened.

'The total, if you please.' Her face was impassive as she studied the enormous bill. She handed it to her sister. 'Is this correct?'

'I—I fear it is. . . I had no idea.'

'These matters are easily overlooked.' Aurelia counted out a pile of sovereigns. 'You should be more importunate, Madame Claudine. You cannot run a business without payment.'

Madame was profuse in her thanks. She forbore to mention that repeated requests for settlement of even a part of the account had met with no response.

She looked with new respect at the slender figure before her. Miss Carrington's dress was not, perhaps, *dernier cri*, but her gentle manner did not disguise a certain air of authority. She signed to her companion and together they began to unpack their pattern books and samples.

Cassie looked uncomfortable.

'Lia, I am so sorry,' she whispered. 'I did not intend that you should pay. Now I cannot order anything new.'

'Nonsense! Did you not assure me that just one outmoded garment will sink us beneath reproach? You shall choose whatever you wish.'

If Madame heard any part of the murmured exchange she gave no indication. She threw open the pages of *La Belle Assemblée* and *Ackerman's Repository of Fashion* and invited the comments of all three ladies.

Later that day she left with a well-filled order book. It had been a profitable afternoon and her black eyes gleamed at the size of Aurelia's commission. She gathered together her samples of tiffany and cham-

bery gauze, sarcenet silks and light muslins, promising
the first of the gowns within three days.

'Lia, you are like to outdo the Regent in extravagance!' Cassie exclaimed. But it was a half-hearted
protest. As the days went by and parcels arrived she
could not hide her pleasure.

'I vow we shall not find time to wear one half of
them.' She sighed happily as she twirled before the
mirror in a pale pink muslin with puffed sleeves. The
low neckline was trimmed with a frill in the same
shade, and a satin ribbon of deeper pink confined it
beneath the bust. 'I am so glad I did not choose that
vile pomona green. It turns my skin to the colour of
cheese.'

Aurelia looked at her reflection in the glass. The
blue reflected the colour of her eyes. It was patterned
in gold, with a gold flounce at the hem, and a ribbon
of the same colour was held with a jewelled buckle at
her breast.

'You do not think this gown a trifle ornate?' she
said doubtfully.

'It is perfect, Aunt Lia. You look like a queen.'
Caro's expression was rapturous.

'That is what I was afraid of. I should not have
allowed you to persuade me, Cass.'

'Nonsense! On a dark person it would be too much,
but on you...well, my dear, it is the height of elegance. Caro, stop pulling at the neckline of your dress.
It is quite low enough for a young girl.'

'Madame Claudine suggested a bust improver to
wear beneath it, mama.'

'Madame Claudine may suggest what she wishes,
but I will not permit it. The very idea! You will fill out
in time, just as your aunt and I have done.' Cassie

looked with satisfaction at her creamy bosom. 'There is no denying that one does need a little flesh to do justice to these styles.'

'I see I shall have to drape gauze scarves about my person,' Aurelia twinkled.

'Do not say so! You are not bony, Lia, though you do not eat enough. If you would but listen to me——'

'Yes, yes, I know. Now, what do you say to a drive? I have hired a chaise. . .'

Cassie looked doubtful.

'Is Jacob fit to drive?'

'I shall drive myself.'

Cassie's dismay caused Aurelia to hide a smile.

'I shall not overturn you,' she promised.

'But the Duke said. . .'

'I do not require Salterne's permission for anything I choose to do. Will you trust me or not?'

'I suppose so.' Cassie stifled her misgivings. The prospect of a drive at the fashionable hour of five was sufficient to persuade her to change her gown, and to hurry Caro into doing the same.

They found themselves in a slow-moving line of carriages. The town had filled up rapidly in daily expectation of the Regent's arrival, and several people looked with interest at the smart little equipage with its elegant occupants.

'Oh, there is Lady Bell!' Cassie waved to a plump little woman who was speaking to a young officer. 'Do bow to her, Caro. We met her in London, you will recall.'

Caroline inclined her head, blushing at the young man's frank look of admiration.

It seemed as if Cassie knew half the world. Aurelia

was forced to stop time and again as greetings and invitations were showered upon them.

'I am so glad we came here.' Cassie was flushed with triumph as they turned for home.

Aurelia smiled at her. She was satisfied with the result of their outing. Now they would be drawn into society. It was clear that during her daughter's season Cassie had made many friends and acquaintances among the *ton*. If there was speculation as to why the lovely Caro was not yet spoken for it was no matter. Salterne's offer was not yet public knowledge.

Cassie, she knew, would be the envy of all match-making mamas when it was known that her daughter had captured the biggest prize of the season, but Aurelia was determined to delay that moment for as long as possible. Once Caro was formally betrothed all chance of further offers being made to her would be at an end, and Aurelia's hopes for her niece would be dashed.

'Do not mention Salterne's offer yet,' she warned next day.

'Why not?' Cassie bridled. 'Not everyone was kind to us in London. Caro had a host of suitors until that odious Mrs Ingleby told everyone that she had no fortune. How I long to give her a set-down. Her own girls are the plainest creatures. . .'

'Not yet,' Aurelia insisted. A spark of mischief lit her eyes. 'Shall you not enjoy the furore when the announcement appears without warning?'

'It will cause a stir,' Cassie said with satisfaction. For the moment she appeared to have forgotten her objections to the match.

'Matthew will drive you if you wish to pay some

calls tomorrow.' Aurelia thought it time to change the subject. 'He is quite capable of handling the chaise.'

'You will not accompany us?'

'No...if you'll forgive me. The scarf I bought at Hanningtons is quite the wrong shade. I shall walk to North Street and exchange it.'

It was a small deception. After the bustle of the last few days Aurelia longed for some time to herself, and during her walks she had seen several bookshops. A quiet hour or two spent browsing would restore her spirits.

Next morning she set off across the Steyne to Mr Donaldson's. She would take out a subscription to his library.

Her slender figure in the new bronze pelisse and bonnet attracted some attention, but she saw none of her acquaintance. She slipped through the crowd outside the shop and made her way to the counter, glancing at her watch.

'I have but one hour.' She smiled at the assistant. 'Will you remind me if I forget the time?' She knew herself of old. How often had she lost half a day in Rye or Tunbridge Wells, absorbed in the treasures on the shelves?

The young man announced himself at her disposal. He produced several volumes for her inspection, including one by a new author.

'*Pride and Prejudice*?' Aurelia glanced at the first page and was struck by the humour of the opening lines. How delightful! She was chuckling aloud when a shadow fell across the book.

'Good morning, Miss Carrington.'

Aurelia stiffened. There was no mistaking that deep voice. She looked up into Salterne's smiling eyes.

'Your Grace.' She gave him the slightest of bows, annoyed to find that the colour had rushed to her cheeks. A multitude of emotions swept through her mind as she gazed at him, but she was appalled to realise that her first reaction was one of joy.

She averted her face, striving to remember that this was her enemy. Had he not insulted her, with his cavalier disregard of the conventions?

She made an effort to regain her composure. She had, she told herself, no wish for his company, but it would be ill-mannered to move away without exchanging a civil word or two.

Salterne took the volume from her hand and looked at the title.

'You have read this?'

'Not yet, but I intend to do so. If you will forgive me, Your Grace, I am pressed for time.' She signalled to the assistant.

'Not even an hour to spare?'

Aurelia blushed. He must have overheard her.

'I will take this for the moment,' she announced.

'Then you must allow me to escort you,' he said coolly. 'I hope to pay my respects to Lady Ransome and to Caro.'

'They are not at home. My sister is paying calls this morning.'

'I shall not object to wait for them.' The Duke led her through the crowds on the pavement. Mr Donaldson had done his best to attract custom by setting out tables where one might take tea, play cards, or read the newspapers. Salterne nodded to his acquaintance. Then he turned towards the seafront. Aurelia stopped.

'My lord, my house is across the Steyne, as you know. We must go straight ahead.'

The grip on her arm did not relax, and through the thin fabric of her sleeve Aurelia could feel the warmth of his hand. For some reason she felt unaccountably breathless.

'You can have no objection to a little exercise, Miss Carrington. Forgive me, but you are looking rather pale.'

'It is not surprising. . .' She bit back the rest of the sentence. She could not admit that his sudden appearance had unnerved her.

'I had not thought to find you still in Brighton,' she said coldly. 'We have not seen you since. . .'

'Since the unfortunate incident with your carriage? May I hope that you have missed my company.'

'You may hope, but it would not be the truth.' Aurelia was tempted to assure him that his ego matched his size, but she bit back the words. It would be too childish to indulge in petty sarcasm.

His lips twitched with amusement as he looked down at her, but he did not take up the challenge.

'I hear from Lessing that your man goes on well.'

'Jacob is recovering, I thank you. Do you not go to London, sir?'

The Duke laughed.

'Anxious to be rid of me, my dear?'

'I was merely making the enquiry. . .but if you care to take my words amiss. . .'

'Why should I do that, Miss Carrington? You are a marvel of tact. I hang upon your every word, it is true. Each pronouncement is—er—pregnant with meaning.'

Aurelia stalked along beside him, too furious to reply, but she found that she was shaking. The less she was in the company of this insufferable creature the better. He had the most unfortunate effect on her, ruffling her feathers, disturbing her composure, and destroying her peace of mind.

'In answer to your kind enquiry, I am come to Brighton for the season,' the Duke continued imperturbably.

'But the Prince is not yet arrived.'

'Perhaps I am come to restore my health.' The grey eyes gleamed with laughter.

'What nonsense! I never saw anyone look better in my life.' Aurelia stopped, and blushed to the roots of her hair, wishing that she could recall the indiscreet remark.

'A compliment! I am overwhelmed. Can it be that you are beginning to discover my true worth, or is this merely another attempt to throw me off my guard?' He was enjoying her discomfiture to the full. 'Appearances can be deceptive, ma'am. You see before you a broken man. . .crushed by your disapproval.'

'You are impossible!' she ground out bitterly.

'So I am told. I should point out, by the way, that you are destroying the volume in your hand. A pity! It is a charming book.'

Aurelia glanced down. In her agitation she had almost crushed the book in two.

'Please to release my arm, Your Grace. I must go home at once, and I prefer to go alone.'

'Do I sully your reputation, my fair adversary?'

'I am aware that your own cannot be tarnished further,' she burst out hotly. 'But I must have some care for my own.'

For answer he settled her arm more comfortably within his own. Then, bending down, he peeped beneath the brim of her bonnet. He was much too close, but in that fashionable crowd she could not struggle without making a scene. He knew it as well as she and the corners of his mouth crinkled with laughter.

'I thought you scorned the opinion of the world, Miss Carrington.'

'I hope I am not so foolish. Only a dowager may flout the dictates of society...' She stopped again, aware that she had given him the opportunity to make some cutting remark.

'And you are not quite that,' he said solemnly. 'Must I remind you, dear relative-to-be, that our acquaintance is beyond reproach? We are almost family, so to speak.'

'Your betrothal is not yet public knowledge.'

'That is easily remedied...an announcement in the *Morning Post* perhaps?'

Aurelia looked at him in alarm. An announcement at this stage would ruin all her plans. She lifted her face to his and gave him her most charming smile.

'Now, in truth, I am worried. Am I to believe that you see me suddenly in a different light?'

'You misjudge me, Your Grace. Perhaps on further acquaintance...?' She hoped that her reply sounded convincing, but she was speedily disillusioned.

'You feel that your antipathy might lessen?' Salterne threw back his head and gave a shout of laughter. 'You raise my hopes, Miss Carrington. I wonder why I imagined that you had taken me in deep dislike at our first meeting?'

'On that occasion you were not yourself, my lord. The long ride...the worry... I appreciate how you must have felt.'

'You are too kind!' He made her an ironic bow. 'We are almost at your door. I will leave you here, and promise myself the pleasure of a visit tomorrow.'

'No!' The sharp refusal was out before she had time to consider.

His Grace raised an eyebrow.

'Then how are we to further our acquaintance, my dear? You do not care to be seen with me in a public place. If we are to learn to appreciate each other's sterling qualities we cannot do so at a distance.'

Aurelia flushed at his mocking tone, but she made an effort to retain her dignity. She knew quite well that he relished throwing her off balance. It should have been easy to treat him with the freezing disparagement she had used to others during her London season, but it was not.

Her own reactions to him puzzled and dismayed her. Antagonism she could handle. It was his teasing, almost tender way of slipping under her defences that was difficult to understand. She was not a child, to be perplexed and thrown into confusion by a word or a smile. The contempt which she had tried to show him appeared to offer him nothing but amusement.

She looked up to find him watching her intently.

'I am persuaded that Lady Ransome and your charming niece will be overjoyed to see me,' he continued. 'I must not be wanting in my attentions. . .'

'My sister is fatigued at present, and after Caro's – er——'

'Escape?' he supplied helpfully.

Aurelia gave him a look of acute distaste.

'I was about to say that after our journey Caroline would welcome the opportunity to recover her spirits.'

'Strange!' he mused. 'When the ladies passed me

not an hour ago they appeared to be in the best of health.'

There was nothing left to say, and as the hard grey eyes gazed into her own Aurelia felt a sense of panic. What a devil he was! He could read her mind without difficulty. She wanted to run and hide...anything to get away from his disturbing presence.

'At a loss for words, Miss Carrington? Surely not?' He was in no hurry to help her out of her predicament. She had told him herself that Cassie and Caro were paying calls, and then she had tried to indicate that they were too fatigued to receive him.

'You intrigue me, ma'am,' he said at last. 'What can you hope to gain by your opposition to my suit? Ransome, I fear, is not like to take it kindly.'

'That wastrel!' Aurelia's hand flew to her mouth. Again she had been betrayed into saying more than was right or proper. However she might feel about her brother-in-law, it was unbecoming in her to speak ill of him to others. She could have wept with vexation. If only the Duke were not so provoking. She could not think of another human being, apart from Cassie, to whom she would have made such an unguarded remark, and Salterne was almost a stranger to her.

The knowledge brought her up with a start. Less than a week ago she had never met him. It seemed incredible. That dark, expressive face was almost as familiar to her as her own. She knew exactly how the laughter began deep in his eyes, suffusing their greyness with warmth, and grew until it lifted the corners of that mobile mouth. And she was aware of every nuance in his voice.

Now it was silky smooth.

'I am glad to see that family feeling has not blinded you to Ransome's faults,' the Duke said softly. 'What a pair we make, he and I. Me with my arrogance, my evil reputation...and this...' He lifted a hand to his scarred face.

'Do not say that!' Impulsively Aurelia reached out a hand towards him. She had almost forgotten the scar, but now she noticed again the thin line, half hidden on his brow by the thick black hair, and curving down his cheek. How nearly the sabre-cut had missed his eyes. He might have been blinded.

'I should be proud to bear that wound,' she said earnestly.

His mocking expression changed, and in his eyes she saw wonder.

'I am half inclined to believe you. Yet it would be a pity to mar that perfect face.'

His words succeeded in robbing Aurelia of speech.

'I shall observe your machinations with great interest,' he observed in a lighter tone. 'You are like to be a worthy opponent, but I warn you I shall give no quarter. I wonder who will win this contest...you or I? Do you care to place a wager on the result?'

'You are insufferable!' All her resentment returned at his taunts.

For answer he raised her hand to his lips, but instead of the conventional courtesy he turned it over and pressed a kiss into her palm. Even through the silk of her mittens she felt that it burned her skin.

He bowed, and to her utter fury she saw that he was smiling as he walked away.

CHAPTER FIVE

AURELIA hurried indoors, blind and deaf to all about her. How could she have allowed herself to be drawn into yet another duel of wits with Salterne?

Her lips tightened. She'd beat him yet. The encounter had been unexpected and it had come as a shock, so that she'd been unprepared. Next time she would be ready for him. If only she had more time, she mourned. She'd been hoping for a breathing space. . . some turn of events. . .perhaps another offer for Caroline which might cause Salterne to withdraw; but it was too soon for that.

And he had spoken no more than the truth. He held all the cards. One word to Ransome and the announcement of the betrothal would appear in the *Morning Post*. Then Caroline's fate would be sealed.

She sat down at her desk and tried to think clearly about the situation. The Duke's attitude puzzled her. He was not lover-like in the least towards Caroline. He had shown no disposition to seek her niece's company either at Marram or in Brighton. He was buying a wife, she thought indignantly, and the transaction did not require him to play the fond suitor. It was an insult to the girl, to say the least.

It was also a relief. She would say nothing of her encounter with Salterne to Cassie or Caro. Time enough to ruin the girl's peace of mind when it could no longer be avoided. In Brighton other diversions might serve to keep the Duke from their door. She had no doubt that he would not lack feminine company. He was a womaniser. His every word and look proclaimed the fact.

Hot colour flooded her cheeks as she recalled her own response to him. She could not treat him with indifference, she lamented bitterly. His touch excited her, though she prayed that he was not aware of it. Yet the man seemed to read her mind with ruthless clarity. The less she saw of him the better, yet in the circumstances that would be impossible.

I won't give up, Aurelia vowed to herself. If Salterne wishes for a trial of strength I'll be happy to oblige him.

She picked up a pile of invitations from the tray. Card parties. . .balls. . .? She was leafing through them when Cass and Caro returned.

'Only think, sister! We are invited to the Broomes' tomorrow.' Cassie's eyes were sparkling. 'I knew Anne as a girl. 'Pon my soul, I believe that all the world is here, and the Regent arrives within the week.'

Aurelia held up a card.

'What do you say to the ball on Thursday?'

'The Old Ship Inn? That is the usual weekly affair. Do let us go! I should enjoy it beyond anything. . .' Cassie's face was lit from within. Once more she was the beautiful Cassandra Carrington, one of the Incomparables.

'I believe I shall wear the jonquil crêpe with the *dents de loup*,' she announced. 'A first impression is of the greatest importance. Caro will look well in her white muslin with the silver sprigs, and possibly a wreath. What of you, Lia?'

'The lavender, I think, with the overdress of spider gauze.'

Cassie looked doubtful.

'It is elegant, of course, but is it not a little subdued?'

'It will suit me well enough,' Aurelia said firmly. 'You would not have me in spangles, like the Prince?'

'Of course not, but——'

'Set your mind at rest, Cass. We shall be quite *à ravir*. I shall send for Monsieur Pierre. He is thought to be a genius with coiffure.' She laughed. 'I wonder how we managed before the refugees arrived from France.'

Her eyes rested on Caroline's face. If the child was missing Richard she gave no sign of it. She had already attracted a good deal of attention, and Brighton was full of eligible beaux, especially the regiment of the 10th Hussars, the Prince's Own. Caro would not lack for partners, and the wider their circle of acquaintance, the more chance there might be of another offer.

She hesitated, knowing full well that she should mention her meeting with Salterne, but that would cast a cloud over Caroline's pleasure. It was apparent that neither she nor her mother knew of his continued stay in Brighton. Aurelia decided to keep her own counsel. Caro should have another few hours' peace of mind.

Then she remembered. Had he not promised to call on the following day?

'I thought we might drive along the coast tomorrow,' she announced. 'If the weather is kind we shall take a picnic to St Mary's Well.'

Caro clapped her hands, but Cassie looked doubtful.

'Had we not better rest? We are promised to the

Broomes for the evening, and, Lia, you know how I freckle in the sun. I am quite out of chervil water as a remedy.'

'Then let us take a morning drive,' Aurelia said patiently. 'You may rest in the afternoon, and we shall deny all callers.'

To her relief Cassie agreed. It was merely postponing the inevitable meeting, but it would serve for the moment.

Her precautions proved unnecessary. On their return she scanned through the pile of calling cards, but Salterne's was not among them. She was seized by the uneasy feeling that he would always be one step ahead of her. Perhaps he intended to lull her into a false sense of security. It would be like him to think of such a devious manoeuvre.

Next day brought Monsieur Pierre and again Aurelia gave instructions to deny all visitors. Even so, she jumped each time she heard a knock at the door.

'Lia, what is the matter with you? Are you not well? I have asked you twice for your opinion on this style for Caro's hair.'

Aurelia gave a guilty start and looked at her niece. The blonde hair had been cropped to form a halo around the girl's face.

'It is cherubic,' she chuckled. 'It suits you quite delightfully, my love.'

The little Frenchman was rightly proud of his reputation. With infinite care he coaxed Cassie's heavy locks into a chignon, training a few tendrils to fall on either side of her brow. It made her look years younger, and as Aurelia caught her sister's eye she was rewarded with a happy smile.

'Now, Miss Carrington, you will trust to my judgement?' Monsieur Pierre regarded Aurelia in the mirror.

'Of course, *monsieur*, but nothing too extreme, if you please. . .'

The Frenchman picked up his scissors with a flourish, ignoring her faint admonishment.

'*À la Grecque*, I believe,' he said firmly. 'We shall not cut these magnificent tresses, but shape them merely.'

Aurelia's misgivings vanished as he combed the cloud of fine fair hair away from her face, and pinned it high into a knot of curls. A swift turn of his fingers caused one or two of them to cascade from the highest point.

'That is better, yes?' He stood back to approve his work. 'Now one may see the full beauty of the eyes, and the classic features. You approve, *mademoiselle*?'

'Indeed, *monsieur*, I like it very much.'

'One sees such styles on Grecian urns. They are in harmony with the present fashion for the draperies of antiquity. And observe how one may continue the theme. . .' He picked up a silver fillet and bound it around her brow. 'One may use ribbons in this way, or jewelled headbands, and sometimes a fillet of three strands. It is a simple matter to catch it at the back of the head.'

He smiled as Aurelia looked doubtful.

'You have perfect carriage of the head, *mademoiselle*, and the style is simple. You may dress it as you will. Perhaps a flower or two besides the curls on top.' To prove his point he chose a cluster of silk roses in the deepest pink and held them against her fair hair.

Aurelia had to admit that he was right. She might

not choose to follow the more extreme of his suggestions, but a flower to match her gown would please her.

That his efforts had been successful was evident when the three ladies entered the ballroom of the Old Ship Inn that evening. A buzz of interest greeted their appearance and a dozen pairs of eyes focused eagerly upon their jewellery and their gowns.

Aurelia scanned the room for the towering figure of the Duke, but he was nowhere to be seen. Satisfied that he was engaged elsewhere, she allowed herself to relax. Perhaps he had returned to London. The Prince liked his friends about him, and he was known to take their absence amiss.

'Lia, do bow! Lady Jersey is beckoning to us.'

Cassie drew her sister's arm through hers and led the way towards the famous London hostess.

'She was kind to Caro,' Cassie whispered. 'We owe her marked civility. Had she not procured us vouchers for Almack's. . .well. . .I do not need to explain what that would mean. The Duchess of Bedford was blackballed, you know, though I hear she was admitted later.'

Aurelia felt the old stirrings of rebellion. It was all so familiar. Arbitrary decisions by the Lady Patronesses of that exclusive establishment could make or break a reputation, and anything was better than the refusal of a voucher to attend. To be without one was to be banished to the outer perimeter of society.

Aurelia found it ludicrous. Almack's rooms were sparsely furnished, the food was indifferent, and the only liquid refreshments permitted were orgeat, lemonade, or the weakest of claret cups. A strange choice of venue for a marriage mart, Aurelia thought to herself, for such was its undisguised purpose.

She moved towards Lady Jersey with a feeling of restraint, and was at once disarmed.

'How pleasant to see you again, Miss Carrington!' Her Ladyship was all civility. 'Country life agrees with you. You are in famous looks.'

Aurelia smiled and thanked her.

'Your father was highly thought of, my dear. I was saddened to hear of his death. Tell me, do you stay in Brighton for the season?'

'For some weeks at least, Your Ladyship.'

'I am glad to hear it.' Lady Jersey nodded her approval. 'When the Prince arrives you may be sure he will invite you to one of his musical evenings.'

She turned away and Cassie squeezed Aurelia'a arm.

'If she speaks to the Regent we are sure to be invited,' she whispered.

Aurelia nodded, though she had no particular desire for such an invitation. But Lady Jersey had great influence with the Prince, and to move in such exalted circles could do no harm to Caro's prospects.

Lady Jersey raised a finger to summon a young man to her side.

'May I present Ensign, the Lord Weekes?' she said. 'I believe he hopes to lead Caroline in the country dance.' She smiled at Caro, who went off happily on the young man's arm.

'Unexceptionable, Lady Ransome.' Her Ladyship at once understood the troubled look on Cassie's face. 'Prince George's officers are beyond reproach.'

Privately Aurelia doubted the truth of that statement, but Cassie was reassured.

'Do you care to dance, Miss Carrington?' Lady
Jersey inspected the crowd of hopefuls standing close
beside them. 'Leggatt, I vow, has had eyes for no one
else since you entered the room.' She beckoned to a
tall young man, clad in immaculate regimentals. 'Will
you take pity on Captain Leggatt?'

Aurelia looked at the eager face. The captain
looked absurdly young, and it would have been churl-
ish to refuse. She took his arm and joined the throng
on the crowded floor.

She felt a little shy at first. It was so long since she
had danced, or even entered into conversation with a
personable young man. But her companion's easy
manner soon set her at ease.

'I have not seen you here before,' he said. 'Do you
know Brighton well?'

'It is some years since I was last in the town,' she
answered. 'I see so many changes.'

'It is a splendid place. There is much of interest
here. . .and yet. . .'

Aurelia looked at the wistful face.

'You would prefer to be elsewhere?'

'Not at this moment, ma'am, I assure you, but I
should like to see some action. We are a joke among
the other regiments. They see us as toy soldiers.'

'That is a harsh judgement. You do not lack courage, I'm sure.'

'Nor does our colonel, Miss Carrington. The Prince
has begged to be allowed to serve in the field, but
permission is always refused.'

'It is hard indeed.' Aurelia gave him a sympathetic
smile. 'Yet the heir to the throne must put his duty
first.'

'I understand that, but we. . .the rest of us? I'm

sorry, I must not bore you. The ladies do not care for military matters. Shall you attend the races?'

'I hope to do so. They are a famous sight.' She stumbled as a heavy foot caught the hem of her gown. The gentleman behind her was profuse in his apologies, but the damage was done. Aurelia glanced down in dismay to find that a length of gauze had been torn from her skirt.

'Clumsy fellow!' Her partner looked his disgust. 'Melton is more at home on the hunting field, I fear.'

'It is no matter, but I must catch it up at once, or I shall be a danger to all about me. Excuse me, sir.'

Her companion led her off the floor.

'I believe there is a retiring-room,' she murmured. 'Please do not trouble to escort me. I shall find my way.'

The rest-room was further away than she remembered, but she found it after passing through a series of small apartments. Torn flounces were no rare occurrence, as the maid assured her. With the aid of a needle and thread the damage was soon repaired.

She had intended to return at once to the ballroom, but the inn had been altered since her last visit, and she was soon lost. In the distance she could hear the sound of music, and she made her way towards it.

It was as she was passing a small embrasure that she noticed an elderly woman lying on a couch. She heard the stertorous breathing, and was alarmed by the pallor of the wrinkled face.

'May I be of assistance, ma'am?' Aurelia paused beside the couch. 'You do not look at all the thing. Perhaps a restorative?'

The papery eyelids opened, and a pair of sharp black eyes inspected her.

'I thank you. . .but my grandson. . .he is gone to fetch something for me. It is just the heat. . .'

'It *is* very warm,' Aurelia agreed. The Regent lived in a hothouse atmosphere, and stuffy rooms were all the rage in Brighton. She pulled up a small gilt chair, and then, disturbed by the old lady's laboured breathing, she leaned towards her.

'Perhaps if I fanned you it might bring relief.' She unfurled her fan, moving it gently to create a current of air.

'That is civil of you, my dear. I am an obstinate creature. Rollo warned me that I should rest, but I paid him no heed.' She lifted her face towards the swaying fan. 'There! I feel better already.'

Even as she spoke she collapsed with a sigh into Aurelia's arms.

'Let me!' The deep voice startled her. Salterne set down the glass of brandy in his hand and took her burden from her.

'I will fetch some water.' Aurelia hurried back to the retiring-room, and returned with a small bowl and a cloth.

'This lady should be taken home at once,' she said quietly. She laid the moistened cloth on the unconscious woman's brow.

'I agree. If I might leave my grandmother in your care for a moment I will order my coach and send a servant for the doctor.'

Aurelia nodded. She poured a little of the water over the old lady's wrists and saw with relief that her patient was recovering consciousness.

'Do not try to speak,' she urged. 'The Duke will be back at once.' She held the brandy to the old woman's lips.

'Stupid of me!' The faint words barely reached Aurelia's ears. 'Rollo is like to be insufferable since he is proved right again.' She gave a low chuckle.

'His Grace will be pleased to find you better, ma'am.'

'You are very kind.' A tiny claw-like hand gripped her own with surprising strength. 'It was fortunate that you chanced by. Will you tell me your name? We have not met before, I think.'

'I am Aurelia Carrington, Your Ladyship. You may know my sister, Lady Ransome?'

'Ah, yes. . . Ransome. . .'

There was a silence which Aurelia did not attempt to break. Was she to be classed with her unscrupulous brother-in-law? She would not blame anyone for repudiating his connections. As she attempted to withdraw her hand the old lady spoke again.

'Your father was very dear to me,' she said. 'What a man he was! You must miss him sadly.'

'I do. No one could have had a happier childhood than my sister and myself.'

'Poor Cassandra. She thought the world well lost for love. And you, miss? Are you of the same opinion? You are perhaps betrothed?'

'No, Your Grace.' From anyone else the question might have been an impertinence, but somehow Aurelia could not take offence.

'You do not answer my first question, Miss Carrington.'

Aurelia smiled and rose to her feet.

'You will tire yourself, ma'am. Then His Grace will regret having left you in my charge.'

'Stuff! Rollo worries too much. 'Tis naught but a dizzy spell and to be expected at my age. It has passed off, as you see.' She struggled to sit up, but the effort was beyond her and she closed her eyes.

'How is she?' Salterne stood beside them.

'A little better, I believe. . .but weak.'

He bent and lifted the frail figure in his arms.

'The door on the left,' he said briefly. 'Will you lead the way?'

Aurelia gathered up the old lady's scarf and reticule. Then she hurried ahead of him.

'Get in,' he commanded. 'I shall need your help.'

Aurelia settled herself in the corner of the coach. This was no time to raise objections. As Salterne laid his burden on the seat she took the Duchess's head in her lap.

Their journey was a short one, but Salterne was out of the coach before it had stopped moving.

'Come!' he said in an abrupt tone. He took his grandmother from Aurelia's arms and ran lightly up the steps of a large house.

Flambeaus burned by the door, illuminating the anxious faces of a group of servants. Brushing aside their offers of help, he called to his steward.

'The doctor?'

'On his way, Your Grace. We are keeping watch for him.'

Salterne started up the stairs.

'Miss Carrington!' It was a peremptory command, and she followed him without question. He threw open the door of a bedroom on the first floor, and laid his grandmother down against the pillows. The frail old lady looked pathetically small in the massive four-poster with its heavily carved upright columns. The roof piece supported a high canopy covered in damask drapery, and curtains in the same material, lavishly fringed and tasselled, were half drawn around the bed.

The Duke thrust them aside impatiently as Aurelia busied herself in removing the satin turban from the Duchess's head. She loosened the ribbons of her upper clothing, and then pulled off her slippers.

'I will attend her, madam.'

Aurelia moved aside as the Duchess's maid bent over her mistress. She was about to leave the room when she heard a whispered request.

'Stay with me, please.'

Aurelia looked towards the Duke, but he was gazing through the window, drumming his fingers on the sill.

'At last!' He strode towards the staircase and hustled the doctor into the room.

Aurelia stood back. There was nothing more that she could do. The Duke took her arm and led her into the corridor.

'She is in good hands,' he murmured, as if to reassure himself as much as Aurelia. His tortured expression went to her heart.

'Pray do not distress yourself,' she said gently. 'The old are surprisingly resilient, and the Duchess appears to have an indomitable will.'

He had been gazing into space, but her words struck a chord. He looked deep into her eyes and then he smiled.

'That is one of her problems,' he admitted. 'Miss Carrington, you have been most kind. May I offer you some refreshment?'

She was about to refuse, but a feeling of pity stayed her. She would wait with him until the doctor had given his verdict.

'I thank you. I must confess I am a little thirsty.'

He led her down to the salon and rang for wine. Then he began to pace the room.

'The Duchess assured me that her disposition was due entirely to the heat,' she offered.

'To that. . .and a heart condition which is like to kill her at any time. . .' His face was grim. 'I begged her not to attend the ball. She should have taken my advice.'

Aurelia did not speak. She had suspected something of the kind from what the Duchess had told her.

'Women!' he went on furiously. 'Of all the stubborn, self-willed creatures on this earth. . .'

Aurelia permitted herself the ghost of a smile.

'Something amuses you?'

'Women do not have a monopoly of such traits, Your Grace.'

He stared at her. Then he put up a hand to acknowledge the hit. 'You are right, of course. I am not myself the best of patients.'

He sighed to his servant to set down the tray beside him. Then he turned to Aurelia.

'You will take wine, Miss Carrington? It is not ratafia, I fear.'

Aurelia blushed. He had not forgotten their first meeting.

'That was ill done of me,' she said. 'It is not. . .not my usual way.'

'You had cause for anger. . .but so had I.'

Aurelia changed the subject. She had no wish to be drawn into a discussion of Caroline's behaviour. She gazed about the room.

'You are interested in paintings, Your Grace?'

The salon had surprised her. Plain walls painted in

the palest possible shade of green formed a perfect
background for a fine collection of pictures. She could
guess at the value of the furniture, which bore evidence of an expert craftsman's skill. It was clear that
the Duke did not share the Regent's taste in matters
of interior decoration.

Her host appeared to have read her mind.

'Astonished?' he said lightly. 'The Prince's "farm-
house" is somewhat overdone for me, though he is a
noted patron of the arts.'

Aurelia felt that she was on dangerous ground. The
Regent's flamboyant tastes were no concern of hers,
and incautious comment might well reach his ears.
She rose to her feet and walked over to the window.
It faced the sea and beyond it the lights of the fishing
fleet were strung out like a necklace of jewels on the
dark waters. Above the sea a rising moon sent a shaft
of silver light towards her.

What an evening it had been! And now to find
herself in the house of her enemy after all her efforts
to avoid him.

She was lost in thought when the doctor entered
the room, and she stayed out of hearing while he
made his report to the Duke. Then she glanced at
Salterne's face with a look of enquiry.

'She is recovering,' he said heavily. 'In future I shall
be firm with her. She must follow the physician's
orders. She still believes that she may go about as she
was used to.' The harsh lines on his face were even
more pronounced, and the scar showed white against
his tanned skin. For the first time in their acquaintance
Aurelia thought that he looked weary.

'I must go,' she said gently. 'Cassie must be
wondering. . .'

'I beg your pardon. I had forgot to mention it, but I sent a message to Lady Ransome to explain. . .'

'That was thoughtful, but even so. . .it is late, Your Grace.' Aurelia gave him her hand. 'Try not to worry, sir. When the Duchess is rested you will see an improvement.'

His eyes searched her face. 'You have some experience, I believe. Your sister told me something of your life at Marram. It must have been hard for you.'

'Not in the least. I loved my father dearly. It is three years since his death, and I miss him yet. We were so close, you see.' Her voice was not quite under control. 'He teased me into forming my own opinions on many subjects. I still feel the need. . .'

'For stimulating conversation?' He had understood her perfectly. 'And for affection too, I imagine. It is hard to lose a loved one. They are not easily replaced. . .'

Aurelia's eyes met his, and she looked away. The depth of misery there appalled her.

'You have a daughter, I understand. She must be a joy to you.'

'Charlotte arrives tomorrow.' Salterne's expression changed. 'She is an imp of mischief, Miss Carrington, and my grandmother indulges her. They are two of a kind, I fear.' His severe look was unconvincing.

'Then you have much to look forward to.' She picked up her scarf and reticule. 'Now, if you will allow me, I must leave.'

'Of course. Forgive me, I am being thoughtless.'

Aurelia murmured a disclaimer, and suddenly felt shy. Tonight she had seen a side of the Duke's character which was totally unexpected. She frowned. Could she have been wrong about him? She was unusually silent for the duration of the journey to the Steyne.

As the carriage stopped Salterne took her hands in his.

'I am in your debt, dear enemy. I shall not forget.'

In the darkness she could not see his face, but the warmth in his voice caused her heart to pound. He was having the most unfortunate effect upon her equilibrium, and to her dismay she found that she had not the slightest wish to draw her hands away from his.

'It. . .it was nothing. I beg you will not speak of it. I was happy to be of service to the Duchess.' Aurelia found that she was trembling, and she could not disguise the fact.

'You are cold. Let me take you to your door.' He handed her down, bowed, and was gone before Cassie could greet him.

'Lia, what happened? You have been gone this age. I was never so surprised as when I received the Duke's message.'

'The Dowager Duchess felt faint. I happened to be there.'

'Is that all? I fancied her at death's door. How uncivil of Salterne to ruin your evening!'

'He did nothing of the kind,' Aurelia said shortly. 'Don't fuss, Cass. I should have done the same for anyone.'

'But you dislike him so! Had he but asked I should have gone myself.'

'There was no time, and you could not leave Caro.'

'You might have stayed with her. . .'

'Cassie, let us forget the matter. Did you enjoy the ball?' Aurelia's patience was wearing thin.

'My dear, what an evening! I enjoyed it above anything...and the invitations we received!' A thought struck her and her face fell. 'Now that Salterne is here we must consider his wishes, I suppose. I confess I was surprised to find him here.'

'Why so? The Prince is expected, and the Duke is a friend of his.'

'I know, but Salterne may not be best pleased to find Caro behaving as if she were unattached.'

'She *is* unattached as yet. And she has not agreed to marry him.'

Cassie's lips set in a thin line.

'She will do so. There is no alternative. Ransome is in desperate case. We must not lose Salterne now.'

'Things cannot be as bad as that.'

'They could scarce be worse. The duns are closing in...' Cassie shuddered.

'How much is involved? I know I said I would not help, but I cannot see you in such straits...'

'No!' Cassie was adamant. 'I had no right to ask you. I would not reduce you to our level.'

'I see.'

'No, you refuse to see. When it is known that Caro is to marry the Duke our creditors will hold off. Salterne scarce knows what he is worth. I could not begin to guess at his income.'

'And Ransome would then feel at liberty to continue his present way of life? Where is it to end, Cassie? I may not like the Duke, but I do not consider him a fool. He will not spend his fortune on a gambler.'

'Neither would he countenance Ransome's bankruptcy,' Cassie persisted stubbornly. 'Salterne bears a great name. He will not see it disgraced.'

'Disgraced even further, do you mean? You seem to have forgot his reputation.'

Cassie shrugged. 'We may discount at least one half of the gossip.'

'The other half would be enough for me.'

'Lia, please! If we can but come about this time, Ransome may have learned his lesson.'

Aurelia stared at her sister in amazement. If, after all these years, Cassie still hoped that her husband would have a change of heart there was no more to be said on the subject.

'I am tired, my love.' She dropped a kiss on Cassie's brow. 'I will speak to you in the morning.'

A disturbed night did nothing to refresh her spirits and the others were up and about before she came downstairs.

Cassie was standing by the window, gazing at the rain-swept street.

'We must forgo our drive,' she said in petulant tones. 'There would be no pleasure in setting off in this miserable weather.'

'Then we shall occupy ourselves indoors, though I confess that I have finished my book.' Aurelia looked up in surprise as a knock sounded at the door. 'Is it not too early for morning callers?'

'It is doubtless Captain Leggatt.' Cassie gave her a mischievous look. 'He asked if he might call.'

'The captain must imagine that he is still on campaign,' Aurelia said drily.

'Perhaps he is. It was clear that he admired you.'

'Now, Cass, you are not to be at your matchmaking already.'

'Of course not.' Cassie bent over her netting, that

Aurelia might not see the twinkle in her eye. 'But did you not say. . .?'

The sentence was left unfinished. Her face changed as the door burst open. She rose to her feet and the netting fell unheeded to the ground.

'Ransome!' she whispered. 'What are you doing here?'

CHAPTER SIX

RANSOME inspected them from the doorway. He was smiling, but his eyes were cold.

'How could I stay away, my love?' He sauntered over to Cassie and caught her by the upper arm. To all appearances he was about to salute her as any man might greet a beloved wife, but she gave a gasp of pain as his cruel fingers nipped her flesh.

'Ransome!' Aurelia's voice cut the air like a lash.

'Yes, dear sister-in-law?' The guileless blue eyes looked into hers. Behind the apparent innocence was a gleam of such malevolence that Aurelia gasped. She had not thought to see such evil in a human face. It was gone in a flash, and Ransome strolled towards her.

'Forgive me!' His smile deepened. 'You are the mistress here, so Frederick tells me.' He bent to kiss her cheek.

'Spare me your embraces!' Aurelia looked pointedly at the red marks on her sister's arm.

'Was I too urgent in my greeting? You cannot blame me. I have been deprived of Cassie for so long.'

'And much against your will, I make no doubt. Your eyesight must be failing, sir. Have you no word for your daughter?'

'I imagined she was trying to make herself invisible.' His tone was smooth, but Caroline began to tremble. 'Doubtless she is attempting to hide her delight at my arrival. Come to me, my dear. Will you not greet your father with a kiss?'

With lagging steps Caroline walked towards him. As she reached his side he seized her hand in an iron grip, forcing her to her knees. Then he dropped a kiss upon her brow.

'Nervous, my dear child? Perhaps the excitement is too much for you, but you must try to contain your transports of joy.' He looked at Aurelia as he spoke, challenging her openly.

'What brings you here?' she asked abruptly.

'My family, of course.' His eyes widened in feigned astonishment. 'It was kind in you to spirit them away so suddenly for—er—a change of scene. . .but now I must insist that they are restored to me.' He shot her a swift look of triumph, knowing that she was power-less to stop him.

Without a word she handed him a card from the pile beside her. He whistled as he looked at the invitation. 'A musical evening with the Prince? You move in high circles, my dear Aurelia. Why this sudden wish to return to society? I thought you con-tent to moulder away at Marram.'

'I have changed my mind.'

'I wonder why? You cannot be hoping for an offer after all these years.'

Aurelia was silent.

Ransome laughed then, and it was not a pleasant sound.

'Have I hit on the truth of it? If so, you must persuade Caro to follow your example. She has some foolish notion that she does not wish to marry.'

'Of course she will marry.' Inwardly Aurelia upbraided herself for antagonising him so quickly, but his cruelty had incensed her. 'Surely another week or two in Brighton cannot signify? If you would but consent. . .'

'Pleading, my dear? That is somewhat out of character, is it not?' Ransome was enjoying himself. 'I know you well, Aurelia. You do not approve of Salterne, is that it?' He gave her a hard look.

'I do not know the Duke well. How am I to judge?'

'Oh, you'll judge! Nothing could be more certain. After all, your standards are so high. No one was good enough for you. Tell me, does your fortune make a warm bedfellow?'

'Ransome, please. . .' Cassie was stung into a reproach, but a look from Aurelia silenced her.

'The Regent will not take kindly to a refusal,' she warned.

'Prinny will understand,' he answered carelessly. 'Cass, make your preparations. We leave today.'

'So soon?' Salterne was standing in the doorway, regarding them with a benevolent gaze. He bowed to the ladies and favoured Ransome with the briefest of nods. Then he walked over to Aurelia.

'I crave your pardon for entering unannounced, Miss Carrington. In view of our forthcoming connection I felt that we might dispense with the formalities.'

He turned to Caro and took her hands, giving her a smile of singular sweetness.

'We go on so well, my dear Ransome,' he murmured. 'Caro has promised to drive with me today. I shall take it amiss if you steal her away.'

Aurelia was tempted to laugh aloud at the look on Ransome's face. Cassie was speechless, and Caroline stood as if turned to stone. Aurelia was the first to recover her composure.

'Do not keep His Grace waiting, Caro,' she said briskly. 'Do you put on your pelisse and make haste. The horses must not stand, you know.'

She turned to Salterne.

'We had not expected you quite yet,' she said in perfect truth. 'The rain was so heavy. . .'

'It is clearing, ma'am.' His expression was imperturbable as he looked at Ransome. 'I hope I may persuade you to delay your departure, my dear sir, but naturally if you insist I must give way.'

'Not at all! I did not know you to be in Brighton, Your Grace. I had imagined, you see. . .' His voice tailed away.

'Yes?' Salterne prompted.

'It is no matter. . .' Ransome looked uncomfortable. 'I was concerned to think that the ladies were alone.'

'A proper sentiment from a loving father and husband.' With exquisite grace His Lordship proffered his snuff-box. 'When Miss Carrington and Lady Ransome approved this delightful expedition I could not believe my good fortune. Such an opportunity to woo my bride-to-be! I trust it has your approval? We should have applied for your permission, but we had no notion as to where you might be found.'

An ugly flush stained Ransome's cheeks.

'I beg that you will allow your anger to fall upon me and not upon the ladies, if you have some objection,' Salterne continued.

Aurelia dared not meet his eye. She had seldom seen her brother-in-law so thoroughly routed, and she kept her countenance with the greatest difficulty. The thought of Ransome chiding this formidable creature brought her sense of humour bubbling to the surface. When His Lordship chose he could be insufferable.

'We dispatched Frederick to beg you to join us,' His Grace said smoothly. 'But perhaps you do not care for Brighton?'

'It is well enough.' Ransome quickly recovered his ease of manner. 'If the ladies had but explained... Aurelia, I fear you have been teasing me.'

'Miss Carrington enjoys a joke,' the Duke observed with a straight face. 'May I beg you to accompany us, ma'am? Lady Ransome will not wish to leave her husband as he is but just arrived.'

'I shall not keep you above a moment.' Aurelia hurried from the room, praying that Cassie would have the wit to support the Duke's story.

On her return she was not surprised to find that he was embarked upon a plausible account as to how and why he had escorted Cassie and his betrothed into Sussex to visit Marram.

'We had scarce hoped to persuade Miss Carrington to join us,' he said without a flicker of expression. 'But I added my entreaties to those of your family and here we are.'

That was doing it too brown. Aurelia's shoulders began to shake as she met his bland look, but her amusement vanished when Ransome spoke to her.

'I may stay here, I suppose? The town is crowded. There is nothing to be had in the way of lodgings.'

Aurelia forced a smile.

'Of course you shall stay. Hannah will see to the arrangement of the rooms.' The thought of having Ransome under her roof filled her with dismay, but there was no avoiding it.

'My apologies, Miss Carrington.' Salterne's voice was low as he handed her into his carriage. 'This can be no pleasant prospect for you.'

'It is no matter.' For her part she was glad that Ransome appeared to be in charity with his wife again. 'I fear you have a vivid imagination, Your Grace. What a tale you told!'

'Merely in the interests of family harmony. Or shall I say rather that needs must when the devil drives? On occasion the normal rules of conduct do not apply. One fights fire with fire. You of all people will know that.'

She refused to rise to the bait.

'You must think me remiss,' she said. 'How is the Dowager Duchess today?'

'She is much recovered, I thank you. It was she who asked me to call upon you. She will be happy to see you.'

'Surely she should rest? Did not the doctor say. . .?'

'He has forbidden all visitors for a day or so, and I have insisted that she obey him.'

Aurelia made an unsuccessful attempt to hide a smile.

'You are quite right,' he told her ruefully. 'It was not easy. I was forced to point out that if she wished to enjoy the Prince's company she must save her strength. They are quite the best of friends. She has known him since he was a child.'

'You know the Prince well, my lord? Caro was asking about him only yesterday. . .' Aurelia attempted to hide her irritation as she looked at her niece. Caro was pale. She had not recovered from the shock of her father's sudden reappearance, but she had been rescued from a difficult situation. If only she would make some effort to be civil.

His Lordship did not seem troubled by her silence. 'I believe I know the Regent as well as anyone may,' he replied. 'His is a complex character, and he has been much abused by his enemies. His country-men are disinclined to favour a patron of the arts, or a connoisseur of food and wine, especially as his pleasures are so costly. Had he been bluff and hearty like the Duke of Clarence he might have been better understood. Yet the Prince has many sterling qualities. . .'

'I was conscious only of his charm,' Aurelia admit-ted. 'And one hears everywhere of his generosity. The old woman who sells gingerbread and apples at the corner of the Steyne? Did he not give her a pension from his own pocket?'

Salterne smiled. 'You are speaking of Phoebe Hessell. Her story intrigued him. She joined the army as a man and followed her lover to the Indies when she was fifteen.'

'What happened to her?' Caroline forgot her fear of the Duke and leaned forward, her face alive with interest.

'She went into battle with the troops and received a bayonet wound.'

'And then she was discovered to be a woman?'

'Not even then. She was tall and broad, and she had a deep voice. It was only when her man was severely wounded that she disclosed her sex. She was sent home with him.'

'And did they marry?' Caroline asked.

'The story had a happy ending. She nursed him back to health, they wed, and enjoyed twenty years together before he died.'

'How wonderful!'

'The Prince shared your opinion, Caro. To save her

from the poorhouse he supports her from his private funds.'

'I am glad that he is so charitable.' Caroline's voice was warm.

'His very generosity adds to his debts, alas, and they, you must know, have always been immense.'

Aurelia looked mystified.

'Was it not said that when he married his difficulties would be at an end? The King and Parliament promised financial help, did they not? I remember my father speaking of the matter.'

'That was the Prince's understanding, ma'am, but it was not as he hoped. His Royal Highness is much embittered. He considers that he was betrayed into a marriage which——'

His eye fell on Caroline and he stopped. He must not discuss her namesake, Caroline of Brunswick, nor the scandals which surrounded that lady. He changed the subject.

'You have not yet seen the interior of the Prince's "cottage"?' he enquired.

Caroline shook her head.

'It is most interesting.' He was smiling as he spoke. 'The Prince is much influenced by Chinese art.'

'I hear that he plans to change the exterior. Will it be in oriental style?'

'It is to be reminiscent of the Indian continent, so I understand. The plans are based on the design of Sezincote, the home of an Indian nabob.'

He glanced at Aurelia's face and his lips twitched.

'Neither to your taste nor to mine,' he said agreeably. 'But the Prince will have his way.'

'An Indian palace by the English Channel. . .?' she

mused. 'Well, it will most certainly be different. . . We have been invited to a musical evening there.'

'You cannot fail to enjoy it.' He turned to Caroline. 'The musicians are of the best, and Prince George has an excellent voice. One cannot help but share his pleasure.' His eyebrows lifted at her look of surprise. 'You are interested in the arts?'

Addressed directly, Caroline grew shy.

'Why, y—yes,' she stammered. She relapsed into silence and gazed through the window.

'Caroline paints,' Aurelia said with a touch of impatience. Really, the child should make some effort to preserve the basic courtesies of social life. Her incommunicative behaviour was becoming a trial.

'Indeed!' The Duke's eyes glazed. Drawing and painting were considered necessary accomplishments for young ladies and he had been forced to examine some dire examples of their effort.

'She has some talent.' Aurelia's eyes glinted. She did not bestow praise lightly, even on a beloved niece. Caroline's work was far removed from the usual daubs.

Salterne sensed her mood.

'I did not know.' He looked at the silent girl. 'Do you prefer portraiture or still life?'

'I. . . I like to paint landscapes,' Caroline said in a low voice.

'Then I shall show you one of the finest sights in England.'

He rapped out an order and the coachman changed direction. As they travelled east the Duke exerted himself to name the villages through which they passed, pointing out the Norman churches, and the ruins of several castles.

Aurelia found that she was enjoying herself. Her companion's extensive knowledge of the countryside surprised her.

When they stopped and he handed her down she found that they had reached a high point of the downs, and in the distance she could hear the sea.

Salterne looked at her yellow kid half-boots.

'The ground is still damp, I fear, but if we keep to the sheep track we may walk a little way.'

Caro was already hurrying on ahead, but Aurelia slowed her own pace.

'Your Grace, I have not yet thanked you for your help this morning. You arrived at a difficult moment. . .'

'You would thank me for my duplicity? You. . .of all people? I am shocked.'

'Please do not jest. I am in earnest. Ransome would most certainly have insisted. . .' Her voice tailed away.

'On removing his family from your baleful influence?' He laughed. 'I guessed as much, Miss Carrington, when I saw him enter the house. It was unpardonable of me to come upon you unannounced, and I had some difficulty in persuading your servant. . .'

'I am very glad you did so,' Aurelia said with feeling. 'I had no power to stop him. I could think of no way to prevent him taking them away.'

'You, at a loss? I don't believe it.'

She caught his eye and blushed.

'We have so many invitations,' she said lamely. 'And it would have been discourteous to refuse the Prince.'

'Quite!' A suspicious quiver lingered at the corner of his mouth. 'And it would not have suited me in the least. However, I am persuaded that Ransome will make no further difficulties.'

She looked at him then and saw that his eyes were dancing. She could think of nothing to say as he strolled along beside her, perfectly at his ease.

'I must compliment you on the speed with which you followed my lead,' he murmured.

Aurelia coloured.

'Do you imagine that Ransome believed your story?'

'It is in his interest to believe it. In any case, it does not much signify, though I must confess that my powers of invention led me on to dangerous ground.'

She gave him a puzzled look.

'I felt that I had gone too far, ma'am, in claiming that you had yielded to my own entreaties to visit Brighton.' The swarthy face was alight with amusement. 'Confess that it almost overset you! We have not been the best of friends, you will agree.'

Aurelia stopped and turned to face him.

'I was unfair to you,' she said frankly. 'Perhaps I was mistaken. . .'

'A sudden change of heart, Miss Carrington? Is it altogether wise? Think of my age, my reputation. . .'

'You are pleased to heap reproaches on my head. I admit that I deserve them. I. . . I am inclined to be hasty on occasion.'

'And fierce in defence of the weak? Your concern for Caro does you credit.'

'It is just that. . .well. . .she is so young.'

'And afraid of me? I shall try to remedy that.'

'I do not understand why——' Aurelia stopped herself. 'I beg your pardon. I have no right to question. . .'

'To question my motives in offering for her, ma'am?

Your niece is a beauty. Had you not noticed? She is unspoilt, and her mama assures me that she is biddable. She will make an excellent wife.'

'Excuse me, if you please.' Aurelia hurried on to join her niece. She was scarlet with mortification at her own want of conduct in quizzing the Duke.

'Aunt, do look at the coastline.' Caroline pointed into the distance. 'We are so high above the sea. This might be a map laid out before us.'

'There to your left you may see almost as far as Hastings.' The Duke raised his gold-topped cane, but Aurelia could not give him her full attention. She wished that the ground might open and swallow her. How could she have been so ill-bred as to question him in such an unmannerly way? She had repaid his civility with what he must only regard as vulgar curiosity.

She hardly dared meet his eye until a firm hand slipped beneath her arm.

'Take care,' he warned. 'This ground beneath you is treacherous.'

She looked up at him then, and the heart-stopping smile made her bones melt. The tension between them was so strong that Caroline must surely sense it. Dear God! She could not go on like this.

With what dignity she could command she moved away, affecting to study the curious lichens growing on a nearby stone. Someone else must act as Caro's chaperon, she thought wildly. In Salterne's company she herself was another person. With him there was always a sense of excitement, and she had never felt more alive. Now she knew why women were said to prefer a rake to more sober-minded gentlemen.

But it would not do. She could not allow him to

steal away her peace of mind. This was but a passing sensation, due, no doubt, to the long years alone at Marram. With an effort she regained her composure, only to lose it once more as he murmured in her ear.

'Take heart!' the deep voice whispered. 'You will come about. Don't sheathe your sword just yet.'

Then he turned to Caroline to discuss the difficulties of capturing the landscape in paint.

'You shall come to see my own collection,' he promised. 'A part of it is here in Brighton. You know the works of Poussin and Claude?'

Caroline's face glowed.

'You have some of their paintings? How I should love to see them.'

'It will be my pleasure, though Turner is thought to be the coming man. You may care to give me your opinion.'

Caroline was all animation. She had forgotten her dread of him. She chattered on as they returned to Brighton, encouraged by his evident knowledge of her favourite subject.

Aurelia spoke little. Her mind was in a turmoil. The Duke had exerted himself to set Caroline at her ease, but his manner towards herself was very different. His easy gallantry, the teasing, and the unmistakable look in his eyes... One might almost suppose that she, Aurelia, was the object of his affection, but that was ridiculous. She could not look at him.

On their return to the Steyne the Duke stayed only to suggest a visit to the theatre that evening. With a promise to call for them at nine he took his leave.

'Did you enjoy your drive, my love?' Ransome was delighted.

'Yes, Father. Did you know that His Grace is

interested in paintings? He has asked if I may go to see his collection. That is—if you will permit me?'

'Of course.' Ransome patted her hand. 'Now go to your mama. She will be anxious to hear your news.'

As the door closed behind her he gave Aurelia a look of satisfaction.

'I must felicitate you, dear sister. You have accomplished what I could not. Caro is quite in charity with the Duke.'

Aurelia could take no pleasure in his words.

'You tried to rush her,' she said coldly. 'You gave her no time to get to know him.'

'Time, for me, is short, as Cassie will have told you. Now it would appear that our troubles are at an end. You have surprised me, Lia. I had not thought you would approve the match.'

'I believe His Grace to have many good qualities,' Aurelia said carefully. She must not arouse his suspicions.

'Do you, by gad?' Ransome's eyes were fixed intently on her face. 'Yet he ain't your style, I think. He's an ugly brute, and he ain't in his first youth. You will know of his reputation.'

She sensed that he was attempting to provoke her.

'He is devoted to his daughter and his grandmother,' she snapped, wondering as she did so why she felt obliged to defend him.

'And to a number of lightskirts...' Ransome's mocking tone infuriated her.

'Then I wonder how you can contemplate suggesting him to Caro.'

'Money, my dear. That would not count with you ...an heiress in your own right. Still, if you care to champion him...'

He gave her a speculative look.

'Ah, I see it now. With Caro wed your poor relations will be off your hands. I cannot say that I blame you.'

'You are off my hands already, Ransome.' Aurelia trembled with anger at his imputation. 'Whatever happens I shall not continue to pay your debts, whether or not the marriage takes place.'

'It will take place. I give you my word on it. I shall speak to Salterne tonight. The announcement will go in the *Morning Post* this week.'

Aurelia was tempted to beg him to give Caroline more time, but she knew it would be useless. She turned to leave him.

'No thought of marriage yourself, I suppose?' His tone was deceptively casual, but Aurelia had developed a sixth sense where Ransome was concerned. She understood the reason for his question. Were she to die a spinster her sister would inherit her fortune.

She could not resist the temptation to annoy him.

'Why else would I be here? An heiress, you will know, must always please. I shall not lack for suitors.'

She was ashamed of her words even as she spoke, but it pleased her to see his angry look.

'Aye. . .if you keep a guard upon that tongue of yours,' he sneered. His eyes roved over her figure. 'You ain't yet run to fat,' he admitted grudgingly. 'But that will of yours is in need of taming.'

Aurelia's nails dug into her palms. She had forgotten how impossible he could be.

'Excuse me. . .' She hurried to her room, resolved to be in his company as little as possible. His presence under her roof was more than she could bear.

'Lia, you look flushed. Is something wrong?' Cassie eyed her sister nervously.

'What could possibly be wrong?' Aurelia gave an ironic laugh.

'I thought perhaps you and Ransome had been quarrelling. I am so sorry. . . I did not intend to foist him on you.'

'It is no matter. At least you are to be allowed to stay.'

A frown creased Cassie's brow.

'He does seem pleased with Caro, but had it not been for Salterne. . . Lia, did you not find the Duke's behaviour strange this morning?'

'You may thank his ready powers of invention,' came the crisp reply. 'He prevented what promised to be a most unpleasant scene.'

'I do not understand him in the least. . .'

'Is it so strange that he should wish to keep you here?' Aurelia said with some asperity. Her head was beginning to ache.

'That he might be with Caro?' Cassie's face cleared.

'He has invited us to the theatre this evening. Did Caro tell you?'

The question was enough to divert Cassie's attention from further discussion of the Duke's behaviour. She slipped away to consider her toilette.

Aurelia summoned Hannah and asked for a tisane. She longed to beg off from the proposed entertainment, but concern for Caro forced her to make the effort to attend. If she could but close her eyes for an hour. . .

When she awoke she found that the tisane had driven away the dull ache in her temples, and she felt able to take an interest in her appearance. She had

intended to wear her pearls with the pale blue sarcenet, but she laid them aside in favour of her diamond
drops. Let Ransome accuse her of flaunting her wealth
if he wished. She intended to look her best, but to
what end she could not quite decide.

Aside from a calculating look at the flashing stones
Ransome made no comment, and when Salterne
arrived he greeted his host with all the easy address
of a man of fashion.

Yet he did not seem to be quite comfortable. Beside
Salterne's massive figure and swarthy countenance
Ransome's classic profile and blond good looks
seemed a trifle insipid to Aurelia's eyes. Both men
were dressed in evening breeches and coats of perfect
cut, but no one could mistake the Duke's position in
life. As always he gave an overwhelming impression
of power and authority.

Caro sensed it too. In her father's presence she
could not be easy with Salterne. As she lingered in
the background, lost for words, Aurelia saw
Ransome's growing annoyance.

'Caro,' she murmured softly, 'do try to be a little
more forthcoming. Today you have enjoyed His
Grace's company, have you not?'

Caro turned her face away.

'I liked him better, but I shall not marry him. If I
cannot have Richard I will marry no one.'

'Be quiet, for heaven's sake! You must not anger
your father. Do you wish him to take you home?' The
words were said in a whisper, and under the cover of
general conversation, but Aurelia looked up to find
the Duke's eyes upon her. Her heart gave a small
unnerving leap. He raised an eyebrow in enquiry, but
Aurelia smiled and shook her head. If Ransome

noticed the exchange he gave no sign. Instead he exerted all his charm to give the impression of a happy family gathering.

Aurelia was undeceived. When things were going Ransome's way he was at his best. Let anyone oppose him and the charm fell away like a cloak, revealing the vicious nature of the man beneath. He lost no time in attempting to embarrass her.

'You have made yet another conquest, Your Grace,' he said slyly. 'My sister-in-law has been singing your praises.'

'An exaggeration, I'm sure. Yet if it is so I am honoured.' The Duke bowed to her, but there was no trace of mockery in his look. He had seen through Ransome's ploy at once and would have no part in it. His face was impassive, but his jaw tightened. She guessed that he was angered by the clumsy remark.

To her relief he suggested that they leave at once if they were to see the opening of the play.

CHAPTER SEVEN

THE exterior of the small theatre in Duke Street had
little to recommend it. The building, of wood painted
to resemble stone, could not be described as anything
other than ugly. A portico above the entrance offered
some pretension to grandeur, but the place had a
ramshackle appearance.

Yet the inside was furnished charmingly, inviting
comparison with the most stylish of London theatres.

Aurelia looked at the scene below from the comfort
of Salterne's box. The performance to come, a revival
of *An Agreeable Surpise*, had attracted a large audience, most of them members of the *haut ton*.

She guessed that speculation was already rife. Her
own appearance and that of the Ransomes, in the
company of the Duke of Salterne, could not fail to
lead to comment. Cassie, she noticed, was already
waving to her friends.

'Lia, do you not see Charles Leggatt?' Cassie drew
her attention to the boyish figure who was bowing to
them from the pit.

Aurelia nodded an acknowledgement. Then, as the
lights dimmed, she settled back to enjoy the play.

It was a slight piece, and she found it impossible to
concentrate upon the action on the stage. Her
thoughts strayed to her conversation with Caroline.
Her niece's unyielding determination to marry
Richard had surprised her. A wry smile touched the
corner of her mouth. It was a family failing. She had

seen it in Cassie, and who could be more stubborn than she herself. Blood will out, she thought with some dismay. At least the girl was steadfast in her devotion.

She looked at her companions. Cassie, secure in her belief that all was well, was on good terms with Ransome. For his part he seemed determined to attract attention. His loud comments on the performance drew angry looks and one or two admonitions to silence from the neighbouring boxes. Caroline had moved away, and was seated in a corner intent on the play.

'You seem preoccupied this evening, Miss Carrington. The performance is not to your taste?'

Aurelia jumped. She had not realised that the Duke was beside her.

'I. . . Yes, of course, Your Grace. I beg your pardon. I was not attending.'

'Something is troubling you?' His words were inaudible to the others. 'If I may be of help. . .?'

'It is nothing, I assure you.' Aurelia found his attention disturbing. The Duke should not single her out in this way. Ransome would be furious to see him by her side when Caro sat alone.

'You would prefer to leave? I should be happy to escort you. . .!'

'Pray do not consider it. Perhaps I am a little tired. At Marram I lead such a quiet life. . .'

Her blue eyes, fringed with dark lashes, looked up at him, and she caught her breath. Some indefinable spark had passed between them in that moment, and it unnerved her. Then the hooded lids came down to veil his expression. It was unfathomable once more.

Aurelia glanced uneasily at Ransome. Where his

own interests were concerned her brother-in-law possessed a sixth sense. He had missed nothing of the exchange between Salterne and herself, and he gave her a inimical look.

With an effort she turned her attention to the play, but Ransome's chatter had ceased. During the interval he came to her on the pretext of offering refreshment.

'Must you make an exhibition of yourself?' he hissed. 'The Duke is not interested in your vapourings. . .'

She was spared the need to reply as the box filled with Salterne's friends.

'What a pleasure to see you again, Miss Carrington!' Charles Leggatt came over to her at once. 'You owe me the favour of another dance, ma'am.'

'You must forgive me. My sister did explain, I believe.'

'And I must claim responsibility.' Salterne stood beside them, dwarfing the younger man. 'It was I who spirited Miss Carrington away. She was good enough to lend me her assistance.' The grey eyes searched one face and then the other. 'I am sorry to have spoiled your evening, Charles.' He moved away.

'Lady Ransome agreed that I might call on you. Did you see my card?'

'I saw several of your cards,' Aurelia admitted with a twinkle. 'You have been unlucky not to find us at home.'

'Then perhaps tomorrow. . .?'

'We shall be happy to see you.'

He flushed with pleasure and stepped aside to allow the other members of his party to be presented to her. She turned to give her attention to the man who was bowing over her hand. He was older than the others, and unlike them he was not in uniform. His flawless evening clothes had an air of understated perfection, contrasting sharply with the ornate dress of his companions. They gave him an air of sophistication which the younger men could not hope to match. His eyes sparkled as he read her thoughts.

'I am quite outshone, Miss Carrington, but I refuse to admit defeat. I have a claim upon your indulgence. Your sister is an old friend.'

'Beware, Aurelia!' Cassie laughed as she tapped his shoulder with her fan. 'Robert Clare is an accomplished flirt.'

'Not so!' Their companion threw up his hands in protest. 'We Irish have a reputation for exaggeration, but tonight I stand on firm ground. We have all Three Graces in this box. Ransome, you are a fortunate man.'

Thus appealed to, Ransome bowed and was at pains to agree, but his eyes were cold. In their depths Aurelia saw undisguised hostility.

She shrugged and looked at Robert Clare with interest. His attractive voice held traces of a Irish accent, and she guessed him to be a member of the Regent's inner circle. Many of the Prince's intimates were of Irish origin. He was said to enjoy their ready wit, their eccentricities, their penchant for late hours, and their love of life. The man beside her appeared to possess those qualities in abundance.

'My countrymen are sadly maligned,' he continued in mock-dismay. 'Our most sincere professions of regard are found to be—er—excessive.'

'Pearls before swine?' she murmured.

'I suspect, ma'am, that I am destined to become

your slave.' His look recorded his appreciation of her sally. 'When wit is allied to beauty I am lost.'

'You are hoist with your own petard, I fear,' Aurelia told him demurely. 'That, sir, is a gross exaggeration.'

She found his manner disarming, and he showed no inclination to leave her side. It was only when the lights dimmed for the resumption of the performance that he rose to his feet. Unlike Charles Leggatt he did not beg for the privilege of calling upon her, but she had no doubt that she would see him again.

She was not mistaken. From then on Robert Clare was a frequent visitor to the house on the Steyne, much to the disgust of Charles Leggatt. The two men vied with each other in proffering invitations to open-air concerts, balloon ascents, and other entertainments.

Aurelia bore Cassie's teasing with equanimity. Neither man had touched her heart, and she suspected that Clare in particular was simply amusing himself.

Ransome, meantime, was growing more surly, and the reason was not far to seek. Caro's betrothal had not yet been announced. Aurelia wondered at the delay, though she was much relieved. Had Salterne decided to play a waiting game, rather than forcing the girl into open defiance?

Her surmise was confirmed when Caroline sought her out.

'We have spoken together, the Duke and I,' she confided. 'He was very kind. I said that I wished to have more time. He looked a little stern, but he made no objection. I was afraid that he might mention it to Father, but he cannot have done so. . .else we should have known.'

Nothing could be more certain. Had Ransome suspected the reason for the delay he would have made their lives unbearable. As it was he grew increasingly morose, and spent as little time as possible in the house.

Aurelia found it a relief. His temper was uncertain, and she dreaded an explosion which might bring matters to a head.

When Salterne called upon them later in the week he brought a message from the Duchess.

'She begs that you will visit her today, Caro, if it is convenient.'

'She is quite recovered. . .? The doctor. . .?'

'Lessing has given his permission, Miss Carrington, and my grandmother has not yet met my bride-to-be.'

'I am so sorry, but Ransome and my sister are not at home.'

'I know,' His Grace said smoothly. 'The invitation is to you and Caro.'

Caroline looked uneasy and Aurelia frowned at her. The Duke gave the ladies a bland look.

'You find some objection, Miss Carrington?'

'Not at all.' It was not quite true. Ransome would be incensed to find that he had not been included in the invitation, but there was nothing she could do. 'It is a splendid idea,' she said hurriedly.

'Then if I might suggest. . .?' Salterne strolled over to the window and looked into the street. 'There is a chill wind this morning, but doubtless the horses will not suffer overmuch if they are kept standing. My groom is looking anxious. . .though naturally I should not wish you to imagine that I am at all impatient.'

'Of course not.' Aurelia's tone was dry. 'How could I have gained that impression.

'My felicitations, ladies!' he exclaimed some five

minutes later. One grows accustomed to a lengthy wait for members of the opposite sex. I trust I was not too importunate?'

'The horses must always be considered, Your Grace.' Aurelia gave him a limpid look.

Salterne chuckled.

'Shall you always pop in a hit when my guard is down, Miss Carrington? I shall come about,' he promised.

He was laughing, and she caught a glimpse of fine white teeth. How could she ever have thought him ugly? she marvelled. When he laughed his face was transformed. The stormy grey of those deep-set eyes could change in a moment into a shining gleam of silver. The lines about them would crinkle and the beautiful mobile mouth would turn up at the corners.

Yet her heart sank as she looked at him. She sensed that she was faced with danger, but not from him. The danger lay in her own heart. He was too much in her mind these days, and she had grown accustomed to his easy camaraderie. She had always been honest with herself, and she could not deny that she looked forward to their gentle *badinage*. What a joy it was to find an intelligent man who relished a battle of wits. He picked up her thoughts almost before she had time to formulate them. She had no need to explain. . .to spell everything out. . . But therein lay the danger.

She folded her hands in her lap. She was becoming fanciful. He had a fine mind, that was true, but of late she could not deny that there was also a powerful sexual attraction. She was not a child, and she could not mistake his look, or her own reaction. She wanted him, she realised now, and the thought appalled her. Of course it was not love. . .just simple animal lust.

She had not imagined herself capable of it, but it was true. She wanted this man to hold her in his arms, to whisper words which she had never thought to hear, and to take her without fear of the consequences.

And he was to marry Caroline. A pang of anguish stabbed her. The child did not even wish to be in his company. What hope of happiness could there be in such a match? Both lives might be ruined.

She was still lost in thought when they reached their destination.

In daylight the house on Marine Parade was larger than Aurelia had at first imagined, and Caroline's eyes grew wide with dread. The size of the establishment served to confirm all her fears, and this was but one of the Duke's houses. She had neither the desire or the ability to take charge of any of them.

Salterne led them up the curving staircase and into the Dowager's room. There, propped up against a mass of pillows, lay the tiny figure of the Duchess.

'So you have come!' The voice was faint, but the black eyes were as sharp as ever. 'And this pretty child must be Caroline. Will you give me a kiss, my dear?'

Caroline moved towards the bed. Although she was shy, and obviously in awe of the old lady, her manner was charming. She dropped a curtsy and bent to kiss the withered cheek.

'I am glad to hear that you are better, Your Grace,' she murmured softly.

'I am well enough, I thank you. It is trying to be confined to one room, but Charlotte does her best to entertain me.'

She threw back the coverlet to reveal a small child,

who gave them solemn look. Then her face gleamed with mischief.

'I was hiding, Papa, and you did not guess.'

She slid down the coverlet and ran towards the Duke, squealing with pleasure as he lifted her to his shoulder.

'I had thought you lost,' he assured her. 'I should have searched everywhere for you.'

'To take me to see the donkeys? You promised. . .'

'Indeed I did, my puss, but you must be patient. Miggs shall take you later.'

The child's lip quivered. 'I want you to come.' A plump little arm crept about his neck.

'We shall see.' Salterne looked at the Duchess. 'I hope she has not tired you, ma'am. You promised to rest. . .'

The old lady snorted.

'Time enough for that in the churchyard,' she snapped. 'Don't fuss, Rollo! Send for Miggs, if you must. It is time for Charlotte's walk.'

The child's face crumpled and she hid her face in the Duke's coat. 'I don't want Miggs. . . I want you to come.'

For once the Duke was at a loss, and the Duchess's enjoinder not to be a watering-pot resulted only in Charlotte tightening her arm about her father's neck.

As she watched his gentle attempts at comfort Aurelia was filled with wonder. She was seeing yet another aspect of this complex man's character, and one which was unknown to her. He bent his dark head, so like Charlotte's own, towards the little girl, and dropped a kiss upon the child's brow. His face had softened, and she heard the tenderness in his voice. With his daughter Salterne was a different person. Gone was the forbidding hauteur of his manner, and the mocking drawl which she so disliked. The love apparent in his eyes made him at once look younger and more vulnerable, and Aurelia found herself smiling at the pair of them with undisguised warmth. The sensation was disquieting and she strove to compose herself.

'I heard a story about a donkey,' she announced to no one in particular. 'His friend was a little girl, but she lived in the sea. Sometimes I look through the window to see if she is here.' She strolled over towards the sweeping curve of glass.

A tearful eye inspected her cautiously, but Aurelia paid no attention. She looked down at the beach.

There was silence for a moment, then, 'Is she there?'

'Not at present, but I can see the donkeys. There ...that is the one; he wears a blue hat. He must be waiting for her.'

'Is she in the sea?'

'I expect so. She is a mermaid, so she can swim.'

'Does the water come over her head?'

'It does, but she doesn't mind. If you come to the window I will show you where she lives.'

In another moment a small hand stole into hers.

'Did you know that a mermaid has a tail like a fish instead of legs like yours?' Aurelia continued conversationally. She settled herself on the window-seat with Charlotte on her knee.

'How does she walk?'

'She doesn't. When the tide comes up to the donkey's feet she reaches up and climbs into his saddle. Then he gives her a ride.'

'Does she talk to him?'

'Oh, yes. Mermaids are clever. They can talk to anyone.'

'Would she talk to me?'

'I believe so. . .if you were lucky enough to meet her.'

'When does she come to see the donkey?'

'She waits until it is quiet. She is rather shy, you see. She doesn't come when the sun is shining because it dries her skin.'

'She could come when it was raining.'

'So she could. That is when the donkey takes her for long, long rides across the sand.'

'To the bathing houses?'

'Far beyond there. Do you see those cliffs? It was there that they found lots of shells.'

The little face brightened. 'I found some shells when Papa came with me. Would you like to see them? I was showing them to Grandmama.' Charlotte reached into her pocket and produced the treasures. 'Papa knows their names,' she said proudly. 'But I have forgotten.'

'They are very pretty. Perhaps you may find some more. Does Miggs like shells?'

'Yes, but she is not as clever as Papa. I could show her, though. . .'

'She would like that. . .' Aurelia looked across at Salterne to find him pulling the bell-rope.

Miggs led the unprotesting child away.

'She is sadly spoiled, I fear. . .' Salterne said heavily.

'Not at all. She is a delight.'

'It is kind of you to say so. In the usual way she is a cheerful child, but her grandmother and I have been away, and. . .'

'And she has missed you? It is but natural. You would not wish it otherwise, I'm sure.'

'Rollo, your daughter has monopolised Miss Carrington! Do you intend to do the same? I shall not permit it. Come here, my dear, and tell me all your news.'

Salterne laughed and strolled towards the bed.

'Caro and I will leave you to your gossip,' he announced. 'She wishes to see the paintings in the salon. . .'

'Then off you go.' The Duchess waved a hand in dismissal. As the door closed she turned to Aurelia.

'You will forgive me for being blunt, but really this will not do. Has Rollo taken leave of his senses?'

'Your Grace, please! I cannot discuss. . . I mean, I have no right to express an opinion. . .'

'Stuff! The child is a beauty, that I'll grant you, and she has a charming manner, but she is not the wife for Salterne. He would be bored within a week. Aside from that, she is afraid of him. You will not tell me that she holds him in regard?'

Aurelia looked away.

'She respects him. That may be enough. . .'

'Fiddlesticks! You believe that no more than I. I do not hold with nonsensical transports of devotion. We are past the days of medieval romance, I hope. But Rollo has suffered enough. He needs a woman of character who will give him more than an heir.'

'Caro is young,' Aurelia offered. 'His Grace may be sure that she will be kind to Charlotte. Then, too, she may develop. . .'

The Dowager sniffed in disbelief.

'Is she like to lose her dread of him? Rollo is no saint. His needs are those of any other man. It would

try his patience beyond belief should she shrink when
he approaches her. No matter what the world believes,
he is not a brute.'

'I am sure of that,' Aurelia told her warmly. 'I place
no reliance on hearsay, ma'am. The Duke has been
all civility.'

A crow of laughter greeted her words.

'You have had no differences, you and he? Do not
ask me to believe it.' With her head on one side the
Duchess looked like some small exotic bird, alert and
sharply aware of the tension in Aurelia's manner. She
had not missed the way in which the colour flooded to
her companion's cheeks when Rollo's name was mentioned, or the highly charged atmosphere in the room
whenever he was present.

'We have not always been in perfect accord,'
Aurelia admitted. 'I find the Duke somewhat difficult
to understand at times.'

'So do I, and never more than at present.' Her
Ladyship settled back against her pillows. 'Now tell
me the truth, Miss Carrington; you like this match no
more than I?'

Aurelia was at a loss for words.

'Yet you do not altogether dislike my grandson, I
believe?' The question was apparently artless as the
Duchess searched among the rumpled pillows for her
handkerchief.

'Our—er—disagreements cannot be laid entirely at
his door.' Aurelia's face was burning with embarrassment. The question was unexpected and she did not
know how to reply. How could she hope to hide her
inner turmoil from the shrewd mind of the Dowager?

Dislike? The word was too mild to describe her
initial reaction to Salterne. She had detested him. But

now? She could not say with honesty that her feelings had not changed. He still had the power to annoy her almost beyond endurance, and of course he had no right to challenge her with his sexuality, as he did each time they met.

No other man had the power to cause those indefinable longings which seized her at his merest touch. With a smile or a look he could throw her into utter confusion. What had happened to the cool Miss Carrington? she wondered. In the past she had always been in command of her thoughts and her emotions.

She looked up to find the Duchess's eyes upon her face.

'I find the Duke an enigmatic person, ma'am. He can be formidable, can he not? Yet when I see him with his daughter and with you I cannot doubt his gentleness.'

'Rollo has a loving heart.' The old lady closed her eyes and lay back among her pillow, but her expression was still troubled. 'Well, they are not yet wed, or even formally betrothed. I had best see Cassandra, I suppose, and Ransome too, though the thought gives me no pleasure.'

Ransome was surprised by the invitation.

'Salterne must have persuaded the old harridan,' he announced. 'We had best put a civil face on it. He won't marry to disoblige her. She has a handsome fortune of her own.'

Peace did not reign for long. When Ransome returned from his visit to the Duchess his face was dark with rage.

'Well, madam, what is your game?' A small vein

pulsed in his temple as he walked towards Aurelia. 'You have set the old hag against me.'

'You need no help from me in that respect,' Aurelia told him coldly. 'This is my house, I must remind you. Either you are civil or you leave.'

'I intend to do so, and I'll take my family with me. We are doing no good here.' He began to curse and stormed out of the room.

'What has gone wrong?' Aurelia turned to Cassie who was sobbing quietly. An ashen-faced Caroline stood beside her. Cassie was incapable of speech. She shook her head and buried her face in her hands.

'Caro, what is the matter?'

'The Duchess was kind, but it was as you thought. She...she said that I would make an excellent wife, but not quite yet. She counselled waiting for some months...' The tears began to trickle down her cheeks. 'Papa is very angry.'

'And Salterne agreed with her. That was the worst of it.' Cassie gasped out the words between her sobs. 'Ransome could scarce contain his rage.'

'I hope he did not disgrace us, Cassie.'

'He would not openly antagonise the Duke. Salterne is very large, you know, and he is said to have a punishing left, whatever that may mean. Ransome did not dare to argue...and that made him worse. I cannot tell you what he said as we left the house.'

'Some tea will restore your spirits. Caro, my love, will you speak to Hannah?'

Aurelia closed the door and returned to Cassie's side.

'Well, sister, what did he say?'

'I had not thought he could be so coarse, especially

with Caro. It was dreadful. He told her that if she encouraged Salterne in. . .in a different way he would not be content to wait. The child was bewildered, Lia. She had no idea what he meant. He said that if she did not know how to go about the matter he would tell her.' Her sobs redoubled. 'He used the foulest language about the Dowager Duchess. I cannot repeat his words. He said also that Salterne could not be much of a man if he allowed Her Grace to lead him by the nose.'

'I notice that he did not care to face the "punishing left",' Aurelia said drily. 'Cheer up, Cass. Nothing appeals to Ransome more than the opportunity to torment his victims. You must not let him think you fear him.'

Cassie raised her head and Aurelia was shocked by the bitterness in her eyes.

'Don't look like that,' she begged softly. 'Ransome shall not have money to gamble away, but I am prepared to pay his more pressing debts.

'You will ruin yourself if you try to help us further.'

'Let me be the judge of that. I cannot allow him to take you away. He must agree to leave you here, at least for the next few weeks.'

Cassie was too distraught to argue further. With an anguished cry she left the room.

It was late that afternoon when Ransome returned.

'Are they ready?' he snarled. 'The carriage is at the door.'

'Then you had best dismiss it. I have something to say to you.'

'You may save your breath.' He thrust his face close to hers and she could smell the fumes of wine. 'I have you to thank for this change in Salterne. Don't trouble to deny it. You want him for yourself.'

Crimson with fury, Aurelia rose to her feet.

'How dare you speak to me like that?' she cried.

'Touched a nerve, did it? It's obvious, my dear. You're behaving like a bitch on heat.'

The crude vulgarity of his words turned Aurelia to ice. She was trembling with anger and the knuckles of her clenched fists whitened, but she made a supreme effort to control herself.

'That remark is all that I would expect from you,' she said quietly. 'Sit down and listen to me. It is to your advantage.'

'Be quick about it, then.' He flung himself into a chair. 'We leave tonight.'

'Is that wise? The Duchess, I understand, has suggested merely a delay.'

It was then that he began to curse—loudly and with great violence. Aurelia scarcely heard him. Her mind was still reeling from his accusations. It wasn't true. It could not possibly be true.

A sick feeling of dismay threatened to overwhelm her, combined with a feeling of self-disgust. She had allowed herself to drift almost imperceptibly into friendship with the Duke. How obvious it must have been to everyone that he sought her company rather than that of Caroline.

She stifled a groan of dismay. Coarse as Ransome's words had been they could not have wounded her so deeply if there were not some truth behind them. In an agony of mind she recalled her own reactions to Salterne's touch. It was all true—she did want him, and honesty demanded that she face the fact.

Wearily she lifted a hand to stem Ransome's flow of words.

'If you will but listen,' she said, 'I am offering you a way out of your difficulties.'

She had his attention then.

'I will give you a letter to my bankers. They will pay your more pressing debts. It will give you time...'

'Aye! If Salterne comes up to snuff...and if that little bitch can be brought to see reason...'

'Curb your tongue! You have not heard my conditions yet.'

'You wish me to kill myself?'

The sneering suggestion did not merit a reply.

'You will leave Cassie and Caro here while you deal with your affairs. If you do not agree I shall not lift a finger to help you.'

He gave her a calculating look.

'I might...if you throw in some blunt as well.'

'You may have one hundred pounds in gold. Give me a list of your debts. As the matter is urgent you should leave at once.'

He shrugged and walked over to her desk. He wrote for several minutes and then handed her the paper. Aurelia was shaken as she looked at the total, but her face remained impassive.

'Is this everything?' she enquired.

'Do you wish to see the accounts?' His laugh was ugly.

'You may show them to my bankers. Give me half an hour and I will write the letter. You had best see Cassie before you go.'

He hesitated, seemed about to speak, and then thought better of it. With a shrug he left the room.

Aurelia dropped her head in her hands. At that

moment she felt that she would never have peace of mind again. She blamed herself entirely. How could she have been so blind? If she had stopped to think ...had considered truthfully where her disturbing emotions were leading her, then she might have avoided her present anguish. Her throat ached with unshed tears, but at last she picked up her pen and began to write.

The letter completed, she reached into her bureau for a leather bag and counted out the gold. She had bought a little time, but to what end? All she had achieved to date was the destruction of her own happiness.

When he returned Ransome looked at her averted face.

'Expecting thanks, my dear? I won't embarrass you with that. Were it not for Cass you would see me rot in hell. My thanks must go to your father, for leaving you so warm.'

She rose to face him then and he recoiled from her look. He turned on his heel and left her.

'Lia, I want to thank you. . .'

At the sound of Cassie's voice Aurelia looked up.

'Not another word! I could not bear it.' Her nerves were close to breaking-point. 'I wish to forget what has happened here today. Did we not promise ourselves to Lady Bellingham this evening? If we dine at seven we shall be in time for Lady Hamilton's performance.'

'Shall you wish to see it?'

'Any performance will suit me well enough, as long as I am not involved.' Aurelia hurried from the room.

CHAPTER EIGHT

LADY BELLINGHAM'S rooms were hot and crowded. As their hostess led them through the crush Aurelia looked about her, praying that for tonight, at least, the Duke would be otherwise engaged.

Now that she had faced up to the truth she could not meet him with any degree of equanimity. Her treacherous heart had led her into the worst of situations. That she could find herself drawn to the man who was to marry her niece did not bear thinking of. At the very least it showed an appalling breach of taste.

Yet she could not repress a most irrational sense of disappointment to find that he was not present. The lights did not seem so bright, and the chatter of the fashionable crowd seemed more meaningless than ever.

She took her seat on a small gilt chair set before an improvised dais which was hidden by a velvet curtain.

'We are almost ready,' Lady Bellingham announced. 'You will forgive me if I leave you for a moment, but I must see Lady Hamilton.'

She bustled away, leaving the audience to await the appearance of the woman whose reputation had set the country by the ears in Nelson's day. Some of the surrounding faces were disapproving, but most were avid with curiosity.

Aurelia sighed as she thought of the tragic ending to the famous love-affair. After Trafalgar and the death of the Admiral a grateful government had showered wealth and honours upon Lady Nelson. Her husband's dearest Emma, the woman he loved with all his heart, had been left in poverty to bring up his daughter as best she might, in spite of his dying wishes. Now Lady Hamilton was eking out a living by relying on the charity of her friends.

'She's drawn the crowd, I'll say that for her.' The speaker behind Aurelia did not trouble to lower her voice.

'Wait until you see her.' There was malicious amusement in the reply. 'She is grown so fat, my dear. One finds it hard to imagine what the Admiral found to admire.'

'She was the loveliest creature in the world.' Salterne took the seat beside Aurelia. Ostensibly his words were for her ear, but the deep voice carried easily to the row behind. 'I saw her once in Naples. So exquisite! She was the jewel among Sir William Hamilton's treasures.'

His words had silenced the gossips for the moment and soothed Aurelia's indignation at their cruelty. She had resolved that when they met again she would keep him at a distance, but now, forgetting her vow, she gave him a warm smile of thanks. It was returned with interest, and she coloured slightly. She would persuade Caro to change places with her... Before she could suggest it, however, the draperies parted. They revealed a figure alone on the stage. It was covered completely by a large shawl. The silence was intense as the audience waited. Then a corner of the shawl was lifted.

Aurelia gasped. The gossips had not exaggerated. It was difficult to believe that this blowsy woman, heavy to the point of grossness, could ever have captured a man's heart. All traces of her former beauty had vanished, obliterated in the folds of flesh.

A lump came into Aurelia's throat. It was tragic to see Nelson's beloved mistress reduced to peddling her notoriety in this way. She had no wish to watch, but escape was impossible. They were close to the stage, every seat was taken, and a number of people were standing by the doors. A sudden departure could only give offence.

'Wait!' A large hand closed over her own. 'You will be surprised.' Once again Salterne had read her mind, but Aurelia would not be comforted. She looked at her sister in despair, but Cassie's attention was fixed on Lady Hamilton.

Aurelia forced herself to look again. Then she leaned forward in amazement. By some curious alchemy the figure was suddenly transformed. Now its very solidity gave truth and dignity to a classical pose. The shawl was drawn further aside, and the white tunic, held only by a ribbon beneath the breasts, fell into graceful lines. The uplifted arms and the curve of neck and head spoke of loss and endless yearning.

In the hush that followed Aurelia knew that she was witnessing true artistry. The enveloping shawl was raised once more as the audience burst into a storm of applause. When it fell to the ground a moment later the figure was supported by another—a young girl kneeling in prayer. A murmur rippled through the room, and stilled in horror as the woman grasped the child's hair. In her other hand she held a dagger. There was not a sound as one emotion after another flickered across the woman's face. Pity was followed by despair, then forlorn desperation gave way to the

first faint gleam of hope. The dagger was cast away as
the child was gathered to her mother's breast.

There were shouts of 'Bravo! Bravo!' and the sound
of tumultuous clapping.

This should be trumpery, Aurelia thought to herself,
and yet it was not. For the next half-hour she watched
enthralled as Lady Hamilton, with the aid of a shawl
or two, a lyre, and a tambourine, took her audience
with her into flights of poetic fantasy with only the
slightest of improvised gestures.

The curtain fell at last, to a furore of clapping and
requests for an encore.

Lady Bellingham held up a hand for silence.

'We cannot ask for more,' she pleaded. 'Lady
Hamilton is too exhausted to appear again. You will
find refreshments in the dining-room.' She stepped
down from the stage and paused by Cassie's chair.

'Did you enjoy the performance, Lady Ransome?'

'Her Ladyship is a true artiste,' Cassie assured her
warmly. 'Lia, I'm sure, will agree.'

'I do indeed. It was a triumph. Your guests will not
soon forget this evening.'

'Poor soul! It is little enough that I can do for her.
She is very low at present.'

'And well she may be!' Aurelia heard the whispered
voice again. 'She is on the verge of bankruptcy, so I
hear. These performances are her only source of
income. Even so, one must question her taste in
dragging the child about with her. . .'

Aurelia turned and glared at the speaker. She was
happy to see that the woman had the grace to blush.

'Lady Hamilton's is a remarkable gift,' Aurelia said
in a high, clear voice. 'We must be grateful to her for
allowing us to share it.'

'I agree, Miss Carrington.' Salterne too had raised his voice. 'It is strange, is it not. . .this magic? I have observed it before. Physical appearance is naught if the gift is there.'

His eyes were half veiled by the thick dark lashes, but she sensed that he was about to give the gossips a set-down.

'The best will, of course, always be a target for the worst,' he observed in the same placid tone. 'I do not refer to Lady Hamilton in particular, though she must always be at risk from vulgar minds.'

Aurelia heard a snort of indignation and the scrape of chairs as the gossips made a hasty exit.

'Thank you,' she said shortly. 'That was somewhat trying. The remarks were unkind, and spoken so loud that I feared that Lady Hamilton must hear.'

'It would not be the first time. She is no stranger to insult, ma'am, and she is accustomed to the censure of the world. When the Admiral was alive it had no power to harm her. . .but now. . .'

'I think you have no taste for hypocrites, Miss Carrington.' Robert Clare had joined them. 'And you are right. Mrs Fitzherbert is still treated like a queen, though the Prince has tired of her.'

Aurelia was still furious. 'That is what I mean,' she said.

Cassie gasped. 'Lia! I beg of you. . .remember where you are! Come, let us find Caro and Leggatt. They are gone into the dining-room.' She rose to her feet, dropping her reticule and her fan in her haste to hurry her sister away. She was relieved to see that the Duke had been drawn into conversation by Lady Bellingham and did not appear to have heard Aurelia's remark.

Robert Clare bent down to retrieve the fallen objects, and then he gave Aurelia a quizzical look.

'Nelson is still idolised,' he said. 'But the gratitude of the country does not extend to his mistress. As to the other matter. . .you have heard the rumours?'

Aurelia looked at him in silence.

'It is said that Mrs Fitzherbert is the Prince's true wife,' he went on. 'Though Fox has denied it in Parliament.'

'That cannot be,' Aurelia protested. 'He married Caroline of Brunswick. It would mean. . .'

'Bigamy?' The room had emptied, but his voice fell to a whisper. 'Remember that Mrs Fitzherbert has never consented to receive Fox since he denied her marriage. . .and there were witnesses.'

'Please!' Cassie was beside herself with anxiety. 'Must we discuss these matters? The world abounds with gossip, and it is naught but hearsay.'

Robert Clare gave her an ironic smile, but he did not pursue the subject. As he moved towards the door, Cassie caught her sister's arm.

'Do take care!' she pleaded. 'Clare is close to the Prince. If your remarks should reach the Regent's ears I cannot answer for the consequences. Neither he nor Mrs Fitzherbert ever forgets an insult.'

'I shall not say another word,' Aurelia promised. 'But it does seem unfair, you will admit.'

'I admit nothing of the kind. It is none of our concern. I wish you will not always be taking up some lost cause or other, Lia. It can lead to nothing but trouble.'

How true that was, Aurelia thought ruefully. Not for the first time she doubted the wisdom of her decision to come to Brighton. It had been a disaster from the first, and what had she achieved? She might as well have stayed at Marram and paid Ransome's debts. Instead she was trapped in a situation which she found intolerable. She could not avoid the Duke's company, sweet torture though it was. She could think of no way to persaude him to alter his manner towards her, and to behave with cool formality. It was the only way they could deal together.

Perhaps if she had a frank talk with him and explained that he should direct his gallantry at Caroline. . . No. . .that would never do. He could only regard it as an impertinence, and in any case the girl would not welcome it.

The answer, she knew, was to return to Marram as quickly as she could, away from his disturbing presence, but for the moment it was out of the question. Caro and Cassie were both dependent on her, and she could not let them down.

The solution to her problem lay in her own hands. Perhaps if she showed an interest in Captain Leggatt, Robert Clare or one of her other suitors Salterne might direct his attentions elsewhere. The town was filled with charmers, many of them beauties, and he had shown that he was susceptible to the female sex.

The thought caused her a pang. There must be other women who could cause that lazy smile to appear behind his eyes. Would he laugh and tease with them as he had done with her? A small green imp of jealousy rose in her heart, but she crushed it at once. A fictitious interest in another man would be her answer.

She was still preoccupied as she walked into the dining-room. Absently she accepted a plate of oyster patties from Charles Leggatt, but she found she could not eat. As she raised a glass of wine to her lips a feeling of nausea assailed her.

'It is so very warm in here,' she murmured to Cassie. I must have some air.'

Without waiting for a reply she walked towards the open windows and stepped into the garden. There was a slight breeze, and the air felt pleasantly cool against her skin. She wandered down the path towards a small gazebo. It had been sited to take advantage of the view. In the night sky the moon was full, paving the sea with a path of molten silver. Above her she could see a scattering of stars.

'You have forgot your wrap, Miss Carrington.' Charles Leggatt had followed her. 'Forgive me if I intrude. . .but I feared you were not well.'

'I found it excessively warm.' Aurelia smiled up at him. 'Pray do not trouble yourself. I wished only for some air. I must not keep you from your friends.'

It was a clear dismissal, but to her extreme discomfiture he attempted to take her hands.

'May I claim you as one of them?' he said urgently. 'I could wish it were something more. Miss Carrington. . . Aurelia. . . I have longed for an opportunity to speak to you alone. You. . .you do not hold me in dislike, I think?'

'Of course not !' Aurelia attempted to draw her hands away, but he held them in a firm clasp. 'We are all sensible of your kindness. It has been delightful to attend the entertainments in your company. . .'

'I do not mean that.' The captain was clearly struggling with some strong emotion. 'I dared to hope that in these past few weeks. . .well. . .you must have suspected—although perhaps you have not.' He sat down on the bench beside her and put his head in his hands.

'Captain Leggatt, please. . . I beg of you. . .' Aurelia had no wish to hurt his feelings, but he was clearly determined to propose.

'Please allow me to tell you of my regard for you. From the moment I saw you I knew that I could love no other woman——'

Aurelia stopped him before he could go on.

'I do not mean to be unkind, but let us not continue this conversation. We are good friends. I should be sorry to find some awkwardness between us.'

He released her with reluctance, and gave her a solemn look.

'My dearest wish is that you become my wife.'

'But I have no thought of marriage.'

'Then your affections are not engaged elsewhere?'

'Captain Leggatt, that is not a proper question, but no, they are not.' To her own ears the lie was unconvincing. Her heart, her mind and her soul were engaged elsewhere, but she must not admit it, even to herself. Had she not resolved to guard her thoughts, directing them away from a tall, athletic figure with a tanned face and laughing eyes? Such infatuations passed in time.

As she saw the expression on the captain's face she knew that her disclaimer had been a mistake.

'That, at least, is one comfort. Perhaps I may hope . . .when we are better acquainted? Lady Ransome gave me to understand. . .'

'My sister wishes for my happiness,' Aurelia told him gently. 'She believes that I should marry, but. . .'

'You do not agree? Will you not tell me why?'

She hesitated. 'It is hard to explain,' she said at last. 'My parents were so happy together, but marriage can be destructive when those concerned are unsuited to each other.' Her look was a plea for forgiveness. 'Each partner must give their heart.'

'You have mine,' he said simply. 'I shall not lose the hope of winning yours.'

Aurelia laid her hand upon his arm. 'Believe me when I say that it can never be. Let us continue to be friends. That is worth something, surely?'

'It is worth a great deal. . .but. . .'

'Let us say no more. Reflect a little. Your own good sense must convince you that without the same feeling on both sides a marriage is not to be considered.'

He gazed at her with stricken eyes. 'I cannot blame you if you do not. . .do not reciprocate my regard; but I thought. . .'

'If I have given you cause to misunderstand me I am sorry, but, believe me, I had no thought of doing so.'

'You did not. . .but I hoped that you would learn to love me.' He was about to launch into another impassioned declaration, when a shadow blotted out the moonlight.

'Miss Carrington, your servant.' Robert Clare stood before them, his eyeglass swinging idly from his hand. 'Lady Bellingham bids me convey her compliments, Captain Leggatt. She is making up her tables and needs a fourth at whist.'

'You were unable to accommodate her?' There was open antagonism in the question.

'Whist is not my game,' Clare said smoothly.

'Just what is your game, may I ask?'

Robert Clare looked amused.

'I am thought to be lucky at Macao. . .and other games where fortune favours the bold.'

It was not the most tactful of replies, and Aurelia

sensed the tension in the air. Before the captain could reply she turned to Robert Clare.

'I had forgot my wrap,' she said swiftly. 'Captain Leggatt kindly brought it out to me. Now I am about to beg another favour of him. Should you see my sister on your way to the tables, sir, will you tell her that I shall be with her directly?'

He had no alternative but to acquiesce, but his rigid back was eloquent as he walked away.

'Your wrap? Well, I cannot deny that the atmosphere was chill.' Robert Clare stifled a laugh. 'Young puppy! I trust that he did not annoy you?'

'You shall not make sport of him,' Aurelia said quietly. 'He is a dear friend.'

'I crave your pardon, Miss Carrington. I was not aware that young Leggatt was a particular favourite of yours. . .'

For once the soft Irish accent failed to charm her, and Aurelia rounded on him sharply.

'Must you be quite so foolish, Mr Clare? Captain Leggatt did not annoy me, but you will most certainly do so if you persist in reading unintended meanings into my words.'

'Am I to suffer your displeasure? You may ascribe my ill behaviour to a violent case of jealousy.'

'Please! You are jesting, I know, but that is unworthy of you.'

'I do not jest, Miss Carrington.' He turned to face her and she saw that he was serious. 'The young have no monopoly of strong affections. I would suggest that only an older man could value you at your true worth.'

'Great heavens!' Aurelia looked about her wildly for some means of escape, but the sinewy fingers were entwined in the long fringe of her shawl. 'Mr Clare, I beg of you——'

'This garment would appear to be entangled.' A long arm reached from behind her and shook the fringe free. 'Miss Carrington, I am charged with a message from your sister. She insists that you rest here quietly until you are feeling quite restored. The lady will excuse you, Clare.'

Aurelia's importunate suitor laughed, and gave way gracefully to Salterne. In no way did he betray is annoyance at being thus rudely interrupted. With a low bow to Aurelia and a wave of his hand for the Duke, he sauntered away.

Aurelia wished that the ground might open and swallow her. She was torn between the warring emotions of relief at her rescue and utter mortifiction at being found at such a disadvantage. Salterne had appeared from the shrubbery, and she had no idea of how much he had overheard or how long he had been there.

He did not leave her long in doubt.

'Do you care for a stroll, Miss Carrington?' He offered her his arm. 'I give you my word that I shall not propose marriage. Three offers in one evening would be the outside of enough. . .'

'You were listening? How could you? You should have discovered yourself, Your Grace. That was not——'

'The act of a gentleman? I believe you mentioned as much to me on another occasion. You are right, of course, but this time I have some excuse. The offers came so thick and fast, there was no time. . .'

Her annoyance deepened as she felt his shoulders shaking. How could he dare to laugh at her predicament? She stalked along beside him, her head held high.

'And then, you know, on these occasions thwarted suitors have been known to get above themselves. Either of them might have called me out.'

'What nonsense!' Aurelia's anger vanished as she tried to stifle a giggle.

'That's better!' He tucked her hand through his arm. 'You lead an exciting life, Miss Carrington. Never a dull moment, one might say.'

'I was surprised myself,' she admitted frankly. 'I came out merely for a breath of air.'

'You did not reckon with the lure of the enchantress?'

'Now you are making sport of me. Forgive me, sir, but I must go back to Cassie. I have been gone this age.'

'You will wish to compose yourself, will you not? These situations can be unnerving.' The gentle teasing did much to restore her spirits, and she was tempted to ask him how he knew. She thought it unlikely that impressionable females were in the habit of declaring themselves to him, only to be rejected, but she did not comment on his words.

'But did you not say that Cassie——?'

'A subterfuge, my dear. I have not spoken to Lady Ransome, but I felt that I should rescue you before other hearts were laid at your feet.'

'It is no laughing matter,' Aurelia said with feeling. 'I have not given either of them the least encouragement.'

'But that is the trouble. A citadel, you must know, is always a challenge.'

'You make me sound cold and unfeeling. . .'

'You? Never!' The warmth of his reply made her heart leap in her breast. 'I should not accuse you of either of those traits of character. Rather the opposite. Moreover, you are a rarity in my experience...a beautiful woman who is neither vain nor a coquette.'

'Really, Your Grace, you must not. . .'

Though she demurred, she was grateful for his words. At least he did not think her a heartless flirt.

'I must not speak the truth? Come, that is unlike you. You set great store on honesty, do you not?'

Now was the time to speak, if ever. After what had happened she had no hope of convincing him that she had any interest in Clare or Leggatt. Taking her courage in both hands, she faced him squarely.

'I do, my lord, so you will forgive me if I speak of a matter which troubles me. It is not easy for me to do so, but it must be said. Ransome has suggested...at least he said...well, the fact is that—er—Caroline is not sufficiently in your company... I mean, by your side.'

She was crimson with embarrassment by the time she had finished the stumbling explanation.

'Please do not think that I mean to criticise,' she continued lamely. 'It is not for me to advise you, but he feels that... Well, I am sure that the fault is mine ...but he imagines that I have been somewhat indiscreet in my attitude.'

The garbled words did not lessen her feeling of discomfort. She was rambling like a fool, and still she had not asked him to avoid her company. Would he understand? It was a humiliating situation and he might well reverse his opinion as to her lack of vanity. She wished that she had not spoken of the matter.

'Does he indeed?' Salterne's eyes were slits of silver in the moonlight. 'That is most interesting.'

'I must go back to Cassie,' Aurelia went on nervously. 'I have been out here for an age. My reputation will be in shreds.'

She heard a cynical laugh.

'Few of Lady Bellingham's guests can boast of unsullied character. Half of them have foisted other men's children on their husbands, and as for the rest ...well, as you know, they thrive on gossip. You do not hope to escape unscathed?'

'I intend to provide them with as little opportunity as possible for the exercise of their tongues, so you see I must return.'

'You disappoint me, Miss Carrington. Who knows what further surprises the night may have in store for you?' Salterne looked up at the sky and shook his head. 'The full moon is said to have a curious effect on the minds of men. I am half inclined to believe it. Will you take the risk? Your next discarded suitor is like to fall upon his sword.'

Aurelia stifled a laugh. 'Really, Your Grace. . .!'

'I am serious,' Salterne said wickedly. 'Think of the scandal, ma'am, and Lady Bellingham's dismay at the possible damage to her carpet!'·

She could contain herself no longer and her peals of laughter rang across the garden. The vision of moonstruck swains was all too much for her composure.

'No vapourings, Miss Carrington? What a relief! I have not a single burnt feather about me at this moment.'

'An oversight, Your Grace?'

An appreciative chuckle greeted her words.

Salterne turned his back on the lighted windows and led her further into the garden.

'Then it is true? Your affections are not engaged? I was not sure... There is a fashionable convention which insists that a lady does not give her consent at once to an offer of marriage.'

'You felt that I was following convention?' Her tone was dry...so dry that he chuckled again.

'I confess it would have surprised me...but you have not answered my question.'

Suddenly Aurelia was seized by panic. Since their first meeting the Duke had shown an uncanny ability to read her mind. She could lie to him, but would he believe her? Here, in the romantic setting of this moonlit garden, with the delicate scent of summer jasmine perfuming the air, she was in danger, and she knew it.

She dared not look at Salterne, but there was no need. His image was forever printed on her mind. The dark, unruly curls, the lean, sardonic countenance, his eyes, his mouth and the graceful poise of his head were as familiar to her as her own face. Pray heaven he would not guess.

Through the thin silk of her wrap he could feel her trembling.

'You are cold?'

'A little,' she lied.

'I have been thoughtless.' He drew her into the lee of the garden wall. 'Will you continue to evade my question?'

'You heard my reply to Captain Leggatt, I believe?' To her relief her voice was under control. 'That is not a proper question, sir.'

'And no business of mine? I must disagree. As I'm

soon to become a member of your family it is very much my concern.'

The recollection of his imminent betrothal to Caroline stabbed Aurelia to the heart. She felt sick with jealousy.

'I have not forgot that you hope to marry my niece,' she said coldly. 'But I must remind you, sir, that I brook no interference in my affairs. I am mistress of Marram, and I may do as I please.'

'Then we must hope that you do not please to throw your life away on some man who is unworthy of you.'

'You believe me to be a poor judge of character?'

'I cannot say, though I suspect that your heart will always rule your head.'

He could not know how close he had come to stumbling upon the truth. How he would despise her if he ever guessed that he was the object of her thoughts and dreams.

Aurelia refused to rise to the bait.

'Captain Leggatt is young,' she said evenly. 'At present he chafes at the restrictions on the Prince's regiment. He found me a willing listener, though I find it hard to understand why any man should seek the miseries of the battlefield.'

'Inexperience, ma'am! One need only take part in an engagement such as Talavera to understand that death and glory do not always go hand in hand.' In the moonlight his face was grim. 'Sickness accounts for much of the army before the enemy is seen. Casualties are to be expected in battle, but it is hard to lose one's friends when the wounded are left untended.'

Aurelia glanced at the harsh countenance. 'Did

you. . .did you meet a Captain Elliott at Talavera?' The quiver in her voice caused the Duke to give her a sharp look.

'Tom Elliott? Was he a friend of yours?'

She nodded, unable to speak.

'Wellington thought highly of him. Were you aware that the great man cried when he saw the list of dead? Elliott was a favourite with all the general staff, and his men would follow him anywhere. They would have died for him. Instead he died for them. You knew that he was killed when trying to save his sergeant?'

Aurelia swallowed the lump in her throat which threatened to choke her. 'No one would tell me anything,' she whispered. 'The details were thought unsuitable for my ears, and. . .and we were not formally betrothed.'

'Then you were the lady?' Salterne stopped and looked at her. 'Elliott had always an air of inner joy. I knew it from my own experience. It comes from the knowledge that one is truly loved, and loves in return. It happened to me, and I understood his secret.'

He did not say more, and Aurelia did not dare to break the silence which fell between them. Long years of private anguish told her that no words of sympathy could ease his pain. It would be insensitive to offer them.

'Will you not tell me something of the Peninsular campaign?' she ventured at last. In the brilliant moonlight the strong planes of his features were etched into light and shade, illuminating the fearsome scar and giving him a sinister appearance, but Aurelia sensed only a fellow human being in need of comfort. Anything she could do or say to draw his thoughts from his dead wife must be of help to him.

For a moment she thought he had not heard her words. Then, with an effort, he gave her his attention.

'It is not a pretty tale,' he said slowly. 'I fear that it may distress you.'

'I want to know,' she insisted. 'In his letters Tom made light of the conditions in Portugal and Spain, but I am not foolish enough to suppose that it was pleasant. I wished to feel close to him, to share the life he lived out there, yet I could understand his wish to spare me.'

Salterne's smile was grim. 'Whatever he told you it would be impossible for you to imagine the heat, the dust, the poisonous snakes, the lack of food and water, and the mosquitoes... My God! The mosquitoes! They feasted well on tender English flesh. Some of the men were a living mass of agony, and the local population laughed at their sufferings. It was too much for one young officer—I will not give you his name... No inch of his skin was free from bites. After days and weeks of such torture he shot himself.'

Aurelia gasped, but she pressed him to go on.

'Our allies failed us, supplies did not come through, and the men were barefoot and ragged. Yet still, in that campaign, they fought with matchless courage to turn the tide against Napoleon. It was the beginning of the end for the French genius.'

'You see him as a genius, and not the monster of popular belief?'

'He is a brilliant man, Miss Carrington. Think of the Napoleonic code...to say nothing of his generalship. The flaw is his quest for world domination. We cannot let him have England.'

Aurelia murmured her heartfelt agreement.

'Thank you for answering my questions,' she said.

'Our brother too was killed at Talavera, and we have wished so much to know of his life in Spain. You knew him?'

'Not as well as I knew Elliott, but I have spoken of him to your sister. She had a look of him, but you. . . you are an original.'

Aurelia sensed that his eyes were upon her face. She began to tremble again.

'Here!' The Duke shrugged out of his coat and placed it about her shoulders. It still held the warmth of his body and the sensation was so intimate that he might have been holding her in his arms. She could detect a faint scent of soap and tobacco rising from the expensive cloth.

She gave a nervous little laugh.

'My brother was used to have two men to help him in and out of his coat,' she said inconsequentially.

'I fear I am too large for such refinements. Besides, I cannot bear to feel constrained.' He looked enormous as he stood before her, the white sleeves of his shirt billowing slightly in the breeze.

'I had best take you back,' he said abruptly. 'You will not care to be exposed to Ransome's insults.'

'He. . .he is gone to London.'

'A sudden departure? I had thought he would not dare.' He looked at her intently. 'Ah, I understand! You have paid his debts once more. I am sorry for that.'

'The decision was mine,' Aurelia said with dignity. 'My sister and Caroline are my first concern. . .' She stopped. She had intended neither to admit to paying Ransome's debts nor to let the Duke know that he was in such desperate straits.

Again he seemed to read her mind.

'The facts are known to me,' he said mildly. 'You need not fear that you have been indiscreet.'

Aurelia was silent as he hesitated, before he continued. 'A word of warning, Miss Carrington. Beware of Robert Clare. He is a dangerous acquaintance.'

'Your Grace, you presume too much,' she said in an icy tone. 'You may not choose my friends...'

In her haste to get away from him she turned sharply and caught her foot in the hidden root of a tree. With a low cry she put out a hand to save herself from falling, and found herself in Salterne's arms. She struggled wildly, but then his mouth came down on hers and she was lost.

His kiss was gentle and caressing, but insistent. The warm lips promised untold delights, robbing her of all caution. Of her own volition she surrendered to his passionate embrace, her hands reaching up to hold him close as she melted into his arms.

'My darling!' His murmured words were soft as he held her to his breast. Beneath the fine cambric of his shirt she sensed the sheer power of the man. His heart was pounding, as was her own, but the sound of his voice brought Aurelia to her senses. With an inarticulate cry of self-disgust she tore herself away from him and fled back along the path towards the house. Her head was reeling. It had taken but a single kiss to destroy her calm resolution to keep the Duke at a distance. And once in his arms she had offered no resistance. At that moment she loathed her own treacherous femininity. Her body had betrayed her at his touch.

Bitterly she remembered Ransome's cruel accusations. His contemptuous words were justified, she knew that now. She had realised the danger in that moonlight stroll, but she had not sought to avoid it. Hers were the actions of a woman lacking in all proper pride. And what must Salterne think of her? Her cheeks burned. Perhaps he had taken advantage of the moment because he'd imagined that she expected it.

She could not forgive herself for her folly. That she, Caroline's aunt, could behave so ill with the girl's betrothed! She would never have peace of mind again.

As she stumbled across the terrace Cassie caught her arm.

'Lia, where have you been? You have been gone this age. I thought you taken faint.'

As the light fell on her sister's face Cassie gasped.

'You are ill! I knew it! Your eyes are wild, and you are so flushed! We must go home at once!'

'Let me sit quietly in this corner behind the curtain. Do you summon the carriage, Cass.' Aurelia sank into the nearest chair as Cassie bustled away. She had only the vaguest awareness of being led through the crowd minutes later. Then they were in the darkness of the carriage, driving towards the house on the Steyne.

It was not until she was safely in bed that Aurelia allowed herself to dwell on what had happened in the garden. She could hardly bear to think about it. Deeply ashamed, she was also furious with both herself and the Duke.

She moaned and buried her face in the pillow. Everything had conspired against her. Salterne had found her first with Captain Leggatt and then with Robert Clare, when any well-bred woman would have been accompanied by a chaperon. In spite of her protestations, no doubt he believed that she had given encouragement to her suitors, permitting liberties as she had done with him.

She had behaved so badly, and she could hardly blame the Duke. To walk through a jasmine-scented garden, with the moonlight turning the trees to silver, and a shimmering curtain of stars above. . . She must have been out of her mind. She might have guessed what would happen. Salterne was a well-known libertine. The normal rules of conduct did not apply to him. He had given her evidence enough of that.

A tear trickled slowly down her cheek. It was no excuse, but for those few forbidden moments she had felt like a woman again instead of an old maid. Her face flamed as she recalled the sensual smoothness of his flesh against her skin.

Once more she had felt beloved, but it was an illusion. The Duke intended to marry Caroline. He had said as much this very evening.

She cried herself to sleep.

CHAPTER NINE

AURELIA awakened heavy-eyed next day. Her head ached, and she felt tired and listless. She was in no mood to cope with Cassie's scoldings.

'To leave those warm rooms and wander about without your wrap in the chill night air – 'tis enough to set up an inflammation of the lungs. . .'

'Cassie, please. . . Doubtless you are right, but I do feel wretched. . .'

Faced with this admission, Cassie was all sympathy, and Aurelia felt a pang of guilt. It was true that she felt out of sorts, but the reason was not a chill. How could she ever face the Duke again? She closed her eye and Cassie tiptoed out of the room.

Until yesterday Aurelia had imagined that nothing could be worse than the difficulties in which she found herself. Now they were compounded. She should have fought against the Duke's embrace, or flayed him with cutting words. Instead she had returned his kiss with a passion that had shaken her to the core.

Her own behaviour had astonished her. Her gentle encounters with Tom Elliott had left her unprepared for the unfamiliar sensations which now troubled her so deeply. If this was infatuation she wanted no more of it.

She blamed herself rather than Salterne. Men, she knew, were said to be carried away by primitive instincts which took no account of civilised observance, but that she should have allowed herself to do the same did not bear thinking about.

The Duke's reputation should have warned her, she thought mournfully, but he had disarmed her over the past few weeks with his quick intelligence and his sense of humour. She had enjoyed his wit and their verbal battles. She could not deny that she was drawn to him, but she had been an easy conquest. A stifled cry of agony escaped her lips.

Writhing as if she were on the rack, she thought of their conversation in the garden. What a hypocrite he was! Had he not told her that she should find a man who was worthy of her? Apparently she had done so. Salterne's lack of integrity was matched only by her own. What man of honour would make an offer for a girl and devote his attentions to her aunt?

She had no doubt that a man of his temperament did not lead a life of celibacy, but surely he might have restricted the fulfilment of his needs to the many lightskirts who already filled the town. The thought gave her no comfort. She could not think of him in another woman's arms even now, when his behaviour had disgusted her. She knew her despair for what it was—a simple case of jealousy.

She rose and dressed and then began to pace the room. Somehow she must recover her peace of mind. In her present mood she was a prey to every kind of nonsensical idea.

After all, the Duke had not tried to rape her. She was refining too much upon a single kiss. As far as he was concerned it was probably but the impulse of a moment, in the worst of taste, considering the circumstances of his attachment to Caroline, but understandable. Easy dalliance was a way of life for him, but she could not be flattered to think that she had been the most recent recipient of his favours. Gently bred women did not expect or welcome such familiarity and, rake though he was known to be, his behaviour had surprised her.

Ransome's words returned to haunt her. He had accused her of wanting Salterne for herself. Surely the Duke could not suspect her motives to that extent? Had it crossed his mind that her stated reasons for wishing to prevent his marriage to Caroline were a sham, and that her own interests were her paramount concern?

The thought was acutely painful. She had done nothing to convince him otherwise...rather the reverse. Self-loathing occupied her mind to the exclusion of all else.

If only her father were still alive she might have taken his kindly counsel. In the three years since his death she had not missed him as she did now.

A wave of homesickness swept over her and she longed to return to Marram. Yet even as she considered the prospect she was seized with doubt. She had been content, but it was a cloistered view of the world. She began to wonder if she knew herself at all. Questions posed themselves and she had no answers. The cocoon in which she had wrapped herself had split. It was she who had changed, and now she wanted all that life might offer her.

Perhaps she had grieved for overlong, for her father, her brother, and Tom Elliott. It was a form of self-indulgence, she realised. Those who turned away from the world would be asked to pay the reckoning, as she was doing now.

She straightened her shoulders. Last night must

serve as a warning to her. She would take good care that such a thing did not happen again. Her next meeting with the Duke might be awkward, but she would not allow him to think that his unseemly behaviour had affected her. If he should mention it, which seemed unlikely, she would put it down to over-indulgence in Lady Bellingham's excellent wine. She must be discreet and, above all, she must put him out of her mind.

She picked up her book. *Sense and Sensibility* promised to be entertaining, and the author's calm good sense and ironic humour would distract her unruly thoughts.

For the rest of the day she revelled in the unaccustomed peace, and fell that night into a deep and dreamless sleep.

'I am glad you are recovered,' Cassie said next day. 'I was persuaded that we should miss the Prince's evening.'

'We shall be there,' Aurelia promised. In spite of her resolutions she was disturbed by the thought of meeting the Duke again, but she had a few days' grace. Would he embarrass her by giving some indication…a look or sly smile…to show that he recalled the memory of their kiss? She would attach herself to some dowager for the evening to prevent an attempt at conversation should the Duke approach her.

On the other hand it was possible that Salterne himself regretted the incident in the garden and had no wish to be reminded of his folly. His visits to the house on the Steyne had ceased abruptly, though Cassie saw nothing to remark upon in this. The

Regent, she surmised, had first call upon the Duke's attention.

Aurelia could only be thankful for the respite. Her peace of mind was only partially restored, but as the days went by she managed to convince herself that the matter was best forgotten. She could now, she felt, meet His Grace with perfect equanimity.

Her fragile confidence was quickly shattered. It was at the fashionable hour of five when she and Cass drove out with Caroline along the promenade.

'Shall you think of bathing, Aunt?' Caro's eyes were upon the blue and red bathing huts at the water's edge.

'I doubt if I have fortitude enough for the waters of the Channel,' Aurelia said with a smile. 'My preference is for Mr Williams' New Baths, which are heated. Cassie, do you not agree?'

A silence greeted her words and Aurelia looked at her sister in surprise.

'Cassie?'

'Over there!' Cassie gestured towards an expensive equipage which had drawn to a halt by the roadside. The occupants were surrounded by a crowd of young bucks.

'It is a trifle *outré*,' Aurelia agreed. 'A lining of pale blue satin would not by my own choice.'

Cassie reddened. 'Look the other way,' she whispered fiercely. 'We cannot recognise those...those creatures.'

'Why, Cass, what on earth...?'

'It is Harriet Wilson...*the* Harriet Wilson...and her sister. The brazen hussies! I wonder that they dare show themselves in daylight and in a public place.'

'How beautiful they are!' Caroline stared avidly as

the crowds parted and the occupants of the carriage were fully revealed. 'Mama, they are dressed like Hussars.'

'Such impudence! To copy the uniforms of the regiment is outside of enough, though it is not surprising. They have formed connections with so many of the officers. . .' Conscious of Caroline's interest, her mother stopped in mid-sentence.

The crush had forced their own carriage to a halt, and curiosity caused Aurelia to glance at the more striking of the two demireps. The woman was a beauty, there could be no doubt. A mass of auburn curls framed one of the loveliest faces she had ever seen, and a pair of glorious blue eyes were trained coquettishly upon a tall figure who had been hidden from their view by a passing horseman.

'Why, Mama, it is the Duke!' Caroline was more intrigued than startled.

At that precise moment Salterne looked up. With a word of apology to the voluptuous young woman who strove to hold his attention, he detached himself from the crowd and sauntered towards Aurelia's carriage.

'Your servant, Lady Ransome. . .and yours, Miss Carrington. Caroline, you are in famous looks today.'

His Grace chose to ignore Cassie's scarlet cheeks. With unruffled composure he lifted Caroline's fingers to his lips. Aurelia attempted to avoid his eye, but he was quick to ascribe her silence to another cause.

'I understand that you have not been well, Miss Carrington. 'I trust that I see you fully recovered from your—er—unfortunate indisposition?'

Aurelia bowed stiffly. She heard the amusement in his tone, but she was determined to ignore it.

'It was nothing. . .nothing to trouble me in the

least.' She gave him a steady look. 'You refine too much upon it, my lord.'

'I am glad to hear it.' His dark eyes were dancing. 'Then we shall meet at the Prince's evening?'

Aurelia bowed again, and left Cassie to exchange a word or two of civil conversation. His Grace then stood back to allow them to drive on.

'Well, really! That man has gall enough for anything! To find him in such company! He had no right to acknowledge us.' Aurelia was pink with indignation, and another emotion, which she had no desire to admit, even to herself.

'There is no need to distress yourself. It was unfortunate to find him in such company, but Salterne, as you know, pays no attention to polite observance.'

'He should have pretended not to see us. . .' Aurelia could no longer pretend that her feelings were other than those of jealousy, but Cassie must not guess.

'I cannot understand you,' Cassie sighed. 'Have you not always been the first to make excuses for such women?'

'That does not mean that I wish——' She stopped, afraid that she might betray herself.

'How little you know of men! What has the Duke's acquaintance with Harriet Wilson to say to anything? Married or betrothed, they will seek amusement in the arms of lightskirts. Anyhow, why should you care how he behaves?'

'*I* do not,' Aurelia announced with dignity. 'But you, I imagined, must have felt outraged.' She glanced at Caroline, who was absorbed in this interesting conversation. 'Had you not best explain to your daughter?'

Caroline flushed to the roots of her hair.

'I... I think I understand,' she said hastily. 'But it does not signify in the least.'

'Sensible girl!' Cassie beamed her approval. 'I must say, Lia, you astonish me! You were not used to be so strait-laced.'

Aurelia held her tongue with difficulty. She was deeply shaken by her own reaction to the sight of the Duke enjoying the company of the lovely Harriet.

The courtesan, so she had heard, had become the mistress of Lord Craven when she was but fifteen. Other lovers, including the Duke of Beaufort and the Duke of Argyll, had followed her original protector, and who could blame them? Those great violet eyes and that spectacular figure were enough to turn the head of any man.

For all she knew Salterne might, at this moment, be planning to give the woman *carte blanche*. Aurelia's nails dug into her palms. What was the matter with her? She was no schoolroom miss. She was well aware that an expensive mistress was an allowable indulgence for a man of fashion, but that knowledge was no comfort to her.

'I had thought better of him,' she muttered fiercely. 'Other men's leavings——' She stopped suddenly, conscious of Cassie's curious look.

'Salterne? My dear...with his reputation? That creature is doubtless but one of many...'

Aurelia lasped into silence, and Caroline seemed momentarily bereft of speech.

But it doesn't matter to her, Aurelia thought sadly. She does not love him. The full import of her thoughts struck her a moment later and she paled. The reasons for her days of depression, her anger and her jealousy were suddenly all too clear. She could no longer deceive herself. This was not simply a foolish infatuation. She had allowed herself to fall in love with Salterne almost unwittingly. The shock of the discovery overset her composure and she began to tremble.

'We had best turn for home,' Cassie said firmly. 'You do not look at all the thing. The drive has been too much for you.'

'Very well.' Aurelia forced out the words through stiff lips. She could not wait to be alone. In her preoccupation with Cassie's troubles she had not paused to consider the true nature of her own emotions. She knew now why she had returned Salterne's kiss with such unbridled passion. It was the reaction of a woman in love.

On the following day Aurelia rose early, determined to occupy herself so fully that she would have no time to think, either of the Duke, her own feelings, or anything at all but the prospect of the Prince's Musical Evening.

In the long reaches of the night she had had time to reflect. Her only hope of contentment or peace of mind was to crush this love which had come unbidden before it succeeded in destroying her. She must banish any hope of a happy outcome, or she might fritter away her life in dreaming.

She gave orders that all visitors were to be denied while the ladies gave their attention to the elaborate toilettes required for the evening entertainment. Monsieur Pierre had been bespoken well in advance, and by early evening the deceptively simple hairstyles were arranged to the satisfaction of Aurelia and Caroline, but Cassie inspected them with a critical eye.

'You do not think, *Monsieur*, that perhaps a turban

or an aigrette for my sister. . .? Her jewels are so fine, and this diamond clasp. . .?'

'If Miss Carrington would consent to the silver hair ornaments which I suggested? Simple bands in the Greek style would be most effective against her fair hair.'

'Cassie, I like it as it is,' Aurelia said gently. 'Your turban is designed to match your gown. I shall wear my diamond earrings and a bracelet. It will be enough.'

'*Mademoiselle* is right. Her beauty needs no ornament; but let us see.' With deft fingers he trained one or two ringlets to fall from the topknot on her head. 'There. . .that is softer. You are pleased, Miss Carrington?'

'Very pleased, I thank you.'

When he had gone she stepped into her underdress of ivory satin. Over it she wore an open robe of crêpe in the same shade, trimmed with blonde lace.

'Aunt, you look like a beautiful lily,' Caroline announced enthusiastically.

'What of your mama? She is like to outshine us all.'

'Fiddlesticks!' Cassie disclaimed the compliment, but she was looking at her best. Her plain round robe of finest white silk was decorated with a formal border of bronze embroidered leaves and edged with bronze ribbon. The Madonna-blue overskirt bore the same decoration around the border of the long train. Her short puffed sleeves were cuffed with the material of the underdress, and the neckline was trimmed with a small ruff of the finest lace.

'You do not think it over-elaborate for tonight?'

'Not at all,' Aurelia said stoutly. 'The Prince is a stickler for tradition. I cannot think how long it is since I wore a train. In any case you know he will put us in the shade.'

Cassie smiled. 'I fear you are right, but I could wish that you had chosen the pink with the black net overdress rather than that ivory crêpe. The trimming on the skirt is well enough, yet I feel that a contrast would have been more striking.'

'The ivory will not clash with the regimentals,' Aurelia said demurely. 'Who can compete with yellow boots, scarlet trousers edged with gold fringe, and a laced jacket dashingly worn across the shoulder?'

Cassie was suitably impressed.

'How clever of you,' she said thoughtfully. Aurelia had described the uniform of the 10th Hussars to perfection. 'Now I am pleased that I did not yield to Caroline's entreaties to allow her to wear pink. She must see how it would clash, and she looks so sweetly pretty in white. The rosebuds are a charming touch. Your bosom-bottle is quite secure, my love?'

'Indeed, mama, it is stitched into the gown.'

'Then you must remember not to bend forward, or you will spill the water for the flowers.'

Aurelia caught her niece's eye and bit her lip, but she managed to preserve her countenance. It would not serve to upset Cassie on this important occasion.

'Let us dine now,' she said quickly. 'You must both be hungry. The Prince does not rise from the table until after ten, and no food is served before the performance. It will be midnight before we are offered refreshment.'

Her prophecy proved to be correct. As they joined a slow-moving line of carriages on the serpentine drive leading to the Regent's villa Aurelia feared that they would arrive later than the appointed time of ten in the evening.

When they reached the portico she hurried her party through into an octagonal ante-hall already thronged with guests.

The smell of the fashionable crowd was nauseating. Mr Brummell might have counselled frequent bathing and changes of linen—he, she had heard, bathed four times a day—but his words had obviously fallen on deaf ears. Not all the perfumes and pomades could disguise the stink of unwashed bodies.

She moved on swiftly into the entrance hall, a larger room which was decorated in soft shades of green and grey.

'But this is beautiful, Aunt Lia. It looks so cool. Did you not tell me that the Prince's taste was for dragons, serpents and other monsters?'

'This is designed as a contrast with the inner rooms. Come through this entrance and you will see.'

Aurelia led the way into a long, low corridor, and Caroline gasped. A myriad flickering candles illuminated the brilliant scene, aided by vast chandeliers. On the walls huge mirrors doubled the apparent width of the gallery and reflected painted murals of peacock-blue bamboos on a background of pink linen.

Everywhere the eye was held by Chinese porcelain figures. Mandarins and pagodas vied with fantastic carvings picked out in scarlet, blue and amber and richly gilded furniture. Oil-lamps of intricate design provided additional illumination.

'Let us stay by the staircase. Just to the side the crush is not so great.' Aurelia managed to find a space by the stairwell, where Caroline might examine the details to her heart's content.

'What a curious choice,' she said in wonder. 'I had not thought that bamboo would be strong enough to support the handrails.'

'A clever imitation, my love. The staircase is cast iron, painted to resemble bamboo. You will find many surprises here. The furniture is of English beech, which also simulates bamboo. And do but look at the windows above the stair. More mandarins, I fear.'

'You do not care for it, Aunt?'

'The workmanship is very fine, but I find the whole somewhat overwhelming, and I do not care to find a serpent by my ankle, though it is only imitation.'

'Thank heavens we are not late,' Cassie murmured. 'The Prince is not yet risen from the table, though I hear that he sat down at six.'

Aurelia glanced at the small watch in her reticule. It was almost eleven. She was about to speak when there was an expectant hush, and the door to the banqueting-room was thrown open.

As the Prince appeared the crowd drew back to allow him passage. He made his way slowly down the line of curtsying women and bowing men, stopping at intervals to exchange a word or two with his guests. There was no mistaking the resplendent figure, though he was much heavier than when Aurelia had seen him last. His coat was of exquisite cut, embroidered down the front with silver flowers, picked out with foil-stones. Beneath it a waistcoat of white and silver tissue echoed the embroidery on the coat. A blaze of decorations completed his ensemble.

Tall though he was, he was dwarfed by the man behind him. Salterne's evening clothes lacked all ornament, but they fitted him to perfection. Those broad shoulders had no need of padding, nor wide revers to emphasise his massive chest. To Aurelia's mind he was the most distinguished-looking man in the room.

As he drew level with their little group the Prince stopped.

'Lady Ransome, I am glad to see you here, and Miss Carrington too. Now, who is this delightful creature? It cannot be your daughter, Lady Ransome. You are much too young.'

'You are too kind, Your Royal Highness, yet it is so. This is my daughter Caroline.'

The Prince was profuse in his compliments, but he was swaying slightly, and Aurelia guessed that he was not quite sober. To her surprise he was carrying an airgun.

'We must have some sport,' he announced. 'Come, ladies, let us go to the drawing-room.'

Seizing Caroline by the hand, he darted off, followed by his guests. As they reached the drawing-room he rapped out an order, and Aurelia realised, much to her consternation, that a target was to be erected at the far end of the room. Her own misgivings were reflected in the faces of the Prince's orchestra, who were seated uncomfortably close to the line of fire.

'Now, my dear.' Prince George pressed the gun into Caroline's unwilling hands. 'Shall you care to try your skill?'

Caroline cast a pleading glance about her, but there was no hope of salvation.

'Will you not show me, sire?' she begged.

'Nothing to it, m'dear.' The Prince took aim and hit the target in the centre. 'Hold the gun so. . .' He stood behind her, enfolding the shrinking figure in his arms. 'Now squeeze the trigger gently.'

Caroline closed her eyes and fired, making a neat hole in the ceiling.

'Well, well. . .better luck next time. Lady Ransome?'

With great dignity Cassie took the gun from her daughter's hands, held it in the prescribed manner, and fired. A yelp of agony followed.

'I fear you have hit a fiddler, ma'am. Now do not distress yourself. The fellow is but grazed. . .' The Prince walked to the far end of the room and handed over a small purse.

He came back beaming. 'No harm done,' he said gaily. 'Now, Miss Carrington. . .'

'Miss Carrington may not be so lucky, sire.' The deep voice behind her startled Aurelia. 'She is so short-sighted as to be almost blind to what goes on about her.'

Aurelia spun round to find Salterne at her elbow. For a second she was tempted to protest, but the thought of being excused from this eccentric target practice was too tempting. She contented herself with smiling at the Prince.

'So!' He bent towards her. 'A pity in one so young, but we all have our afflictions, ma'am. I myself am a martyr to gout.'

He paused for a moment, lost in thought. 'I have it, my dear—you will be able to enjoy the music, at least.'

With the courtesy for which he was renowned, he led her to the far end of the room and seated himself beside her.

'Do you care for glees and catches, m'dear?' He signalled to the leader of the orchestra. 'You shall join in. We do not stand on ceremony here.'

He began to sing in a pleasant bass, with so much

enjoyment that Aurelia found herself infected by his own enthusiasm.

'These are your favourites, sire?' she asked.

A piercing blue eye regarded her. 'Shall you like to hear the best of all?'

Aurelia smiled her assent and the Prince began his solo—'By the gaily circling Glass'.

A burst of loud applause and cries of 'Encore!' marked the conclusion of his song, but their host rose to his feet, shaking his head. He bowed to Aurelia and to Cassie and moved away to join his other guests.

'Is he not perfection?' Cassie was glowing at the signal mark of favour shown to her family by the Regent.

'He was certainly very kind,' Aurelia agreed in an absent tone. It was difficult to give Cassie her full attention when her glance would persist in straying towards the tall figure standing by the Prince's side.

It would not do. If they could but steal away unnoticed now that the music had ended. . .

Cassie would have none of it.

'How can you think of such a thing?' she demanded. 'We should never be forgiven. Besides, I long to see that odious Mrs Ingleby. Tonight she has been given the set-down she deserved. I doubt if she will put on her airs with me again.'

Aurelia resigned herself to the inevitable, but she had no intention of putting herself in the Duke's way. She allowed Robert Clare to find her a seat in a corner half hidden by a Chinese screen, and accepted his offer to bring her a glass of wine. The hothouse atmosphere of the room had made her drowsy, and she guessed that it was late. A glance at her watch showed her that it was after midnight. If only Cassie would return. . .

She was roused by the sound of voices.

'I hear that Harriet Wilson has her hooks in yet another noble lord. . .' The speaker was very close.

'And this time there is talk of marriage. . .' A sneering laugh accompanied the reply. 'It may be the only way to stop her publishing her memoirs.'

'She has threatened to do so?'

'Indeed! And Harriet means it. She has caused a certain *frisson* among the *bon ton*, but this latest *affaire* may put an end to it. The thought of becoming a duchess will doubtless weigh with her.'

Aurelia froze. Could this be the reason for the delay in announcing Caroline's betrothal? And why the ravishing Harriet had been seen in public with Salterne? Yet the Duke could not possibly be contemplating marriage with a Fashionable Impure. She could not believe it. Yet she had seen him conversing on easy terms with Harriet, and the woman's previous ducal suitors were known to have tired of her.

If Harriet had the means in her possession to injure him. . .? No, he would never submit to blackmail, she was sure of it. Sir John Lade might take to wife a woman with a past, but Salterne would not stain his ancient name by marriage to such a creature. The speaker must have been referring to some other duke, but try as she might she could not think of a suitable candidate.

'Lost in thought, Miss Carrington?' The subject of her preoccupation seated himself beside her.

Aurelia gave a start at the sound of that familiar voice. She knew only too well why her heart was pounding, and to her dismay she found that her hands

were shaking. Why must he seek her out? His nearness made it so difficult to hide her true feelings. She
gave him a faint smile and looked away.

'Are you absorbed in the study of this curious piece
of furniture?'

'I. . . I had not noticed it.' Pehaps if she gave him
no encouragement he would seek more congenial
company.

'Really! You surprise me! Personally I feel that the
place for an Egyptian river boat is on an Egyptian
river. The crocodile feet are charming, of course, but
this gilded prow is inclined to catch one at a painful
angle.'

The laughing eyes sought her own, expecting her to
share his amusement, but Aurelia averted her head.
She was about to make some excuse to leave him
when Robert Clare appeared.

'Your wine, Miss Carrington. My apologies for the
delay, but the rush was appalling.' He gave Salterne a
pointed look, but the Duke showed no disposition to
relinquish his seat.

'I see I have been supplanted,' Clare remarked
cheerfully. 'Perhaps later, Miss Carrington?'

Aurelia nodded. She would not insult her companion in front of Clare, but courtesy dictated that he
should have given way to her supper partner. She was
about to speak when he forestalled her.

'I believe I mentioned Clare to you before.' There
was a hint of steel in his voice.

'And I believe that I informed you that you may
not choose my friends. You will perceive that I make
no comment upon your own.'

He looked at her for a long moment, and she saw
the glint in his eyes.

'Ah. . .the lovely Harriet. . . I see. . .'

'How dare you, my lord? No gentleman would mention such – er——'

'Barques of frailty?' he supplied helpfully.

'I was about to remark that such subjects are unsuitable in mixed company.'

'But you brought this one up yourself, my dear.'

'If you will excuse me, Your Grace. . .' Aurelia gave him an icy look, and rose to her feet.

'No! I think not. Sit down, Miss Carrington.' A firm had closed about her wrist and, short of indulging in an undignified struggle, she had no choice but to obey. 'We were speaking of Robert Clare. . .'

'*You* were speaking of Robert Clare, and I may say that I find your attitude offensive.'

'But you do not know the reason for it, do you?'

'Jealousy, my lord? Clare is close to the Prince, I believe. Do you think that he will supplant you?'

'It is unlikely, and you are mistaken. My reason for warning you against Clare is other than that. He is a dangerous man.'

'I do not believe you. He has been kind and courteous and. . .and all attention.'

'That is a part of his stock-in-trade. A surly manner would not serve him well.'

'I wonder if you realise just how insulting you are?'

'My intention was not to insult you, Miss Carrington, but to open your eyes, if possible.'

'How would that help me, Your Grace, if I am thought to be so short-sighted as to be blind to all about me?'

'Come now.' The corner of his mouth lifted. 'Confess that you were happy to be rescued from a trying situation.'

'I should have begged to be excused from attempting to hit the Prince's target.'

'You might not have succeeded. Prince George can be most persuasive, and I feared that with a gun in your hand you might have aimed elsewhere...quite by accident, of course. I was resolved to stand behind you, should you attempt the feat. One quarry was brought down, you will recall.'

Aurelia's composure was sorely tried. The memory of Cassie in full court dress, with plumes in her turban, was all too much for her. Her shoulders began to shake.

'I shall treasure that moment always,' the Duke observed mildly. 'It will be a comfort in my declining years.'

Choking with laughter, Aurelia attempted to hide behind her fan.

'Cruel!' she gasped reproachfully. 'The man might have been badly hurt.'

'But he was not. I believe he was more astonished than injured, as were we all.' His grave look set Aurelia off again.

'Careful, Miss Carrington! I shall begin to suspect you of unbecoming levity. Had you not heard that a polite simper is all that is allowable in society? Laughter mars the features, and is the cause of wrinkles, so I understand.'

'You are impossible,' she told him frankly. 'I cannot imagine why I let you tease me into a better humour when I am determined to be cross.'

'But we deal together extremely, do we not?' A large brown hand reached out and covered her own. 'Will you not trust me in this matter of Clare? It is not personal pique, I assure you. There are reasons, but they are not mine to give at present.'

Aurelia snatched her hand away as if she had been stung. His touch was too disturbing. The warmth of his flesh against her own brought back vivid memories of that night in the garden which she now regretted so bitterly. What to him was casual friendship, or even a mild flirtation, now meant everything to her. And she would never drive him from her mind if she was forced to see him, to hear his voice, and, worst of all, to be so close to him.

Silently she prayed that he would leave her.

'Look at me!' he commanded. 'Do you believe that I have your interests at heart?'

His tender expression set her heart beating wildly, and she rose to her feet, afraid of betraying herself.

'I believe that you mean well, Your Grace, though I cannot understand your aversion to Clare. My sister has known him for years. He is an old friend. . . Now, if you will excuse me?' She was relieved to find that her voice was well under control.

'My grandmother asked me to come in search of you. Will you spare her a few moments?'

'Why did you not say so, my lord? I should not wish to keep her waiting.'

Salterne picked up her scarf and draped it about her shoulders. Did the strong hands linger longer than was strictly necessary? Aurelia stiffened, but she did not speak.

He led her to an ante-room, tapped on the door and entered. The Dowager Duchess was propped up on a sofa, laughing immoderately at one of the Regent's stories. The Prince broke off as Aurelia walked towards them.

'Now, ma'am, that piece of gossip is not fit for tender ears,' he warned. 'Miss Carrington will think me no fit company for a gently bred young lady if you give me away.'

Aurelia murmured a polite disclaimer, but Prince George shook his head.

'Come, Salterne! Let us leave these ladies to their coze. Then, ma'am, you shall obey your doctor's orders. Your carriage will be at the door in precisely fifteen minutes.'

The Duchess smiled indulgently as the two men left the room.

'The Prince has a generous heart,' she said. 'In many ways he is the best of men. . .'

'You have enjoyed this evening, ma'am?'

'I have. The Prince is a matchless mimic. He was reminding me of his uncle. One might almost think to hear the old man speaking, with his grunts and his broken English, but done without malice, my dear. . .'

'His manner is so very affable,' Aurelia said shyly. 'Is he not called The First Gentleman of Europe?'

'He is, and the tile is well-merited, but it was not of him I wished to speak. I heard that you had not been well.' The sharp black eyes scanned Aurelia's face. 'You look vastly elegant tonight, but you are not yourself, I think.'

'I am well enough, ma'am.' Aurelia's heart sank. Did she give herself away so easily? It was becoming more and more difficult to hide her secret. She longed to explain her difficulties to the Dowager. That wise old head held years of accumulated wisdom. Yet Salterne was her beloved grandson, and she would never doubt his integrity. To speak of his behaviour, and particularly of her own reaction to it, was impossible.

'I am glad to hear it, as I can now pass on to you a message from a faithful admirer. . . Charlotte longs to see you again. Will you not come to visit us? Salterne is with the Prince for much of the time, and I am ordered to rest each day. The child worries me. She is growing subdued, with so little company aside from that of the servants. . . Perhaps I should not ask. . . It is an odd request. . .to bear company with a six-year-old. . .'

'Ma'am, I should be happy to see her,' Aurelia answered warmly. 'Charlotte is so interested in the world about her.'

Her sympathy had gone out at once to both Charlotte and the Dowager, but on reflection she knew that it was unwise to be drawn even further into Salterne's affairs. She sighed inwardly. Events never ceased to conspire against her avowed resolution to put him from her mind.

CHAPTER TEN

'LIA, have you seen Caro?' Cassie looked about her with a frown.

'You will scarce discover her in this crush. Do you stay here and I will find her. Then we must go. It is very late.'

'I suppose so.' Reassured by Aurelia's words, Cassie turned back to Lady Bellingham.

Aurelia walked swiftly through the thinning crowds, but Caro was not to be found. Perhaps the grounds? Aurelia's cheeks burned as she recalled her own experience a few days earlier. Had Caro been tempted into the gardens by some young buck intent on a stolen kiss or two?

Her niece was not within the building. That much was certain. There was nothing for it. She must venture out herself. At least Caro was wearing white. Her gown would be visible in the darkness.

Aurelia looked about her before she stepped on to the terrace. She had no wish to provide food for gossip. Wagging tongues would be quick to credit her with an assignation if she was seen to leave the villa alone.

No one glanced in her direction, so she caught up her train, opened the long window and hurried out of sight around the corner of the building.

'Another promenade in the evening air, Miss Carrington?' The deep chuckle brought her to an abrupt halt. Salterne, of all people! She could have cried with frustration.

'My lord, as you appear to spend your time on these occasions lurking in the shrubbery, perhaps you will tell me if you have seen my niece?'

'Unjust, my dear! But in answer to your question I saw Caroline not half an hour ago. She was walking towards the Prince's stables.'

'Alone?' She could have bitten off her tongue even as she spoke.

'Alone,' he agreed smoothly.

'Then what in the world. . .?'

'The architecture is thought to be very fine. Prince George considers that his horses are better housed than he. It is difficult to appreciate the finer points in darkness, of course.'

'Oh, you. . .you. . .'

'Give yourself time, Miss Carrington. You will find a suitable word to describe my character. Meantime, if you care to go in search of your niece I shall be happy to accompany you.'

'Yes. . .no. . . oh, that foolish girl! She can have no idea. . .'

'None whatever,' he agreed politely. 'Will you take my arm? The ground is somewhat uneven. There is every chance that you may stumble.'

Aurelia's face flamed. So he had not forgotten the false step which had thrown her into his arms. She was tempted to withdraw her arm and order him to leave her, but the grounds were large and lonely, and ahead of her the stable block loomed dark against the night sky.

'How pleasant this is,' the Duke observed in an

affable tone. 'I am glad that you share my enjoyment of a stroll before retiring.'

He might have been making civil conversation in a drawing-room, but Aurelia was seized with a strong desire to give him the worst set-down of his life. No suitable epithets came to mind, so she vouchsafed no reply. Instead she scanned the rising ground in the hope of catching a glimpse of Caroline.

'In here, I believe.' Salterne indicated a narrow doorway in the great stone wall.

Aurelia stopped and faced him, dreading what she might find.

'You will not. . .?' she breathed.

'No, I shall not accompany you. I fear I should be *de trop*.' With a bow he turned and left her.

Aurelia felt both humiliated and furious. That Caroline should put any member of her family in this position! She marched inside the building, and made her way along a narrow corridor. A dim light burned at the end of the passageway, and as she reached it she heard whispering.

'Caroline!'

She heard a gasp. Then Caroline appeared with a young man by her side.

'We are ready to leave.' Aurelia's tone was icy. This was neither the time nor the place, but she would have much to say to her niece when they reached home. Meantime she would give the young man a piece of her mind. She paused in surprise as he stepped into the light.

'I *had* to see Richard.' Caroline was nervous but defiant. 'I have made no secret of my feelings for him, Aunt, and they have not changed.'

'And you, Mr Collinge? What have you to say to

me? I had thought better of you. This sneaking way of going on is not to my taste. Have you no thought for Caroline's reputation?'

'No one saw me leave the villa,' Caroline told her sullenly.

'Then how is it that the Duke of Salterne was able to tell me where to find you?'

'I might have known,' came the bitter reply. 'Am I to be spied on for the rest of my life?'

'Hush, Caro.' Richard Collinge moved towards Aurelia. 'I hear. . .' He cleared his throat. 'I hear that Caro is not yet betrothed. We had hoped to find some way. . .'

'My niece knows of my desire to help her, but clandestine meetings will not serve, Mr Collinge. This is the height of folly. You may be thankful that His Grace did not accompany me.'

'Is. . .is he waiting outside?' Caroline's courage was fast deserting her. 'He shall not harm Richard. I could not bear it.' She threw herself into her lover's arms and burst into tears.

'The Duke knows only that you entered this building.' Aurelia crossed her fingers behind her back. The Duke, as she knew from his remarks, was in no doubt that his bride-to-be had an assignation with another man. If he chose to ignore her foolishness that was his privilege, odd though it might appear.

'What do you suppose might have happened had my sister found you together?' she continued.

The two young people looked at her in silence.

'You know quite well, I believe. Caroline would be taken home at once to face her father's wrath. Did you think of that, Mr Collinge?'

'She has been badly treated,' the boy said in a low

voice. His face was pale, but determined. 'I cannot let her suffer.'

'Her suffering is like to be far worse if you do not heed me. Caro, I am surprised at you. Did you not give me your word?'

'I promised only that we should not elope. I did not say that I should not write to Richard, or try to see him.'

Aurelia felt a surge of pity as she looked at the two wan faces. It was mixed with a certain admiration. She had underestimated Caroline. None of the lures thrown out to her, the compliments, or the obvious admiration of the men who clustered about her daily, had changed her devotion to this stocky young man.

'You have two minutes to make your farewells,' she said. 'Caro, I will wait for you by the outer door.'

She knew when she was beaten. Caro had received no formal offers, but whether this was due to her want of fortune or a lack of encouragement she had no way of knowing. She suspected a combination of both.

She was half tempted to release Caroline from her promise. An elopement might be the answer after all. Caro would be safe from both her father and the Duke. Yet Cassie must be thought of too. Aurelia shuddered. She could imagine her sister's treatment at Ransome's hands should such a thing occur.

'Has the Duke gone?' Caroline's voice was a mere whisper.

'I do not see him. You may give thanks for his discretion, Caro. It is more than you deserve.'

She hurried her niece across the deserted lawns, uneasily aware that their light-coloured gowns made them conspicuous as they left the shelter of the trees. They gained the villa undetected, though a scattering of guests still clustered in the entrance hall. Aurelia had feared a tirade from Cassie, but her sister was still deep in conversation with Lady Bellingham. As the ladies whispered together she guessed that some particularly juicy snippet of scandal must be under discussion.

'Cassie, here is the Prince.' Aurelia curtsied deeply as the portly figure of their royal host came towards them.

'Lady Ransome...Miss Carrington...you have enjoyed this evening?' He appeared to be gratified by their expressions of pleasure. 'You do me honour, ladies. Now tomorrow we have the fireworks. Shall we see you at the display? I can promise you something out of the common way.'

They thanked him prettily as he handed them into their carriage.

'Did you see Mrs Ingleby's face?' Cassie was enjoying her triumph. 'If looks could kill we should be lying dead at her feet.'

The lack of response from her companions did not appear to trouble her.

'Only think, my dear!' She leaned towards Aurelia. 'That creature Harriet Wilson has hopes of becoming a Duchess.'

Aware that she had Aurelia's full attention in response to this startling piece of news, she glanced at her daughter, but Caro was staring into the darkness, lost in her own thoughts.

'Marriage, Lia! What do you say to that? I could not credit my ears. What is the world coming to...?'

'I do not believe it.'

'But it is true. I had it from Lady Bellingham. His Lordship made the offer last week...'

'And. . .and you do not mind?' Aurelia forced out the words with difficulty. So this was why Salterne was so unconcerned about the evening's events. He had lost all interest in Caroline. She felt as if a giant hand had clasped her throat, choking her in its grip.

'Mind? Why should I mind? It has naught to do with me. If the young man is lost to all sense of propriety then his father is not. The old Duke offered to buy her off. . .'

'The. . .the young man? And. . .the old Duke?'

'That is what I said. What is the matter with you, Lia? One might suppose that you are deaf. You know the parties concerned, though I must name no names.' She gave a significant nod in Caroline's direction.

'Then Salterne is not involved?' Aurelia clenched her hands as she waited for the answer.

'Only to the extent that he has succeeded where the old Duke could not. The slut professed herself insulted by the offer of an annuity, or even a lump sum. As though it were possible to insult a whore! She had her eye on the family wealth. All seemed lost until Salterne spoke to her. He is believed to have issued a certain warning. . .'

'Is. . .is the matter ended?' Aurelia felt weak with relief.

'I believe so. You look oddly, sister. I pray that you have not taken another chill.'

'Cassie, you worry about me over-much,' Aurelia chaffed. She bent a mock-frown upon her sister. 'Had you but heard the questions about my health tonight. Do not, I beg you, continue to fancy me at the gates of death.'

'You must make light of it, I know, but sometimes I think. . .Oh, well, if you do not wish to tell me. . .'

'I am perfectly well, I assure you. Was it not kind of Prince George to invite us to the fireworks? If he claims that the display is to be out of the common way it is sure to be extraordinary.'

The remark served to divert Cassie's attention, and she continued to speculate upon the forthcoming entertainment until they sought their beds.

'I shall not rise early,' Cassie announced. 'It is already past three in the morning. I vow I shall not open my eyes before noon. We shall all sleep well tonight.'

Aurelia agreed, but sleep did not come easily. A niggling feeling of guilt assailed her. She groaned as she thought of the twinkle in Salterne's eyes when she had been indiscreet enough to mention Harriet Wilson. She had not actually spoken the woman's name, but he had taken her meaning at once.

She had been all too ready to impute the worst of motives to him. Yet this evening he had shown himself to be a marvel of tact when faced with Caroline's folly.

She tossed uneasily in her bed until she came to a decision. She must apologise, if he would allow it, and thank him for his discretion. She would be on dangerous ground. A prospective bridegroom might reasonably be expected to take violent exception to unfaithfulness on the part of his betrothed. Again she wondered why he seemed unperturbed. That he knew of the assignation she could have no doubt. What was the matter with the man? He did not lack courage. Perhaps he had waited for Richard and challenged him. Her blood ran cold at the thought. But would he call out a mere boy? No, she would not think that of him.

The thought served to calm her, and she found herself growing drowsy. There was something... something at the back of her mind which she could not quite recall. She went over every word of their conversation, and then it came to her. He had asked for her trust.

That in itself was strange. Was she not his acknowledged enemy? Her cheeks grew warm as she remembered that lazy voice and the gently smiling eyes, yet she had seen something behind them. A flicker of steel?

She tried to crush her growing unease. Was he playing some deep game? It would account for so much which she found inexplicable... She drifted off to sleep at last.

She was roused by a bustle in the street below and the sound of knocking at her door. Aurelia looked at her watch. It was almost noon. She rang for Hannah and was dismayed to learn that Ransome had returned from London. It was to be hoped that he had settled his affairs. She dressed and went down to the salon.

Her brother-in-law greeted her cheerfully. He appeared to be in the best of spirits.

'I may stable the curricle here?' he asked. 'It will not crowd the phaeton.'

Aurelia forebore to ask if the vehicle was a recent purchase. Ransome's pride in it was evidence enough.

'You saw my bankers?'

'Yes, my dear, and all is well. I thank you.'

His unusual civility disturbed Aurelia. What mischief had he been up to? She might be sure that some nefarious scheme was afoot. Either that or his luck had changed, and he had won heavily at the tables.

'You seem in good spirits, Ransome,' she observed.

'Why not, my dear Aurelia? Your generosity brought me good fortune. Your gold has multiplied.' He pushed a leather bag towards her. 'Naturally I shall wish to repay your loan.'

Aurelia's heart sank. Now she was more convinced than ever that trouble must follow as surely as night must follow day. She straightened her shoulders. Why should she doubt his words? Fortunes were won and lost each day at White's and Watier's. It was not impossible that he was speaking the truth.

'I thank you.' She picked up the bag of gold and locked it in her desk. 'You have seen Cassie?'

'Not yet. . .not yet. . .but I hope to surprise her.' He patted his pocket significantly. 'Just a trifle which I hope will give her pleasure, and something for Caro too.'

He left her then, and Aurelia sank into a chair. In spite of his assurances she could not trust Ransome. He had not mentioned Salterne. Did this mean that the proposed marriage was not now of the first importance? His win must have been large indeed. A feeling of dread swept over her. She should be happy to find him so much changed, and yet she was not. With an effort she put Ransome from her mind, and proceeded to give her orders for the day.

It was a radiant Cassie who came tripping down the stairs.

'Is it not wonderful?' she cried. 'Ransome has had such luck at the tables. See, Lia, he thought of me.'

She held out a trinket in the form of a golden melon. As she pressed a spring at the side the fruit opened out into quarters, each section containing a different perfume.

'Is it not charming?' Cassie allowed a drop or two

to fall on the inside of her wrists. 'Only the French can create such things.'

'Then how did Ransome come by it? All trade has ceased since Napoleon conquered the European mainland.'

'Doubtless it came from one of the refugees. Poor creatures! When they fled the Terror they brought their prized possessions. Now, I suppose, they are forced to sell to keep themselves alive.'

'I see. It is gold, is it not?'

'Of course. Oh, Lia, you will not complain of his extravagance? I am so happy to have it.'

Aurelia forced a smile.

'And for Caro. . .well, you cannot imagine. It is the sweetest brooch. . .a double circle of pearls and diamonds. It will look delightful with her chamerry gauze. That is, if you think it warm enough for gauze this evening? We shall be out of doors. . . Well, perhaps we may carry our Kashmir shawls.'

Aurelia tried to hide her dismay. At that moment she longed to run away. If she could but saddle up her horse and ride back to Marram she vowed silently that she would lock the door against all callers, and to perdition with the Prince's fireworks.

Instead she expressed her admiration for Caroline's brooch, and allowed herself to be drawn into a discussion of a suitable toilette. In defiance of Cassie's pursed lips she elected to wear an underdress of silver-grey tiffany covered with an open robe of her favourite spider gauze. It was understated, but Aurelia felt that it matched her mood. She was unaware that the slender silver column was a perfect foil for her flawless skin, and that it did not detract from the beauty of her hair and eyes.

The Prince was in no doubt.

'Venus rising from the foam,' he announced that evening. 'Clare is right when he speaks of the Three Graces. Salterne, you must agree with him for once?'

'I do, sire.' Salterne bowed, but his eyes were for Aurelia alone, and the warmth of his expression discomfited her. That look should be for Caro. After all, it was she to whom he had offered marriage. His open admiration for herself, and the way in which he almost ignored her niece. . .well, not only was it embarrassing, but it was not the behaviour of a man of honour. Her face was cold as she turned away. How could she have grown to care for someone who lacked integrity?

'Ladies, we must make sure that you are settled in a point of vantage.' The Regent fussed about them. 'You will see to it, my lord?'

He moved away, leaving Salterne to guide Aurelia's party across the park.

Ransome, she noted in surprise, was less than cordial to the Duke. Could it be that his sudden access of fortune had changed his mind about the desired connection? She hung back as her brother-in-law strode ahead with Caro and Cassie on his arm.

'Your Grace, I have something to say to you.' Aurelia kept her voice low, partly from shyness and partly from a wish not to be overheard.

'My time is always at your disposal, Miss Carrington. The matter is urgent, I presume? Shall we—er—lurk in the shrubbery? As you know, it is a favourite haunt of mine. . .'

Aurelia's face flamed. Perhaps he was merely referring to her acid comment on the previous evening, but she could not be sure. She suspected that he was recalling to her mind that dreadful loss of conduct on

her part when she had allowed him to kiss her, and
. . .she could not deny it. . .she had returned that kiss
with such fervour.

'I wish you will not joke,' she said as calmly as she
could. 'I wished merely to say. . .at least, I feel that I
should. . .'

'More sackcloth and ashes, Miss Carrington?' She
heard the laughter in his voice. 'Oh, dear, I hope not.'

'Not at all.' Would he never be serious? 'It is merely
that I wished to thank you for your. . .your forbearance with Caroline last evening. I had feared that. . .
that. . .'

'That I might call the gentleman out?'

'Oh!' she cried in exasperation. 'You are the strang-
est lover I can imagine. Don't you care? You seem to
take these matters so lightly.'

'There you are mistaken.' The light tone had vanished. 'But your fears are unfounded, my dear. Your
niece's youthful peccadilloes do not interest me in the
least.'

'They most certainly should.' Aurelia was indignant.

A pair of large hands rested lightly on her shoulders
and the Duke swung her round to face him.

'Must I ask you once again to trust me? The facts,
my dear. Remember that you must have *all* the facts.'

'But if you intend to marry her?'

His smile was enigmatic as he drew her arm through
his and led her towards the others.

Aurelia drew her Kashmir shawl closer about her
shoulders. The slight breeze from the sea promised to
increase in strength, and the delicate gauze of her
overdress offered little protection. The Duke felt her
shiver.

'You ladies have my admiration,' he remarked. 'I

cannot understand why fashions which originated in ancient Greece should be thought suitable for the English climate.'

'I have thought the same myself,' Aurelia admitted, and was rewarded by a chuckle. She stole a glance at him. What a mystery he was. She would never learn to understand him. What other man would have turned aside her apologies for Caroline's behaviour to speak of the present fashions? He must be possessed of an iron self-control.

He raised an eyebrow in enquiry.

'Another question, Miss Carrington?'

'I was admiring your panache, Your Grace. Your self-discipline amazes me.'

'It also amazes me, my dear. In the last few weeks my resolution has been sorely tried.'

The words were spoken lightly, but there was something unnerving in his tone.

'You do not care for the present fashions?' she said quickly. It was best to follow his earlier lead and attempt to conduct their conversation on more acceptable lines.

Was he suggesting that he was losing patience with Caroline's delaying tactics? Aurelia's heart sank. If Salterne wished to marry without further delay he might override his grandmother's advice.

'The fashions are charming when they are worn by an enchantress with fair hair and eyes as blue as the summer sky,' he said softly, but his words enraged her.

'I find extravagant compliments foolish and distasteful. Oh, dear, I sound so priggish, but it is true.'

'So is the compliment, my dear, but if you wish I

will change it. Shall I tell you that you are obstinate and headstrong, and also impatient of restraint?'

Aurelia laughed.

'I fear it is a fairer assessment of my character, your Grace. Appearances mean so little. . .'

He did not pursue the subject, and led her back to Cassie.

'Ransome, may I suggest that you move your party closer to the shelter of the trees?' he said agreeably. 'There the ladies will be more comfortable, and you will have an excellent vantage-point.'

Ransome gave him a careless nod and moved away. When Aurelia next looked round the Duke had disappeared.

'Is it not delightful to be *en fête*?' Cassie's eyes sparkled with pleasure. 'Look, Lia!' She pointed as a Horizontal Wheel blazed into the night, decorated with Roman candles and Pots de Brins. Gillocks of Brilliant Fire followed it in quick succession. Then came the transparencies in Rayonant Fire, and Maroons, but by that time Aurelia was trembling with cold.

'I do not propose to stay out here for the finale,' she told Cassie. 'I will wait for you at the Prince's villa. Pray do not hurry yourselves.'

'But you will miss the discharge of the Pots de Grades and the Illuminated Bomb Shells,' Cassie protested. 'Ransome shall fetch you another wrap.' She looked round for her husband but he was nowhere to be seen.

'Don't worry, I shall be perfectly comfortable. It is but a step to the villa.' Aurelia moved away before her sister could argue further.

She found the villa deserted except for the servants.

They were clustered by the tall windows, enjoying as much of the entertainment as they could see.

Thankful to be out of the wind, Aurelia made her way to a retiring-room on the ground floor. The breeze had disarranged her hair. She must tidy it before the later crush prevented her from finding a mirror.

It was the work of a moment to secure her topknot in place. Thank heavens she had yielded at last to Cassie's plea to wear the silver fillets. The sides at least were smooth. She combed back the straying tendrils of curls which marred the perfection of the front, and glanced at her reflection. A flush rose to her cheeks as she remembered Salterne's extravagant compliment. It was a flush of annoyance rather than pleasure, she told herself severely. Had he not only moments before expressed his impatience for the delay in his wedding plans? Not only did he lack integrity, he was also insincere. Had she thought his words came from the heart...well...that was quite a different matter. One might not then be quite so irritated to be termed an enchantress. Her colour deepened, and then faded.

She was forgetting. A rake must, of necessity, know how to please, and the Duke's success with women was not in doubt. And she had succumbed to his charm as easily as many others. The thought disgusted her. She frowned and turned away.

In the distance she could hear the boom of the shells which signalled the end of the display. If she made her way to the entrance hall she would be certain to find Cassie.

It was as she passed an ornate archway that she heard the sound of voices raised in anger. Surely that

was Robert Clare? His Irish accent was unmistakable.
Anxious not to embarrass him, she hesitated. He was
too close to the door to allow her to slip by unseen.

Then she froze. The second voice was even better
known to her, and Ransome was in a towering rage.

'You'll remember my position, damn you!' he
shouted. 'Who are you to tell me what I may or may
not do?'

'Be quiet, you fool, and keep your voice down. Do
you wish to be charged with treason?'

'I shan't be taken alone.'

'No, my friend? Remember that I am an Irishman.
I cannot be held guilty here. England is naught to me.'

'The Regent would be glad to hear it. And the law
may not make such a fine distinction.'

'Then use your head. Your circumstances are well-
known, yet you come here in the latest curricle, with
the kind of horseflesh only the wealthiest can afford.
Not satisfied with that, you must present your daughter with a costly gift of French design, which she wears
tonight for all to see. I cannot credit such stupidity.'

'A gaming win accounts for all,' Ransome
announced in a surly tone.

Aurelia heard a sneering laugh.

'A gaming win? Who will support your story?
Where did you play, and who were the unfortunate
losers?'

'Must the place be well-known? St James's street is
not the only——'

'It is the only place where play is high enough to
warrant such a win. And would not the tale be all
over London?'

'Who is like to challenge my word?'

'Everyone who knows you, at a guess. And not least

those whose eyes are already on the loss of gold to France. Did I not warn you to avoid any alteration in your way of life?'

'My sister-in-law has paid my debts. I do not care who knows it.'

'Miss Carrington is not a fool. The world thinks highly of her common sense. Not even for her sister's sake would she give away her fortune.'

'That's true!' Ransome sounded bitter. 'She keeps a close eye on the guineas.'

Aurelia was too horrified by what she had heard to take exception to the lie. She was trembling violently, and the world seemed to spin about her. If they should suspect that she had overheard. . .

Panic seized her as a hand closed over her mouth.

'Don't struggle,' Salterne said softly. 'You are perfectly safe.'

Drawing her arm through his, he strolled calmly into the room ahead of them.

'Ah, Ransome, there you are. We have been charged to find you. The entertainment is ended and Lady Ransome was wondering. . .'

'I. . .I felt the need for refreshment.' Ransome's face was grey with shock, but he made an effort to recover himself.

'A splendid idea. I had just suggested to Miss Carrington. . .Do you care to join us, gentlemen?'

'I think not, Your Grace. Affairs call me away, if you will forgive me.' Clare was at his most urbane, though Aurelia sensed the tension in the air. Did he wonder how much of the conversation might have been overheard? If so, he gave no sign.

He left them and Salterne turned to Ransome.

'My lord?'

'No, I cannot. I must find Cassie and Caro. Aurelia, will you come with me?'

A warning pressure on her arm enjoined Aurelia to silence.

'Miss Carrington felt the chill of the evening air,' the Duke murmured. 'I fear she has not yet fully recovered her strength. May I take it upon myself to find her a glass of ratafia? It will restore the colour to her cheeks.'

A glance at Aurelia convinced Ransome that his sister-in-law was far from well. Her face was ashen. With a muttered word he left them.

Aurelia sank into a chair and buried her face in her hands.

'Miss Carrington. . .Aurelia. . .look at me!'

Aurelia shook her head. She could not speak.

'You heard everything?'

She nodded.

'My dear, you must be more careful. You might have placed yourself in the greatest danger. So much is at stake. . .'

She looked at him then with swimming eyes.

'You. . .you know?'

'Let us say that I have suspected for some time. Gold is most certainly being smuggled to France to pay Napoleon's troops. The profits are enormous. In Paris an English guinea sells for half as much again. For that kind of money men will stop at nothing.'

'Blood money!' Aurelia said faintly. 'And Ransome is involved. I might have known, yet, blackguard though he is, I had not guessed him to be a traitor.'

'Hush, my dearest.' A comforting arm slipped about her shoulders. 'There is nothing you can do. Events must take their course.'

'But my sister...and Caro?' Aurelia's eyes were wild. 'How are they to bear the disgrace? Yet that is not the worst of it. Our own troops die at Ransome's hands as surely as if he had fired the guns.'

'I asked you once to trust me. I could not explain, but now you know some part of it. The rest I will tell you when it is safe to do so. Do you understand?'

Aurelia was too shocked to do more than stare at him.

'What am I to do?' she whispered. 'Please tell me. I cannot stand by and pretend that I know nothing.'

'If you do not you will be as guilty of costing lives as Ransome himself.' There was a note in Salterne's voice which she had not heard before, and it frightened her.

'We owe it to those who have already died to stamp out this villainy. Would you have others follow them?'

She shook her head.

'Ransome and his kind must be stopped or this French war will go on for years. You of all people know what it has cost in human suffering.'

The reference to her dead brother and her lost love forced a sob from Aurelia's lips, and the arm about her tightened.

'I know what I ask of you,' the Duke said softly. 'And it will be hard. For the next few days you must carry a heavy burden. The net is closing, but we must have them all. Will you...can you bear it?'

Aurelia sat with folded hands. She longed to beg for time to think...to decide...but in her heart she knew the answer.

'I will do as you ask,' she said.

'You are a truly remarkable woman. I knew you would not fail me.' Salterne cupped a hand beneath her chin and gazed into her eyes. He gave her a smile of singular sweetness and Aurelia's heart turned over. How could she ever have doubted him, or thought him ugly? Her hand went out to him and he pressed it to his heart. Then he turned it over and kissed her palm.

'Be very careful,' he warned. 'The danger is extreme...You must give no hint of your suspicions.'

He took her arm and led her back to the entrance hall.

Aurelia could not look at Ransome, but she was aware that Robert Clare's keen eyes were fixed upon her face. She turned to Lady Bellingham.

'Do you attend the races, Miss Carrington? I vow I shall apply to you before I venture on a wager. You know I cannot tell one beast from another...'

'I shall do my best to help you.' Aurelia felt that she was moving in some dreadful nightmare. 'Appearance is not everything. The jockeys are not always honest; there has been talk of pulling...' She rattled on, only half aware of what she was saying, but Clare seemed satisfied, and he moved away. She longed for their carriage to be announced. If he should engage her in conversation she doubted her ability to convince him that nothing was amiss.

'Miss Carrington, would it be uncivil of me to say that you look somewhat out of countenance this evening?' The soft Irish voice held only sympathy, and she realised with a start that he was close behind her.

'Aurelia felt so chilled at the display.' Unwittingly Cassie came to her rescue, putting her arm about her sister's waist. 'See, here is the carriage. Tomorrow you shall rest. You will excuse us, Robert?'

Clare stepped back at once and made them a deep

bow, but Aurelia felt uneasy. She was under no illusions as to his quick intelligence. Ransome might claim all the advantage of rank, but it was Clare she feared.

She took her seat in the carriage, leaned back, and closed her eyes, expecting Ransome to make some comment about her sudden appearance with the Duke. He was so quiet that she stole a glance at him. The handsome face wore a surly expression, and even Cassie's constant chatter did not bring the usual snarling rebuke.

A wave of nausea swept over her as she considered the full enormity of his guilt. Then her eye fell on Cassie and she clenched her hands. What a price her sister had paid for a youthful infatuation! If only she could be spared the worst of the disgrace... Ransome might deserve a hideous fate, but why should Cassie suffer too?

Her only hope was Salterne. In these shifting quicksands of intrigue and deception he alone offered some hope of salvation for Cassie and her daughter. He had asked for her trust and she had given it unconditionally. She would keep her promise to him.

'Tired, Lia?' Cassie laid a soft hand on her arm. 'I blame myself, my love. I have persuaded you to do too much. Tomorrow you shall have peace and quiet.'

She was as good as her word, but Aurelia could not rest. At the back of her mind was the awful spectre of what would follow when the conspirators were taken. She forced the images away. They were too horrible to contemplate. She would live from day to day, even from hour to hour. For the moment her task was to avoid arousing suspicion.

It was easier than she hoped. Ransome had left the house before she rose next morning.

CHAPTER ELEVEN

'SHALL you care to drive out, Lia? The air might do you good.' Cassie cast a troubled look at Aurelia's face.

'I am promised to the Dowager Duchess this morning, but do you take the chaise. I shall not need it.'

Her forbidding expression stifled any argument. If she had had misgivings about the wisdom of her promised visit to Charlotte they vanished with the certainty that in Salterne's house she would run no risk of meeting Robert Clare.

As she walked along the promenade her thoughts revolved around a number of mysterious questions. What part had Salterne played in the discovery of the plot, and how could he contemplate marriage with the daughter of a traitor? Was this the reason why his attachment to Caroline appeared to be, at best, lukewarm? How long had he suspected Ransome? And worse, had he offered for her niece in order to watch Ransome without arousing suspicion? She could think of no satisfactory answers.

Her mind was still preoccupied as she mounted the steps to the Duke's front door. Then her attention was distracted by a tapping at the window. Looking up, she caught sight of an eager little face which disappeared as she rang the bell.

Aurelia stepped diffidently into the lofty entrance hall. She should have insisted that Caroline accompany her. It was her niece's place to get to know

Charlotte better, but the Dowager had not included Caro in her invitation. Aurelia sighed. It was all so very difficult. Then Charlotte ran towards her.

'Miggs said that I should wait for you in the salon, but I could not. Was that very bad?'

'Poor Miggs! Has she lost you again? She must think you are a little eel which wriggles away and hides.'

The anxious expression on the child's face gave way to a mischievous smile.

'She would not do that. Papa says that eels have no legs...Oh, dear, I have forgot my curtsy.' Frowning with concentration, Charlotte sank to the ground, and promptly tumbled over.

'Are you hurt?' Aurelia reached down to help her to her feet.

'No...I do it all the time. I wobble too much, you see.'

'It isn't easy,' Aurelia agreed gravely. 'But it will come with practice.'

'Grandmama would like to see you.' A small hand slipped into hers. 'She is tired today, so she is still in bed. We must be very quiet.'

Aurelia allowed herself to be led upstairs to the great bedroom which overlooked the sea. A glance at the Dowager's face convinced her that Charlotte had not exaggerated. Lying amid the mass of silken pillows, the Duchess looked more fragile than ever. Her face was ashen, and Aurelia noticed with misgiving the bluish tone of the skin about her lips.

'It was good of you to come, my dear.' The old lady managed a faint smile. 'I am not at my best today, so I shall be poor company.'

Aurelia bent to kiss her.

'Ma'am, you must rest,' she said in a low voice. 'With your permission I shall take Charlotte for a walk.'

'Would you? Miggs has a heavy cold. Charlotte should not be too much in her company lest she catch the infection.'

'Do not worry, I beg you. We shall enjoy ourselves on the beach.' She looked at Charlotte who was nodding in delight.

'We should not trespass so upon your time,' the Duchess murmured. 'Salterne has been seeking a governess, but the child is over-young, and her old nurse is too infirm to travel.'

'Your Grace, it will be my pleasure. Charlotte has much to tell me and to show me.'

Her words were spoken in all sincerity. Aurelia could think of nothing at that moment which would please her better than to spend an hour or two with this artless little creature who found so much interest in the world about her.

'Will you curtsy to your Grandmama?' she suggested. 'Perhaps if I held your hand. . .?'

Thus supported, Charlotte's curtsy was a triumph.

'It makes it easier not to wobble,' she announced. 'My coat is here. I can nearly fasten all the buttons and the ties, but if you help me it will be quicker.'

Five minutes later they were walking hand in hand along the promenade.

'I haven't seen the mermaid yet,' Charlotte said earnestly. 'But the donkey with the blue hat is over there.' She cast a glance of longing at the patient animals.

'Would you like to ride him if I walk beside you?'

Charlotte's look of rapture was all the reply she

needed. Once astride the donkey she was speechless with delight, and Aurelia felt a surge of affection for the indomitable little girl.

'Now who is this fearless rider who is galloping like the wind across the beach?' The Duke had suddenly appeared beside them, and Aurelia jumped at the sound of his voice.

'Papa, you must not tease. Blue Boy is not galloping; he is walking quietly so that I do not fall off.'

'I beg your pardon, Charlotte. You must excuse me. He is such a matchless steed that the mistake is understandable.'

'He is beautiful,' Charlotte said with reverence.

Aurelia glanced down at the ancient animal. The donkey was the picture of dejection. Head down, he plodded along as if even Charlotte's weight was too much for him. Her lips twitched.

'I think we must agree that beauty is in the eye of the beholder, Miss Carrington?' Salterne's dark face was alight with amusement. The breeze had disarranged his thick black hair, and as he threw back his head and laughed Aurelia caught a glimpse of strong white teeth. His delight in Charlotte made him look like a boy again.

'Will you ride him back again, my puss?'

Charlotte nodded, and the Duke signalled to the attendant to take the rein.

'You are too kind, Miss Carrington.' The teasing note had vanished from his voice. 'May I hope that my grandmother's request was not inconvenient for you? Perhaps we are overly concerned for Charlotte's welfare.'

'Not at all. I admire you for it. Children, I feel, are sometimes left too much in the care of servants. Their parents seldom see them. Perhaps it is the way of the world, but I cannot think it right or sensible.'

'I agree. Such parents miss so much pleasure, and the children lack guidance. . .' His fond glance rested on his daughter. 'She was too young to remember her mother well, but one wonders. . .'

Aurelia's feelings threatened to overwhelm her. She longed to offer words of comfort, to gather him to her breast, and to wipe away all memory of the past with her caresses. Reason told her that she must not love him, but she could not listen to reason. How could she convince herself that the man beside her was a roué or that he lacked integrity, when beneath the sophisticated mask she had found a caring heart? His love was not for her, it was true, but his affection for his child proved that he was not the monster she had thought him.

'Again, Papa! Again!' Charlotte's excited voice broke into her thoughts.

'Certainly not!' Salterne reached out to lift her down from the saddle. 'Too much riding on one day means that tomorrow you will be eating nuncheon standing up.'

'Why?'

'You will be saddle-sore. You are not yet accustomed to ride for any length of time.' He looked at Aurelia. 'I thought she might have a pony of her own when we get back to Salterne. Do you advise it? She may be too young. . .'

Charlotte trembled with excitement, but her eyes were fixed on Aurelia's face.

'I think it a splendid idea.' Aurelia was not allowed to continue. She was almost overset as the small body hurtled towards her and wrapped a pair of chubby arms about her knees.

'I knew you'd say yes. Oh, thank you, thank you. . .'

'Charlotte, where are your manners, my dear? You must not tear about like this. Miss Carrington does not care to be tumbled in the sand.'

'I'm sorry. Did I hurt you?' Charlotte's lip quivered.

'No, you did not. Now give me your hand. Were we not going to look for shells?'

'An inspiration! Shells, I confess, are a passion with me. I shall accompany you.' Salterne smiled down at them and Aurelia's heart turned over. She moved ahead so that he might not see the expression on her face. Loving him as she did, she could not fail to betray herself.

'I had thought you occupied with the Prince today,' she said in a voice that was not quite under her control.

'Today the Prince meets with members of the opposition,' Salterne replied. 'These political factions are not to my taste. They lead to much dissension.' He did not elaborate and changed the subject at once.

'I am glad to see you looking more yourself. To learn what you did must have been a severe shock.'

'It was,' she agreed. 'To be frank, I have always considered Ransome capable of any villainy, though I had not thought of treachery. Now I cannot bear to look at him.'

'Yet you will dissemble, as I asked?'

Aurelia nodded.

'It is Clare I fear,' she said quietly. 'He is too quick by half.'

'You are right, but you must not give yourself away. I cannot over-emphasise the danger.'

'What is this, Papa, and this?' Charlotte ran back to join them, bearing a pile of shells. To her delight Salterne was able to name them all.

'Your claims are justified.' Aurelia attempted to lighten his mood and her own. 'You have indeed a passion for shells, Your Grace.'

'Among other things.' His face was inscrutable. 'Did you doubt my words, Miss Carrington? Shall I beg you again to give me your trust?'

'I do trust you,' she admitted in a low voice. Her face was rosy as she bent to pick up the shells. 'Now if you will excuse me. . . Cassie must be wondering. . .'

'Always Cassie?' His tone was dry. 'Will you never consider yourself?'

Aurelia was about to reply when she caught sight of Charlotte's stricken look.

'Is something wrong?' She stooped down to the little girl.

'Are you going home? I thought you would stay with Papa and me. Don't you like us?'

'I do indeed! You are my friend, are you not?'

Charlotte hid her face in Aurelia's skirt.

'You could stay for nuncheon. I am supposed to have mine in the nursery, but sometimes Papa allows me. . .' She peeped hopefully at her father.

'You are a witch!' Salterne tugged gently at a shining curl. 'But you remind me of my manners. Miss Carrington, may we not persuade you. . .?'

He stood very tall and straight beside the tiny figure of his daughter. Two pairs of grey eyes, so much alike, were fixed eagerly on her face, and Aurelia had not the heart to refuse; but still she hesitated. The child must not grow too fond of her.

'A message shall be sent to Lady Ransome, if that is what is troubling you. . .'

'Then I thank you. You are very kind.' Aurelia made a quick decision. Perhaps it was sheer folly, but she could not disappoint the child. Nor, a small voice deep inside insisted, did she wish to disappoint herself. Every moment spent in the company of the Duke and his daughter was precious to her.

At nuncheon a joyful Charlotte kept them entertained with her plans to learn to ride the promised pony.

'John will help me,' she said earnestly. 'Then, when I am very good, I shall be able to ride with you and Papa.'

Aurelia had not the heart to explain that she would never visit the great house at Salterne until after the Duke and Caroline were married. And not even then, if she could avoid it, she told herself.

Dear as Caroline was to her, she could not face the prospect of seeing the man she loved wed to another woman. Her own plans for Caroline's future had come to naught. It was clear that the girl was still in love with Richard Collinge, and Caro had received no other offers. If the Duke could bring himself to wed the daughter of a traitor the marriage might yet take place, but even if it did not. . . Depression overwhelmed her. Salterne did not love her, and what hope did she have that he might ever return her affection? She too was tainted with Ransome's betrayal of his countrymen. Unseeing, she allowed her thoughts to wander.

'Miss Carryton, you look sad!' Charlotte tugged insistently at Aurelia's hand. 'Shall we play a game to make you smile?'

'Miss Carrington, if you please, my puss.'

Charlotte tried again, frowning in concentration.

'It is very difficult,' she announced. 'May I not call you Aunt Lia, as Caro does?'

'That is not respectful,' the Duke said sternly. 'I doubt if Miss Carrington will permit it.'

'Of course I will. It is much easier to say.' Aurelia smiled, though she felt a pang of regret, knowing that she should not encourage the child in any form of intimacy. But what did it matter? When she returned to Marram she would not see the Duke or his daughter again.

'Papa and I play a splendid game,' Charlotte confided. 'It is called "Guess what I am?"'

Aurelia looked up at the Duke. Did he think her too forward in allowing Charlotte to call her by her given name? His face reassured her. He was gazing at his daughter with an expression which she could only describe as smug.

'We play in the Grand Salon,' Charlotte explained. 'Papa needs plenty of space when he is pretending.'

Aurelia gave in to temptation.

'Now that I should like to see,' she admitted.

'I go first,' Charlotte told her, once they had entered the salon. Without more ado she got down on all fours. 'I'll do an easy one first because you haven't played before. I'll be an animal, and you have to guess which one.'

She pretended to lick her imaginary fur, miaowing like a cat.

'Gyp the dog?' The Duke lay back in his chair, his eyes closed in concentration.

'Papa, it isn't your turn, and I'm not a dog.'

Aurelia pretended to think hard.

'You must be a cat,' she said.

'Yes, I am. You win, so you may go next.'

'Your papa is disappointed because he did not guess correctly. Will you allow him to go next?'

Charlotte nodded, quite missing the expression on the Duke's face.

'Thank you very much, Miss Carrington,' he said with heavy irony. 'I see that you cannot wait for my performance.'

'I am all impatience, Your Grace.' Aurelia smiled.

Salterne gave her a withering look and walked to the far end of the room.

'Will you do the frightening one, Papa?'

'Only if you promise not to tell Miss Carrington what I am supposed to be.'

Charlotte took Aurelia's hand.

'Don't be afraid,' she said. 'Papa is only pretending.'

The Duke shambled towards them, rolling his head from side to side and growling.

'Can you guess?' Charlotte whispered in a conspiratorial tone.

Aurelia shook her head.

'You must try. If he reaches us before you guess he will eat us.'

'I have it now,' Aurelia whispered back. 'Your papa is pretending to be a mouse.'

A peal of laughter rang through the room.

'No, no. . .not a mouse. Papa is a fierce bear.'

Charlotte rolled about the floor in glee, only to be scooped up in the Duke's arms and nuzzled.

'Right, my puss. Now it is Miss Carrington's turn.' Salterne grinned at Aurelia. 'I shall promise you some inspired guesses, ma'am.'

Aurelia thought for a moment. Then she sat down

before them, blinking solemnly and hooting like an owl.

'My turn to guess,' the Duke announced. 'Now, Charlotte, you must not help me, even though I am puzzled. This cannot be an animal. . .Miss Carrington is much too pretty. . .'

'She is, isn't she?' It was a stage whisper, 'She looks like the princess in my book, Papa.'

'So she does!' The Duke grinned again as Aurelia blushed. 'Do you think she is pretending to be a rose?'

Aurelia threw him a reproachful look.

'No? Then perhaps the morning star?'

'Only one more guess, Papa. . .then it is my turn.'

'Perhaps she is the princess after all, though I cannot guess which one. Was there not a lady who was awakened. . .?'

'With a kiss? I remember. . .but Papa, do you not see? Aunt Lia is pretending to be an owl.'

'So she is! I should have known. The owl. . .who is the wisest of all creatures. . .'

The Duke was unrepentant at having been the cause of Aurelia's blushes.

'Wisdom dictates that I return home, Your Grace.'

'You are offended? I beg your pardon. The temptation to repay you in kind was too much.'

'I am not offended, but I must go. . . I thank you for a most delightful day.' Aurelia bent to drop a kiss on Charlotte's brow.

'You will come again, Aunt Lia? You promise?'

'I will.' She could promise that at least before she returned to Marram.

Charlotte clung tightly to Aurelia's hand.

'I don't want you to go,' she whispered tearfully.

'You are importunate, my puss.' The Duke swept

her up in a pair of massive arms. 'We cannot keep Miss Carrington with us, much as we should like to do so.'

He stretched out a hand to Aurelia.

'What can I say? We are much in your debt, my family and I.'

'And I in yours,' Aurelia admitted shyly. 'Today I have forgot my worries, thanks to Charlotte.'

'And to me, I hope. It is not given to everyone to see my impression of the bear.' The fine grey eyes were full of humour as they looked down at her.

At that moment Aurelia loved him more deeply than ever. Once again he had surprised her. She had not thought to see this tough, intimidating man so far forget his consequence as to romp like a boy. That he loved his daughter she could not doubt, but he also had a deep understanding of the child's needs. He realised that it was not enough to provide Charlotte with material possessions. She also had a claim upon his time and his attention, and those he gave gladly.

She could not wish for a better father for her own children, should she be lucky enough to have them. A shadow crossed her face. She was dreaming again and it was naught but folly. Salterne was not for her.

Then she looked up and his expression startled her. Blue eyes were held by grey, and something passed between them. She could not be mistaken. His look was both tender and passionate and her own feelings must be plain for him to see.

She stood as if mesmerised until Charlotte reached out to her.

'Another kiss?' she begged.

'Take care! You may awaken the sleeping princess,' the Duke said softly.

'Papa! You have forgot the story. It is the prince who kisses her.'

'Not the Duke?' Salterne moved towards Aurelia with his daughter still in his arms.

Aurelia felt unable to stir. Her heart was pounding so violently that he must surely hear it. It was only too clear that he had not forgotten that night in Lady Bellingham's garden. She flushed to the roots of her hair. He could not intend to kiss her again?

With an effort she moved back a pace, though her legs were trembling so that she doubted if they would support her. He was much too close, and once again she was aware of the faint scent of fresh linen, soap, fine wool and tobacco.

As he lowered the child towards her she found herself wishing that he would gather both of them within the circle of his arms. There she would feel both safe and. . .beloved? No, that could not possibly be. She disengaged herself from Charlotte's embrace as gently as she could.

'I will order the carriage for you,' the Duke said quietly.

'If you please. . .I should prefer to walk back to the Steyne.'

'As you wish.' The grey eyes rested intently upon her face. 'Do you attend the races tomorrow?'

'I believe so.' Aurelia tied the strings of her fashionable bonnet, thankful that the brim protected her in some sort from that searching gaze. She would not ask if he too would be there. His eager look assured her that he welcomed the prospect of another meeting. She must do something. . .anything. . .to stop the exquisite torture of being in his company. Was she not beginning to suspect that he returned her love? She must be out of her mind. If it was so then he was playing a dangerous game, and it did him no credit. Off with the old and on with the new while he was still unofficially betrothed...?

A prey to a thousand conflicting emotions, she walked back slowly along the promenade.

By next day the wind had dropped and the clouds had blown away. The sun shone from a sky of flawless blue as Aurelia and her party set out towards the east of the town, attended by Captain Leggatt and two of his friends.

Ransome had not returned to the house on the Steyne, but no one remarked on his absence, as much for Cassie's sake as for any other reason. Her spirits were much depressed.

'He will appear at the races, never fear,' Aurelia whispered. 'Cheer up, Cassie. You must not play the part of the injured wife.'

Cassie's depression lifted at the sight of the fine horseshoe course, built on the downs within sight of the sea. The gaiety of the three young men, and the brilliant spectacle of the crowd, served to chase away her sombre mood. Within minutes she was engaged in greeting her acquaintances as the ladies, in their light cambrics and muslins, strolled by escorted by the splendidly uniformed officers of the militia.

Captain Leggatt pointed down the course.

'The Prince, you must know, prefers to keep to his barouche. Over there...with the six black horses, and Sir John Lade on the box.'

'The crowds do not trouble him?' Cassie eyed the Regent in wonder.

'He is all good nature, ma'am. . .and they think the better of him for his easy manner.

Aurelia gave a rueful smile. As a patron of the arts the Prince might expect only scorn from his fellow countrymen, but when it came to the sporting life that was a different story. On a day such as this he could bask in unaccustomed popularity.

She glanced at the men in the barouche, but Salterne was not among them, nor was he to be seen in the stand. She felt a pang of disappointment, for which she at once took herself to task, deploring her own inconsistency.

Common sense dictated that she must avoid his company, but in view of the dreadful knowledge of Ransome's treachery she would feel safer with the Duke at hand. It was easier to be brave with him beside her.

She could only be thankful that Ransome and Robert Clare were also absent from the gathering. The Duke had counselled courage and expressed the belief that she would not fail him, but she would prefer not to have that courage put to the test.

'Do you care to go down to the paddock before the races start?' Captain Leggatt looked into the distance. 'If you wish to place a wager I will arrange it for you.'

'May I go, Mama?' Caroline looked as if she expected a refusal.

'You may, my love, and I will go with you. Lia, do you care to come?'

'I think not. I shall stay here. Oh, wait! Here is the Dowager Duchess come to join us.'

Caroline looked uncertainly from one face to the other as the old Duchess, leaning heavily on Salterne's arm, made her way towards them.

'No, no. . .off you go!' An imperious wave of her silver-topped cane dismissed the party of young people. 'Rollo was against this expedition, but the day is so fine, and all the world is here.' She looked about her in some satisfaction, daring her grandson to contradict her. A slight twitch of the lips was his only reply to this admission of disobedience. 'I am told that Basset is the horse to beat in the first race,' she continued. 'Is that so?'

'I should not care to wager on him myself,' Salterne said with a smile. 'Warren and Sherry will know his form.' He beckoned to the men behind him.

The Dowager Duchess was soon involved in a discussion of the merits of the various horses and their jockeys. At last she made her choice and turned to the others.

'Aurelia, do you care to wager? Rollo will see to it.'

'I think not, I thank you. Not for the moment, at least.'

'Cassie?'

'I cannot resist.' Cassie picked up her reticule. 'Since Ransome won so heavily in London I must believe that luck is with us.'

A silence greeted her words. The Honourable George Warren raised an eyebrow and looked at Sir Francis Sherry. Both of them glanced at Salterne, but his countenance was inscrutable.

'Is. . .is something wrong?' Cassie had sensed the tension in the air.

'Not at all, my lady. It is some time since we left London. We had not heard of Ransome's good fortune. I felicitate you.' Sherry's smooth words had a hollow ring, and his lie was unconvincing. They had travelled down from the capital on the previous day, as Aurelia knew.

'We are wasting time,' Salterne said quickly. 'The race will be over before we have settled on the horses.' He strode away, taking his two companions with him.

At the sight of Aurelia's stricken expression the Dowager turned to Cassie.

'I trust that Caro makes use of her parasol? In my young day we were used to dread the sight of freckles. Do you believe in crushed strawberries or chervil water as a remedy?'

Her words reached Aurelia through a mist of terror. Should a doubt arise in Cassie's mind about the fictitious gaming win, her sister might question Ransome, and Cassie could be persistent when she chose.

The possible consequences were too terrible to contemplate. With an effort she forced her attention back to the conversation.

'I am persuaded that distilled water of pineapple is the best, Your Grace, though Caro will take care. She is so fair, and her skin is like to suffer in the sun.'

The Dowager Duchess directed Cassie's attention to the Regent's barouche.

'Prince George is in spirits today,' she observed. 'He has waylaid Sir Francis, as one racing man to another. Sherry is one of his favourites.'

'I do not doubt it.' Cassie blushed a little. Sir Francis had not attempted to hide his admiration when they were introduced.

'I vow I never laughed so much as when he told me the story of Lady Haggerstone.'

'Is she not Mrs Fitzherbert's sister? I beg you will share the joke.'

'It is a piece of nonsense, but I confess I was much diverted. The lady, you must know, was taken with the fashion for rusticity. If Marie Antoinette could play the milkmaid then so would she. She transformed her garden into a farmyard, hired three Alderneys, and invited the Prince and his friends.'

The Duchess paused for effect, her black eyes gleaming.

'And then?' Cassie prompted.

'Why, then, my dear, out she came from her dairy, attired in the most fetching milking-hat and with the sweetest little apron over her silks. She carried a stool and a silver pail. Her intention was, I believe, to offer Prince George a fresh syllabub.' The Dowager's composure threatened to desert her. She raised a handkerchief to her lips.

'Do go on, dear ma'am.'

'Her Ladyship essayed to milk the nearest of the cattle, but the animal was of the wrong sex.'

'A bull?' Cassie's peal of laughter caused heads to turn in their direction, and Aurelia too was smiling.

'I hope the creature did not take offence,' she said.

'He did not take it kindly, Aurelia. Milady was forced to flee to her dairy. She did not appear again.'

'And the Prince?'

'A marvel of tact, my dears. His manner did not falter. He remarked upon the neatness of the farmyard, and the fineness of the day, before he returned to his carriage. One may imagine his amusement later.'

'Poor Lady Haggerstone!' Cassie wiped her eyes.

'Pray do not waste your sympathy on her. Such nonsense! I have no patience with these sentimental fancies. Neither she nor the French Queen had the least idea of how the rustics live. Some small experience would soon shatter that idyll.'

'More scandalous stories, my dear ma'am?' Salterne had reappeared beside them, his tone of reproof belied by the fond glance which he bestowed upon the old lady. His keen eye searched the faces of the other two ladies and, attuned as she was to his every mood, Aurelia sensed that he was not displeased to find them laughing together. 'You distract Lady Ransome and Miss Carrington,' he continued. 'They are like to miss the start of the race.'

'We have been waiting for you.' The Dowager tapped him with her fan. 'How it can take so long to set a man upon a horse I do not know.'

She continued to mutter at intervals, claiming to have lost her reticule, and searching for her shawl, until Cassie was only too pleased to accept an offer from Salterne to escort her to the paddock.

The Duchess turned to Aurelia.

'What is amiss, my dear? I thought you about to faint when Sherry and Warren disclaimed all knowledge of the gaming win. Is Ransome up to his tricks again?'

'I have not the full story, Your Grace. . .'

'I shall not upset Cassie, if that is what you fear, though I do not doubt that he had lied to her.'

Aurelia was silent.

'It will not be the first time that a man has deceived his wife. . .nor the last, I fear. . .But why should it frighten you so?'

'Are my feelings so obvious, ma'am?'

'Perhaps not to others, but you are grown so dear to me. Is Salterne involved?'

The sudden question took Aurelia by surprise. She

cast about wildly for a reply, and jumped as Salterne answered for her. She had not known he was so close.

'I must always be involved when Miss Carrington's interests are at stake. . .and Caroline's too, of course.'

'Of course!' The Dowager's ironic tone was not lost on him and he gave her a disarming smile.

'Sherry begged the privilege of escorting Lady Ransome,' he explained. 'I could not refuse.'

'So you hurried back to me?' The irony was even more in evidence. 'I am flattered, but you shall not change the subject, Rollo. I hope you know what you are about.'

Salterne sank into the seat beside her and stretched out his long legs.

'Why, ma'am, I believe I do.' His voice was calm and untroubled as he took her tiny claw-like hand and raised it to his lips. 'You have all my thanks. I know I might trust to your diplomacy.'

'I cannot come at your meaning, Rollo.'

'I think you can, my dear ma'am.'

'Such a farrago of nonsense! Diplomacy? Trust? Half-hints and the like. It sounds like a hum to me.'

'On the contrary, it is extremely serious.' He was still smiling, but the Duchess straightened suddenly as her eyes met his.

'This girl is frightened,' she said grimly.

'She will not be harmed if she follows my advice.' Half unconsciously he moved closer to Aurelia.

'Very well. I shall say no more.' The Duchess closed her eyes and took no further interest in her companions.

Salterne drew Aurelia a little apart.

'We cannot speak here,' he said in a low tone. 'Shall you attend the concert in the park tonight?'

'I cannot say, but I will speak to Cassie. Ransome is still away. . .'

'He will not return tonight, and nor will Clare. Shall we say at nine?'

His face was impassive, but Aurelia's feeling of dread returned. Some of the brightness had vanished from the day. She longed to ask him what was afoot, but his look enjoined her silence.

It was in no contented frame of mind that she set out for the park that evening. Salterne's suggestion of a meeting had disturbed her. She guessed that he would not be the bearer of good news.

To add to her worries Sir Francis Sherry approached them with a message which she could not welcome.

'I am charged to tell you that your son is in Brighton, Lady Ransome. I chanced to meet him at the races. He will wait upon you presently.'

'Frederick is here?' Cassie shot a nervous look at her sister.

'Your elder son, I believe. He expressed an urgent wish to see you. I mentioned that he might find you here this evening.'

Aurelia stifled a feeling of dismay. A true son of his father, Frederick's visits invariably heralded trouble of one kind or another. Pray heaven he was not involved in Ransome's dealings with the French.

On reflection she decided that it was unlikely. Frederick was a loose fish. When foxed with drink he would not guard his tongue. None of the conspirators would trust him. He would give their game away within a week.

'I cannot understand it, Lia.' Cassie took advantage of a particularly stirring military march to whisper to her sister. 'How is he able to afford to travel here? Ransome may have offered to fund him, of course... though he did not mention it to me. And where is he to stay? The town is full.'

'You may ask him yourself. Here he is...'

Frederick strolled towards them in a group of his cronies. He greeted Aurelia's party civilly enough, kissing his mama, and bending low over his aunt's hand. As handsome as his father, Aurelia thought cynically, and just as untrustworthy. Frederick seemed to sense her thoughts.

'Don't worry, Aunty, dear, I shall not trouble to ask for your hospitality.' His lips were close to her ear, and the words were inaudible to the others. 'It would scarce be offered willingly, but I have no further need of your crumbs of charity.'

'I am glad to hear it, Frederick. And to what do you owe this sudden access of fortune?'

'A run of luck.' He waved his hand in an expansive gesture. 'No need to mention it to Mama.'

Aurelia was strongly tempted to box his ears. She quickened her pace to catch up with the others. Caro, as always, was surrounded by a bevy of admirers, and Cassie was deep in conversation with Sir Francis. There was no sign of Salterne.

Aurelia glanced at her watch. It was long past nine. Perhaps he had been called away. If events had overtaken him he might be in danger at this moment. She prayed that her fears were unfounded. Without his support she felt lost and vulnerable.

Then she saw him. He was walking towards her in company with the Prince. Her heart sank. Now there would be no opportunity for him to speak to her in private.

The Regent was at his most affable.

'More music, Miss Carrington? I see you are of the same mind as myself. There is nothing like it to lift the spirits, but we are too far away. You cannot see the uniforms of the band. I designed them myself, you know. Let us go closer and you shall give me your opinion.'

'Your fan, Miss Carrington. I believe you dropped it.' Salterne held out the pretty trifle, and pressed it firmly into her had.

Aurelia was about to disclaim ownership when his expression stayed her.

'How careless of me!' She was conscious of Cassie's eyes upon the fan.

'Are you not mistaken, sister? Look at it close. I do not recognise the design.'

Salterne intervened before Aurelia could reply.

'Sadly it is broke. The fall has damaged the sticks.' With a barely perceptible movement of his fingers he gave a slight tug at the central ribboning and the fan opened to reveal a solid core between the struts. She caught a glimpse of writing, but she had no time to read it before he snapped it shut.

'A charming object! May I see?' The Prince took the fan from Aurelia and examined it with the eye of a connoisseur. 'I commend your taste, Miss Carrington. These Chinese brisé fans look delicate, but see how the copper end sticks protect the inner ones of ivory. Were you aware that some of them hold secrets?'

To Aurelia's dismay he pulled at the ribbon. The fan separated, but after one brief glance the Regent closed it and returned it with a bow.

'I was mistaken,' he said easily. 'It is of a different

type. The struts are damaged, but it is not beyond repair. The less it is handled the better. May I suggest that you put it in your reticule?' Still chatting about the programme of music, he led the way towards the bandstand.

'I vow I am green with envy, Lia. Where did you buy that lovely thing? I have not seen ought to match it.'

'The shops are full of such trifles, Cass. Try at Hanningtons, if you can tear yourself away from the muslins.'

Aurelia's face gave nothing away. She continued to smile and chat to the others, but her mind was filled with dread. Something must be sadly wrong for Salterne to risk passing her a message in such a way.

In her preoccupation she was scarcely aware of the music, but to her relief the end of the concert was followed by yet another display of fireworks, and all eyes were fixed on the sky. A burst of fiery stars followed the flight of each rocket, lighting the faces about her. She felt in her reticule for the fan, opened it, and waited for the end of the display.

On this occasion the Prince had outdone himself. He had ordered a representation of the eruption of Mount Vesuvius as the *pièce de résistance*.

Aurelia glanced down at her lap. In the reddish light which illuminated the grounds she could read the message easily. It was brief, giving only a time and a place.

She looked towards Salterne, to find his eyes upon her. She nodded. Then she rose to her feet to accompany the others as they walked back to the Steyne.

CHAPTER TWELVE

'You may go to bed, Hannah. I shall not retire just yet. An hour with my book is what I need.'

'What you need, Miss Lia, is a rest.' With the licence permitted to one who had known her mistress from the cradle Hannah sniffed. 'Burning the candle at both ends...and after an inflammation of the lungs? I shouldn't wonder if you were carried off before the end of the month.'

'I did *not* have an inflammation of the lungs, and that will do, thank you.'

Hannah showed no inclination to be snubbed, and it took a great deal of wheedling and a promise to read but a single chapter before she could be persuaded to retire.

As her footsteps died away Aurelia sighed with exasperation. Hannah had insisted on helping her into her bedrobe and unpinning her hair. She could not dress it high without help so she tidied it as best she could. Old retainers could be so...so officious.

A search through her wardrobe revealed one of her old gowns. It was a round dress of grey cambric, high at the neck, and with long sleeves. And there should be an all-enveloping cloak, which she was used to wear at Marram. She threw it about her shoulders, drawing the hood close.

Then she opened her door the merest crack. The silence from below was reassuring. Thank heavens that Caro had elected to share her mother's room since Ransome was away. Their candles had been snuffed, so she guessed that they were both asleep. She stole quietly down the narrow staircase to the hall.

The heavy iron bar across the door almost defeated her efforts to remove it, but she dared not leave the house by the passage to the stables. Matthew was a light sleeper, and devoted to his charges. At the least sound he would rouse the household, convinced that thieves were about to rob his mistress of her prized bloodstock.

Aurelia redoubled her efforts and at last the bar slid back. One glance at the deserted Steyne assured her that the coast was clear. She hurried across the road to the closed carriage waiting in the shadows.

The door opened at her approach. Then Salterne reached out for her hands and drew her in beside him.

'I had to warn you,' he said in a low tone. 'Matters are coming to a head and you are all at risk. I fear for your sister, in particular. Should she question Ransome. . .'

'I had thought of it. It was unfortunate that she should mention Ransome's supposed win before Sir Francis and his friend.'

'She could not know that he had lied. Sir Francis is discreet, but there were others in the company. Clare cannot fail to hear the gossip. He has informers everywhere.'

'But. . .but even if Ransome were to admit his treachery to her she cannot testify against him, as his wife.'

'She would not be given the opportunity to do so.'

Aurelia froze. 'You cannot mean. . .?'

Salterne gathered her trembling figure in his arms, and in her terror Aurelia clung to him.

'They would have no alternative but to silence her, my dear.'

'You cannot mean it!' Aurelia's blood turned to ice. Dear, foolish Cassie, with her passion for clothes and trinkets, and not a thought in her head of treachery.

'Clare would not harm her. He is a friend.' Her voice quavered as she tried to convince herself.

'He might be given no choice. There are others in high places who have even more to lose than he.'

'He has known my sister for an age.'

'He does not trust Ransome.'

'Then why did he include him in this. . .this plot?'

'Your brother-in-law has excellent connections on both sides of the Channel. You will forgive me for saying this, but he is known to have no qualms of conscience where money is concerned.'

'What you say is true, but Cassie. . .? Oh, what shall I do?'

'You must be prepared to leave Brighton at once should the need arise. Go to Salterne. There you will be safe. No one will follow you, but I will warn my people, just in case. . .'

'Then you think. . .you think. . .'

'I can only guess at the probable outcome of tonight's meeting at Newhaven. Ransome is already in disfavour. Clare warned him not to draw attention to himself, but the temptation to boasting and extravagance was too strong. He will be lucky to escape with a whole skin.'

'You cannot mean. . .?'

'Clare has already been taken to task for including

Ransome in the plot. To protect himself he will agree to the majority decision.'

'And if it goes against Ransome?'

'I do not know, but we must be prepared. Now give me your word. You will go at once if I ask it of you?'

'Of course.' Aurelia forced out the words through stiff lips. 'Yet suppose Ransome is able to convince the others that no harm has been done? He may return to Brighton.'

'That is my fear, Aurelia. Should he realise that he is under suspicion he may cut and run to save his own skin. It is more than likely that he would come to you.'

'He has no love for me,' she cried harshly. 'He knows that I should not protect him.'

'Not even for your sister?'

'She would be better off without him.'

'He knows that, my dear, but it would not be affection for his family that would draw him back to Brighton. You keep gold in the house, I imagine, and I have often admired your jewels. To a man on the run money is essential.'

'He need expect no help from me.'

Salterne took both her hands in his.

'My dearest girl, I know you better than that. At the first threat to Lady Ransome or to Caro you would give him all you had.'

The tenderness in his voice caused Aurelia to release her grip upon his coat, but she seemed to have no control over her shaking limbs.

'May we not go now...tonight? I must get them out of danger. If we leave within the hour...'

Salterne was silent for what felt like an eternity, and when he spoke it was with difficulty.

'Allow me to explain. Ransome may yet persuade the others that he is still of use to them. If he returns to find you gone he will sense that something is amiss. He may give the alarm. Then, if his fellow conspirators bolt, we shall lose them.'

'And they will continue to trade with France?'

'I fear so.' His voice was hoarse and almost unrecognisable. 'I should not ask this of any woman, but I must. Will you do it? Will you stay? The choice is yours, and my offer holds. You may leave for Salterne tonight if you wish. . .'

'No!' Aurelia had already made her decision. 'Cassie will never be safe as long as Ransome is at large. Should she learn the truth at any time he would fear that she might betray him. And apart from that . . .I cannot condone treachery.'

'What a jewel you are!' He drew her close and his lips were against her hair. 'I knew you could not fail me.'

Aurelia's heart was pounding, but now it was from another cause. She longed to reach up and lock her arms about his neck, drawing his face to hers. How dear he was! And how his nearness set her blood afire!

She disengaged herself from his embrace.

'I am so sorry,' she whispered. 'It can be no pleasant thing to learn that your betrothed is the daughter of a traitor.'

'Can it be that you have not yet understood?' Salterne sounded incredulous. 'I had to get close to Ransome in a way that would not arouse suspicion.'

'I. . .I have wondered. . .' Aurelia's heart leapt.

'As well you might. I thought I had made my

feelings plain. Must I assure you that I have not the slightest interest in your niece?'

Aurelia's face grew warm. The conversation had taken an unexpected turn.

'She. . .she is very lovely.'

'She is indeed. Her beauty was the key to the whole. Even an ageing roué like myself might be so affected as to offer for her.'

'Suppose she had accepted you?' Aurelia gave him a demure look which was full of mischief.

'A child of that age confronted by a monster of iniquity? It was unlikely, and then, you see, I had made enquiries. Her heart, I knew, was given to another.'

'What a devious creature you are, my lord! And how you bamboozled us when you came to Marram with your horsewhip at the ready! You might have enjoyed success on the boards.'

She heard a low chuckle.

'I flatter myself it was a good performance. I might have enjoyed it more had Caro not been so distressed. Ransome ill-treated her sadly and I am sorry for it.'

'I shall not soon forgive him. . .for anything,' Aurelia promised fiercely.

'I am glad to hear it. Let it stiffen your resolve. You will need all your splendid courage, my dearest.'

The endearment made her feel shy.

'I must go,' she said quickly.

'Not yet.' He bent his head to hers and sought her lips. As the cool, firm mouth came down on hers Aurelia sensed that his need matched her own. As she had done before she found herself responding with all the fervour of a woman deep in love, in the throes of a dizzying passion.

'I adore you, my enchantress,' he murmured husk-
ily. 'Now go, while I still have the strength to allow it.'

Half dazed by his embrace, Aurelia slipped away
into the darkness. All her fears had vanished, to be
replaced by a sense of joy which threatened to overwhelm her. He loved her. . .he loved her. . . Had he
not said so?

She had left a single candle burning in her room,
but it was not until she slipped off her cloak that she
noticed the motionless figure sitting in the corner,
almost invisible in the shadows.

She raised a hand to her mouth to stifle a scream.

'Where have you been?' Cassie's voice was cold
with anger. 'Are you so sunk beneath reproach that
you must sneak out at night like any common trollop?'

A furious reply rose to Aurelia's lips, but she bit it
back,

'You forget yourself, Cassie. I need not account to
you for anything I choose to do.'

'This man? Is he so far beneath your touch that he
cannot approach you with propriety, as a gentleman
should?'

Aurelia did not reply. An explanation was out of
the question.

'Pray do not tell me it is nothing of the sort,' Cassie
continued. 'I should not believe you.'

'I do not intend to lie to you,' Aurelia said steadily.
'You may think what you wish.'

'Indeed! The creature is married, I suppose. I wish
you joy of him, though doubtless the gossips will have
the tale within the week.'

'Doubtless, but do not allow it to distress you.'
Aurelia's tone was stiff. How could Cassie believe that

she would allow herself to become entangled in some unsavoury liaison?

'Could you not have confided in me?' Cassie burst into tears, rocking to and fro in anguish. 'I know how unhappy you have been in these last few years, but this...this affair will bring you further grief. How I wish that we had not come to Brighton. Nothing has gone right since we arrived...and now Ransome has disappeared.'

'Ransome is used to come and go without explanation. Did you not tell me so yourself?' Aurelia put her arms about her sister and hugged her close.

'Something is amiss, I know it.' Cassie's sobs redoubled.

'You will feel better in the morning. You are overtired, my dear.'

Cassie still looked heavy-eyed when they assembled for a late nuncheon on the following day, and Aurelia sighed. She too had had a troubled night. Her joy in the knowledge that Salterne loved her was already tinged with sadness.

Her own connection with Ransome meant that she herself was tainted with treachery. Anger threatened to choke her. The man sowed the seeds of ruin all about him. His behaviour had crushed any hope of happiness which she might cherish. Even should Salterne wish to marry her she could not accept in the knowlege that she would stain his name. The man she loved was as far out of reach as ever.

She looked up as Frederick was announced.

'Is your father come with you?' she asked in a curt tone.

'I have not seen him, ma'am.' Without a by-your-leave Frederick seated himself at the table and began to pile his plate with food.

'No need to stand on ceremony is there, Aunty? In Brighton, so I understand, we dispense with the conventions.' His sly grin persuaded Aurelia that he was in possession of information which boded no good for someone.

'Do you stay long in the town?' she asked. 'We did not see you at the races.'

'I was there. Here, there and everywhere, one might say. And sometimes in the most unexpected places.'

Aurelia's expression did not change. He was hinting at something, but what? She had been so careful. He could not have seen her leave the house. . . She waited for his explanation, but Frederick addressed himself to his plate.

'Must you always be making a mystery, brother? Cannot you say what you mean for once?' Caroline's voice was unexpectedly sharp, and Frederick turned to stare at her.

'So!' he sneered. 'The worm has turned at last. Is this due to Aunty's influence? You had best not let Father hear you.'

'Why not?' As the harsh voice reached them from the doorway Aurelia's blood turned to ice.

Ransome swung his riding crop impatiently against his boot as his gaze roved from one face to another. Aurelia hid her trembling hands beneath the table. She must have managed a few words of greeting, for he appeared to find nothing strange in her manner, but later she could not recall a word that she had spoken. Anyhow Ransome did not reply. It was clear that he was under an appalling strain. A muscle jerked incessantly in his temple, and his eyes were unnaturally bright as he regarded them with a fixed smile.

Aurelia looked around the table. As always in her father's presence Caroline's face wore a hunted look, but Cassie stared straight ahead. Only Frederick seemed at ease.

'No word of greeting for me, my love?' Ransome walked over to stand behind his wife's chair and rested his hands on her shoulders. She winced as the curved fingers dug into her flesh, and turned her head as if to make a sharp retort. Then she caught Aurelia's eye and muttered something unintelligible.

'I beg your pardon, my dear? I did not quite hear that, but I am prepared to believe that you are over joyed to see me.'

'Will you not join us, Ransome?' Aurelia gestured towards the food in an effort to draw his attention from her sister.

'I'll take some wine.' He flung himself into a chair, drumming his fingers on the polished surface of the table until Aurelia thought that she must scream. She cast about wildly in her mind for some topic of conversation which might lift the tension in the room.

'Are you not surprised to see Frederick?' she asked. 'We did not expect him, you know.'

Ransome looked at his son.

'How came you here?' he said abruptly. 'I thought you had not a feather to fly with. . .'

'I had good fortune at the tables, sir.'

The stem of Cassie's wine glass snapped in her hand. She looked down dully as a few bright drops of blood fell on the skirt of her gown but she did not move.

'Oh, my dear, I am so sorry. This is the second time

within a week that we have had such an accident. It is all my fault. I had doubts about the quality of the glass when I bought it.' Aurelia felt that she was babbling as she tried to staunch the flow of blood with her handkerchief.

Ransome's eye were fixed intently upon his wife's face.

'Come, Cass, the wound must be bathed at once. Hannah will find linen for a binding,' Aurelia urged.

'I will see to it.' Ransome seized Cassie by the wrist.

'There is no necessity for you——'

'You have some objection?'

Aurelia stared at him helplessly. She could think of nothing to say.

'Ma'am, Mr Robert Clare has called. He wishes to see Lord Ransome, if that is convenient.' Jacob stood in the doorway. 'I have shown him into the salon.'

'You had best go to him, Ransome.' Little as Aurelia wished to see Robert Clare, she blessed his opportune arrival. Ransome, she knew, would force the truth from Cassie at the earliest opportunity. Her sister was unable to dissemble, and he had known at once that something was wrong.

She left Cassie in Hannah's capable hands and made her way to the salon. As she neared the door she heard raised voices, but as she was about to enter Jacob admitted another visitor.

'I trust I see you well, Miss Carrington?' Salterne was immaculate in a dark blue coat of Bath superfine and buff pantaloons. His starched cravat fell in snowy folds, and he carried a clouded cane.

Aurelia hurried to him with shining eyes. He saw the relief in her face.

'Remember we are enemies,' he warned as he

looked beyond her. 'Caro, my dear, I felicitate you on that charming gown. How well it becomes you. I vow you will take the town by storm.'

He nodded to Frederick, who had accompanied his sister to the salon, and stood back to allow the ladies to precede him.

'Ransome, your servant. . .and yours, Clare. Such a pleasure to see you.' The underlying sarcasm in his tone brought a flush to Ransome's cheek, but Clare stepped forward with every sign of satisfaction.

'The pleasure is mutual, Your Grace. We are all, I see, unable to resist the charm of Miss Carrington and her family.'

'And Lady Ransome? She is well, I hope?' The question was casual, but Aurelia was quick to notice that the Duke's hand had tightened on his cane.

'My sister has suffered a slight accident,' she said at once. 'It is not serious. The stem of a wine glass broke and cut her skin. She will join us directly.'

'Let us hope so.' Salterne favoured the company with his most charming smile, and turned to Aurelia and Caro. 'I am charged with messages for you. The Dowager Duchess hopes that you will do her the honour of calling upon her. She is at home tomorrow.'

Caro joined Aurelia in thanking him.

'She much enjoyed your company at the races,' the Duke continued. 'I am very much afraid that she has another fund of scandalous stories for you.'

'We need not look far for scandal,' Frederick broke in. 'You might look to your household, Aunt Lia. Closed carriages and females slipping through the gate at night are not at all the thing.'

The cold hand of fear closed tight about Aurelia's heart but her expression did not change.

'What *can* you mean?' she said calmly.

'Exactly what I say.' His words were accompanied by a leer. 'I was too far away to catch the wench, but you may take my word for it.'

Salterne raised his quizzing-glass. Centuries of power, of wealth and of influence were behind his look and Frederick squirmed.

'Remarkable!' the Duke pronounced at last. 'Such concern for the morals of the lower classes! If only I might claim the same devotion to their welfare. Alas, I find the nocturnal activities of my servants of not the slightest interest to me.'

The snub was severe, and it silenced Frederick, who took his leave with the air of a man who had just survived an encounter with a striking snake.

'Do you attend the cricket match today?' His Grace turned to Clare with his customary affability. If he had seen the strange glitter in Ransome's eyes he affected not to notice. 'And you, my lord? Cricket is one of your many interests, is it not?'

He was interrupted as Cassie came into the room. Under cover of a chorus of greetings Aurelia moved aside, hoping to regain some semblance of composure. For Frederick's words had shaken her to the core. They had not gone unnoticed by either Ransome or Clare; that she knew. Ransome had betrayed himself with a sudden start, and though Clare had more self-control she had seen him stiffen. She was forced to admit that her worst fears had been realised. Salterne had done his best to dismiss the incident, but she doubted if either man believed him. A closed carriage for an assignation with a servant? The idea was incongruous.

She shot a look at Ransome from under lowered

lids. That heightened colour, his jerky movements and the tell-tale tic beside his eye told her that he was close to breaking-point. She could almost smell his fear.

Clare, on the other hand, betrayed no trace of anxiety, though his eyes did not leave her face. To her horror he strolled over to stand beside her.

'Do not take it so hard,' he advised kindly. 'One cannot forever be keeping an eye upon the servants. It was ill-advised of Frederick to mention the matter in public.'

'In private I should not have minded quite so much.' Aurelia hoped that her downcast eyes would convince him that her manner betokened embarrassment and nothing more.

Clare helped himself to a leisurely pinch of snuff.

'Perhaps it was fortunate that Frederick was too late in his pursuit of her,' he murmured smoothly.

'I should not care to be brought from my bed to deal with a hysterical girl.' Aurelia forced a smile.

'Of course not, though one cannot help but wonder. I doubt if your maid would have an assignation, and your cook, I believe, is no longer young.'

'It could have been one of the kitchen-maids,' Aurelia said with resolution.

'Ah, yes, to be sure. What beauties they must be to warrant a closed carriage. . .!'

'Forgive me.' Aurelia sent a plea for help in the Duke's direction. 'His Grace, I believe, is anxious to speak to me.'

'I am entirely at your disposal, Miss Carrington.' The Duke came to her at once. 'Shall you think me importunate if I mention that the match is due to start quite soon? I believe you ladies expressed a wish to see it from the beginning. That is, if Ransome has no objection. . .?'

Ransome gave his consent with barely concealed impatience. Aurelia gained the impression that he could not wait to be rid of them. Both men, she surmised, would wish to discuss the mysterious figure who had left the house the previous night. She felt an unwelcome lurching in the pit of her stomach. Not even the presence of the Duke could dispel the fear which consumed her.

'You will be ready to leave tonight if necessary?' Salterne had fallen behind the others, and his voice was low.

Aurelia's attempt at a smile was pitiful. She looked at him with terror in her eyes.

'My darling. . .don't. . . I cannot bear it. I want to take you in my arms and keep you safe for always. This is almost at an end. Will you be brave for just a little longer, my own true love?'

His presence steadied her. He was so large and so . . .so dependable. Had he not promised that she would be safe? She could refuse him nothing, whatever the cost.

'What has happened? Has Ransome convinced the others of his good faith?'

'They are under no illusions, but they have let him run. They need him for one more night. He does not know it, but the verdict went against him. He is to be . . .disposed of.'

Aurelia felt sick. She stumbled, but a firm hand held her upright.

'Does he suspect?'

'You have seen him, Aurelia. He goes in fear of his

life. Clare has been ordered to make sure he does not escape.'

'We cannot go back to the house,' she murmured in anguish. 'Do not ask it of me. Should he be cornered. . .'

'You must not distress yourself. You will not return until he has gone. There is little time left to him, and he must decide. . .'

'You do not know him as I do. If he should slip away from Clare he might return for Cassie.'

'He will not encumber himself with your sister. His enemies are implacable. . .on both sides of the law.'

'I wish that we might never see him again,' she burst out passionately. 'I do not hope for his death, but if he would go away and never return. . .'

For answer he relieved her of her frivolous little parasol, and appeared to struggle with the catch.

'Do not open it,' he warned. 'This is but a precaution, but you will feel safer if you have it by you. You know how to use a pistol?'

He returned it to her and she felt the added weight. Then he increased his pace to catch up with the others.

'Lady Ransome, the Prince was distressed to see the damage to your sister's fan. He begs that you ladies will accept these trifles. They are oriental curiosities.' He handed each of them a fan, smiling at their exclamations of delight. 'They are murderous objects, I fear. Let me show you.' A slight pressure of his fingers caused Aurelia's fan to fall apart, disclosing a sharp knife. 'They are known as dagger fans,' he said cheerfully. 'I do not suggest that you use them for their original purpose, but they make excellent paper knives.'

'The blade is very sharp,' Caroline said doubtfully.

'I should be afraid to cut myself, though it was kind of His Royal Highness to think of us.'

Aurelia suspected that nothing would surprise the Prince more than to be thanked for his gifts. She guessed that he knew nothing of the weapon which lay so innocently in her palm.

'Let me keep yours for you, Caro,' she suggested. 'See, I will put it in my reticule. Then you will not lose it. Cassie?'

Cassie shook her head.

'I will keep mine by me,' she muttered.

'Shall you come to the Prince's villa for cards this evening?' Salterne's question betrayed no more than casual interest. His eyes were fixed on the player at the stumps, but a slight pressure on her arm persuaded Aurelia to acquiesce. She was more frightened than she had ever been in her life, and the fact that Salterne had seen fit to offer her a pistol and a knife convinced her that they were all in grave danger.

'I. . .I believe we are promised to it,' she faltered. 'Cassie is fond of cards. Is that not so, my dear?'

Cassie stared at her with dull eyes. She made no reply.

'And Caro enjoys the parties,' Aurelia continued brightly. She looked at her niece, but Caro's thoughts were far away.

Aurelia turned to Salterne with a pitiful little smile, and something in her expression caused him to bend towards her with a look of such warmth that she could not mistake his regard.

'Do not look so,' he whispered softly. 'You try my resolution. You will come to no harm, I promise you. Nor will you be asked to defend yourselves. I thought merely that you would feel safer with a weapon.'

For the rest of the afternoon he appeared to be engrossed in the cricket match, and spoke of nothing but the merits of the players. Aurelia made a valiant effort to take an interest, but her nerves felt as tight as bowstrings, and she was filled with dread at the thought of returning to the house on the Steyne.

'May we not stay to watch the foot-races?' she begged when the match had ended. She would do anything to delay their return.

'As you wish.' His look was a caress, and she found herself recalling the way he had drawn her close the previous evening. She had thought that it was simply an attempt at comfort. He could not know how deeply she loved him, but she treasured those moments in the carriage when she had allowed herself to rest against that broad chest and had realised for the first time that he had no thought of marriage to Caroline. She had put her own soul into that single kiss, believing then that her affection was returned. Now, with every nerve a-quiver, she became a prey to uncertainty. Was he simply using her for his own ends?

He had offered for Caroline, knowing that he would never wed the girl. Excusable, perhaps, when the safety of his country was at stake, but it had shown that he would stop at nothing where duty was concerned.

Had duty led him to make love to her? He had seemed sincere in his profession of love, but then, he had proved times enough that he was a master of deception.

Her face burned. She could never marry him, but there was no need to trample on her heart in order to persuade her to give him the help he needed. She would have given it gladly even if he had not spoken of his feelings.

'Doubting me again?'

Aurelia looked up, startled by his perspicacity. What she saw in his eyes resolved her doubts once and for all, and she began to breathe quickly. Only a fool would mistake that expression for anything other than the love she craved.

'I trust you, my lord.' She spoke the words in all sincerity as his eyes held hers for a long moment. Then he transferred his gaze to a point beyond her shoulder, and she looked round, dreading what she might see. The only person close to them was a shabbily dressed man who scratched gently at his ear.

'You are in no danger,' Salterne murmured. 'Ransome has left the house.'

She was tempted to ask him how he could be so sure, but she decided to believe him. She turned to Cassie. 'We have little time to dine and change,' she said cheerfully. 'Let us go back at once. The Prince makes up his tables early, and we must not keep him waiting.'

They would be safe indoors. She took her leave of Salterne and followed Cassie into the house.

'Shall you wear your new apricot sarcenet with the black net overdress, Cass? The contrast is so striking. It is quite one of Madame Claudine's most successful gowns.'

Cassie stared at her without a word.

'Hannah shall dress you first,' Aurelia said briskly. 'Then you shall talk to me while she does my hair.'

She ached with pity, but there was little she could do to comfort Cassie.

She tossed aside her half-poke bonnet, and cast off

the dress spencer which she had worn for warmth over her sprigged muslin. A bathe in cold water helped to refresh her, and the knowledge that Ransome was no longer under her roof served to lift her spirits further. She slipped unaided into her gown of primrose lustring as she considered what jewels she might wear with it.

When she turned she caught sight of her reflection in the long dressing-glass, and was surprised. Somehow she looked different. The change could not be ascribed to the high-waisted robe, which set off her figure to perfection. She stepped closer and looked at her shining eyes. There was no mistaking their message. She might as well have announced her love for Salterne to the world, she thought ruefully. For the first time in years she felt truly alive, and it showed in her animated expression. She blushed and wondered if he was aware of it.

Her joy was short-lived as memory flooded back. Had she not told herself that her love could never be? There seemed to be no end to Ransome's destructive influence. She rued the day that Cassie had ever met him.

Pushing her vain regrets aside, she reached into the drawer for her jewel box. As she opened it she gasped.

The box was empty and the key to her money chest had vanished.

CHAPTER THIRTEEN

AURELIA reached into the bottom drawer of the tall-boy, moving a pile of clothing to one side. The small chest was still there, but she did not need the lack of weight to assure her that it was empty.

Doubtless the bag of gold which she kept locked in her writing desk would also have disappeared.

So Ransome had gone. She felt only an overwhelming sense of relief. The theft convinced her that he did not intend to return. If that was so he was more than welcome to her money and her jewels.

A knock at the door caused her to close the drawer. She turned to face Cassie with a smile.

'I was right,' she said cheerfully. 'That gown becomes you well.' She did not comment on her sister's lack of bracelets, earrings, necklace, or even a locket.

'Mama, I cannot find my pearls!' Caro hurried into the room in a state of high anxiety.

'My love, I forget to tell you. Had you not noticed that the clasp was loose? I sent them to the jeweller this morning. Are not the rosebuds ornament enough? Ought else would be too much, especially as you are wearing a wreath upon your curls.'

Caroline sat down upon the bed.

'Then you approve my gown, Aunt Lia?'

'It is altogether charming.' Aurelia's hasty explanation about the missing necklace had satisfied her niece, but Cassie remained silent.

'Will you wear your diamond drops, Miss Lia?'
Hannah stood back to admire her mistress's toilette.
As Monsieur Pierre had directed, Aurelia's fair locks
were caught high with a length of primrose ribbon
embroidered with silver thread.

Aurelia was careful to avoid Cassie's eye. She stood
before her mirror, apparently considering whether or
not she would wear the diamonds.

'I think not.' She picked up her scarf. 'Let us make
haste, my dears. There is little time to dine before we
go.'

Relieved though she was to think that Ransome
had disappeared, possibly for good, she could not
repress a feeling of deep unease. Her efforts at conversation met with no response from Cassie, and
finally even Caro gave up the pretence that all was
well with her mother.

Aurelia caught her niece's eye and shook her head.
This was no time for questions. Cassie was close to
breaking-point and an incautious word might snap her
self-control at any moment.

Perhaps in the company of her friends her sister's
mood might change. With this in mind Aurelia moved
quickly through the crowds in the outer hall of the
Prince's villa. She was searching for a familiar face. . .
Lady Bellingham. . .or even the odious Mrs Ingleby—
anyone who might capture Cassie's attention.

She led her sister into the gallery. It was a favourite
lounge for the Prince's intimates, but though she stood
on the first step of the ornate staircase to raise herself
above the crowd the faces turned to hers were those
of strangers.

For once the figures of the Chinese fishermen bearing their lamps aloft failed to charm her. The gilded

carvings of dragons and serpents seemed to have taken on a strange life of their own. She shuddered. It was all so macabre. The atmosphere of the place had a subtle tinge of nightmare.

She pulled herself together at once. Tonight she was allowing her imagination to run riot. The shock of discovering the loss of her jewels and her gold had unnerved her...that was all. She must forget these fanciful notions.

Perhaps they should not have accepted the Prince's invitation for this evening, yet a last-minute refusal would have given offence to His Royal Highness. Taking Cassie's arm, she moved into the south drawing-room.

Sanity returned as she looked at the tables, already set out and awaiting the players. The tall figure of the Regent was easily recognisable. He was deep in conversation with a group of *émigrés*, moving from French to Italian and then to German with equal ease.

As she hesitated in the doorway he looked up and saw her. He came to her at once.

'Will you not join us?' His pleasant deep voice was confortingly familiar. 'We are indulging in a little frivolous chatter before we begin the serious business of the evening.' He gestured towards the tables.

Aurelia looked into the bright blue eyes. As always, in spite of his vast bulk, she could see traces of the handsome young man who had captured the affections of the townspeople some thirty years earlier.

'Melton is in form tonight,' he observed. 'I must ask him to tell you the story of Bullock's race.'

No stranger to depression, he had sensed at once that Cassie was not herself, and he exerted himself to cheer her.

'Bullock was not of the *ton*, Lady Ransome. I doubt if you have heard of him, but he was an unusual character, and of a vast size. Come, Melton, you have the tale at your fingertips. It will divert the ladies.'

Aurelia recognised Melton as the man who had stepped on her gown at the Old Ship Inn. He gave her an apologetic look. Then, encouraged by her smile, he launched into his story. It lost nothing in the telling and the Prince slapped his thigh with glee as Melton described Bullock's wager with Lord Barrymore.

'You must remember, ladies, that the man was hugely fat. When he offered to beat My Lord Barrymore in a foot-race for a purse of gold, His Lordship accepted at once. Being young and healthy, he agreed to Bullock's terms—the choice of time and place, and a thirty-five-yard start. The man was cunning, one must allow. He chose the narrowest passage-way in the town, and Lord Barrymore could not pass him.'

A shout of laughter greeted the end of his story and Aurelia was happy to see that some of the colour had returned to Cassie's cheeks.

'Lady Ransome, do you care to take your place for the gaming?' The Prince glanced about him as the room began to fill. 'Allow me to seat you here. You know Lady Bellingham, I believe, and Broome and his wife will make up the number.'

At his bidding Cassie sat down, and the Regent turned to Aurelia.

'May I beg your indulgence, Miss Carrington?' he said in a low tone. 'The Dowager Duchess is here alone tonight. Salterne is called away, and I fear my old friend is inclined to over-tax her strength. You are a particular favourite of hers. Will you sit with her for

a time? She must not spend too long at the tables. . .
but perhaps later?'

Aurelia at once assured him of her willingness to
forgo the gaming.

He led her through to his private sitting-room,
excused himself, and left to rejoin his guests.

'Well, miss, and how do you go on?' The Duchess
was resplendent in a gown of oyster satin beneath a
heavily embroidered tunic in the same shade. A
matching turban, ornamented with plumes, sat atop
her thinning hair. As she looked up it slipped to one
side, and she gave it a tug of exasperation.

'Allow me, Your Grace.' Aurelia settled the head-
dress firmly in place.

'Much better, my dear, I thank you. But you do not
answer me. . .'

'I am well, ma'am, as you see.'

'But troubled still, I fancy. Well, Salterne has
warned me that I must not question you. . .though I
cannot abide a mystery, I will confess.'

Aurelia was silent. The news of Salterne's sudden
absence had left her feeling vulnerable and very much
alone.

'How is Charlotte, ma'am?' It was an effort to make
conversation when her thoughts were elsewhere, but
the Duchess answered her readily enough.

'The child is as mischievous as ever, my dear. At
present she has a passion for riding along the promenade in the goat-carts which are for hire. Now she
must tease Salterne for an animal of her own.'

A twinkle came into Aurelia's eye.

'He has agreed?'

'Not yet, but he is weakening. The child needs a
mother, Aurelia. My grandson is too easily swayed. . .'

'And you are not, dear ma'am?' The teasing note in her voice brought a sparkle to the old lady's eyes.

'Perhaps, my dear, but I could wish——'

She was interrupted at that point. The door opened to admit the Prince, accompanied by Salterne.

A flush of colour suffused Aurelia's face, and her heart began to pound. She was careful to avoid the Duke's eye as she pretended an interest in a bowl of roses close beside her.

'Now, Duchess, you shall come with me. Here is your grandson returned, and I have promised him that you do not play high tonight.' The Prince proffered an arm and was promptly taken to task.

'Stuff!' the Dowager said briskly. 'Do not listen to him, sire. I have no patience with his namby-pamby ways.'

This description of the formidable figure standing by her side caused Aurelia's lips to twitch, but the Regent preserved his countenance.

'Salterne is a sad case,' he agreed drily. 'But I am inclined to missishness myself, so you must bear with me.'

The old lady gave a crow of delight at this piece of impertinence and suffered herself to be led away.

Aurelia sat down suddenly. She felt that her legs would no longer support her. Salterne's grave manner had told her at once that he had news.

'Is it over?' she whispered faintly.

'The leaders are taken, Lia, but. . .'

'Something is wrong?' She had sensed his mood at once. 'Please tell me. . .'

'Ransome and Clare were not among them,' he said slowly.

'Is that all?' She felt light-hearted with relief. 'Pray

do not concern yourself. Ransome is gone these several hours, and I cannot believe he will return.'

'What has made you so sure?' As he looked at her the implications of her lack of jewellery struck him at once. 'He took everything?' he asked grimly.

'It is not of the least importance.' Aurelia laid a placatory hand upon his arm. 'The loss is nothing if it means that we shall not see him again.'

'If only I could be sure. . .'

'Surely he would not dare to return? He will be far away by now.'

'And you have no idea of where he might have gone?'

'None! And I do not care to know. He has harmed my family for the last time.'

'I hope you may be right. Does Lady Ransome know of his departure?'

'She knows,' Aurelia said bitterly. 'Though she will not speak of it. I had not thought to see my sister so distressed. She has been used to give up her possessions to him, but now she fears disgrace, and worse. I am thankful that she does not know the whole.'

'It is doubly hard for you,' he murmured. 'I know how much you care for her.'

'I cannot bear to see her so changed.' Aurelia's voice shook with emotion. 'What is to become of her?' She buried her face in her hands.

A strong arm slipped about her waist and the Duke drew her close.

'Do not give way, my dearest. All may yet be well.'

Through the fine fabric of his shirt Aurelia could hear the thudding of his heart. She allowed her head to rest against his shoulder, wishing that the moment could last forever. Then she pulled away.

'Your kindness weakens my resolution,' she whispered. 'I am become a watering-pot and...and I do not mean to be so foolish. I beg you will forgive me.'

'You speak of kindness? Lia, look at me! Do you doubt my love for you? God knows, I have made it plain enough. You are all I want, my darling. Will you not say that you will become my wife?' He bent his head to hers and sought her lips, but she put up a hand to stop him.

'I cannot, my lord. You must know that. Oh, please, this is impossible... To continue can only cause pain... We must go... Someone is sure to come upon us.'

'In the Prince's private apartment? No, my dear. That will not serve.' He possessed himself of her hands and felt her quiver beneath his touch.

'Is marriage such a dreadful prospect?' he asked in a low voice. 'Your happiness will be my first consideration always. You have heard stories, Lia, but they are not true. Something of an evil reputation was needed for my purpose, but I am not the rake you may think me.'

Involuntarily she put up a hand to his lips to stop him.

'I do not think you a rake at all.' Aurelia's eyes were bright with unshed tears. 'I know you for the man you are.' Her fingers traced the long line of the white scar on his cheek. 'I...I have a high regard for you, Your Grace.'

He kissed her then, with infinite tenderness at first, and then with growing hunger. Aurelia abandoned herself to the warmth of his lips until she felt herself drowning in a sea of passion. She made a despairing effort to struggle free of his embrace.

'I beg of you, do not try me further,' she whispered. 'You cannot offer me marriage. If you will not consider yourself you must think of Charlotte and the Duchess.'

'Aurelia, you will not tell me that my grandmother might disapprove of you? She has been scheming for this moment since we met. And Charlotte is still looking for her mermaid. . .' His eyes were filled with private laughter.

She could give him no answering smile.

'You have not considered, my lord. In future the taint of treachery must always be upon my family. I would not. . .could not allow your own to suffer.'

Salterne's face hardened.

'Will you let Ransome destroy you? I cannot believe it. I should want you for my wife had he been hanged at Tyburn.'

Aurelia shuddered.

'He might yet return. You hinted as much yourself. Think of what that would mean. . .for all of us.'

'My dearest, will you not think of yourself for once?' He made as if to seek her lips again, but she turned her head away, feeling as if her heart must break.

'Please go.' Her words were scarcely audible. 'This is too painful. . .for both of us.'

He did not reply and she turned to him at last with a question in her eyes.

'My lord?'

'I am waiting, Aurelia.'

'For what? I have explained. . .'

'I am waiting for you to tell me that you do not love me and that I may not hope. Say that and I will leave you.'

The room was so quiet that she could hear the ticking of the ornate clock which stood upon the mantelshelf. The scent of roses drifted towards her from the bowl beside her hand. It lent an added poignancy to the scene. Roses for love, she thought inconsequentially, and now, with her next few words, she must destroy any hope of future happiness. The constriction in her throat was choking her, and she felt that she could not breathe.

'Well?'

He would never know what it cost her to do so, but she forced herself to meet his eyes.

'You are mistaken, Your Grace. My regard for you is that of a friend. . .and nothing more. I am sorry if I have led you to believe otherwise.'

He looked as if she had struck him, and the colour drained from his face.

'I see,' he said abruptly. 'Do not blame yourself, Miss Carrington. It was wrong of me to force my attentions on you. I had imagined. . .Well, it does not signify. I should have realised that my case was hopeless from the start. You will not soon forget the deception I have practised on your family.'

'Oh, please!' An involuntary cry of protest broke from her lips. 'You had little choice, and the stakes were high. I honour you for the course you took. You must have found it repugnant.'

'Not all of it.' His twisted smile cut her to the heart. 'I found you, and from the first moment of our meeting I hoped that when this terrible business was done I could come to you and offer you my love. What a fool I have been! Yet even now I can't believe——'

'We should not suit,' she told him firmly, but the tremor in her voice betrayed her.

'Lia, my love. . .' Again he attempted to take her in his arms, but she drew away.

'This is not kind in you, my lord. You must believe me. I do not feel those sentiments for you which would lead me to accept your offer, though I am honoured. . .'

'Good God! Will you send me away with words such as those? You might have learned them by rote. Are we nothing to each other?'

'Not. . .not in the way you would wish, but I shall always stand your friend.'

His face closed and when he spoke his voice was bitter.

'You surprise me, ma'am. For a female whose affection is not involved you gave an excellent performance.'

Her own hurt betrayed her into an angry retort. 'It could scarce rival your own, Your Grace.'

He laughed then, and it was not a pleasant sound.

'It is to be spinsterhood, then? The condition will not suit you, Miss Carrington, or else I am no judge.'

'Who better? Your experience of women is so wide, is it not?' His cruel reference to her own response to him incensed Aurelia.

Salterne's face paled, but the expression in the glittering eyes caused her to shrink back. Then he bowed. 'I shall not trouble you again.' He strode out of the room.

Aurelia sat motionless, exactly as he had left her. A ladybird crawled slowly up the stem of one of the roses and, unthinking, she followed the progress of the little insect. The heavy perfume of the flowers drifted towards her. She had always loved their scent, but now she found it cloying. It might have been a drug which had robbed her of all will to move. A sense of deadly inertia possessed her, and her brain refused to function. She knew that feeling must return in time, and with it an agony which she dared not contemplate.

He had looked so...so stricken. Her throat ached with unshed tears. How could she meet him again and continue to pretend that she did not care?

Salterne was angry now...and hurt...but when he had time to think he would guess that she was lying. She rose to her feet and began to pace the room. Her refusal had been so ridiculously formal, she thought wretchedly. She had acted like some simpering miss who wished to keep a suitor dangling. What must he think of her? She had sounded so unlike herself.

And there lay the danger. If he forgave her she would not be proof against a renewed appeal on his part. She must take herself far out of his reach. Not to Marram. He could find her there. She must think... but not of the love which she had so recently refused.

She would go to London. There she could see her bankers, replenish her funds, and seek refuge in some unfashionable quarter of the city while she considered her future plans.

Her sorrow was too deep for tears. Those plans could not include him. Above all, she must convince herself of that. And now, before she could change her mind, she must find Cassie and explain...

She came to an abrupt halt. Of course...Cassie and Caro. She had not just herself to think about. Since Ransome had gone they were dependent upon her. And how could she explain to her sister that she was fleeing from the Duke's love?

She threw out her arms in a gesture of despair. She

was trapped in a tangled web from which there could be no escape. She sat down suddenly, feeling that her legs would no longer support her, and buried her head in her hands.

'Lia, my dearest girl, what on earth has happened? Rollo stalked past me looking as if the world had come to an end. You have quarrelled?' The Dowager Duchess laid a sympathetic hand upon her shoulder.

Aurelia nodded, searching for her handkerchief.

'Take mine.' A scrap of lace-trimmed cambric was pressed into her hand. 'Do not distress yourself, my love. Rollo can be hasty, but he doesn't mean one half of what he says. His temper, you know...'

'He...It was not his fault, ma'am. I alone am to blame. I beg your pardon; I thought you were at the tables.'

'I pleaded exhaustion.' Aurelia heard a low chuckle. 'What a busybody I am! Yet I could not sit by when two people who are dear to me are at such odds with each other.'

'You guessed?'

'I know my grandson, Lia. I have not seen that look on his face before...at least, not since Elizabeth died.'

'Oh, do not say so! I cannot bear it. I have been so cruel.'

'He has offered for you?'

Another sob was her answer.

'Well, then, my dear, that is no cause for sadness. His love is not given lightly, I assure you.'

'I...I refused him.'

'You must have had cause, Aurelia, for you do return his love, I think?'

'I said that I did not...' The muffled words were almost inaudible.

'And he believed you? Great heavens! The man must be wandering in his wits, and so I shall tell him.'

'Oh, please do not! I cannot marry him, Your Grace. There are reasons, believe me. It is impossible. Forgive me, but I dare not say more.'

'Then the secret is not your own?'

Aurelia shook her head.

'Harrumph! My dear, I am an old woman. I have seen much unhappiness in this world and much of it was self-inflicted. Will you not reconsider?'

'I cannot.'

'Very well. I will say no more. Now you shall compose yourself and come with me to find Cassie and Caro. Ransome is not here tonight?'

'No.' The word was spoken with great violence, but though the Duchess looked up sharply she did not comment. Instead she took Aurelia's arm and, leaning heavily on her gold-topped cane, she walked towards the door. There she paused for a moment.

'This will pass, believe me. Now hold up your head and brave it out. Let us not set the gossips' tongues a-wagging.'

Together they walked slowly through the crowded rooms, pausing to greet an aquaintance here and there. The Duchess was careful to avoid lengthy conversations, pleading the lateness of the hour, but she contrived to draw attention from Aurelia with a few salty remarks in her usual style.

'What riff-raff the Prince draws about him in these days!' She remarked succinctly. 'And what airs they give themselves! Letty Lade, so I hear, complains of the admission of the wives of cits to the assembly. For a strumpet that is coming it too strong.'

She did not trouble to lower her voice, and heads

turned in her direction, but recognition brought only indulgent smiles.

'Fools!' the Duchess said briskly. 'You will please to note, Aurelia, that to do and say as one pleases one must be very old or very rich. Fortunately I am both.'

In spite of her deep unhappiness the forthright words brought a faint smile to Aurelia's pallid lips. She felt a surge of affection for the Dowager, appreciating the way in which the old lady had protected her, covering up her distress until the blessed moment when she might call her carriage and return to the house on the Steyne.

'May I give you a word of advice, my dear?' The satin turban had slipped askew once more, but the eyes beneath it were wise. 'You have been under a strain. I don't know why, and I must not ask, but you are overwrought. Will you give yourself time to reconsider?' She did not wait for Aurelia's reply, but turned to greet the Prince. He came towards them swiftly, a frown marring his normally amiable countenance.

'Duchess, I am charged with a message for you. Salterne is called away. May I provide you with an escort to your home?'

He looked about him, and raised a finger to call Melton to his side.

'Pray do not trouble, Your Royal Highness. We are leaving now, and shall be happy to accompany the Duchess. If you will allow me but a moment I will find my sister. . .'

'Then Melton shall summon your carriage, ma'am.' He stayed beside the Dowager, engaging her in conversation, as Aurelia excused herself and went in search of Cassie.

She was not much surprised to find that her sister

had left the tables and was sitting on a sofa with Caro by her side. The set look was still about Cassie's mouth and Caro's attempts at conversation were falling on deaf ears. Aurelia forgot her own misery, and in her concern she did not notice her niece's heightened colour, nor her air of suppressed excitement.

'Come, my dears,' she said gently. 'We are to take the Duchess home.' She shepherded her party to the entrance hall and shook her head in a plea for silence as the Dowager glanced at Cassie's face.

Aurelia could not shake off a sense of foreboding which had nothing to do with her refusal of the Duke. Perhaps it was her imagination, but no one seemed quite themselves. The Prince's normally cheerful manner had vanished, and in his eyes she detected a curious mixture of anger and regret.

'Something is troubling Prince George.' As they settled themselves in the carriage the Duchess put Aurelia's thoughts into words.

'Ma'am?'

'No doubt it is his debts again. Still, if one is inspired to pay ninety guineas each for handkerchiefs trimmed with Brussels lace it cannot be wondered at.' The old lady gave a sniff of disapproval.

'Is that true, Your Grace?' Caroline's eyes were round with astonishment.

'It is perfectly true, I assure you. When the Prince is beset by his creditors he must needs spend more in order to raise his spirits.'

Caroline chuckled at the dry remark, and the Duchess continued to divert her, drawing her attention from the evident worries of her mother and her aunt.

Uncharacteristically, Cassie preserved an uncompromising silence, oblivious of the need to hide her feelings. She seemed incapable of speech.

Aurelia was deeply troubled. For the first time in her life she felt that Cassie was beyond her reach. Nothing she could say or do brought a spark of interest to her sister's eyes, or drew her thoughts back to the present. Cassie had retreated into a world of her own, and what her thoughts were Aurelia dreaded to imagine.

Her own dejection turned to icy rage as she thought of Ransome. She had prayed never to see him again, but now she longed for the chance to...to do what? Perhaps to crush him like the vile reptile he was. As handsome as Lucifer, she thought savagely, and just as evil.

She clenched her hands in a effort to control her fury. He should never be given the opportunity to harm Cassie again. She must be calm. If only she could think, but for that she needed a cool head. The Duchess had advised her to give herself time. It was excellent counsel, if only it might be obeyed.

Her thoughts returned to Salterne. It was unlike him to abandon the Dowager Duchess without a word. What could have drawn him away on such an urgent errand? When the answer came to her she began to tremble. It could only be Ransome or Clare. He must have had some message.

Hideous pictures formed in her mind, and try as she might she could not shut them out. The two conspirators were desperate men. If he had followed them alone he might be in deadly danger, even at this moment. She must not think of that, or what might follow.

If they had not quarrelled he might have taken her into his confidence. If only he had told her something to set her mind at rest. Perhaps he was accompanied by troops? It was a forlorn hope, and she knew him better. He would go alone, still hoping to find some way of protecting her sister and Caro from disgrace.

She roused herself to bid the Duchess farewell, but it was with a heavy heart that she sought her bed that night.

She was awakened by the sound of voices, but they seemed far away. Late revellers in the street, she thought drowsily.

Then a hand grasped her shoulder. She opened her eyes to find sunlight pouring through the half-opened curtains, and Hannah bending over her.

'Miss Lia, it's Lady Ransome! Will you come?'

'What is it? Is she ill?'

'I don't know, ma'am. She will not speak.'

Aurelia threw on her robe and ran to Cassie's room. On the threshold she stopped, appalled. She might have been facing a marble statue. Cassie stood motionless, holding a letter in one hand.

Aurelia drew it gently from the nerveless fingers and began to read. The content brought on such a wave of nausea that she felt faint. She threw her arms about Cassie's rigid form, but her sister did not respond.

'Warm blankets, quickly!' Aurelia ordered. 'And bring me some hot, sweet tea. Lady Ransome is in a state of shock.'

She read the letter again. The words danced before her eyes, but the message could not be mistaken.

If you wish to see your daughter alive, come to the crossing at Ditchling on the Lewes Road. You will be met at noon. Tell no one. You are being watched. If you are followed the girl will die.

CHAPTER FOURTEEN

AURELIA heard a low moan. She turned to see Cassie sliding to the ground.

'Lift her on to the bed.' She signed to Jacob and Matthew who were standing in the doorway. 'What o'clock is it?'

'It is eight, Miss Lia.'

'I shall want the phaeton and the greys at once.'

'But ma'am, there is no need. Matthew shall fetch the doctor.'

'No!' Cassie's eyelids fluttered open. 'It is but the effect of my sleeping draught. I felt a little dizzy.'

Jacob looked at Aurelia.

'You heard Lady Ransome...no doctor.' Aurelia fixed him with a quelling eye. 'Now have the horses put to.'

She turned to Hannah.

'There is no necessity to wake Miss Caro. Lady Ransome will soon be well.' In her haste to reach Cassie's side she had not thought to look in the cot in her own room.

'Miss Caro ain't in the house, and well you know it, ma'am. Did I not try to rouse her too?' Hannah's eyes were full of suspicion. 'She's never run off again?'

'Hold your tongue, Hannah. I shall bring her back before she is missed. Lay out my riding habit, please.'

Hannah tossed her head and left the room.

'Lia, I beg of you...you must not go.' Cassie's face

265

had aged in minutes. 'The letter was sent to me. I was to tell no one, else they will kill her.'

'Can you drive the phaeton?' Aurelia demanded. 'Don't be foolish! They will not fear a woman.'

'We cannot be sure of that.' Cassie wrung her hands. 'I don't know what to do. Salterne is most nearly concerned, apart from ourselves. Had we not best ask him?'

Aurelia hesitated. Cassie was right, but, though she longed for the Duke's protection, to involve him might place Caro's life in danger, and there was no time.

'He is gone away from Brighton. In any case, the instructions are clear. No one else is to be involved.'

'Then what can we do?'

'Not you, my love. I shall go alone.'

'No, you will not! Caro is my daughter. We shall go together.'

Aurelia looked at her in amazement. Cassie's colour had returned and she held her head high.

'I shall not hold you back,' the latter said firmly. 'But I must go with you.'

Aurelia wasted no words on further argument. She could only be thankful that Cassie's sanity had returned. At one time she had feared for her sister's reason.

They left the house together in the teeth of Hannah's furious reproaches and worried looks from Jacob and Matthew.

Aurelia gave her horses the office, and then she turned to Cassie.

'I heard nothing in the night, did you?'

'No. Caro must have been tricked into slipping out. She may have thought to meet Richard. . .' Cassie's lips trembled. 'I paid no attention to her, even when she came to bid me goodnight.'

'You were not yourself, my dear.'

'If only I had not taken the sleeping draught. . .I must have heard her leave.'

'You must not blame yourself.'

'But Lia, what can this mean? All the world knows that we have no money. Do they believe that I can pay to have my daughter returned to me?'

'We cannot know until we meet them.' Aurelia glanced at her watch. 'I had best spring the horses. Shall you mind?'

Cassie shook her head. 'I am sorry that Ransome took your jewels,' she said suddenly. 'The gold, too, is gone?'

'Everything, but it is no matter. We have more important concerns. . .'

Cassie was silent for some time. Then she said, 'Ransome must be involved in this. I am sure of it.'

'You must be dreaming, Cass. To take his own child? What can he gain by it? He does nothing, as you know, without advantage to himself.'

'We shall see.' The set look was back on Cassie's face, and Aurelia hastened to divert her attention.

'This is Ditchling,' she announced. 'And here is the turning for Lewes. Do you see anyone?'

'Not a soul. Have we misjudged the place?'

'Look!'

In the distance a solitary horseman was silhouetted against the skyline. As they watched he raised a beckoning arm.

Aurelia lost track of the twists and turns in the country lanes as she followed him in the phaeton. He was leading them far from the well-used roads.

'I should have come alone.' Cassie's face was ashen. 'There may be danger. I should not have allowed you to accompany me.'

'You couldn't have stopped me.' Aurelia felt in her pocket and her hand closed about the comforting solidity of her little pistol. She felt oddly elated. Better by far to confront the enemy openly than to struggle blindly in a web of intrigue and deceit.

They had entered the confines of a wood, and the path ahead was little more than a track. Overhead the trees leaned towards each other, blocking out the sun.

'How dark it is. Do you see anyone?' Cassie's voice was but a whisper.

'It's lighter up ahead. There's a clearing and a hovel.' Aurelia brought the phaeton to a halt. This must be their destination, for the path did not run beyond it. The place appeared to be deserted.

Cassie made as if to step down.

'Stay where you are,' Aurelia warned. 'Up here we have the advantage.'

'Quite so,' drawled a familiar voice. 'For that reason you would be wise to relinquish the reins, Miss Carrington. May I assist you?'

Aurelia looked into the smiling face of Robert Clare. Instinctively her hand tightened on her whip.

'I should not advise it,' he said smoothly. 'We have much to discuss. Let us preserve the niceties.'

Aurelia sprang down, ignoring his outstretched arm, and moved round the phaeton to help Cassie.

'Where is Caroline?' she asked coldly. 'And what is the meaning of this charade?'

'Where would your niece be but with her father?' Clare asked in mock-surprise. 'Shall we return her to her fond mama?'

As he looked towards the doorway of the hovel Ransome appeared, dragging Caroline by the hand. The girl was filthy and dishevelled, and a purple bruise had closed one eye.

'You beast!' Aurelia moved towards him so fast that Clare was unable to restrain her. She raised her whip and struck Ransome hard across the face.

With a curse he started for her, the blood running down his cheek, but Clare stepped between them before he could reach her.

'Please to control your temper, my dear,' he reproved. 'We must not let our passions run away with us. At least, not yet.'

Caroline was in her mother's arms, weeping incoherently, but Cassie looked beyond her to where Ransome stood. He was attempting to staunch the flow from the wound, and he did not meet her eye.

'What do you want of us?' Cassie spoke quietly, but her voice was so changed as to be unrecognisable.

'I hoped to restore you to your husband,' Clare said with great good humour.

'That you will never do. Come, Aurelia, let us go.'

'Not so fast! You do not fully understand, Lady Ransome. Your husband and I are in some little difficulty. Matters have not gone well for us of late. All might have been well had you not harboured a spy within your midst.'

'You are insane!' Cassie turned to help Caro into the phaeton.

It was then that Clare's composure vanished. He dragged Caro down again and thrust her roughly towards her mother.

'Take care!' he warned. 'Do not try me too far, or I

may be tempted to leave you to your husband's tender mercies. Would you prefer him to explain, or shall I?'

'Get on with it!' Aurelia flung the words at him through gritted teeth.

'It was stupid of you to leave the house at night, Miss Carrington, and the carriage was Salterne's, was it not? Oh, yes, you were recognised, but not by Frederick. He had only to describe your height and your slender build for me to guess.'

'What is that to you? Are you the guardian of my morals?'

'If it were only that! But you must not try to gammon me, my dear. Those who play a deep game must take the consequences. Doubtless you have informed your sister of Ransome's part in our plot.'

'She knows nothing. I was told not to speak of it to anyone.'

Her hand flew to her mouth. With those few words she had confirmed his suspicions.

'It does not signify. She cannot testify against her husband, but you. . .now, that is a different matter.'

'A plot?' Cassie stood perfectly still. Her eyes were fixed on Ransome's face.

'You really did not know? I have misjudged Miss Carrington. Your husband, dear Lady Ransome, has been assisting us. It was merely a matter of moving—er—currency to France.'

'Treachery?' Cassie stood very still.

'If you will have it so, but we are wasting time. The question is, what are we to do with Miss Carrington? She bears no love for either of us.'

'I told you what to do.' Ransome's chilling expression left Aurelia in no doubt as to his meaning.

'An extreme solution, my friend. You forget that I

have a *tendre* for the lady. If she will but consent to be my wife...'

Aurelia laughed in his face.

'Have you taken leave of your senses? Nothing would persuade me...'

'No?' Clare looked beyond her to the shrinking figure of Caroline. 'We have the girl and she lays no claim to fortitude. If you had but heard her screams when her father attempted to show her her duty...'

Aurelia heard a light click, and looked down to see the gleam of metal. Cassie had opened the dagger fan. In one swift movement she stepped behind her sister and lunged at Clare with the wicked-looking knife.

He brushed her aside with a gesture of disdain, and she fell heavily to the ground.

'Enough of this!' Clare's veneer of sophistication was wearing thin. He bent to retrieve the fan. 'You see our dilemma, Miss Carrington? But for Salterne we had been wealthy men. Now we shall be hunted from one end of the kingdom to the other.'

'You deserve far worse,' Aurelia cried hotly.

'Possibly, but that is a fate which we intend to avoid. You have a choice, my dear. Either marriage to me—in which case Ransome and I will make good use of your fortune—or the unfortunate course which Ransome does not cease to urge upon me. The result would be the same, as I understand that your sister will inherit.'

A silence fell upon the glade. Overhead the sun shone from a cloudless sky, the birds were singing, and a pair of squirrels chased each other around the bole of a tree.

This can't be happening, Aurelia thought in disbelief, but the smiling face before her was implacable.

Bereft of speech, she put out a hand to help Cassie to her feet.

'Have you no pity?' Cassie pleaded. 'I will go with Ransome gladly and I shall not speak of what has happened here, but please...I beg of you...Caro is but a child, and my sister will not harm you. Let them go... I will vouch for their silence.'

'How touching!' The sneer brought a flush to Cassie's cheeks. 'You have forgot the trifling matter of money. Now, Miss Carrington, must you have a demonstration of our determination?'

He picked up Aurelia's whip and beckoned to Caroline.

'Come here, my dear. I trust you are in good voice?'

'Stop! You shall not touch her.' Aurelia's voice was high with panic.

'Very well. Ransome, get the parson!'

Aurelia stood as if turned to stone as Ransome lurched towards the hovel. He was holding a pistol when he reappeared, but she was only half aware of the weapon. Her attention was fixed on the thin figure of a small man in clerical garb who walked towards her.

Her fingers closed about the gun in her pocket. When the parson was close enough to shield her from Ransome's line of fire she brought it out swiftly and took aim.

'Stand back!' she cried. 'Cassie, put Caro in the phaeton. You will manage the team as far as the road to Brighton.'

'No! Lia, you cannot... I shall not leave you here.' A sudden blow from her husband caught Cassie full across the mouth and sent her reeling.

For one vital moment Aurelia's attention was distracted. It was enough. She gave a cry of agony as Clare raised the whip and struck her hard on the wrist, knocking the pistol from her hand.

'No more tricks!' he warned. 'Ransome has been under a strain. His finger is over-light upon the trigger.'

Aurelia glanced about her wildly, praying that someone might come upon them—a swineherd or a charcoal burner—even a poacher—but there was no sound within the wood.

'Aunt Lia, you cannot. . .' Caroline mumbled the words through bruised and swollen lips. The tears were streaming down her face.

'I agree, Miss Carrington; you cannot and you shall not.' Salterne's voice came from behind them.

With a sob of relief Aurelia swung round. He was strolling towards them with a wicked-looking pistol in each hand.

'God damn you!' Ransome fired once and the glade erupted in a haze of gunsmoke, flying metal and tattered flesh.

Aurelia looked down at the mangled, bloody figure at her feet and then she fainted.

She opened her eyes to find herself seated in her own phaeton, supported by a pair of massive arms. As memory flooded back she moaned and turned to bury her face against a comforting chest clad in a coat of Bath superfine.

'Don't dwell on it, my love,' the Duke said gently. 'Ransome did not suffer. His death was instantaneous.'

'What. . .what happened? When he fired I thought he must have killed you.'

'The gun exploded in his hand. It is not unheard of.'

Aurelia shuddered. The horror of the sight still filled her mind.

'Lia, you must believe that it was for the best. He will not now stand trial.'

'I know. . .but Cassie. . .'

'Your sister did not see it. When he struck her she was stunned.'

'And Caro? She was standing close to him.'

'She is unharmed, though she was dazed by the blast.' He looked across the glade to where Caro stood beneath the trees, locked in the arms of Richard Collinge.

'How came he here?' Aurelia said blankly.

'I made it my business to seek him out.' The dark face gazed at her fondly. 'You will recall the night that Caro met him in the Prince's stables?'

Aurelia nodded.

'I—er—accosted him as he left. I managed to convince him that he might serve both Caro and his country if he would lend me his assistance.'

'He is but a boy,' Aurelia said in wonder.

'There you are mistaken, my dearest. He is a man, and a sensible one. He was unknown to the conspirators, and could show himself where I could not. I have great hopes for him. There is an old head on those young shoulders.'

Aurelia sank back against his broad chest.

'Then you have forgiven both of them for deceiving you?'

'I can be magnanimous, my darling. I have even forgiven you for deceiving me.' His laughing face was very close to hers, but as she looked up at him she saw fresh lines of strain about his eyes.

'I confess that I was very glad to see you, my lord.'

'Well, that is something, I suppose. I must be thankful for the odd kind word.'

Aurelia sensed that his chaffing had a purpose behind it. The light, teasing words were intended to calm her and to prevent her from dwelling too much on Ransome's hideous death. She was thankful for his understanding, but panic still gripped her as she looked about the clearing. Ransome was gone, and she could not feel regret, yet there was another. A man who terrifed her far more than her wastrel of a brother-in-law.

'And Clare? Where is he? I pray to heaven that he was taken, for I shall not soon forget. . .' she looked about her fearfully.

'Clare escaped in the confusion. It is better so. The prince would not wish to have it known that one so close to him was an enemy of England. But I too shall not forget.' His face was grim.

'But. . .but if he should return. . .?'

'He will be shot on sight. He knows it. Whatever else, the man is not a fool. His greatest mistake lay in recruiting Ransome. You may be easy in your mind, my love. You will not see him again.'

Aurelia could not control her shaking limbs.

'It was so horrible,' she whispered. 'That dreadful parson! I. . .I thought he must be sure to marry us.'

'What a horror you have of parsons,' the Duke teased tenderly. 'I must hope to change your mind.' His arms tightened about her. 'The man was a dupe, Aurelia. He played no part in the smuggling. He agreed to Clare's plan for gain.'

The glade was full of men, most of them in military uniform. No one had so much as glanced in her direction, but now she noticed one or two grinning faces. Belatedly she remembered the proprieties and struggled free of the Duke's embrace.

'I must go to Cassie,' she murmured.

Salterne jumped down from the phaeton and held up his arms.

'Come,' he said. 'She is inside.' He gestured towards the hovel. 'We did not wish her to see. . .'

A wave of nausea threatened to overwhelm Aurelia as she looked towards the spot where she had last seen Ransome. The only evidence of the accident was a patch of scorched brown earth, and some darker stains where the grass looked wet and sticky.

She shuddered and averted her head. For the rest of her life she would carry with her the memory of that terrifying day.

Later she could remember nothing of the drive to Brighton. Her mind was filled with images of that dreadful scene in the clearing. She could not bring herself to think of the outcome had Salterne not arrived in time. Wearied to death, she closed her eyes.

When she opened them it was to find that the phaeton had drawn to a halt before the Duke's mansion.

'No, not here,' she demurred. 'I should like to rest. We must go back. . .'

A large hand covered her own.

'No one will trouble you, my love, and Hannah is waiting upstairs.'

Aurelia was too tired to argue further. She expressed no surprise to find her maid in the bedroom which was prepared for her. She suffered herself to be tucked between the silken sheets without a word.

It was dusk when she awoke. A candle was burning

in one corner of the room, but a screen had been placed before it to shield her eyes.

For a moment she could not think where she was. Then Hannah crept over to the bed to look at her.

'Cassie? Where is Cassie?' Aurelia attempted to struggle to her feet.

'Lady Ransome is still asleep, and Miss Caro too. Now do you lie still, Miss Lia. His Grace has given orders that they are not to be disturbed.'

'His Grace does not give *me* orders,' Aurelia said with dignity.

'But, Miss Lia, he is right. You would not wish to wake them after what has happened. . . Is it not best that they should rest?'

'That may be so.' Aurelia hesitated. In her desire not to be beholden to the Duke she ran the risk of behaving foolishly, but to remain under his roof? That would never do.

'His Grace knows what is best,' Hannah said smugly.

Aurelia threw aside the coverlet, suffering a stab of pain as she was reminded of her injured wrist, now bathed and bandaged.

'I must see him,' she announced. 'We cannot stay here, and I must make arrangements. Help me with my hair, Hannah. I cannot go down to him like this. . .'

'You are not to go down at all. Your supper will be sent up here. His Grace says——'

'Hannah! The Duke has been most kind, but he does not rule me or my servants. That must be understood.'

'Then you had best tell Jacob and Matthew, ma'am. The Duke has sent them to the Steyne to fetch your clothes.'

'They are here too? Great Heavens! I must speak to him at once. . .'

'His Grace is not at home.' Hannah's face wore a look of triumph. 'He was summoned to the Prince.'

'Then I will see the Dowager Duchess,' Aurelia said coldly.

It was clear that Hannah approved whole-heartedly of the Duke's high-handed ways, and it was time that she was disabused of such notions.

'Now, Miss Lia, don't you go flying into the boughs. His Grace means all for the best.'

'Hannah! How many times must I tell you? I will not be beholden. . .I mean. . .I am grateful, of course, and I will thank him. . .but he shall not dictate to me.'

Aurelia dressed quickly, pointedly ignoring the smile on Hannah's face.

'Where is the Duchess?' she asked.

'Waiting for you in the salon, ma'am.'

'Oh, sometimes I could slap you, Hannah! Why did you not tell me?'

'His Grace——' Hannah stopped at the expression on Aurelia's face.

'I'll wear the muslin, though it is badly crushed, but the Duchess will understand. . .'

'Very good, Miss Lia. When your other gowns arrive I'll hang them up at once.'

'Oh!' Aurelia gave a cry of exasperation and left the room.

She found the Duchess lying on a day-bed in the salon. As Aurelia entered the Dowager put her book aside.

'What a time you have had, my dear!' She held out both her hands. 'I am so sorry! Rollo was like a man possessed when Hannah came to say that you had gone.'

'Hannah?'

'Why, yes. Did she not tell you? Your man brought her to us before you had been gone five minutes. Rollo was in a rare state. He could not think why you did not ask for his help.'

'We were warned that the house was being watched,' Aurelia said simply. 'Cassie wished to tell His Grace, but I. . .I thought him gone away. . .'

'And that was the only reason?'

'We parted on the worst of terms, ma'am, as you know.' Aurelia looked down at her hands.

'My dear! A lovers' quarrel was enough to persuade you to risk your life. . .and Cassie's too?'

'I must explain. We did not know that Ransome was involved. Who could imagine that he might abduct his daughter?'

'You could scarce expect whoever took her to be other than a rogue, Aurelia.'

'You need not remind me that I have been foolish beyond belief, Your Grace, but we did not know what to do. I thought that if we followed their instructions . . .and if I offered to pay for her release. . .You see, they threatened to kill her.'

'I understand. . .but I doubt if you will convince Rollo. He thought he had lost you, Lia. I hope never to see him in such case again.'

Aurelia looked at her steadily.

'Nothing has changed, my dear ma'am. Ransome is dead, but he was yet a traitor. The stigma must always be there. I cannot marry your grandson.'

'So what are your plans, Aurelia?' The old lady had

lowered her eyes, and appeared to be searching through her reticule.

'I shall go back to Marram, and take Cassie with me. I may be able to persuade her that Richard Collinge is a suitable match for Caro. . .'

'You think it likely?'

'The child has been constant in her love for him,' Aurelia said warmly. 'Not all the pleasures of Brighton, nor the beaux, have swayed her. She asks only to be his wife.'

'A laudable ambition!' The Duke's voice startled Aurelia and she blushed to the roots of her hair. He looked directly at his grandmother.

'Ma'am, may I beg your indulgence? I have much to say to Miss Carrington, and I believe you would not care to hear it.'

The Dowager's eyes snapped.

'Now, Rollo, do not get up in your high ropes, I beg of you. Miss Carrington will be no more pleased than I to be scolded and ordered about as you are used to do.'

'Indeed not, ma'am, I assure you.' The light of battle was in Aurelia's eye.

The Duke strode over to the door and opened it.

'You will grant me a word in private, if you please. Or do you stay here in the hope that my grandmother will protect you?'

The taunt was enough to bring Aurelia to her feet. With her head held high she swept past him and into the hall.

'In here.' He thrust her before him into the library and closed the door. With folded arms he leaned against it and regarded her with a steely gaze.

'You will please to give me an explanation of your folly,' he said without preamble.

Aurelia's anger rose to match his own.

'I beg your pardon, My Lord Duke,' she said crisply. 'You shall not take that tone with me.'

Even as she spoke she could understand the reason for the change in his manner towards her. The tenderness which had been so apparent when he'd first come to her rescue had given way to rage. She had known the same reaction herself when danger threatened Caro. A first surge of relief to know that the girl was safe had led at once to a need to vent her feelings in a furious outburst.

'I am under an obligation to you,' she went on more calmly. 'And I am more grateful than I can well express. I owe you my life, but I will not brook your ordering of it.'

'Indeed!' The grey eyes snapped. 'Please to go on, Miss Carrington. I'm sure that you have much more to say.'

She threw him a smouldering look.

'You have removed my staff to your home without my permission, and now you see fit to question my actions. You have ordered my maid to follow your instructions and. . .and you have even dispatched my men to fetch my. . .my. . .'

'Baggage!' he supplied helpfully.

He was not referring to her trunks, as she well knew, but she ignored the gleam of amusement in his eyes.

'Perhaps I do owe you an explanation,' she continued. 'We had no choice but to follow Caroline.'

'It did not occur to you to seek my help?'

'I believed you to be away,' she said stiffly. 'And then. . .I thought. . .'

'You could not imagine that I might refuse? Oh, Lia! How little faith you have in me!'

'It was not exactly that,' she said in some confusion. 'The message was worded in such a way that we. . .I . . .felt we must go alone.'

'I read it.' His eyes never left her face. 'Hannah brought it to me. You dropped it in your haste.'

'So that was how you knew where to find us?' Her eyes fell before his. 'Cassie wished to send for you, you must know, but I would not hear of it.'

'Headstrong and wilful as always,' he observed. 'I am to understand that you receive a message which threatens murder and you plan to handle the matter yourself?'

'I. . .You gave me a pistol.'

'And much good it did you. I have always thought you sensible, my dear, but on this occasion your sister showed more judgement.'

Aurelia sat before him like a recalcitrant schoolgirl, gazing at her hands.

'Cassie suspected that Ransome was involved,' she said wretchedly. 'I would not hear of it. I. . .I could not believe that he would threaten to murder his own daughter.'

'Did you not assure me that he was capable of anything?'

'Anything but that! I. . .I thought it must be someone who saw the chance of gain. I believed myself to be the target.'

'And so you were, but to offer yourself as the sacrificial lamb. . .!'

'What else could I do? I...you...' Aurelia was on the verge of tears.

He came to her then and took her in his arms.

'I am out of reason ill-humoured, my dearest love, but I thought that I had lost you. You cannot know the torture of that journey... We mistook the way when we left the Lewes road, but thank God we were in time.'

'We?'

'The Prince called out the militia. Clare and Ransome had been seen twice on the previous night, but they escaped the net. It was when I read the note that we were certain of their whereabouts.'

'But how did you know that the message came from Clare and Ransome?'

'It was obvious.' Salterne's expression was grim. 'It could scarce be coincidence that the bait was offered so quickly.'

'And I took it like a gudgeon!'

'A beautiful gudgeon, my love.' He kissed the nape of her neck.

'Ah! Do not...I have not changed my mind, Your Grace.'

'Then I must try to change it for you.' He kissed each eyelid tenderly, and sought to find her lips.

Aurelia averted her head.

'I cannot forgive myself,' she said in a low voice. 'You have made it all too clear that I was the victim of my own failings. I have been obstinate and over-sure that I was right.'

'A sad character indeed! But I do not despair of you. In time you may learn to mend your ways.' The grey eyes were dancing.

'It is not kind in you to mock,' she cried indignantly.

'The thought did not enter my head. Though when one is perfect, as I am myself, it is hard to understand the vagaries of others.'

A gurgle of laughter escaped Aurelia's lips, but the Duke frowned in mock-reproof.

'It is not at all flattering to think that my claim to all the virtues is greeted with such merriment.' He shook her gently. 'Let us be done with the sackcloth and ashes, Lia. It is not in your style.'

He cupped a hand beneath her chin, and as his lips found hers she was swept away into a dizzying vortex. Her head was spinning when he released her.

'Darling, maddening Lia! How I fought against my love for you. You were the threat to all our plans. Had Ransome guessed. . .'

'He accused me of—er—attempting to attach your interest.' Aurelia coloured and rested her burning cheek against his coat.

'He was cleverer than I. You were always so cool and distant in my company. . .'

'Not always, my lord.' Her blush deepened.

'That's true!' His eyes were filled with private laughter. 'I might have ruined all that night at Lady Bellingham's, when my resolution failed me. I had vowed to wait until I might approach you with propriety, but I was sorely tried. . .I longed to hold you in my arms, and when you stumbled I was lost.'

'The night conspired against us,' Aurelia said in a dreamy tone.

'Thank heavens it did! I had welcomed our growing friendship, and hoped that you were losing your contempt for me. . .'

'Never that!' she said softly. 'I found you arrogant, and I could not understand your wish to marry

Caroline, but I soon discovered that I was mistaken in my judgement of your character.'

'How well you concealed your change of heart! I suffered a number of sharp set-downs, my love, and lost much ground when you found me in conversation with Harriet Wilson.'

'I was jealous.' Aurelia hung her head. 'That was when I first discovered. . .well. . .it is no matter. I was not kind to you.'

'A masterpiece of understatement,' he said drily.

'I wished to discourage your. . .your unseemly behaviour, sir. Not only were you a shocking tease, but you appeared to lose no opportunity to—er——'

'Behave like a man in love?'

'I did not know that at the time. I found you over-familiar in your manner.'

'But you are irresistible, my enchantress. . .and a challenge to any man.'

'My lord, I wish you will not say such things. They are quite untrue.'

'Are they, my dearest?' His eyes grew serious as he cupped her face in his hands and forced her to look at him. 'I cannot think so.' He bent his head to hers as if to kiss her again.

'Papa, are you pretending to be the prince?'

Blue eyes and grey stared at Charlotte in confusion as she stood before them clutching a battered doll.

Salterne sighed.

'Which prince is that, my puss?'

'I mean the one who wakened the princess with a kiss.'

'Er. . .something like that.'

To Aurelia's amusement the Duke looked almost shy in the face of Charlotte's interested expression.

'Did it work?'

'You must ask Miss Carrington.' A slight flush darkened his tanned skin.

Aurelia gave him a reproachful look. It was unfair of him to enlist the services of the child she loved so much in an effort to overcome her scruples.

'Did it waken you, Aunt Lia?' Charlotte scrambled on to her lap. 'Grandmama said that I must be very quiet this morning because you were asleep.'

'Well, now, as you see, I am awake.'

'It works! It works!' Charlotte slid to the ground and began to dance about the room. 'Papa always said it did, though Grandmama and I did not believe him.'

Salterne grasped his daughter firmly by the shoulders.

'You will find your great-grandmama in the salon,' he announced. 'I believe she wishes to speak to you.'

'Oh, yes. Now I shall be able to tell her. . .' Charlotte assumed an expression of great importance as she ran towards the door. Then she stopped.

'And you will marry the prince, Aunt Lia, won't you?'

'Shoo! Away with you.' Salterne flapped his hands at her.

'Oh, dear, I hope that she does not. . .' Aurelia felt acutely uncomfortable.

The Duke reached out and drew her close. Her heart began to pound as she was enclosed once more in that dear and familiar embrace.

'Aurelia, you are the most chivalrous and the most generous person I know. You are also the most honest. I will ask you again. Do you love me?'

'I love you so much that I cannot agree to harm

you. We spoke once of friendship. Will not that serve?'

'Like this, you mean? And this?' He pressed his lips against the inside of her arm, and then into the hollow of her neck.

A delicious warmth began to pervade her body. Instinctively she began to stroke his dark head as she murmured inarticulate endearments. It was only when he raised his eyes and gave her a quizzical look that she answered him.

'You know I have no thought of marriage,' she protested faintly. It was a last despairing effort to withstand him.

The Duke's shoulders began to shake.

'You shock me deeply, Lia. Only consider the scandal!'

'Oh, how can you? You know that I did not mean what. . .what you are suggesting.'

'I am suggesting that you become my wife. Had you not best consider it? Your judgement is at fault again, I fear.'

'I suppose it is,' she agreed breathlessly.

A lingering kiss destroyed the last vestiges of her resistance. Dizzy with joy, she clung to him. Then he looked into her eyes.

'We are no strangers to affection, you and I. We have both loved before, but you, my darling. . .You are my last enchantment.'

And after that there was no need for words.

SERENA

by

Sylvia Andrew

Dear Reader

Love, laughter and some tears, drama, a sense of style, a flavour of the language of the period—these are what attract me in writing 'Regency Romances'. And since I am, after all, a woman of the twentieth century, I like the idea that women of that period, unlike their Victorian daughters, were allowed to display spirit and intelligence.

In writing *Serena* I was fascinated by the idea of a cold and arrogantly cynical aristocrat, who falls deeply in love for the first time in his life—with a woman he knows only as 'Serena', who provokes, intrigues, amuses and finally enchants him. He is determined to marry her. But you, dear Reader, know more than he does! You know from the first that 'Serena' is also Sasha Calvert, a 'Jezebel' my hero has sworn to destroy, one of the hated Calverts, who thirteen years before, had brought death and deep unhappiness to his family . . . What happens when he finds this out? I hope you enjoy reading about my lovely, spirited, golden-eyed heroine as much as I enjoyed writing about her.

Sylvia Andrew

Sylvia Andrew taught modern languages for years, ending up as Vice-Principal of a sixth form college. She lives in Somerset with two cats, a dog, and a husband who has a very necessary sense of humour, and a stern approach to punctuation. Sylvia has one daughter living in London, and they share a lively interest in the theatre. She describes herself as an 'unrepentant romantic'.

Other titles by the same author:

Perdita
A Darling Amazon
Eleanor
Serafina
Francesca
Rosabelle *Volume One* ⎫
Annabelle *Volume Two* ⎭ The Christmas Belles

CHAPTER ONE

THE late afternoon sunshine pierced the blinds over the veranda, dazzling in its intensity. Reluctantly Serena moved to close the slats. It was very hot, and the breath of wind coming off the sea had been welcome. She returned to her seat and waited for her visitor's reaction to her plan. 'Well, Lady P.?' she asked finally. Very few people on the island were permitted to use this mode of address for the governor's lady, but Serena, a Calvert of Anse Chatelet and one who had known Lady Pendomer for most of her life, was one of the privileged. However, Lady Pendomer, normally the most placidly optimistic of creatures, said firmly, 'You will never manage it, my dear! You can have no notion of the cost of a London Season—it was more than enough for us, I assure you, and, sad though I am to have to say this, your circumstances are not such that you could afford anything like the amount needed!'

Serena lifted her chin, and the look she gave her guest was slightly cool.

'You needn't give me one of your father's stares, either, Serena. I would be doing you a disservice if I did not speak plainly now, rather than later. The project is doomed from the start—you simply do not have the resources to carry it through properly. And unless you do the thing in style it is better not to do it at all.'

Serena said with a teasing smile, 'You are suggest-

ing that we lack the necessary style, Lady P.? I am
surprised.'

'You lack the necessary funds, my dear! If you wish
the ton to take note of you, you will need to hire a
house with an impeccable address, and have an extensive and fashionable wardrobe—shoes, fans, shawls
and all the other bits of nonsense. And then you will
need servants, a carriage and horses. It's not as if you
have any sort of base in England—you would be
arriving with everything to find! When we launched
Caroline we were at least able to stay at Rotherfield
House with Henry's cousins. You have no one. No,
no, it is quite beyond your means! Unless Lord
Calvert left some secret Eldorado which I know
nothing of?'

This time Serena's smile was bitter. 'No, there were
no pleasant surprises in my father's will. The family
fortunes are quite as you describe them. The estates
bring in just about enough to keep us and to repay a
little of the mortgage each year.'

'You are surely not contemplating raising more
money on the plantation?'

'I doubt we could.'

'Well, then. . .?'

'I have managed to put a little aside. And I have
some jewellery——'

'No, Serena! You must not! If and when you ever
agree to marry anyone, that jewellery will be your
dowry! And if you do not marry it will be your only
safeguard for the future. You must not spend it on
Lucy!'

'I wouldn't have to sell all of it, Lady P. Possibly
just the Cardoman necklace——'

'The Cardoman necklace! Sell the Cardoman necklace?'

'Why not? It's not even particularly beautiful——'

'But it's a priceless heirloom! Serena, I really think you are not yourself. It may not be beautiful to modern eyes, I grant you—it is, after all is said and done, over a hundred and fifty years old—but how many families can boast of a necklace made for one of their ancestors by a king? There are those who say that King Charles would have married Arabella Cardoman if he could. No, no, you must not let it go out of the family. Besides, you would never find a purchaser.'

'Now there I fear you are mistaken. I have one already. And as for the family...have you forgotten that Lucy and I are the last Cardoman Calverts? The name will disappear when we marry—or die. And Lucy must be given a chance to...to escape, before it is too late. The loss of the necklace is a triviality compared with that.' Serena walked over to the edge of the veranda, released one of the blinds, and gazed out over the sea. The dying sun had laid a path of golden light across the waves, which rolled lazily into the cove below that gave the estate its name. 'You seem surprised that I have never married. Tell me, if your Caroline had been forced to stay on the island, or if she had not met Lord Dalcraig during her Season in London, would you wish to see her accepting an offer from one of St Just's "eligible bachelors"?' She turned back to look at her old friend and, without waiting for a reply, she continued, 'Of course you wouldn't. You were wise enough to see that both of your children left the island while they were still young. This climate seems to bring out the worst in the men who stay here. They are either weaklings, sapped of energy, lacking in any kind of enterprise, content to let others direct them...or they become self-indulgent, vicious——' She broke off suddenly, and turned away again. After a small pause she said, 'Lucy is a lovely, high-spirited girl. I will not see her married to someone who would break that spirit, nor yet to someone whom she would eventually despise.'

'You are very harsh in your judgement of island society, Serena.'

'Have I not good cause?'

There was another, longer silence. Finally Lady Pendomer sighed and said, 'I know the importance you place on seeing your niece safely established, and I cannot deny that the possibilities here on St Just are few. But the cost of such an enterprise as a Season in London for the two of you——'

'Oh, but I should not go!'

'Not go? Why not? Who would look after Lucy?'

'Lucy would take Sheba with her to England, and my Aunt Spurston would chaperon her. I could not leave the management of Anse Chatelet in the hands of anyone else for such a length of time. The situation is precarious enough.'

'But you must go!' said Lady Pendomer, quite forgetting that she had been protesting just one moment earlier that the whole scheme was impossible. 'If there is to be a trip to England at all then you must go too, Serena! You are so concerned for Lucy's future—surely you should be thinking of your own?'

'Oh, come, Lady P.! Who would look twice at me— a middle-aged spinster, with no dowry to speak of? No, we must concentrate on happiness for my niece.'

'Serena, I could become very angry with you if I did

not know how hard you have fought to keep Anse
Chatelet in the family. You are twenty-six, not middle-
aged. You may be somewhat thin, but that is because
you do not look after yourself. You could be a very
handsome girl if you bothered to dress properly. And,
whatever fears I may have had for you when you were
a child, they have now disappeared——'

'Fears? Surely you mean disapproval, Lady P.?'

'No, Serena, I was afraid for you. Wild, hot-headed,
lacking any kind of discipline or self-control—faults I
lay completely at your father's door, I may tell you.'
Serena's chin lifted again and she stiffened. But Lady
Pendomer swept on, 'And you were both so completely dazzled by Richard... Everyone was, if it
comes to that. But even after the rest of us knew your
brother for what he was, you and your father still
idolised him. Your hero-worship I could understand—
both your brothers were so much older than you—but
your father...he should have known better——'

'He was cruelly punished for his blindness. We all
were.'

'Yes, Serena.' Lady Pendomer bit her lip. 'Forgive
me. I did not mean to remind you of the past.' She
returned to her former theme. 'I should not be at all
surprised if you were to find a match for yourself as
well as for Lucy in London! You rate yourself far too
low.'

'You are mistaken! It is rather that I rate myself
too high!' Serena smiled at Lady Pendomer's exclamation of disbelief. 'Let me explain. My brothers
almost ruined Anse Chatelet before they died, and
you know as well as anyone how we have fought to
save it ever since—I am still fighting. I never had the
sort of girlhood I have tried to give Lucy——'

'You could have had one with your great-aunt in England, Serena. She invited you to live with her long ago.'

'I know, and I was grateful to her. But you must know how impossible it was. There was Lucy. . .and as my father grew older he depended on me to run the estate—there was no one else. And indeed, I think I have done as well as any man—better by far than my brothers would have done. I assure you, I wouldn't marry and give up control of Anse Chatelet, not after all these years, unless I found a husband I could trust to manage it better than I can myself. And if such a paragon existed—I say if—he would surely find a better match than a spinster of uncertain age with a run-down estate in the West Indies!'

'Yet you say you rate yourself too highly?'

'Yes. I rate myself too highly to accept less. In any case, what man could tolerate less than total control of his wife's estates? Would I respect him if he did?' She smiled at Lady Pendomer. 'No, I am doomed to die an old maid. And now let us talk of something else. Lucy may come in at any moment.'

But Lady Pendomer was not to be deflected. She said obstinately, 'Whatever rubbish you talk, Serena, I will tell you that I still consider you eminently suitable to be a dutiful and loving wife to any man fortunate enough to win you.'

'You make me sound such a dull creature!'

'Nonsense, my dear! In fact, I think you might well make a very good match. And I might just be persuaded to help in this ridiculous scheme of yours if you were to accompany Lucy to London. Surely Will Norret could run Anse Chatelet for one year? Pendomer will keep an eye on him. And there are

other ways in which I could be of some assistance—
your wardrobes, for example. I fancy Maria might be
of some use...' Serena's eyes lit up at this. Lady
Pendomer's maid had at one time worked for
Madame Rosa, the noted London *modiste*. If she
would make some dresses for Lucy there would be a
great saving. But Lady Pendomer was continuing,
'And, most important of all, I shall be very surprised
if you can persuade Lucy to go without you. Think it
over, Serena. Your mad scheme will very likely fail in
any case. But if you force Lucy to go alone——'

'Sheba would be with her!'

'A slave!'

'Sheba is a freedwoman, Lady P. We have no slaves
on Anse Chatelet.'

'That might be so, Serena, but, slave or not, Sheba
is as ignorant of England as Lucy herself. A former
nurse is not quite the company Lucy needs! If, as I
said, you force her to go without you, then you are
being quite unnecessarily cruel to the child. And I will
not help you in that.'

After Lady Pendomer's departure Serena was left in
a most unusual state of indecision. For years she had
practically run the estate, for her father, the nominal
head of the family, had been a sick old man, and there
had been no one else to shoulder the burden and
make the decisions which affected all their lives. Now
her father too had died, and Anse Chatelet was hers—
hers, that was, except for the massive mortgage which
had been raised years before to pay off the family's
creditors. She lived in constant fear that she might one
day, through mismanagement or some oversight, fail
to pay the instalments as they fell due. The agent in

Barbados had left her in no doubt that the creditor
for whom he was acting would foreclose. It would be
folly to risk such a disaster by leaving Anse Chatelet
to the care of someone else, even for one year.

On the other hand... Lucy was growing up fast.
She was now well past her seventeenth birthday, and
if she was to be prepared for presentation to London
society then a voyage to England could not be long
delayed. And go to London she must! It was unthink-
able that her beloved niece's beauty and vivacity
should be wasted here on St Just. If Caroline
Pendomer, who was a girl of very moderate charms,
could capture a gentleman of such breeding and fortune as Lord Dalcraig in her first London Season, then
Lucy's success would be certain, and her future secure.
And at least one of Serena's private worries would be
set at rest.

At this point Lucy came running on to the veranda.
'Sasha, Joshua and the others are having a crab race
on the beach—do come and watch it!' She grabbed
Serena by the hand and attempted to pull her back
through the house.

'Wait, Lucy! I have something important to discuss
with you. And how many times——'

'Must I tell you to call me Aunt Serena?' finished
Lucy in chorus with her aunt, adopting a disapproving
frown. 'Lady Pendomer has been here.'

'If you know that, why weren't you here to speak to
her?'

'I didn't know—I just guessed it from your
expression—you've got your Aunt Serena face on.
And you're not often stuffy, Sasha. Do come down—
Joshua won't wait much longer!'

'Lucy, my love, you're no longer a child.' Serena

hesitated, then went on, 'You know I've always tried to do what is best for you. . .'

'Goodness, Sasha, what a Friday face! What has Lady P. been saying?'

'Nothing that need concern you. But I think it's time we talked about your future. I have been thinking of a Season in London for you.'

Lucy's eyes grew large, and she sat down rather suddenly on the stool by Serena. 'We can't possibly afford it!'

'Yes we can, with a little planning and management. I shall sell the Cardoman necklace.'

'But, Sasha, that's a Calvert heirloom!'

Serena said innocently, 'Oh, forgive me, Lucy, I thought you didn't like the necklace? But, of course, if you wish to keep it, then there's no more to be said. . .'

'I think it is hideous! But it's been in the family for such a long time, Sasha——'

'Too long! Your grandfather was considering whether to sell it when he died. It would fetch a pretty little sum—enough to pay most of our expenses, at least. What better use can there be for it?'

'It's yours, Sasha. You mustn't sell it for my benefit.'

'Why not, pray? Let us talk no more about it. We are the last of the Calverts, Lucy, and if you do not wish me to keep the necklace in trust for you, then it will be sold—in an excellent cause.' Serena smiled lovingly as her niece's anxious scruples gave way to excitement and she threw her arms round her aunt.

'Oh, thank you, thank you! I hadn't thought. . . I never imagined I would ever see England! Oh, Sasha! It would be beyond anything! I've always dreamed of London, but I never thought I should go there! And

to make my come out... I can't believe it! London!
Oh, how soon are we going?'

'Wait a moment! I'm not sure that I can come with
you.' Serena put her hand over her niece's mouth.
'No, listen to me, Lucy. Our resources are not great
even if we sell the necklace, and it is important that
they are wisely spent. You will need clothes, lessons
in deportment, a suitable background, and lots more
besides. If I came I should also need clothes and the
rest. It's not as if you would be alone in England.
Sheba will go with you, and I am sure Aunt Spurston
could sponsor you in society better than I could. And
you know the estate needs my attention here.'

'*I* need your attention, Sasha. How could I manage
without you? Can't you forget Anse Chatelet, just for
once?'

'Anse Chatelet is our only real asset, Lucy. It is a
far greater part of the family heritage than the
Cardoman necklace. I dare not forget it.' Serena
watched as the bright hope on Lucy's face faded.

'Of course. It was stupid of me. But if we cannot go
to England together, then I do not wish to go.' Lucy
walked out on to the veranda and Serena's heart sank.
This was worse than she had bargained for. She
started to follow her niece but then changed her mind.
She would avoid further confrontation for the
moment. Lucy was impulsive, but essentially reasonable, and when she had had time to consider the
advantages of a Season in London she would probably
agree to the plan.

In the weeks that followed Serena was able to judge
how wrong she had been. Lucy remained adamant in
her refusal to go to London without her. Reason,
persuasion, threats—all failed. Lucy merely said that

she could enjoy nothing without the company of her aunt, and that they could perfectly well be two old maids together on St Just. When Serena turned to Lady Pendomer for support, her old friend merely replied, 'I have never been one for saying "I told you so", Serena, but did I not warn you that this would happen? And much as I disapprove of Lucy's refusal to obey you, I do in fact agree with the girl. I'm afraid you must reconsider your position. Either you both go to England—and I have already expressed my doubts on that head—or Lucy must make do with St Just!'

So Serena was already weakening when a letter arrived from England which took the decision out of her hands. Aunt Spurston offered to accommodate them in Surrey, and to help in preparing Lucy for presentation to society. However, for Aunt Spurston herself, a London season was out of the question, her doctor would not hear of it. Serena, as Lucy's guardian, must accompany her niece.

Serena was resigned, Lucy was overjoyed, and Lady Pendomer exerted herself on their behalf. She wrote to her friends in London, she spoke to her husband to engage his help in overseeing Will Norret's work on the plantations, and, best of all, she commissioned her maid to make some dresses for them. The necklace was sold and preparations were soon under way for a voyage to England.

Lucy's début was of enormous importance to herself and her aunt, but they would both have been very surprised to hear that four thousand miles away someone else was looking forward to their departure from Anse Chatelet and their arrival in London with an eagerness that almost equalled their own...

CHAPTER TWO

To THE discerning eye the gentleman striding through Grosvenor Square in the direction of Upper Brook Street was unmistakably wealthy. His buckskin pantaloons and dark blue superfine coat were plain, but superbly cut, and his starched muslin cravat was secured with a very fine diamond pin. His cane was discreetly mounted in gold, and his boots were of the finest quality and polished to gleaming perfection. His dark hair was fashionably dishevelled under his beaver hat. This was no fop, however. There was a suggestion of power in the broad shoulders and lithe figure, and he had an air of one accustomed to command. Many would have called him handsome, but there was an indifference, a coldness even, in his ice-blue eyes, and a hardness about the well-shaped mouth which was not prepossessing.

The gentleman turned in to one of the houses at the nearer end of the street, where he was met by Wharton, his butler, and two footmen.

'Bring a bottle of Madeira to the library, Wharton. I am expecting Mr Bradpole,' was all the master of the house said as one of the footmen reverently received hat and cane.

'Yes, my lord. Your lordship may wish to read this before Mr Bradpole arrives.'

Lord Wintersett, for that was the gentleman's name, took the card which the butler offered him and looked at it impassively. 'When did Mr Fothergill call, Wharton?'

'Shortly after your lordship went out.'

'If he calls again, tell him I'm not at home.'

As Lord Wintersett closed the library door behind him and Wharton disappeared to the wine-cellar, the two footmen retreated to the rear hall. Here they lost their professional stiffness and became more human. 'Cold fish ain't 'e?' said the younger one. 'Wonder if old Fothergill will call 'im out?'

'Not if he wants to live, he won't. And you mind your tongue, Percy. If Wharton hears you, you won't last long in his lordship's service, even though you are my own sister's boy.'

'I'm not sure I'd mind. A proper frosty-face 'is lordship is, no mistake. I don't know what all those gentry females see in 'im.'

'His wealth, that's what they see. And as for you— let me tell you, Percy, you don't know a good place when you see one, you don't. His lordship may be a touch cold in his manner, but he's fair. You could do a lot worse, a lot worse. Anyway, what makes you say that Fothergill would want to call his lordship out?'

'I thought you'd know. They're saying 'e seduced old Fothergill's daughter.' Percy looked in astonishment as William burst into chuckles.

'Not another one!'

'What do you mean?'

'I'll bet you a tanner it's a try-on. The Fothergills aren't the first aristocratic coves who've had an eye on the Wintersett gelt and attempted a bit o' genteel blackmail. But they'll be like all the rest. They won't get far with him.'

'You mean——'

'I mean it's time we cut the gabble-mongering and did our jobs. Off you go, young Percy, I can hear a carriage. That'll be Bradpole.'

'Oo's that?'

'The lawyer, you nocky!' Once through the door to the entrance hall they resumed their air of stately indifference and went to stand by the door to the street.

After Mr Bradpole had been received with dignity he joined Lord Wintersett in the library. First they spent some time clearing up odd bits of family business, and then the lawyer was offered a glass of Madeira and a seat in a more comfortable chair by the fire. These he accepted with pleasure, saying as he sat down, 'I have something further of interest to your lordship.'

'What is that?'

'News from our agent in the West Indies.' Lord Wintersett frowned.

'And?'

'Lord Calvert is dead. He died at the end of May.'

There was a pause during which Lord Wintersett got up and poured some more Madeira. Finally he said, 'I'll drink to that. Damn him!'

'My lord!'

'Oh, we're all damned, Bradpole, but he, I fancy, more than most. Who inherits?'

'His daughter.'

'Sasha Calvert. Or has she married?'

'Not yet.'

'She's unlikely to do so in the future. Whatever her attractions were in the past, they must have faded by now—the tropics are notoriously hard on women, and she must be nearly forty. Over thirty, anyway. And

her fortune is small enough. I'll drink to her dam-
nation, too.'

'My lord, I must protest. You do not even know the
lady.'

'But I know of her, Bradpole. Oh, I know of her.'

'Lord Wintersett,' said the lawyer gravely, 'have
you never considered that Mrs Stannard, your sister-
in-law, might have been influenced by her own very
natural feelings in presenting the circumstances of
your brother Anthony's unfortunate death. It all happened so long ago—some thirteen years, I believe.
Would it not be better to. . .to forget the past? After
all, Lord Calvert and his sons are now all dead.'

'But Sasha Calvert is still alive, Bradpole—and has
inherited everything, you say?'

'There's also a granddaughter, Rodney Calvert's
child—but she has no share in the estate, merely a
small sum of money. I understand that Miss Calvert is
her guardian.'

Lord Wintersett said swiftly, 'I have no quarrel with
the granddaughter.' He sat down on the other side of
the fireplace. 'So. . . Sasha Calvert is now mistress of
Anse Chatelet—but for how long? Now that the
father is dead, surely the estate cannot survive?'

'I understand from our agent in Barbados that Miss
Calvert has been running the estate herself for some
years now. Indeed, he is full of admiration for her
courage and spirit—in the past year or two Anse
Chatelet has made some recovery——'

'A lady of many talents, it seems. But I don't
believe she can keep it up forever. And the estate will
survive only as long as the mortgages are paid,
Bradpole—paid on the day they fall due and not
a second later. Do you understand me?' Lord

Wintersett's lip curled. 'There is to be no extension of time, no soft-hearted response to appeals from a lady in distress.'

Mr Bradpole looked at his client in silence. Finally he said, 'Am I to understand that you wish to deprive Miss Calvert of Anse Chatelet if you can?'

'I not only wish to—I shall, Bradpole, I shall. One of these days she will make a mistake—and then I shall have her.'

'Before that time comes you will have thought better, I hope,' said Mr Bradpole soberly. 'I very much doubt that your lordship could take pleasure in such a victory.'

'Pleasure! No, there isn't much pleasure in the whole damn business. When the Calverts drove Tony to his death they ruined the lives of half of my family—you know that as well as I do myself.'

'And in return your lordship has done his best to ruin the Anse Chatelet estate ever since. Yes, I know the story.' The lawyer chose his words carefully when he next spoke. 'Lord Wintersett, do you think what you are doing will improve the state of your mother's mind? Or make Mrs Stannard happier? Or give your nephew the use of his legs?'

Lord Wintersett's voice was glacial as he replied, 'Bradpole, your family has served the Wintersetts for many years. You are one of the few people in this world in whom I have confidence. But I will not tolerate further doubts on this matter. Do I make myself plain? I intend to deprive Sasha Calvert of her home and her happiness.'

Mr Bradpole started to put his papers together in silence.

'God's teeth, Bradpole, why do you feel the need to

defend the woman? She's a harlot, a Jezebel. My poor
brother was so ashamed of falling victim to her that
he——' Lord Wintersett swore and turned to the window. His back to the room, he said, 'On the whole I
do not admire my fellow creatures, and with few
exceptions remain indifferent to them. But Tony was
. . .unique. A gentle scholar who loved the world—
when he noticed it, that is. I would have sworn that
his honour and integrity were beyond question. That's
why he shot himself, of course,—having betrayed his
marriage, and with such a woman, he could no longer
bear to live.'

Mr Bradpole started to say something, then stopped
as Lord Wintersett swung round.

'I wish to be kept informed of every circumstance
on St Just, do you hear?'

'Of course, Lord Wintersett. I will see to it. Er. . .
there is something else, in fact. I understand that Miss
Calvert is thinking of bringing her niece to London—
to present her during the next Season.'

'Sasha Calvert in London, eh?' A most unpleasant
smile on his lips, Lord Wintersett added, 'Good! Not
only will Anse Chatelet be left in less watchful hands,
but Miss Calvert will be within my reach at last—and
on my ground. Excellent! Let me know as soon as you
hear of her arrival in London.'

Mr Bradpole's face was impassive as he left the
room, but once outside the house his expression
revealed his worry. He had long known Lord
Wintersett's feelings on the subject of his brother's
death, and, convinced as the lawyer was that the true
facts had yet to be established, he had frequently
attempted to argue his client into a more temperate
frame of mind. In everything else Lord Wintersett was

scrupulously fair, capable of objective judgement—
almost inhumanly so. But in this one matter he
was unapproachable. Mr Bradpole returned to his
chambers filled with foreboding.

It was unfortunate that Mr Bradpole's departure
coincided with Mr Fothergill's return, for that gentleman took advantage of this to force his way into Lord
Wintersett's presence. William and Percy would have
removed him, but with a resigned wave of the hand
Lord Wintersett took him into the library and shut the
door.

'I've come to demand satisfaction, Wintersett.'

'Pistols or swords, my dear fellow?'

Mr Fothergill stammered, 'No, no you misunderstand, by gad. I mean that I...we—my wife and
I—expect you to make an offer for our little
Amabel—after the situation you placed her in last
night, that is. She was very upset.'

'You surprise me, Fothergill,' murmured Lord
Wintersett. 'I quite thought that it was the lady who
had placed herself in the "situation", as you call it.'

Mr Fothergill shifted uncomfortably under Lord
Wintersett's cynical gaze, but the memory of his wife's
words as he had set out, and even more the consciousness of what she would say if he returned without
result, spurred him on. 'Amabel wouldn't compromise
herself—for that is what being found in a private room
with a man of your reputation must mean—without
encouragement! My daughter knows what's expected
of her!'

'Now there I am in complete agreement with you,
Fothergill,' said Lord Wintersett with a sardonic smile.
'She does indeed—a very able pupil. Who coached
her? Your wife?'

'What do you mean by that?'

'I mean that I am far from being the flat you think me. If I were green enough to be taken in by the kind of trick employed by your wife and daughter last night, I would have been married long since. Do you think they are the first to have tried? Believe me, the ladies find me almost irresistible.'

'You take pride in that, do you?'

'None at all. I find it excessively tedious—what tempts them is my wealth, not my person. I assure you, Fothergill, whatever your wife may have said, your daughter's good name has not been damaged by me—I have learned to be far too wary a bird. At worst she might be accused of a slight indiscretion—which will be forgiven because of her youth and high spirits. But her chances of making a respectable match will be much reduced if society hears how you have pursued me this morning. Bad losers are never admired.'

'But the private room! My wife said. . .and your reputation——'

'——is not for seducing young and innocent girls. You may be assured of that. Your daughter followed me into Lady Glastonbury's winter garden—which can hardly be described as a "private room"—without my knowledge, let alone my encouragement. I think she realises that now. Go back to your wife—tell her that I am neither worthy nor desirous of Miss Amabel's attentions. She is a pretty enough girl, and should look elsewhere.'

'But——'

'My man will see you out. No, really, I have had enough. And Fothergill——' He waited till Fothergill turned. 'I am indifferent to what society thinks of me.

But I should warn you that you will only make your-self even more ridiculous if you persist in these accusations.'

After Fothergill had left Lord Wintersett found him-self unable to settle. He was conscious of nothing so much as an overwhelming sense of boredom. The scene that had just been enacted was not the first such. London was full of pretty, empty-headed little dolls, whose chief, if not only, ambition was to marry a wealthy man. The thought of marriage to such a one appalled him. Yet he ought to find a wife before long. He could not in all conscience let the title and all the responsibilities of the estates fall to young Tony—delicate since his birth and now confined to a wheel-chair. He frowned as he thought of his nephew. Perhaps he should take more of an interest in him. The boy was intelligent, but hopelessly spoiled. Alanna was far too indulgent. . .

His gloomy thoughts were interrupted by another unexpected, but far more welcome, visitor. A warm smile transformed Lord Wintersett's face as Lord Ambourne came into the room.

'Ned! What are you doing in town? Is Lady Ambourne with you, or can you dine with me tonight? I need you, dear fellow, how I need you! I was rapidly falling into a melancholy.'

'I can and shall dine with you. Perdita is down at Ambourne, supervising the packing. We are off to France in three days.'

'Well, then, where shall we go? Or would you prefer to dine here? Albert has a way with a capon which I think you would find acceptable. And I have a very fine white burgundy. . .'

After it had been decided that Lord Ambourne should dine in Upper Brook Street, and orders to that effect had been sent to the kitchen, the two men settled down with a bottle of wine in the most comfortable chairs by the fire.

'What's wrong, James? Or can I guess? Fothergill?'

'You heard? No, that's nothing. I'm used to it.'

'From what I hear, you were not very kind to the young lady.'

'I should think not, indeed. If I were, she'd have cast herself on my bosom and matters would have been much worse. The chit will recover.' His tone was indifferent.

Lord Ambourne's face was troubled. He hesitated, then took the bull by the horns. 'Probably. However, there have been others who have not found it easy to recover from the public set-downs you have given them. I dare swear they have deserved them. But do you have to be quite so brutal, James? Perdita and I do not enjoy hearing what society says of you.'

'I am indifferent to what society says of me. You should try not to care, too.' James glanced at Edward's set face. 'I mind what you and your family think of me, Ned. Am I such a monster?'

Edward sighed in exasperation. 'You've always been the same! The best friend a chap could have, but the coldest fellow in creation towards anyone else. Why don't you find a wife?'

James smiled derisively. 'You think that would cause me to love my fellow creatures more, Ned?'

'Perhaps not. But at least these poor girls would stay away from you. Though I'd feel sorry for your wife. Unless...'

'Unless what?'

'Unless you found someone like Perdita.'

James laughed, a warm, human sound. 'Impossible! Perdita must be unique. If you can find me her double I'll marry her on the spot. Now, you've done your duty, let's change the subject. Tell me what you've been doing.'

Later that night, after Lord Ambourne had returned, with a certain deliberation of movement, to Rotherfield House, James thought over what his friend had said. Ned was right, he ought to get married. He promised himself that after he had settled the affair with the Calverts once and for all he would seek out some amenable débutante, the least stupid he could find, and beget some heirs. Meanwhile he would wait patiently for Sasha Calvert to walk into his parlour...

CHAPTER THREE

SERENA kept her expression of polite attention firmly in place as she wondered for the third time in as many minutes how much longer the visitors would stay. They were sitting in her great-aunt's drawing-room, a somewhat dismal apartment made gloomier by the heavy grey skies outside. She and Lucy had been staying with Lady Spurston ever since their arrival in England two weeks before, and it seemed to Serena that she had not seen the sun in all that time. In spite of the large fire the drawing-room was chilly, though Mrs Galveston and her daughter seemed not to notice. For the moment Serena was free to follow her own thoughts, for Mrs Galveston, an imposing dowager in plum silk and an amazing hat, had finished with her, and was now quizzing Lucy. Miss Eliza Galveston was timidly displaying her velvet reticule to Lady Spurston, her fingers twisting the strings nervously as she explained how she had painted it. Mrs Galveston was one of her great-aunt's closest friends, and a member of one of the first families in the county. Aunt Spurston had said it was important to please her for a number of reasons, the chief one being that she had an elder daughter, Maria, married to a peer of the realm, whose own daughter was about to make her début. . .

Though Serena herself had been amused rather than intimidated by the dowager's trenchant remarks, she was anxious about Lucy. But her niece had so far done well, answering Mrs Galveston's questions with charming deference and remembering not to put herself forward. This was not easy, for some of Mrs Galveston's remarks would have been considered impertinent even among 'colonials'. The constant guard on tongue and behaviour which her great-aunt deemed essential for Lucy and Serena were not apparently necessary for this dreadful old woman. The corners of Serena's mouth lifted in a hint of a smile as she listened. Lucy was not giving anything away, for all her pretty ways.

'Serena?' Lady Spurston's voice was reproachful. 'Miss Galveston was asking about the flora of Jamaica.'

'I must tell you, Miss Calvert, that I positively dote on Nature. I have quite a collection of pressed flowers at home, have I not, Mama? Perhaps you would like to see them?'

Before Serena could reply Mrs Galveston cut in tartly, 'Do not encourage her, Miss Calvert. She spends far too much time as it is with her collections. But there, what else is there for the poor fool to do— unless it's daubing paint on velvet!' She turned to Lady Spurston and pronounced her verdict. 'Miss Lucy has a pretty way with her, and once she acquires more polish might well take. But it won't do for Miss Calvert to be her niece's sole chaperon.'

'Why not?' asked Serena in astonishment. 'I'm Lucy's guardian.'

Mrs Galveston eyed her with scorn. 'Whatever they might do in the colonies, Miss Calvert, it is still necessary here for a chaperon to be married! You are not married, I take it?'

'No, but I have surely reached the age of discretion.'

'No spinster, of any age, not even Eliza here—and she is well into the age of discretion, one might say almost beyond it!—can be a young girl's sole chaperon—not in the kind of circles I imagine you wish to move in. It is unfortunate that your great-aunt's indisposition makes it impossible for her to be with you in London, but without a chaperon to assist you you may as well abandon the whole scheme.'

Serena looked at her in some consternation. Was her beautiful plan for Lucy's future to fail after all? Mrs Galveston looked speculatively at Lucy, and then back at Serena.

'Perhaps Miss Lucy should meet my granddaughter and her mother, Lady Warnham. Maria's as much a fool as Eliza—I am singularly unfortunate in my daughters—but at least she married well. Isabella is the same age as your niece, and is making her come out at the same time. We might be able to arrange something. . . I will see.' She looked with disapproval at Serena's sober dress. 'It would not be impossible to find you a husband, too, Miss Calvert. . . Some respectable widower, perhaps. But you are sadly brown—I'll send some Gowland's lotion round. You won't find it here in the depths of Surrey, but I have a supply from London. Applied nightly it might repair some of the damage done by the tropical sun.' She cast another speaking glance at Serena's dress, but decided to say no more and got up to go. She took her leave of Serena and Lucy, then kissed Lady Spurston's cheek. At the door she stopped and said, 'See that Miss Calvert takes some of Dr Massinger's beef extract, Dorothy. She's far too thin. Come, Eliza!' She sailed out with supreme assurance.

After Mrs Galveston had gone Lucy said passionately, 'I would rather die than spend another second in that woman's company! Do not, I beg of you, Sasha, have any more to do with her!'

'That will do, miss!' said Lady Spurston sharply. 'It is kind of Mrs Galveston to take such an interest in you. She is extremely well connected, and you might consider yourself fortunate indeed if she decided to help with your début. You must curb that unruly tongue of yours, Lucy. Pert young ladies are not admired.'

'My dear aunt,' Serena said swiftly before Lucy could reply, 'After this afternoon I am sure you must agree that we may have every confidence in Lucy's ability to behave well, whatever the provocation.'

'Provocation? What provocation, pray?'

'Surely Mrs Galveston's questions passed the bounds of discretion?'

'Serena, you do yourself no credit in taking exception to Mrs Galveston's very natural interest. She must satisfy herself that you are both worthy, before assisting a young girl from the colonies with little dowry and only a maiden aunt to protect her.'

'We are nevertheless Calverts of Anse Chatelet, Aunt Spurston,' said Serena, always sensitive about her family's name. 'I should have thought our credentials were sound enough for anyone, however well-connected they may be.'

'Besides, Mrs Galveston is so unkind!' Lucy cried. 'Sasha doesn't need her Gowland lotion and. . .and. . . beef extract!'

'How many times must I tell you to call your Aunt Serena by her proper name, Lucy? Mrs Galveston may be somewhat blunt in her pronouncements, but she knows the world as you do not!' She looked at

Lucy's downcast expression and said more gently, 'I am sure you are fond of your aunt and would not wish her to have wasted her efforts in bringing you to England. So you must exert yourself to conform—I cannot tell you how important it is. And now I would like to have a word in private with your aunt.'

Lucy glanced at Serena, saw her nod, and reluctantly went out. Serena waited calmly for her aunt to speak. Finally Lady Spurston began, 'Why are you here in England, Serena?'

'You know why. I want Lucy to meet the kind of man I would wish her to marry.'

'Have you any matrimonial ambitions for yourself?'

'Oh, no. Mrs Galveston may confine her good offices to Lucy. They would in any case be futile—I cannot imagine who would be interested in me. I have too small a dowry to attract a man in search of a rich match, I have neither youth nor looks to attract a romantic, and I'm afraid I lack the docility required by a man simply looking for a wife to run his household. No, my ambition is purely to see Lucy settled, after which I shall return to Anse Chatelet.'

'And die an old maid. Not a very attractive prospect.'

'I fear that is the only prospect left for me.'

Lady Spurston considered this for a moment. Then she said briskly, 'I am not yet convinced of that, Serena, but at the moment I wish to discuss your niece's future, not your own. Lucy is very pretty, and her liveliness will do her no harm in the eyes of the young men. She will take, no doubt of that. But the world in general will judge her as much by your demeanour as her own—you are her guardian, after all. If you wish her to move in the very best circles,

you must pay more attention to your own dress and
behaviour. That slave you brought with you from St
Just – Bathsheba——'

'Sheba is a freedwoman, Aunt Spurston. She could
have stayed behind on St Just, but came with us
because she can't believe we could manage without
her,' Serena said, smiling.

'Well, whatever she is, she seems to manage to
dress Lucy well enough. Why does she not do the
same for you?'

'I suppose I don't ask her to!'

'Exactly so! At the moment you are careless, dowdy
even, and there is altogether a want of ladylike formality about you. These colonial manners will not
pass in London. Try for a little elegance. Learn what
is acceptable behaviour for a lady. Lucy looks to you
for her example, and never forget that you are on trial
as much as she.'

Serena coloured, but forced herself to remain silent.
Her aunt was probably right. If she only knew how
hard it was, how Serena longed for the sunshine and
freedom of her life on St Just! The weeks she had so
far spent here in this damp, cold climate, hemmed in
on every side by strictures on 'acceptable behaviour
for a lady', had seemed like a year—a century. The
trouble was that for too long she had been her own
mistress. For years she had ranged the plantation in
complete freedom, exercising the authority her father
had given her. If truth were told she knew that the
English inhabitants of St Just were not so very different from their London cousins. Her independent ways
had more than once shocked them, though the Calvert
name kept them silent. But at least there she answered

to no one. Here she felt stifled—'cabin'd, cribb'd, confin'd'.

'You are silent, Serena. I hope you are not indulging in a fit of the sulks.'

'No, no, Aunt Spurston. Forgive me, I was... I was thinking. You are quite right of course. I will try to mend my ways.'

Serena did her honest best in the weeks that followed to meet her aunt's exacting standards. Whereas before she had always hurried Sheba along when dressing, now she was patient with her maid's attempts to dress her properly. Together with Lucy, Serena stood docilely while they were fitted for morning dresses, walking dresses, carriage dresses, ball dresses; they learned to walk elegantly, sit elegantly, eat elegantly, converse elegantly; they practised the quadrille and the waltz, though Serena had no intention of dancing in London. They learned the subtle differences of curtsying, bowing the head and offering a hand, how to encourage welcome approaches and how to depress pretension. Lady Warnham proved to be as amiable as Lady Spurston had said, and Lucy struck up a most unexpected friendship with her daughter Isabella. In fact, Lucy seemed to be enjoying every minute, but to Serena the endless trivialities to be learned by a lady who aspired to Society's approval were stifling. She wanted to be alone, to feel free, to rid herself of her resentment in a burst of energy. At home on St Just she would have taken off on her horse for the day, but here that was impossible. A tame stroll round the dank gardens, a gentle trot with a groom round the park, were the only available forms of exercise. The very notion of a lady walking or riding out unaccompanied was unheard of.

But just when she was at her most desperate, salvation appeared—a course of action that was highly risky, unquestionably not 'acceptable behaviour for a lady', but all the same a perfect answer. It came in the unlikely form of Mrs Galveston, who one day brought with her a bundle of clothes which her grandchildren had outgrown.

'They're for your wretched charity, Dorothy. The Society for the Relief of Indigent Gentlefolk, or whatever you call it. Improvident, more like. However, Isabella hardly has room as it is for her clothes, and now Maria has ordered more for the chit. It's all quite unnecessary, as far as I can see. One or two pretty evening gowns and a presentation dress are all Isabella requires, but there, Maria was never noted for her common sense. Some of Michael's things are in the bundle as well. They're quite old, but too good to give to the villagers—they would not appreciate them. No, do not thank me. I am glad to find a use for them.' She turned to Serena. 'By the way, Miss Calvert, it is rumoured that the Cardoman necklace has been sold. Surely that was part of the Calvert heritage?'

Serena was ready with her answer. 'My father always disliked the necklace, Mrs Galveston. It is notoriously unlucky. But I wonder where it has been since he decided to get rid of it? I thought it had been sold in the West Indies, I must confess. Can you tell me more?'

Much to Serena's relief, Mrs Galveston was unable to enlighten her, for apparently the purchaser had remained as mysterious in England as he had in the

West Indies. As for the clothes, they were taken to a closet in one of the unused bedchambers where such items were housed until they were bundled up and sent away. But Serena sought them out, for an audacious idea had formed in her mind as soon as she had seen the boy's garments. She tried them on behind locked doors—breeches, frilled shirts with one or two cravats, a waistcoat, and a warm jacket. A large forage cap in a military style successfully hid her hair, and there were even some boots which almost fitted. She secreted her treasure trove in the West Lodge—a cottage which had fallen into disuse since the drive to the western side of the park had been permanently closed after Sir George Spurston's death.

When her aunt and Lucy next went visiting Serena pleaded a headache. She waited till Sheba had stopped fussing and had gone to the kitchens, then slipped out to the stables. They were deserted, except for the stable lad and Trask, the elderly hunter. Saddling him presented no problems, and she was soon in the cottage, feverishly changing. She had left her petticoats in her bedroom, and it was simple to replace her dress and light slippers with shirt, cravat, breeches, jacket and boots. One other thing she had brought from her bedchamber—something which she had kept hidden away in a special pocket in her valise, for her aunt, if she had known of its existence, would have most strongly disapproved. This was a small pistol. On St Just she had carried it whenever she went any distance away from the house, for the danger of poisonous snakes or renegade slaves was very real. Now she slipped it into a pocket in her jacket which could have been made for it. She had no idea what dangers she might meet in England—but it was better to be sure.

Once Serena's hair was bundled into the cap she made a very fine boy, helped, no doubt, by the lack of curves and the brown complexion so displeasing to Mrs Galveston. She would be safe from detection in any casual encounter, she was sure. And she did not intend to meet anyone at all!

Half an hour later she was enjoying the wide views and invigorating air of the North Downs. The ground was too hard and Trask too elderly for her to let fly as she would have wished, but the sense of freedom was intoxicating. After a good run she paused on the highest point for miles round. Far away to the north she could see the smoky haze of the city, but up here...up here the air was clean and the hills empty of any visible dwelling. For the first time since leaving St Just she felt happy. It was a far cry from the tropics, but it was beautiful. Away to the south the slanting winter sun exaggerated the folds and furrows of the land, and the fields below formed a patchwork of black and brown, russet and green. Something tugged at her mind, a line of poetry she had recently read and not fully appreciated till now. It was about hedgerows... '"Once again I see these hedgerows——" she murmured slowly. '"Scarcely hedgerows——" She frowned and tried again. 'No, that's not right. "Hardly hedgerows... hardly hedgerows. . ." but what comes next?'

'"Hardly hedgerows—little lines of sportive wood run wild,"' said a voice behind her. 'And who the devil are you?'

Serena nearly jumped out of her skin, and Trask took exception to the sudden tug on the rein and took

off. After the initial surprise Serena knew she would
have no difficulty in bringing her horse under control—she had dealt with horses of greater mettle than
this. But she allowed him his head for a while—she
had no desire for closer contact with the stranger, and
she just might escape. It was annoying therefore to
hear drumming hoofbeats behind her and to see a
lean hand stretch out to take hold of the reins and
bring Trask firmly to a halt.

'Let go! I don't need your help!' she said furiously.

'I think you do, you ungrateful whelp!' said the
stranger looking at her in lazy amusement. 'And
unless you express yourself more gracefully I'll take it
upon myself to teach you some manners.' His voice
was still amused but there was steel in it, and in the
hand that held the reins. 'We'll start again. Who are
you?'

She remained silent.

'Are you playing truant? Is that it?'

A fugitive smile touched the corners of her mouth
and she nodded.

'You may safely tell me who you are. I'm no tale-
bearer.'

She looked at him, unable to hide a lurking amusement in her clear amber-gold eyes. If he only knew!

The gentleman saw the amusement. His face was
suddenly cold, the eyes diamond-hard. He tightened
his grasp on the reins. 'I warn you—I intend to find
out who you are, one way or another. What are you
doing on my land?'

Serena tried to pacify him. 'How did you know what
I was trying to say—about the hedgerows? You must
be pretty clever. I've been trying to think who wrote
it. . .?'

'Wordsworth—William Wordsworth. And I'm still waiting for an answer to my questions.'

He was not to be put off, it seemed. Serena realised that if she were not to be discovered on her very first outing she must satisfy him, somehow. She cleared her throat, and adopted the sulky tone of a schoolboy. 'I'm sorry. I didn't know it was private land. I didn't do any harm, just enjoying a ride. It was boring at... at home.'

'Gave your tutor the slip, eh? Where do you live?'

Serena waved her arm vaguely. 'Over there.'

'And what is your name? You shan't go till you've told me, you know.'

'It's...it's William.'

'Shakespeare or Wordsworth?' There was scepticism in the gentleman's voice. He wasn't so easily deceived.

Serena let herself look puzzled. 'Neither. It's... It's Blake. May I go now?'

The stranger laughed in genuine amusement—and Serena gazed in astonishment at the change in him when he did so. He was suddenly altogether more approachable, more human. 'You mean the "Tiger, tiger, burning bright" Blake? The golden tiger eyes match it, but I'm not so sure about the rest.'

'What do you mean, sir?'

'I mean that there's a whiff of poetic fishiness about you! Blake indeed!'

Serena said with dignity, 'My family is connected to the other Blake, sir——' which was no more than the truth ' – Robert the Admiral, not William, the poet.' She hesitated, then pleaded. 'They'll soon be looking for me. Keeping me here is almost as bad as telling.'

'Very well, William Blake. We can't have the truant

caught. But you will promise me not to do it again, if you please.' He held her eye until she reluctantly nodded. 'And in future keep your wits about you when you're riding. You could have taken a nasty toss. Off you go!' Serena was about to protest again that she had not needed his help, but he said softly, '"Waste no time in words, but get thee gone"—and that's by the other William.'

She smiled impishly, replied, 'I believe the correct reply is—"Sir, I go with all convenient speed"—that's by Shakespeare, too!' and rode off followed by the sound of his laughter.

For a short while Serena stayed circumspectly within the grounds of her great-aunt's house. Much as she had enjoyed her encounter with the strange gentleman it had brought home to her the enormous risk she had been running. She could not imagine what Lady Spurston would say if her great-niece were discovered to have been masquerading as a boy, but Mrs Galveston would surely wash her hands of them all. Lucy's future might be at stake.

So Serena contented herself with pleasing her aunt. This was not always easy, for Lady Spurston had grown so set in her own ways since the death of her husband that the addition of two young ladies to the household often made her irritable. She enjoyed talking of her youth, however, and Serena would spend hours with her great-aunt looking at old pictures and souvenirs of the past. Lady Spurston was appreciative of her audience and one day said, 'You are a good girl, Serena. And very good to Lucy. I dare swear the greater part of your dress allowance for London was devoted to her. Well, I have a surprise for you. In that

bureau over there you will find a small box. Be so
good as to bring it over to me, if you please.' Serena
did as she was asked. The box though small was heavy.
'Put it on the table here. Thank you.' Lady Spurston
opened the box and took out a small picture. 'This is
a portrait of your mother when she was Lucy's age. It
is for you.'

Serena examined the heart-shaped face with its
large blue eyes, delicate colouring and blonde hair
wreathed in roses. 'I'm afraid I am not much like her.
She must have been much admired.'

'She could have been a duchess. But, though your
father was so much older than she was, she fell in love
with him and his stories of the tropical islands, and
nothing would move her.'

'Othello to her Desdemona,' murmured Serena.

'I beg your pardon?'

'It's a Shakespeare play, aunt. Desdemona fell in
love with Othello for the same reason.'

Her aunt looked at her disapprovingly. 'You run
the risk of being thought bookish, Serena, if you
continue to quote Shakespeare on every occasion.'

'The Bible, my mother's edition of Shakespeare,
and a few books of poetry were all we had to read on
St Just, Aunt Spurston. I think I know most of them
by heart! Did my mother ever come back to visit
you?'

'No, we never saw her again after your father took
her to St Just.' Lady Spurston paused, then said, 'We
didn't want your mother to marry Lionel Calvert, you
know—a widower with two boys not much younger
than she was herself. The older one—Richard, wasn't
it?—was a charming rogue. I don't remember the

other one—he would be Lucy's father. What was his
name. . .?'

'Rodney.'

'That's it, Rodney. He was a very quiet boy.' There
was a short silence. 'She had always been so biddable,
such a loving, obedient child. . .' said Lady Spurston,
gazing into the fire. 'But she would not be dissuaded,
and in the end your grandfather was forced to agree.
And then she died when you were born. . .' Her voice
faded away again. Then she suddenly raised her head
and said sharply. 'There was some sort of scandal
later, wasn't there? Not enough to damage Lucy's
chances, I hope?'

'No, no. The scandal was all over long ago, Aunt
Spurston. Thirteen years, in fact. And my father saw
to it that the affair was all hushed up at the time. In
any case, Rodney was not involved—he was already
an invalid.'

'Good!' said Lady Spurston and then added, 'The
other things in the box are also for you.'

Serena carefully put down her picture and looked
inside the box. In it were some jewels and a fair
number of gold coins.

'I haven't much to leave you, Serena. When we saw
that there were to be no children of our own, Sir
George arranged an annuity which will die with me.
These baubles would have been your mother's had
she lived. They are of more use to you now, I think,
than after I am dead. And you may spend the money
on clothes for yourself—yourself, mind, not Lucy.'

Serena got up and embraced her great-aunt warmly.
'I. . . I don't know what to say, Aunt Spurston. Thank
you.'

Her aunt's expression softened, but she said sharply,

'Control yourself, Serena. A lady does not display excessive sensibility in public. Oh, if only my stupid disability did not prevent me from accompanying you in London...but there, Maria Galveston—or Lady Warnham, as I suppose I should call her, she's been married these twenty odd years—was a good girl, and I have no reason to suppose she is very different now. Her mother will see that she helps you. We still have a little time before the season begins, and I will spare no effort to see that you are prepared.'

Serena managed to amuse herself well enough with these conversations with her aunt and other rather tame pastimes, but finally the lure of another ride proved irresistible. It was for consolation, more than anything else. To Serena's mingled pleasure and regret Lucy, who had always been so close, was at the moment increasingly deserting her aunt in favour of her new companions. It was not surprising. For years Lucy had been denied the company of young people of her own age and class, and here in England she was not only learning the manners of the young ladies of English society—she was learning from Isabella and Isabella's brothers and sisters their amusements and interests, too. The preparations for their forthcoming début, which Serena found so tediously dull, were viewed by Lucy and Isabella with happy anticipation. Even Sheba seemed to have settled into an English household better than Serena herself, and spent much time in the kitchens, gossiping, regaling the other domestics with gruesome stories of voodoo and the like, and incidentally keeping warm. In short, Serena was lonely, and when she found that Lucy had apparently forgotten that it was her aunt's birthday, she grew very low in spirits.

Serena had always despised people who felt sorry for themselves, and she decided to take action. So once again she took out her boys' clothes and made her way to the top of the Downs. Here she dismounted, tied Trask to a tree, and walked to the edge of the ridge. The weather seemed to reflect her mood, for the sky was heavy with rain clouds and the fields looked dull and grey. A most unaccustomed feeling of melancholy overcame her in which the battle for Anse Chatelet hardly seemed worth the effort and her own future looked as drear as the fields below. With a heavy sigh she turned to go back. The tall gentleman was standing by Trask.

'Well, if it isn't my young friend William!' he said genially. 'Which one are you today?'

'Sir,' said Serena, trying wildly to remember what she had said her name was.

'Wordsworth, I think you said.'

'No, sir,' Serena replied in relief. 'Blake. My name is William Blake.'

'Ah, yes, forgive me. My memory occasionally fails me——' a slight pause ' – too.'

Serena could not resist it. She said gravely, 'I expect it's your age, sir. My grandfather was very absent-minded.'

He glanced at her sharply, but she managed to return a look of limpid innocence.

'Hmm. I am not yet in my dotage, however. And I clearly remember letting you go in return for your promise that you would not do this again.'

Serena started to enjoy herself in spite of the risk she was running. She looked injured. 'I am not sure what you mean by that, sir. A Blake does not break promises, I assure you.'

'Oh? So you're not playing truant again? Tutor broken his leg, has he?'

'His arm, sir. A most unfortunate fall.' Serena looked sideways at the gentleman, and what she saw caused her to say hastily, 'I was only joking. I've been given a holiday—today is my birthday.' She lowered her head as the memory of Lucy's defection returned.

'That has the ring of truth. But why aren't you celebrating it at home? Where are your parents?'

'They're dead.'

'I see.' There was a pause. 'May I join you on your ride?'

Serena looked at him suspiciously, but he was serious. She eyed his bay mare, cropping the grass a short distance away.

'Could you ride her?' The gentleman's voice broke in on her wistful thoughts. She turned to him, her eyes glowing.

'Oh, yes!'

'Sure?'

'Oh, please let me try! I'll go carefully, I promise.'

He laughed at the eager face before him, and then he frowned.

'What is it? Aren't you going to let me, after all? I'm sure I can manage her.'

'I believe you can—and anyway, Douce is like her name, although she's so fast. I was just puzzled for a moment. . . Where have I seen those eyes? No matter. Come, I'll help you up.'

But Serena had already mounted the mare, who was pawing and nodding playfully. 'She's beautiful! Do hurry!'

The stirrups were adjusted and, while he was occupied in fetching Trask and mounting, she furtively

checked her cap to make sure it was secure. They set
off along the ridge. At first Serena was careful to hold
Douce to a steady walk, getting the feel of the animal's responses. But then they came to a piece of
open land and she gave way to temptation. She let the
mare have her head.

Serena had never experienced anything like it. The
mare fairly flew over the soft, springy English turf,
and the air rushed past, intoxicating in its cool, damp
freshness. For five minutes she was in heaven. When
she finally slowed down, Trask and the gentleman
were nowhere in sight. It was as well. Her cap was
thoroughly askew and her cravat was flapping wildly.
Both had to be restored to order before she returned,
somewhat apprehensively, to look for her companion.
When she came into view he pulled Trask up, and sat
waiting for her in silence. He was, quite understand-
ably, very angry.

'You deserve a whipping, my boy,' he said unpleas-
antly. 'Get off that horse.'

'I'm. . . I'm sorry,' Serena faltered. She thought of
flight, but dismissed the idea. Riding off with the
gentleman's horse would only make bad worse.

He saw how her hand tightened on the reins,
though, and said menacingly, 'Don't even think of it.'

'I wasn't, not really.' Then, pleadingly, 'I'm truly
sorry, sir.'

He dismounted and came towards her. She quickly
jumped down and clutched his arm. 'Please don't be
angry! You've just given me the best birthday present
I've ever had. Don't spoil it!'

The gentleman looked down at the hand on his arm
with a frown, and then, surprisingly, stepped back. He
turned to mount Douce, but stopped with one foot in

the stirrup. 'Perhaps it is I who deserve the whipping,' he said harshly. 'You might have broken your neck. When you disappeared I was afraid for a moment that you had.'

'Oh, no! It was. . .it was magnificent! I cannot thank you enough! I felt as if. . .as if. . .as if I was "an angel dropp'd down from the clouds, to turn and wind a fiery Pegasus——"'

Once more he completed her quotation, '"And witch the world with noble horsemanship." So you're acquainted with the history plays as well. And I think you're right. You certainly know how to ride. Well, I'll overlook the fright you gave me—this time. Come, we must get back. It looks as if it will rain before long.'

The clouds were gathering fast as they rode back down into the valley, and by the time they reached the high road it was raining heavily. The gentleman was apparently absorbed in his own thoughts, and Serena was cold and wet, her elation of a short time before quite vanished. Suddenly he said, 'We'll stop here till the rain eases. Old Margery will give us shelter—and perhaps even something to eat—though it won't be quite a birthday feast. In here!'

They turned into a narrow lane, at the end of which was a tumbledown cottage. Serena was seized with apprehension.

'No, I. . . I must get back——'

'Don't be ridiculous, boy! You cannot go on in this downpour! What would your guardians say? The cottage may look decrepit from the outside, but Margery always keeps a good fire going. We'll be dry in no time.'

Nervously Serena dismounted and followed him

inside. The cottage was empty, though a fire was laid ready.

'She must be working at the farmer's down the road. She won't mind if I light this, however. We can reset it before we leave. Now I'll get this going, and you can fetch more kindling and wood from the shed. Then we'll take our wet coats off and dry them. It won't take long. . .'

He was busy with the fire. Serena slipped out, tiptoed to Trask, and led him quietly to the end of the lane. Then she leapt up and rode for her life along the high road.

CHAPTER FOUR

THE fire was burning brightly. In a few minutes the cottage would be warm and they could get dry. Not before time—the rain had penetrated his thick riding coat and the boy must be chilled to the bone. He heard a step outside. 'You've been a time! Could you not find any?'

'Whatever are you doin', my lord? Oh, I beg y'r lordship's pardon. But if I'd a knowed y'r lordship was comin' I'd 'a made sure things was ready! 'Ere, let me do that!'

James Stannard, sixth Baron Wintersett, straightened up and surveyed the newcomer. 'Good day to you, Margery. We took the liberty of sheltering in your cottage while the rain was so bad. What were you doing out in it? When you weren't here I thought you must be at Rufford Farm for the day.'

'I 'ad ter go down the road a piece after the goat. She'd gotten loose, the bothersome thing. Y'r lordship's welcome to whatever 'e can find. There isn't much, though. I'll fetch some more wood in for the fire, shall I?'

'Where's the boy? He should have brought some in by now.'

'There's no boy 'ere, my lord—just the two of us.'

'What? Of course there's a boy!' He strode outside. The rain had stopped as quickly as it had started. Douce was placidly sheltering under the lean-to shed. Of Trask and the boy there was no sign.

'I see'd a boy ridin' off down the high road as I came up the lane,' offered Margery, who had followed him out. 'In a terrible 'urry, he were. Ridin' as if the devil 'imself were arter 'im.'

'In which direction?' Lord Wintersett's first instinct was to leap on Douce and ride in pursuit, but then he changed his mind. Let the ungracious whelp go! 'No, it's of no consequence. I expect he had to get back.' He looked at the cottage. 'I'll send someone round to repair this roof, Margery. It's leaking yet again. You should move into the village; this hovel isn't fit to live in.'

'I'll end my days 'ere, thanking y'r lordship,' said Margery, her face settling into obstinate lines.

'Very well. But if you should change your mind, let Rossett know. He'll find you somewhere to live.' And, slipping some coins into Margery's hand, Lord Wintersett mounted Douce and set off for home. As he rode his mind was puzzling over the boy's behaviour. An odd mixture, William Blake—if that was his name, which he doubted. It was strange to have this conviction of the boy's integrity, when so much of what he said was open to question. Whoever was teaching him had managed to instil a love of poetry, that was clear. But they were undoubtedly careless in their supervision. He was too often left to his own devices. The lad was probably lonely—he had certainly been unhappy when they had first met today. The slender figure standing at the edge of the ridge had had a melancholy droop to the shoulders. It had been that more than anything which had resulted in his own impulsive offer of a ride on Douce. James Stannard smiled grimly. He must have been mad! How his London acquaintance would stare if they had

seen it! Frosty Jack Wintersett, for he knew what they
called him, giving way to a kindly—and ill-con-
sidered—impulse! And then to be rewarded with such
cavalier treatment. . .

In spite of his efforts to dismiss the boy from his
mind, the thought of 'William Blake' continued to
plague Lord Wintersett, and one particular aspect
more than the rest.

That evening they were three at dinner, for his mother
had appeared just before the meal had been
announced. At first James had been delighted, but
Lady Wintersett had acknowledged neither her son
nor her daughter-in-law, and was now lost once more
in a shadowy world of her own. Alanna Stannard sat
between them, dressed in a very pretty lavender gown
which enhanced her Irish colouring—black hair,
speedwell-blue eyes and a wild rose complexion. It
was difficult to believe that she had been a widow for
so long, the mother of a child who had never known
its father. James wondered briefly why she had never
remarried. She looked very little older than the girl of
nineteen who had most unexpectedly captivated his
brother Tony—Tony, who had never looked twice at
any woman before, Tony, who had always been
immersed in his books and his plants, gentle,
unworldly Tony, who had been a near genius. What
had there been in Alanna to attract such a self-
sufficient man? And what had Alanna found in Tony?
It had been a most unlikely match, for behind her
pretty face Alanna was an empty-headed butterfly—
or so James had always thought. He had wondered at
the time of Tony's marriage whether Alanna had
made a mistake—had she been seeking a rich young

man who would give her the social life she wanted?
But he had misjudged her—she had remained in
retirement here at Wintersett since her return from
the West Indies, a widow with a tiny, delicate baby,
born prematurely after Tony's death. James's face
saddened as it always did when he thought of his
brother. He glanced at his mother, still sitting silently.
She had been a lovely woman, too. Now she was like
a ghost.

Alanna had kept up a flow of inconsequential chatter throughout the meal, but she now interrupted it to
ask what was wrong. 'For I have asked you twice
whether you can obtain some French lace caps for
your mama and me, and you have made no reply.'

Lord Wintersett glanced at the figure at the other
end of the table. 'Would you like a new lace cap,
Mama?'

A sweet, infinitely sad smile was the only response.
Lady Wintersett slowly rose and left the room. With a
little sigh Mrs Stannard got up to follow. 'I think you
should come down more frequently, James,' she said.
'You seem to be the only one of us who can get any
response from Mama.'

'A smile? Before she slips away?'

'It's more than anyone else gets, I assure you. She
spends hours at little Anthony's bedside, but her face
never changes. She is like a doll sitting there. I would
be so obliged if you could procure the lace caps.'

'Isn't my nephew any better? Why is he in bed this
time?'

'The winter is always bad for Anthony. He is very
listless, and his limbs ache, he says.'

A sudden picture of a face glowing with eagerness
as the boy on the ridge, who called himself William,

pleaded for a ride, an image of Douce and the boy
flying off into the blue, poetry in motion, filled his
mind. He dismissed it, and said, 'Well, of course
Tony's limbs will ache, damn it! He never has any
exercise! You'd do better to get him out and about
instead of mollycoddling him. In a chair, if necessary.'

Alanna's blue eyes looked at him reproachfully.
'Your mama would not like to hear you swear, James;
I am sure she would prefer you to keep your oaths for
your club. And, forgive me, but how can you possibly
judge what is best for my darling? You hardly ever
see him! Dr Charlesworth——'

'It is my considered opinion that Dr Charlesworth
is a quack! All he does is echo your own wishes!
What's wrong with Galbraith?'

'Oh, no! Dr Galbraith is impossible! I have tried
him and he is quite unsuitable. He would kill little
Anthony in no time at all with his fresh air
regimes——'

'Little Anthony! He is nearly thirteen, Alanna! You
are far too protective of him——'

'And why shouldn't I be? Is he not all I have left?'

Alanna's eyes were large with tears. James got up
and went to the fireplace. He had lost interest in this
argument. It was one which frequently occurred
between them, and always ended in Alanna's tears.
Since tears irritated him, and since he was in any case
not prepared to stay at Wintersett Court to see any
reforms carried through, discussion was fairly point-
less. Mopping her eyes, Alanna made to leave the
room.

'Wait! If you please, Alanna, we must talk. Come
and sit down.' His sister-in-law came back to the table,
her head drooping, and waited while James carefully

closed the dining-room doors. Then he poured two
glasses of brandy and, ignoring her shake of the head,
put one of them in front of her. 'You might need it. I
have something to tell you which might upset you.'
He paused, then said abruptly, 'Sasha Calvert is coming to England.' Alanna's head jerked up, her hand at
her throat. Her face was suddenly colourless.

'What did you say?' she whispered.

'Have a sip of brandy, it'll do you good. Sasha
Calvert is bringing her niece to England. It seems that
the girl is now of an age to be presented to Society.'
His lip curled. 'The society of St Just isn't good
enough for Miss Calvert's ambition.'

'She mustn't come to England, she mustn't!'
Alanna's voice rose hysterically. 'James, you must stop
her!'

'Oh, no, my dear. Even if I could, I would not
dream of doing anything of the sort. It suits my plans
quite well to have her four thousand miles from Anse
Chatelet.'

'Be quiet, James! Be quiet! You don't understand!'

'Pull yourself together, Alanna!' he said coldly. 'It
shouldn't matter to you whether Sasha Calvert is in
England or in the Antipodes. You have no need to
meet her. Indeed, it's better that you shouldn't. You
never come to London, so any encounter is very
unlikely. You could even spend the summer in Ireland
if you wish.'

Alanna looked at him with haunted, terror-stricken
eyes. He forced himself to speak more kindly. 'I do
understand your feelings, believe me. I hate the
Calvert name as much as you—and with nearly as
much reason. Thirteen years have not diminished the
memory of their infamy. But this time I will deal with

its last member once and for all. Have confidence in me, Alanna.'

In spite of his reassurances she remained unconvinced, pleading with him again and again to prevent Sasha Calvert's journey to England, refusing to believe he could not prevent it even if he wished. She became quite distraught, and in the end he sent one of the servants for her maid, saying that Mrs Stannard was unwell and should retire to her room.

The thought of the boy continued to haunt him that night and throughout the next week. Several times he took Douce up on the Downs, and found himself scanning the area for the slight, quaintly dressed figure on horseback. 'William Blake' nagged at his mind like the toothache. There was something elusively familiar about him, and yet James was convinced they had never met before. And then—he had to face it, to bring it into the open—when the boy had put his hand on James's arm, James had felt a totally unfamiliar sensation, one which was strangely agreeable. He had been profoundly shocked at the time, and had wondered if he was going mad. The obvious explanation seemed so ridiculous that he refused to entertain it for one moment. Nothing in his past had ever suggested anything of that nature. There must be another reason. He went over their meetings again and again, recalling every detail. Slowly an incredible suspicion began to take root. He grew impatient to see the boy once more, so that he could test his theory. But though James stayed at Wintersett Court for much longer than he had originally intended, the landscape remained empty of both boy and horse.

* * *

Serena had made up her mind that her excursions were too dangerous to be repeated. She could hardly bear to think of what might have happened in the cottage. What excuse could she have found for keeping her soaking jacket on? What would have been the gentleman's reaction on finding out how she had deceived him?

Even after she reached the comparative safety of the Lodge her difficulties were not over. It took some time to remove her wet things and drape them over whatever she could find in the Lodge. When she arrived in the house, dressed but without her petticoats and with wet hair, Sheba was waiting for her.

'Where you been, Miss Serena? Your hair's all wet, and you got no petticoats! Shame on you!'

Serena hurried to her room with Sheba in close attendance. If her great-aunt saw her now she really would be in trouble. She was only halfway through changing when Lucy came in.

'Goodness, Sasha, where have you been? Out in the rain, I imagine—your hair's wet. I've been looking everywhere for you. What have you been doing, aunt of mine?'

Serena tried not to say anything, but Lucy would not be put off. Finally the fear that Lucy would continue questioning her in front of Aunt Spurston caused Serena to confess that she had been out riding on the Downs. The gentleman was not mentioned. Lucy was highly amused.

'And to think I thought you had become totally stuffy, Sasha! Oh, my dearest aunt, I do so love you!' She hugged Serena tightly, saying, 'And I will never breathe a word, I swear! Now, I have something for you.'

She ran out of the room and soon returned with a very pretty reticule, wrapped in silver paper. 'It's for your birthday!'

Serena was unable to speak. The reticule was exquisitely painted with poinsettias, delicate orchids and ferns. The work must have taken Lucy hours to do.

'Serena?' Lucy's voice was uncertain.

'I. . .' Serena cleared her throat. 'It's beautiful. Thank you.' She looked at Lucy's anxious face. 'Lucy, it's the most beautiful thing I've ever seen! Thank you, oh, thank you, my love.'

'That's all right, then. I thought for a moment you didn't like it. Now tell me about your rides.'

'Not at the moment,' said Serena firmly. 'Great-aunt Spurston will be waiting downstairs. I don't want her to start asking questions—they might be difficult to answer!' So Serena brought the boys' clothes back into the house and put them with the other things for her great-aunt's charity. She returned her pistol to its special place in her valise and applied herself resolutely to her duties, determined to forget her new acquaintance. In the days that followed this proved to be more difficult than she had imagined. She was surprised how sharply she regretted the thought that she would never see him again.

One reward for Serena's concentration on improving her behaviour was Lady Spurston's approval.

'You are growing more presentable by the hour, Serena! I'll swear the lotion Mrs Galveston sent is doing your skin a vast amount of good. You will never be a beauty, but your complexion is much less sallow—and I do believe you are filling out a little. Certainly your new dresses are most becoming! And that woman of yours is learning fast.'

Serena privately thought that it was lack of sun which was causing her tan to fade, but in accordance with her new mode of life she smiled, and when she next saw Mrs Galveston she thanked her gracefully.

Alas for Serena's good intentions! Her great-aunt forgot to have the charity clothes ready when the agent next called, and they were left for another month. The weather improved, and the fresh scents of an English spring proved too enticing. Once again the clothes were rescued from their storage place, the pistol was tucked into the jacket, and, after a lively argument with Sheba, Serena stole away to the stables. With the assistance of a friendly stable lad, Trask was saddled and removed unseen to the Lodge. Excited, her heart beating nervously, Serena set off through the country lanes towards the Downs.

Trask himself also seemed to be feeling a springtime renewal of energy. Together Serena and he had a good run, until they both ended up on the ridge, panting. The advancing season had turned the patchwork of fields into a medley of greens. The air was brilliantly clear—Serena could see for miles. Entranced, she slipped down from Trask and stretched voluptuously, breathing in the scents of the countryside. The tropics had their own beauty, but this air was like champagne. She felt quite warm, but did not open the jacket or remove her cap. It was most unlikely that the tall gentleman would appear again after all this time, but she dared not risk it. . .

It was as well. Douce and her rider were emerging from the trees, almost as if they had been waiting for her. A warm glow of satisfaction spread through her veins, astonishing her with its intensity. She suddenly felt exhilarated. It was worth any risk to feel like this. 'Hail, Caesar!' she cried gaily.

His face was inscrutable as he dismounted and stood beside the horse for a moment.

'Hail to thee, blithe spirit! Bird thou never wert——'

Her eyes grew intent. 'I've not heard that. Where is it from? I don't think it's Shakespeare, is it?'

'Not Shakespeare. Nor Wordsworth. Nor Blake, my boy.'

He spoke with a curious inflection. What was wrong? He even looked menacing. For a moment she felt frightened and thought of flight, but he suddenly smiled and she was reassured. She must be imagining things! 'Then who, sir?' she asked.

'It's by Shelley—Percy Bysshe Shelley. Have you heard of him?'

'No.' He was now quite close. He was menacing— he seemed to loom over her, and she suddenly felt breathless.

'How. . .how does it go on?'

'Hail to thee, blithe Spirit! Bird thou never wert——'

His face and voice were hard as he added, 'Or should it be "boy thou never wert"?' He put out a long arm, pulled off her cap, and breathed a long sigh of satisfaction as her dark hair tumbled out over her shoulders. 'I thought so,' he said. He regarded her in silence while her face flamed and she stared back at him, mesmerised. Finally he smiled and, drawing her to him, he kissed her hard. 'I thought so,' he said again with satisfaction. 'You've been haunting me, my little changeling,' he murmured, covering her face in little kisses. 'I've had some sleepless nights over you.

Now you must pay.' His fingers were undoing the
buttons of her jacket.

Serena came to life. 'Stop! Stop it, I say!' She tried
to get free, but he held her easily, laughing at her
struggles.

'Don't bother to pretend. You've led me a pretty
little dance, my dear, but it's over now. The game is
over. I'm willing to admit you're an original. Unlike
most of your sisters, you've at least succeeded in
catching my interest.' He bent his head again, whispering against her lips, 'We'll discuss terms later.' He
pulled open her jacket, took her even more firmly into
his arms and started to kiss her again, more passionately than before.

Serena was in a state of panic. She had never felt so
helpless. No man had ever kissed her like this before,
held her so roughly, talked to her in such a manner.
But soon her pride and spirit came to her rescue. She
managed to kick Trask, who snorted and jibbed in
surprise, and, taking advantage of a momentary relax-
ation in the man's grip, she tore herself free and
backed away. Before he could catch her again she
pulled her pistol out of her jacket pocket and cocked
it. 'Don't take another step!' she said. He made to
move, and she pointed the pistol at his knees. 'I mean
it! I'll shatter your kneecap.'

They regarded one another in silence, Serena's eyes
watchful and her hand steady.

'The devil!' he said then with a laugh. 'I believe you
would, too.'

'You may count on it,' Serena said grimly.

'Hmm. Perhaps I was wrong after all. Does this
mean—forgive me if I seem somewhat obtuse—that

all this was *not* part of a plot to become—er—more closely acquainted with me?'

'I would rather have a closer acquaintance with a boa constrictor. Whatever made you think I would?'

'What the devil else was I to think? Oh, point that pistol somewhere else; I give you my word you're safe from me.'

'I'd rather keep it where it is for the moment. So far I have no reason to take your word for anything.'

'In that case we're quits, William Blake—or is it Wordsworth? What *is* your name, girl?'

She hesitated, then her lips began to twitch. 'It's Serena. But that's all I'll tell you.'

He gave a great shout of laughter. 'Serena! I refuse to believe it! You've made it up!'

'No, it's my real name.'

'Serena! Oh that's rich, that's really rich! Wait! Er . . .do you expect to ride Trask back?'

Serena turned her head to see Trask moving slowly out of sight. She gasped in dismay and moved to go after him, but before she had taken a step an iron hand had caught her wrist and forced her to drop the pistol. An exclamation of pain escaped her and she looked at him with a fear she could not conceal. But though he did not release her, he made no attempt to kiss her again.

'If you promise not to point it at me any more you may have it back,' the man said quietly, holding her gaze. 'I intend you no harm. Do you believe me? Will you promise?' Serena nodded and he picked her pistol up, made it safe, and handed it to her. She hesitated, then put it carefully away. Her wrist was aching and she furtively rubbed it. He saw the movement, and stretched out to take it. She backed away nervously.

The gentleman raised his hands and smiled. 'I mean no harm. I'm sorry I hurt you, that's all. And I apologise for my behaviour a moment ago. I think we owe each other an explanation, don't you?'

'Trask?' she croaked out of a dry throat.

'Douce will soon overtake him. In fact, if you wait here I'll fetch him for you now.'

Trask was brought back and tied up, while Serena restored herself to order.

'Now, Serena!' His lips twitched and he said, 'A less suitable name would be difficult to find——'

'Prudence?' suggested Serena. He burst into laughter. She went on, 'I may not be very serene, but I have been even less prudent, I'm afraid. But you have no notion how stifling it is to be a woman.'

'Tell me,' he said. 'Why did you have to turn into a boy?'

She looked at him uncertainly. How far could she trust him? He said, returning to a colder manner, 'I have given you my word, Serena. I do not in general force myself on unwilling females, once I am sure they are unwilling, that is. Not many of them are. But you have convinced me of your reluctance in the plainest possible way.'

She made up her mind. 'You misunderstand. I was wondering how much to tell you, not whether you were about to...to attack me again. I accept your word on that. Though why the discovery that I was not a boy should lead you to the conclusion that I would be...would be...a woman like that, willing to be treated in such a way, I am at a loss to understand!'

'Dammit, how could I think otherwise? Modest young females don't normally roam the countryside with no one to protect them! And modest young females don't normally dress like boys—or ride astride, if you'll forgive my mentioning it.'

'But why should you assume that I was doing all this just to attract you? Or do you take that for granted? I have to tell you that I find you guilty of a fault worse than any of mine.'

'What? What fault?'

'Your conceit!' She was pleased to observe that this remark had struck home. A faint pink appeared in his cheeks, but then he drawled,

'I have been pursued by the fair sex, Serena, ever since I was old enough to notice. But I am not so green as to believe that they loved me for myself. My family's fortune is famous. It's only too obvious where my attractions lie.'

'If your riches are your only attractive feature, that may well be true!'

'Is that your opinion? That my wealth is my only attraction?'

'We have agreed, have we not, that attraction is not a question between us?' said Serena loftily. She spoilt it by adding, 'In any case, I had no idea—still have no idea—who you are, so how could your riches appeal?'

He bowed. 'I am Wintersett.'

'Well, Mr Wintersett——'

'Lord Wintersett. And my given name is James. So now we have settled the question of our relationship—or rather the limitations to our relationship, shall I say?—isn't it about time you told me why you had to be a boy? So far we have only established that being a woman is stifling.' He indicated a fallen tree-trunk at the edge of the track, and they sat down. Serena, in spite of his assurances, took care to keep her distance.

'Till recently,' she began carefully, 'I have led a less

restricted life then I have to at the moment. Don't
misunderstand—my former life was completely
respectable, just more. . .perhaps "independent" is the
word.'

'You're not old enough to be a widow! Are you?'

'You may speculate as much as you wish. I will not
tell you anything more than I choose. But I was able
to go much my own way.'

'And now?'

'Now I have to set an example to someone younger
than myself.'

'You're a governess. I find that incredible, too.'

'Perhaps. Perhaps not. And sometimes, just sometimes, I cannot stand the restraints any longer. I have
to get free.'

'But why the disguise?'

'You ask that! When you have just demonstrated—
and so roughly, too—what happens to women who—
what was your phrase?—"roam the countryside with
no one to protect them".' Can you imagine the disgrace if it were discovered that the very person who
should be setting an example was breaking every rule
in Society's book? No,' she continued bitterly, 'I
thought my disguise would give me the freedom
I longed for without hurting people I——' she looked
at his intent face—'to whom I owe my loyalty. As for
not riding side-saddle—have you ever seen a boy who
did?'

'That's true! Yes, I can see that one followed from
the other. And now?'

'And now I shall have to confine myself to "acceptable behaviour for a lady".' She sighed deeply. 'Walks
round the garden, morning calls, which are *always*
paid in the afternoon, polite conversation, in which

one never, ever says anything worthwhile. Do you know that I am thought "bookish" because I enjoy Shakespeare? I shall probably finish by pressing flowers and painting on velvet.'

His laugh rang out again. 'May heaven preserve you from such a fate! I must confess, you intrigue me, Serena. It's clear that you are no governess—you occupy a superior position in society than those unfortunates—and I'm fairly sure you're no widow, either. What possible circumstances have combined to give rise to such a life as yours?'

Serena looked at him in alarm. He was too intelligent. Before long he would learn everything from her. 'I must go!' she said hurriedly, and went to pick up her cap, which was still lying where Lord Wintersett had dropped it.

'Oh, no!' he said and calmly appropriated the cap. 'You don't escape so easily. Like you, I spend much of my life with people who bore me beyond measure——'

'I didn't say that! I love my——' she stopped short. She had almost told him more. His face changed, and he looked like a stranger. His voice was icy as he said,

'Have I been mistaken yet again? Can it be that you seek relief from a boring lover in these... escapades?'

'No, no!' His face remained cold, so she said desperately, 'I'm. . .a kind of chaperon. The person I love is my charge.'

'You're not old enough!'

'I am seven and twenty.'

He looked flatteringly astonished. 'I will not express disbelief,' he said. 'You must know how old you are, and can have no reason to exaggerate your age. But I would not have guessed it.' Then a new thought occurred to him. 'If you are a chaperon, then you must be married—or a widow?'

'Neither. That is why I must be so circumspect.'

'Of course. As you are. Indeed. I have seen it myself.'

Serena chuckled. 'You, sir, have seen my alter ego. It is unkind of you to mock me. Now, if you will give me my cap. . .'

'I did not finish what I had to say, Serena.' He looked down at the vivid face lifted to his, the golden eyes half laughing, half anxious. 'I have found more amusement in half an hour of your company than in a year of most of my acquaintance. I do not intend to do without it.'

'But. . .but I cannot spend more time with you now!'

'Why not?'

'You must see it is impossible! Pretending to be a boy so that I can have some time to myself is one thing. Slipping out in disguise to an assignation is something very different—indeed, it would be shameful! And I will not do it!'

'I would never have thought you so poor-spirited. Or so conceited!'

'Conceited?'

'Yes, Serena. How can you be so quick to accuse me of conceit, when you suffer from the same fault yourself? What makes you think I want an assignation with you? Those I can have whenever I choose.'

'Of course,' she murmured. 'That wealth of yours. . . What would you want of me?'

'Companionship, friendship—call it what you will. I enjoy your company, and do not wish to lose it.'

'I'm afraid you must. I cannot agree to meet you clandestinely.'

'I fear, dear Serena, you will have to!' She started to make an angry protest, but he overrode her. 'For if you do not agree to ride here in your boy's clothes, let us say once a week, when I am at home——' he held her gaze ' – I will seek you out where you live and reveal all. It would not be difficult to trace you if I really tried.'

Serena looked at him in horror. 'You wouldn't do such a thing!'

'I agree I probably will not. You will have seen reason before it becomes necessary.'

'But that's blackmail!'

'Quite. I am glad your understanding is so quick.' When he saw that she still didn't believe him he said slowly and clearly, as if speaking to an idiot, 'I will find out who you really are, and you will be disgraced, unless you agree to continue our acquaintance.'

It was obvious that he meant every word.

'You. . .you scoundrel!'

'Come, you are disappointing me, Serena. What am I asking you to do that you were not doing already? I have told you that I have no wish for an alfresco love-affair. And I would not suggest for a moment that we meet anywhere but here on this open ridge. No, it will be as if you are the boy I first thought you. I will even call you William if you desire me to.'

She looked at him uncertainly. 'But you know I am not a boy. It is. . .it is embarrassing to be in br. . . breeches, when you know I am a woman.'

His voice quivered as he said, 'I promise never to look at your br. . . breeches.'

'You will call me William?'

'All the time.'

'And not help me, or coddle me as you would a woman?'

'I will be as severe on you as on the toughest of the members of my own club.'

'And you won't think badly of me for this masquerade?'

'I'm beginning to think badly of you at this very moment, Serena——'

'Ha!'

'I shall call you Serena while you continue to act like a woman. At the moment you are suffering from a totally feminine inability to face the inevitable. If you wish to be thought a man, then you must begin to think like one—logically and clearly.' He held up one hand and counted on his fingers.

'One: for no reason other than your own pleasure, you chose to dress as a boy and ride out on the Downs. Am I right?'

Serena nodded reluctantly.

'Two: at the risk of being accused of conceit, I will say that you have enjoyed our conversations as much as I. Correct?'

Serena nodded again and he looked satisfied.

'Three: if you do not agree to continue these very pleasant activities, you will suffer some very unpleasant consequences. Where is the choice?'

Serena was going down fighting. 'How can I possibly enjoy something I am doing under constraint?'

'Humbug! You want to, you know you do, constraint or no. But it's time to put an end to this unnecessary discussion. Are you to be Serena or William?'

'If I agree, you won't attempt to find out where I

live or who I am? I can only carry this out if I feel my
two lives are totally separate.'

'Hand on heart!'

'You'll let me ride Douce occasionally?'

His face, normally so cold, was transformed by his
smile. 'Of course you may, my boy! Now, if you wish.'

Serena took a deep breath and said, 'Done!'

That was the first of several outings. Aunt Spurston,
whose health improved as the weather got better,
decided that she would visit Mrs Galveston every
Friday in Reigate. Here Lucy could join Isabella in a
dancing class with other young people of the district—
all under strict supervision, of course—while Aunt
Spurston herself renewed old acquaintances. Serena
was excused from these excursions as the carriage was
really only comfortable for two, and Aunt Spurston so
much enjoyed the opportunity to gossip with her
cronies.

'You will have time to yourself for a change, Serena.
There will be little enough occasion for that once the
season starts.'

It was as if everything conspired to smooth the way
for Serena's meetings with Lord Wintersett. Sheba
scolded, but helped her. Her great-aunt, naturally,
always took the coachman and groom with her, and
Tom, the stable lad, became one of Serena's staunch-
est allies. Trask enjoyed the exercise after several
years of neglect. As for the outings themselves—they
soon became the focus of Serena's week.

CHAPTER FIVE

SERENA'S life had till now been active and rewarding, but not really a happy one. Her childhood had often been lonely, in a household dominated by two strong-willed males—egomaniacs, both of them—her father and her brother Richard. Looking back, Serena could see now that Richard had always been selfish and unscrupulous, but she and her father had worshipped him, blinded by his charm and reckless courage. 'The looks of a lion, with a lion's heart,' her father had said of him. Richard and her father had both bullied Rodney unmercifully, and had at the same time despised him for allowing it. For a while Rodney had managed to escape them through his marriage with Lucy's mother. But when she died he had returned to Anse Chatelet with his little daughter, and in the end he had found another, more dangerous way to forget-fulness. Serena had been so anxious to avoid the same contempt that Anse Chatelet had been haunted by her tiny figure fiercely determined to win Lord Calvert's approval or Richard's admiration by acts of reckless daring. By the time she was fourteen she had learned to shoot, to ride, to sail almost as well as they did themselves.

Later, in a sadder and wiser time, she had worked unceasingly to keep Anse Chatelet out of the hands of the creditors. The work had been rewarding, but very demanding, and the consciousness of her twin responsibilities—for Lucy and for the estate—had weighed heavily on her.

Now, here in the heart of the English countryside, she learned what it was to be unreservedly happy. Together she and Lord Wintersett explored the hills, valleys, lanes and fields of Surrey. They seldom met anyone, for they kept to the unfrequented paths and byways. But her favourite place was still the top of the ridge, for there she could feel as if they were on the roof of the world, far removed from the restrictions of life below.

They explored each other's minds, too. The love of poetry they already shared, but Serena, conscious of her lack of other knowledge, listened avidly to her companion's accounts of his journeys in Europe, of the people he had met and the sights he had seen. New worlds were opening up before her, and she soaked up knowledge as a sponge soaked up water.

For his part, James talked more freely than he had ever done in his life before, and he waited with a quite unaccustomed interest for anything she might say or ask in response. She never disappointed him. Her quick intelligence, her strong sense of humour, the freshness of her views, were a constant source of pleasure to him. He delighted in the mobile features, golden eyes now sparkling with laughter, now wide with wonder, the generous brow wrinkled in concentration, the sensitive mouth soft with compassion or set in determination. Almost the only barrier between them was her fixed resolve to keep everything about her other life completely hidden. He sensed that this was her defence against any stirrings of conscience about her behaviour, and respected her wishes, never seeking to trap her into betraying herself. Any indications he gleaned from things she said he stored up in his mind, but he gave them little importance. He, too, liked the feeling of isolation from the rest of society, in the world which they had created for themselves on the top of the hill.

They had differences, of course. Serena had already experienced Lord Wintersett's ruthlessness in pursuit of something he wanted. She was occasionally repelled by his coldness, his indifference to the feelings of others—even of those he liked. And he soon found that Serena was touchy about her independence and very fond of her own way. Worse than that, she had a temper. He could see that years of discipline had taught her to control it, but once it was released it blazed like a furnace, leaving her with no thought for the consequences.

On one memorable occasion he actually had to use force to save her from catastrophe. They had wandered further afield than usual, and came upon an isolated cottage in front of which an ugly scene was being enacted. The cottagers—an elderly couple—were being forcibly removed from their home. Two men were throwing pathetic scraps of furniture out on to the grass in front of the cottage. The woman was wailing, and her husband had a bruise on his forehead—graphic evidence of the treatment they had received. Serena rode forward and said imperiously, 'What are you doing there? Stop what you're doing immediately!'

The two bailiffs looked round in surprise, but when they saw a mere boy confronting them they turned back to resume their activities.

'I told you to stop, you hog-grubbers!'

One of the men thus addressed turned round swiftly

and said, 'You saucy young buck! Be off and stop
interfering with what don't concern you! This here lot
has to be got out by tonight or else! We don't need
you to teach us our jobs.' He turned round. 'Here,
you!'

The old woman had scrambled to the pile of furniture and was trying to take it back inside. The bailiff
went over to her and pulled her away so roughly that
she fell into the mud. Serena, her eyes flashing molten
gold, jumped down from Trask and ran to pick the
woman up. This was the point at which James thought
it prudent to intervene before "William" ran into
disaster. He rode into the clearing and interposed
Douce between the bailiff and the boy.

'What's the trouble?' he asked coldly.

The bailiffs took off their caps. 'Pardon, sir. We was
just doin' our duty when this young gentleman
appears.'

'And your duty consists of throwing a woman old
enough to be your grandmother to the ground?'

The men flushed darkly, and one of them muttered,
'The old biddy must 'a tripped. She wouldn't do what
we told 'er. Troublemakers, that's what they are.'

'Can't they pay their rent?'

'It's not that, sir. The master wants the land for
another purpose. And the cottage ain't fit fer man nor
beast to live in. They've been offered somewhere
else.'

'But this is their home!' cried Serena. 'Why do they
have to leave if they don't want to?'

'If the landowner wants the land and has offered
them an alternative they have no choice,' said James.
He turned to the men. 'But see that you go gently
with the old people. Come—*William!*'

'I'm not going till I'm certain that they're all right,' said Serena hotly. 'Where is their new home?'

'In the work'ouse, young maister!' shouted the old man. 'And Sal and me are goin' to 'ave to live apart!'

'Well, what's wrong wi' that? You ain't much use to a woman at your age, old man,' jeered the other bailiff.

'That's monstrous! How dare you!' cried Serena. She dodged round Douce and kicked the unfortunate bailiff in the shins.

''Ere!' he roared, and grabbed Serena by the scruff of the neck.

James was there in a flash, almost breaking the man's arm as he knocked him clear. 'You,' he snarled, 'lay another finger on my nephew and you'll be the worse for it. Who is your master?'

'Sir Oliver Camden,' muttered the bailiff resentfully, picking himself up. 'You'd best be careful—Sir Oliver don't like interference with his concerns. And he's a magistrate, as well!'

'I know Sir Oliver. I don't believe he would wish this. I'll speak to him about it. Meanwhile leave the old people alone, do you hear? William—get on your horse. We're leaving.'

'But——' Serena started to protest.

'I said get on your horse!' When she would have argued James picked her up under one arm and carried her, kicking and protesting, to where Trask was patiently waiting. Here he threw her up on to the horse, called Douce to him, and they were soon riding away, with Trask's reins firmly held in James' hand.

Serena was furious. 'Let go! I said let go! You're every bit as bad as they are!'

James rode on in grim silence. Ignoring Serena's

worst efforts, he guided them both until they were
well clear of the wood. It was a superlative display of
horsemanship. But as soon as he stopped Serena
immediately wheeled Trask round and urged him back
the way they had come. She was quickly overtaken,
and this time James forced her to dismount. They
stood facing one another in the quiet lane. Serena was
still angry. 'How dare you treat me as if I were a
child? Those people needed my help! I shall go back.
You cannot stop me!'

James was every bit as angry as Serena, but he was
in control of himself. He said coldly, 'You're a fool,
Serena! Do you wish to make a public spectacle of
yourself? You were within an ace of discovery back
there! If I hadn't stopped him that bailiff would have
found he'd got more than he bargained for when he
held you by your collar! Pull yourself together!'

'But that old man—and the woman!'

'Forget them! Sir Oliver is within his rights, you
know he is!'

'But he's going to separate them—after all those
years together!'

James regarded her curiously. 'Why are these people so important to you?'

'It's not that—it's just that it's wrong to deprive
anyone of their...their dignity like that. If you have
people in your care you have to treat them with
humanity. I've met people like them. Separate them
and they'll die without each other; I've seen it
happen.'

'They'll die anyway soon enough. Forget them!'

Serena looked at him in disgust and turned away.
They stood in silence for a while.

'I'll speak to Sir Oliver,' he said finally. 'He can

probably find some cottage in the village for them,
though he might well wonder what business it is of
mine. Still—will that satisfy you?'

In an instant she had turned round, her face glowing
with gratitude. She came close and clutched his arm.
For a moment James thought she was going to kiss
him, and he experienced such a unexpectedly strong
surge of feeling that, before he could stop himself, he
had put his hand over hers, clamping it to his arm.
'Serena!' he said fiercely. She looked up, startled. For
a moment they stared at each other, and then they
both took a step back as if they had reached a sudden
abyss.

'You. . .you promised always to call me William,'
she said uncertainly.

James strove to regain mastery of his feelings. He
knew that this next moment would be decisive. If
Serena even suspected how powerfully she had
affected him she would refuse to see him again, he
was sure. If that happened. . .his mind shied away
from the possibility. Her friendship and trust had
become more important to him than he had realised.
He must not lose them because of any transitory
feelings of desire. Those could be satisfied cheaply.
The value of this relationship with Serena was beyond
price.

She was waiting for his response. He took a deep
breath.

'As I think I've said before, when you behave as
irrationally as you have just done with those men, I
shall call you by your woman's name,' he said coldly.
'Act sensibly and you will be William again to me.'

Serena was reassured by this. In all their other
meetings, apart from the one when he had discovered

her to be a woman, Lord Wintersett had behaved impeccably. He had treated her and spoken to her like the boy she was pretending to be. If he had ever hinted at a warmer feeling she would have been forced to abandon her excursions, even if he carried out his threat to expose her. A moment ago she had been afraid that this might be the case, but his reply had hardly been that of a lover! She must have been mistaken. She was surprised how passionately relieved she felt, that she was free to continue with this strange friendship.

It was astonishing that such a brief moment could have such a profound effect on both James and Serena—the very opposite of what might have been expected. Each had recognised the danger of the moment. But each had also realised the value of their relationship, the importance of preserving it. So an incident which might have led to a reserve, a wariness between them, in fact served to draw them closer.

But the disadvantage of their precarious relationship was brought home to Lord Wintersett when Serena did not appear at her usual time the following week. The trust between them was now so absolute that he had no thought of carrying out his threat of finding her if she refused to meet him. But he was worried. Had she had an accident? Had she reached wherever she lived safely after the last expedition? Was she ill? He had no means of knowing without exposing her—the last thing he wanted. When she did not immediately appear for the second week he was so anxious about her that he was debating whether to set off to look for a clue—anything—as to where she might be. His relief therefore was enormous when she appeared over the hill, and he strode to meet her.

'Serena! What happened?'

'Last week? I must say I was quite relieved not to see you riding up the drive to...the place where I live, like Nemesis. I suspect you are a humbug, Lord Wintersett. I should have tested your threats before now.'

'What happened, Serena? Did you have an accident? Were you waylaid?'

'No, My...the person I live with was unwell. I could not leave her.'

They suddenly realised that James was holding Serena's hands, and she moved away self-consciously. 'You promised to call me William, Lord Wintersett!' she said almost angrily.

'I know, I know!' he replied. 'It's sometimes damned difficult to remember that. I've been worried about you. You may dress like a boy, but you are a woman when all is said and done. And vulnerable.'

Serena laughed as she flourished her little pistol. 'Not while I have this, my friend.'

'Much good that toy would have done you had you fallen off your horse and broken your leg.'

He was obviously seriously upset, and Serena, not without some secret amusement, set herself to coax him into a better mood.

The weeks flew by, and Serena was aware that she would soon have to think of removing to London. She had received a letter from Lady Pendomer saying that Sir Henry's cousin, Lord Ambourne, was prepared to sublet a small house in Dover Street at a very moderate rent for Serena's stay in London. Serena had written to Lord Ambourne, and had had a very civil reply offering her the house, together with its staff, as

soon as she needed it. He regretted that he would
unable to make her acquaintance as early as he had
hoped, since he and his Countess were spending the
early part of the summer on his estate in France.

Lady Warnham and her family were leaving Surrey
within the month to open up the Galveston mansion
in Portman Square, and Lucy was growing impatient
to be gone. Her and Serena's wardrobes had long
been ready. The small finishing touches, such as shoes,
fans, shawls and the like, would be bought in the
warehouses and shops of London. Little remained to
be done in Surrey, and yet Serena lingered. She was
sure she would meet Lord Wintersett in London, and
was fairly certain that their friendship was secure
enough to withstand the transition, but it would not
be the same. In London she would be 'Miss Calvert',
or 'Serena'—never 'William'.

When she mentioned her imminent departure to
Lord Wintersett he seemed to feel regret, too. 'I take
it you are going to London for the Season—your
"charge" is no doubt to be presented? Oh, don't look
at me like that, William! I have not pried into your
affairs all this time, and you have no reason to suspect
me of doing so now! Well, it is perhaps as well. This
could not continue forever, much as I have enjoyed it.
Will you be in London? Shall I meet you there?'

She nodded.

'It will seem strange,' he continued. 'I feel I know
you better than anyone of my acquaintance, and yet
we shall have to appear to be strangers. Do you realise
that I have never even seen you in a dress?'

She looked at him doubtfully. 'Don't expect too
much, my friend. Remember my position as a
chaperon.'

'Now that really will be a piquant situation! The thought of seeing how William the Turbulent is transformed into Serena the Respectable Chaperon almost consoles me for the loss of our present meetings. Almost. But not quite.'

They had ridden up to the ridge and were looking down on bright green fields and sprouting hedges. "Hardly hedgerows. . ."' Serena murmured.

'"Little lines of sportive wood run wild". I shall miss William, Serena.'

'He has to go, Lord Wintersett. But he will always treasure the memory of how good you have been to him.'

'Serena——'

'No! I shall be Serena in London,' said Serena quickly. 'Wait till then. When do you plan to move to the town?'

'I live most of the year in London. My home here is not a very happy place, I'm afraid, and I am not often to be found there. This spring has been quite exceptional.' He smiled down at her. 'I think you know why, William.'

But Serena was thinking of what he had said before. Breaking her own rule, she asked, 'Why is your home not a happy one?'

'My nephew is confined to a wheelchair when he is not actually in bed. My mother is also an invalid, and recently she has been getting worse.'

'Can she be cured?'

'Who knows? Her illness is not physical, but the result of two shocks, the one rapidly following on the other. Both my father and my younger brother died within a month of each other. She has never been the same since.' Then he added abruptly, 'But don't let us

spoil a beautiful afternoon with such gloomy thoughts.
It might be one of our last. Come—is Trask fit for
another gallop—or do you wish to ride Douce?'

Serena smiled. 'What an unnecessary question!'

Serena told James the next time they met that this
was their last meeting. He looked at the wide view
below and wondered why the devil it all had to look
so bright. Rain would have been more appropriate.
He forced himself to speak calmly.

'You told me last time that you were soon going to
London, so it comes as no surprise. And I will soon
in any case be unable to spend much time here in
Surrey—I have business of my own in London.'
Serena shivered. 'You're cold?'

'No. Someone walked over my grave, I think.' She
looked at him with troubled eyes. 'Or was it because
of stories I've been hearing about a certain Lord
Wintersett?'

'Stories?'

'I haven't been prying. I respect your privacy as
much as you have respected mine. But now that our
London début is so near, my charge and I have been
subjected to a great deal of advice and gossip... I
have heard your name mentioned several times. The
Lord Wintersett I hear of then does not seem to be
the man I know.'

'No?'

'No. I hear that Lord Wintersett is cold, heartless,
indifferent to others. That any lady who attempts to
attract him runs the risk of a severe set-down. That
even his paramours—forgive me, I am still speaking
in the character of William, so I can mention these

things—never know when his interest will wane and they will be discarded.'

He said harshly, 'They are right, Serena—you see, I have already said goodbye to William, so you must now be called by your right name—I do not deny these stories.' Serena looked at him gravely and something in her eyes made him continue, 'You once said that I could have no notion how stifling it was to be a woman. But you have no notion of what it is like to be a very rich man. You once called me conceited because I assumed that you were pursuing me. My experience would never have led me to think otherwise. I will not bore you with other and different stories. But I think every trick known to woman has been tried to trap me—not my person, you understand, but my wealth. As for my paramours—they run the risks of their calling. They are well rewarded.'

Serena swallowed and looked away from him and down into the broad valley.

'What is it, Serena?'

'In one breath you excuse your lack of concern for others because you think they seek you only for your wealth. In another you use your wealth as a substitute for concern. "They are well rewarded," you said. It does not reassure me, Lord Wintersett.'

He took her by the shoulders and turned her towards him. 'The stories may be true. But one thing my critics have never been able to say. Look at me, Serena, for this is important to me.' She looked up, her golden eyes serious. 'No one has yet been able to say that I have broken any promises.'

'I suppose that is something. But it is not enough. I think you lack. . .'

'What?'

'I don't know. Kindness?'

'Is that important to you? Universal kindness, I mean?' he asked in surprise.

'I think it is.'

'Strange. It is not a quality I have sought to cultivate. One is kind to idiots or well-meaning fools. I have always avoided them where possible.' Serena was still looking troubled. He felt a sudden urge to remove the worried frown from her brow. 'Do you wish me to make promises to you? Is that it?'

'No!' she said vehemently. 'No! Now is not the time to be promising anything. This situation between us . . .is too artificial——'

'I sometimes feel it is the only real thing in my world,' he said whimsically.

'But the world you talk about is here, on this hill. It isn't real, either,' she said sadly.

'Serena, believe me, the world of London society is infinitely more artificial than any make-believe world we have here. You will be flattered and cozened, as I have been——'

' "Taffeta phrases, silken terms", Lord Wintersett?'

'Exactly! "Words, words, mere words, no matter from the heart." What a splendid thing quotation is! But please, Serena, don't change when you get to London.' A small frown creased his brow. 'I am strangely afraid that I am going to lose you. Can we not take some kind of vow? I am willing, if you are.'

'Lord Wintersett, if, when we meet again in London, you still wish to make a promise of any kind—for friendship, for loyalty or. . .of any kind—then I will listen to you. Not till then. And now I must go.'

'Then farewell till then, Serena. But first there's

something I must do.' He drew her gently to him and
kissed her, and was jubilant to feel her total response,
untutored though it was. 'Whether you realise it or
not, you have just made a promise all the same,
Serena,' he said as they drew apart again. 'Serena, my
"bright, particular star".'

Serena, still looking at him with wonder in her eyes,
said nothing.

'Till London, then,' he said, holding her chin in his
hand. She nodded silently. He kissed her once again,
then let her go, and stood watching as Trask carried
her away from him down into the valley.

As James returned to his home he had the
unpleasant feeling that an idyll had just ended. What
would take its place he had no means of knowing, but
he feared the effect of London on their relationship.
Serena had called their situation artificial and he
supposed it was, but they were able to be more natural
with each other here than in any conceivable situation
in the city. Would Serena be different when she put
her skirts on? He couldn't imagine her fluttering and
twittering like the rest of society's vapid females, but
she was almost certain to lose that wholly natural
spontaneity which so delighted him. Especially as she
was a "kind of chaperon". Who was her charge?
Among the local families he rather thought the
Warnham girl was of an age to be presented—but she
had a perfectly adequate family, including the Gorgon
figure of Mrs Galveston. Speculation was useless—he
would find out soon enough.

Alanna's hysterical outburst when she had heard that
Sasha Calvert was coming to England had not been
repeated, but she was pale and tense and feverishly

active. James had offered to send her to her parents
in Ireland for the summer, but she had refused,
especially when he told her that young Tony would
stay in England where he belonged.

'You would not separate us, James!' she exclaimed.

'I'm beginning to think it might be the best thing
that could possibly happen to the boy,' he said brutally. 'Tony will never make the attempt to be normal
while you are constantly hovering over him assuring
him he is delicate. Where is he now?'

'He's up today,' she said eagerly. 'In his room. He
has even been working with his tutor.'

James went along to Tony's room. It was a sunny
room on the ground floor, with a large window which
opened on to the garden. But the windows were
always closed, sometimes even shuttered, and the
child often lay in darkness for hours on end. James
hated visiting him. This boy was all that was left of his
beloved brother, yet he could see nothing of the older
Tony about him. Born at seven months, the infant had
grown slowly from a puling, sickly baby into a pale,
lethargic invalid. There was nothing of his father's
gentle courage, none of Tony's eagerness to learn of
the world around him. He remained confined to his
bed or a wheelchair, watched jealously by an over-
anxious mother. Of all the casualties of the tragedy on
St Just this was the most pathetic.

Tony was sitting in his chair, but his tutor was
missing. The boy looked up as his uncle came in.

'I've been ringing the bell for ages. No one came.'

'Where's Mr Gimble?'

'He's gone to look for some book in the library.
Uncle James, would you pass me that box of comfits
from the table by the bed?'

'The wheels of that chair—they can be pushed by hand, can't they?'

'Yes.'

'Push them, then. It's not far to the table.'

The boy opened his eyes in astonishment. 'But. . . but——'

'Go on. If you can do it I'll bring one of Flossie's pups to see you.' The boy's face brightened and he leaned forward to grip the wheels. His frail hands whitened as he pushed.

'It moved!'

'Of course it did,' said James, surreptitiously moving the chair a fraction further with his foot. But then Alanna, who for some reason could never bear to leave James alone with her son for long, came in. When she saw Tony straining to turn the wheels she shrieked in horror and ran forward to stop him.

'No, Mama! I must do it! Uncle James says he'll bring a puppy for me if I can.'

'A puppy! You must surely be mad, James! Anthony would be coughing and wheezing half the night if an animal came in here. Come, my darling, Mama will get you what you want. This box, was it?'

James gave an exclamation of impatience and left the room.

The next morning there was a note from Bradpole, requesting an interview with Lord Wintersett. Sasha Calvert was expected about the middle of April, and would be staying in a house rented from the Earl of Ambourne in Dover Street. James gave a twisted smile at the thought. It was ironic that Ned should give shelter to a Calvert, for Ned and he had been at school together and the Earl was one of James's few

close friends. Not that Ned knew anything of the
events on Anse Chatelet so long ago, for the story of
Tony's suicide in the West Indies had remained a
well-kept secret. Alanna had wished it so for the sake
of her son, and the Calverts had had their own reasons
for hiding the truth. The world at large had been
allowed to think that Tony had succumbed to the
tropical climate.

When they met, Mr Bradpole's manner was grave.
'I have been unable to ascertain which packet boat
Miss Calvert and her niece took from the West Indies.
The passenger lists are most inadequate. But numbers
of people are arriving in London every day for the
season, and I have learned from Lord Ambourne's
man of business that he is expecting his tenants to
move in next week. Are you still as adamant, Lord
Wintersett?'

James hesitated. In truth he had recently had
occasional feelings of distaste for this vendetta against
the Calvert family. But it was not in his nature to
reveal weakness or lack of decision, so he evaded a
reply. 'What about affairs on Anse Chatelet?' he
asked.

'News travels slowly between England and the West
Indies, and even more slowly between Barbados and
St Just. I do not expect to hear for some time.'

'Tell me when you do. I'll decide then what action
to take.'

Soon after that he tried to persuade Alanna to talk
about the past. 'Believe me, Alanna, I am far from
wishing to raise any ghosts. But the time is approaching when I must decide what to do about Sasha
Calvert, and I need your help. I need to know what
really happened.'

Alanna's blue eyes filled with tears. 'I have told you over and over again,' she whispered brokenly. 'It was a nightmare, James. Why do you force me to remember?'

'Try. Were you and Tony happy before you went to St Just?'

'Oh, yes!' she cried. 'We were deliriously happy! And on the island, too. Right up to the moment it happened. Yes, we were happy.'

'You were living at the house—Anse Chatelet?'

'Yes. Lord Calvert had invited Tony to stay there while he explored the island and sought out new plants.'

'Who else was living there at the time?'

'Let me see... Lord Calvert was there, and Sasha, and Rodney—but he was an invalid. And the elder brother—Richard, I think he was called. And little Lucy.'

'And what happened?'

'That woman—Sasha. She hardly ever spoke to us in the house. But she followed Tony everywhere on his expeditions.'

'Where were you during these expeditions?'

'I stayed behind at the house, at Anse Chatelet.' She said defensively, answering his unspoken criticism, 'I suppose it would have been better if I had been able to go with Tony, but it wasn't what I was used to! I found the heat too much.'

'What about Tony? Surely the climate was new to him, too.'

'He was so fascinated by the plants out there that he didn't seem to notice it. Or me.' She added forlornly, 'He was always out.'

'When did you learn that Tony was having an affair with the Calvert woman?'

'She was so clever, James! She never went near him in the house. And when they were out everyone thought she was just guiding him through the forests. It never entered my head that she would appeal to him, for she wasn't at all like me. She was not at all feminine. But all the time... My poor Tony! My poor darling Tony!' She began to sob.

James set his teeth. 'I've nearly finished, Alanna,' he said as gently as he could. 'Tell me, if you can, what happened before Tony died.'

'I will, I will, James. But not now. I must go to see Anthony——'

'Mr Gimble is with Anthony. Tell me what happened, Alanna.'

She sat down again. 'I... I wasn't feeling well. I told Tony about... about the baby, and... and that's when he confessed. That he was in love with Sasha Calvert, and he wanted to leave me. There was a dreadful scene. I was distraught after it. Perhaps I should not have done what I did.'

'What did you do?'

Alanna paused and wiped her lips with her handkerchief. Then she continued, 'I went to Lord Calvert, to tell him how badly his... his daughter had behaved. He didn't believe me at first, but finally he said he would confront them. We were waiting on the terrace when they came in. When her father accused her Sasha just laughed.' Alanna was white to the lips, and she closed her eyes as she said, 'I shall never forget that laughter. It is still ringing in my ears.' She said this with such genuine anguish in her voice that James was moved to pity. He was about to suggest that

Alanna should rest for a while, but she was already continuing,

'Can you imagine how Tony felt when she said. . . she said—— Oh, James, with such an expression of scorn!—she said she despised him, that she had no intention of taking him away from me, however besotted he might be. That one lover more or less made no difference to her, she had plenty, and any one of them was more thrilling than a tame little botanist. That I was welcome to him and could take him home with her good will.'

With an muffled exclamation James got up and brought his fist down on the mantelpiece. 'Go on!' he said harshly.

'Lord Calvert was beside himself with rage. He must have known what sort of a woman his daughter was, but he pretended to blame Tony. He swore to ruin him, to throw him off the island, and to see that he was never allowed back anywhere in the West Indies. I don't think Tony heard any of it. He was. . .he looked like a ghost, a zombie they call them out there. Then he went to our rooms. I followed him a few minutes later but. . .you know the rest.'

'And Richard Calvert?'

'Richard? What about Richard? What has Richard to do with this?'

'Didn't he die about the same time?'

'Later—after Tony. But the deaths were unconnected, I think.' Alanna swallowed. 'Richard fell off a cliff on his way back to Anse Chatelet. He was drunk. I believe he usually was.'

'They were a pretty lot! But now only Sasha is left. What shall I do about her? Anse Chatelet may be said to be mine if things go as planned. Is that enough?'

Alanna's pretty face showed her distress as she pleaded, 'I don't want you to take Anse Chatelet! Leave Sasha Calvert where she belongs, where we will never see her again. Send her back, James! Don't even try to see her! Send her away!'

'You are talking nonsense! How can I send Miss Calvert away? And why should I?'

'You do not know her! She is a wicked liar—she casts a kind of spell over her victims till they do not know what to believe. They said on the island that she had learned the arts of voodoo. Look at the way she dazzled my poor Tony until he was driven to his ruin.'

'She is surely not such a Circe now! She must be well into her thirties.'

Alanna ignored him. She was becoming hysterical again. 'Send her away! Make it impossible for her to remain in England. She ruined our lives once and she will do so again unless you get rid of her!'

'I suppose that is one way,' said James thoughtfully. 'To disgrace her somehow in the eyes of society so that she has to leave England. It would be a kind of poetic justice, after her father's threats to Tony. But it would not be easy to do anything like that without involving the niece, too. And that must be avoided, for neither she nor her father were involved in this sordid affair.'

'Why are you so scrupulous about the niece? The Calverts are all the same.'

'Lucy Calvert is innocent and must be protected,' said James firmly. 'But have no fear, Alanna. Sasha Calvert will pay for Tony's sufferings—and yours.'

'I like your idea of poetic justice, James. If you destroyed the Calvert woman's credit in the eyes of the world, then no one would believe her stories,' said Alanna slowly. She smiled for the first time that evening. 'Oh, yes, James! I think that would be the best idea of all! If you wish, I'll help you in that. In fact I think I have the beginnings of a plan already. Why don't you leave it all to me!'

'Alanna, you are too impetuous! Sasha Calvert is not yet in England. When she arrives she should be given time to become known in society, and to establish her niece. Then we shall see.'

CHAPTER SIX

SERENA and Lucy, together with Sheba, were carried
to London in a hired post-chaise. The chaise was
comfortable, and the journey not long, so they arrived
in Dover Street in reasonably good order. The Earl's
agent was waiting for them. He introduced himself as
Etienne Masson, and they found to their surprise that
he was French. 'Though I prefer to describe myself as
Norman, *madame*,' he said with a smile.

He introduced the footman, John, and the housekeeper, Mrs Starkey. Mrs Starkey curtsied and said in
a soft, West Country voice, 'Your rooms are ready,
ma'am. Shall I lead the way?' While John supervised
the unloading of their many valises and had them
carried up to the rooms, Masson gave them the direc-
tions for the best shops and the sights he thought they
would like to see.

'John knows London very well, madame. He will
accompany you anywhere you go.'

'Always?' asked Lucy in astonishment.

'It is the custom, *mademoiselle*,' the agent replied
apologetically, with the smile that Lucy always seemed
to attract.

'And I for one am grateful for it,' said Serena.
'From what I have seen of it so far, the size and bustle
of London appals me.'

'Forgive me, *madame*. You have only just arrived.
You will soon see that London is in fact very small—
the part of it which you will need to know, that is.

Er. . . Lord Ambourne seemed to think that since you are a small household Mrs Starkey might combine the services of steward and housekeeper. She is experienced in both kinds of work. She has a number of domestics to help her in the house, but if you would prefer to engage maids for yourself and Miss Lucy Calvert I will arrange it.'

Serena was secretly relieved that the household expenses would be so much lighter, but simply replied, 'It is kind of Lord Ambourne to take such trouble. We have brought our own maid with us from St Just, and I think she will be enough, but I will let you know a little later what we decide.'

'Then I will take my leave. I hope you will enjoy your stay here.'

After Monsieur Masson left, Serena and Lucy explored the house. It was delightful.

'How can Lord Ambourne bear to let it out? Does he not use it himself?' Serena asked.

'The Dowager Countess occasionally stays here when she is on her own. But when the Family are in London,' said Mrs Starkey, and Serena could hear the capital in her voice, 'they stay in Arlington Street—at Rotherfield House. They are all in Normandy at the moment, but I believe they will be here later in the season.'

'I hope so,' said Serena, 'for I should like to thank Lord Ambourne in person for his kindness.'

Mrs Starkey smiled. 'It's probably her ladyship you ought to thank, Miss Calvert. Very particular, Miss Perdita is, about her house. Lady Ambourne, I should say. She lived in it before she was married, you see, and his lordship kept the lease on because she likes it

so much. But I'm forgetting my duties. Would Miss
Lucy or yourself like a refreshment?'

Serena had wondered somewhat apprehensively
about the domestics in Lord Ambourne's establishment. The servants at Anse Chatelet had all known
her since she was a child. Betsy, the housekeeper
there, had been Serena's nurse, and Sheba had been
Lucy's. For many years Serena had relied on all of
them to help her in keeping Anse Chatelet viable, so
the relationship between household staff and mistress
had been more informal than was usual. She had
heard dreadful stories from Mrs Galveston and her
friends of maids who were more conscious of position
than their mistresses, of footmen who despised anyone
who did not know his place. It had been impressed on
her that she must always keep her distance with
London domestics, otherwise they would 'take advantage'. Another source of worry had been Sheba's
position in the household. Would London domestics
accept Sheba? But the stories were all proved false as
far as the servants in Dover Street were concerned,
and Sheba, with her tales of magic and her warm grin,
quickly made herself as popular in the servants' quarters here as she had been in Surrey. Mrs Starkey had
known Lady Ambourne before her marriage and
admired her enormously. Indeed, she was devoted to
the whole Ambourne family, and was prepared to
extend her good will to any of their friends who
happened to be staying in Dover Street. It was impossible not to like her, for she was a sensible, kindly
woman, who soon took the interests of both her young
ladies to heart. 'But Mrs Starkey,' cried Serena when
she heard herself thus described, 'You mustn't call me

a young lady! I am supposed to be Miss Lucy's chaperon!'

'If you'll forgive my saying so, Miss Calvert, it's hard to believe that, when you're looking so handsome.' She regarded Serena admiringly. They were standing in front of the cheval mirror in Serena's bedchamber, where Mrs Starkey had been helping Sheba with the final touches for her two ladies' first appearance in society. Whether it was Mrs Galveston's lotion, or the new wardrobe, or something quite different from all of those, Serena was blooming. Her dark hair was now fashionably cut and arranged, her dark-fringed, amber-gold eyes glowed with well-being, and her skin was pearl-like. A conventional beauty she would never be, but she was striking. Too striking. With determination Serena took off her topaz-yellow silk dress, undid her hair and, while the bewildered housekeeper looked on, ordered Sheba to plait it into a tight chignon on the back of her head. Mrs Starkey might have disapproved of the freedom with which Sheba voiced her objections, but she heartily agreed with her sentiments.

'Sheba, that is enough! You have had your say, now do as I tell you!' said Serena. 'And fetch the green dress, the one with the high neck, if you please.'

Still grumbling under her breath, Sheba brought out a dress in a dull, greyish-green, and helped her mistress put it on.

'Sasha! What are you doing?' cried Lucy when she saw her.

'Looking like a chaperon,' said Serena grimly. 'We came to England to give you a London Season, Lucy, not to make a spectacle of me. It's you who must shine.'

'But I do!' said Lucy, twirling gaily round. 'Apart from you in your yellow dress, I'm the most beautiful thing I've ever seen! I'll swear this creation by Maria is more exquisite than any to be found in London! Lady Pendomer is a trump!'

'Lucy! Wherever did you pick that up?'

'Oh. . .' Lucy blushed. 'I beg pardon, Sasha. It's something Isabella's brother says.'

'Good God! About you?' asked Serena, looking at her niece in amusement. Growing even redder, Lucy nodded. 'Well, I'm sure the sentiment is admirable. But the word itself should not be any part of a young lady's vocabulary!'

'I'm sorry, Aunt Serena. I should have said that Lady Pendomer possesses the attributes of a very good friend!' She laughed and danced away, then came back to ask mischievously, 'Is it all right to say "Good God"?'

Lucy and Serena joined Lady Warnham at Mrs Galveston's mansion in Portman Square, prepared for the culmination of all Serena's plans—Lucy's introduction to London society. Lucy was nervous, but this merely gave a sparkle to her eyes and a becoming colour to her cheeks. At the rout party which followed Serena sat firmly with the chaperons, and only with difficulty did she disguise her pride. The daughters of most of the best families in London were there but, in Serena's eyes at least, not one of them could hold a candle to her niece. She noticed with some amusement that there was at the party a sort of magic circle of Lucy's Surrey friends, who tended to regard intruders with uneasy suspicion and were ready to see them off. But Lucy handled them all as if born to it. The girl was a credit to her training. When the two Misses Calvert returned to Dover Street that night they were both extremely satisfied with the evening.

Serena had not looked to see Lord Wintersett at Mrs Galveston's. The party had been specifically for the younger section of society, with the purpose of giving Isabella and Lucy some experience before they were launched into the deeper waters of a full-scale ball. It was hardly an occasion which would be graced with his lordship's presence! But he was never far from her mind. However busy she was, matching silks, trying on shawls, walking in the parks, occupied in the hundreds of activities which made up the London Season, she was always aware that he might suddenly appear round the next corner. She grew increasingly nervous of seeing him again. What would he think of her? Each time they went to a ball or some other grand affair she took out the topaz silk dress, wondering whether Lord Wintersett would be there. But each time she put it away again and put on something more modest. She was Lucy's chaperon.

It was Lucy herself who was instrumental in persuading Serena to change her mind. Lucy's nature was sunny, and here in London she was having the time of her young life. But one day she came in from a walk in the park with a face like a thundercloud. Serena was unable to find out what was wrong, but was even more concerned when Lucy refused an invitation to spend the next afternoon with Isabella. When she finally extracted the cause of Lucy's displeasure she didn't know whether to be relieved or annoyed.

'I've quarrelled with them,' said Lucy.

'Why?' asked Serena in astonishment. 'You've

always been such friends with Isabella. Whatever was
it about?'

'It wasn't Isabella. It was the other girls. They were
being unfair.'

'To you.'

'No, about someone else.'

It was clear to Serena who this was. There was only
one other person who could rouse Lucy to this
passionate defence. 'About me?'

'They called you a dowd, Sasha! They said you had
spent all your money on me, and had none left for
yourself. They started to make fun of you. It's not
true, is it?' Lucy was worried.

'Of course it isn't! I have lots of dresses, you know
I have.'

'Well, why don't you wear them?'

Lucy was seriously upset. Serena remembered that
Great-aunt Spurston had told her that Lucy would be
judged by Serena's appearance as well as her own,
had even given Serena money and jewels for this
purpose. Had she been selfish to ignore her great-
aunt's advice? Was it protection that she had sought
among the quietly dressed chaperons? Serena started
to get angry not only with herself, but with those who
had made her darling niece unhappy.

'Spend the afternoon with your friends, Lucy. Try
not to let what they say about me make any difference. They don't understand. But just between ourselves—just between ourselves, Lucy, my love—I
think they might be in for a surprise. . .'

So that night Serena put on her topaz silk dress,
together with the diamond drop earrings and bracelet
which her great-aunt had given her. Her black hair
was swept into a knot on top of her head and secured

with a diamond pin, and loose waves and curls framed her face. Her slender throat rose proudly from the low-cut neckline of her dress. Sheba's face was one big grin, and Mrs Starkey was very impressed. Lucy was ecstatic. 'You'll eclipse everyone there, Sasha! Oh, indeed they will be surprised!'

'Tonight, Lucy, I want you to exert yourself—as I shall. You will call me Aunt Serena, and we shall both remember all our lessons in the manners of the ton. We shall be very grand—true Calverts of Anse Chatelet. Do you agree?'

'Oh, yes,' breathed Lucy, her eyes shining.

The occasion itself was also grand—a ball at the Duchess of Stockhampton's, no less. Serena was aware of curious eyes on her as they mounted the huge, curving staircase, but she put her chin up a touch higher and ignored them. Her blood was up, and generations of Calverts marched with her. A chaperon she might be, but Lucy's aunt was no dowd!

Mrs Galveston greeted her in typical manner. 'Good evening, Miss Calvert! How well you look! I was beginning to wonder whether you would have been happier left in Surrey, but now I see I was mistaken. We may well find you a match, after all. Indeed, I doubt a respectable widower would have a chance with you tonight! Perhaps we should look higher?'

'I am not,' said Serena coolly, 'in search of a husband, Mrs Galveston. But I am touched by your compliments. May I return them? Town life obviously suits you.'

Mrs Galvston almost smiled. 'Your great-aunt would be proud of you. She always said you'd repay dressing, and there's no doubt you have an air about you tonight.'

Serena smiled and moved on. One of Lucy's beaux, a handsome, well set-up young man who was looking rather nervous, came up to ask if Lucy would stand up with him for the country dances.

'Thank you. May I first introduce you to my aunt? This is Michael Warnham, Aunt Serena. I believe you are acquainted with his mother?'

Serena hastily disguised her involuntary laugh with a cough and inclined her head slightly. As the young man took Lucy off with a sigh of relief, that maiden gave her aunt a very arch look.

Serena was soon besieged by various ladies with requests to be allowed to introduce Lord This and Sir That. She smiled charmingly at her admirers, and answered their eager questions willingly enough, but refused all requests to dance.

About halfway through the evening Lord Wintersett came into the room and gazed casually round. His eye lighted as if by accident on the chaperons' corner, and then moved on. Serena was not there. He surveyed the scene before him. She was not dancing, either. He had hardly expected it. Perhaps she had gone with her charge to the supper-room. He was about to leave the ballroom when an animated group on the other side of the room caught his attention, and he glanced at the central figure. She was surrounded and her head was bent. But he knew instantly who it was, and at that very moment Serena looked up and their eyes met. His widened as he saw the proud lift of the head and recognised the sparkle of diamonds in her ears. He looked briefly in the direction of the winter garden, and she closed her eyes once. No more was needed. A few minutes later he was standing at the end of the path, half hidden by the lavish arrangement of plants, when he saw Serena coming towards him.

James had not known what to expect—he had imagined everything from a sedate, quietly dressed ladies' companion, to a girl/woman uncomfortable in society and ungraceful in skirts. But he had never imagined anything like this cool, poised beauty. The diamonds in her ears and at her wrist, the pin in her hair, the exquisite dress—these were merely the trappings of a most unusually lovely lady. He was almost afraid to speak to her, almost afraid that he would find that his Serena had gone forever. Then she smiled, her eyes glowing with happiness, and he knew he had not lost anything. Nothing at all. He had gained more than he could ever have imagined.

'Lord Wintersett? You are shameful, sir! We have not been introduced, and yet you invite me to an assignation in the Duchess's winter garden!' Her amber-golden eyes were brimming with laughter. 'I dare swear you will even say I took it upon myself to follow you!'

'Serena! I am overwhelmed!' He took her hands in his. 'William was never as lovely as this!'

'Alas, poor William in his hand-me-downs! No! I am wrong. Fortunate William!' She gently released herself. 'At least in the short time allowed him he was free from observation and criticism—except by you, of course. Here in London it is very difficult to escape at all.'

'From your admirers, no doubt.'

'From my critics, rather! I must not stay long. The chief function of a chaperon is to prevent her charge from behaving as I am doing at this very moment! I must not be found out!'

'You! A chaperon? I know you said you were, but I find that impossible to believe. How can you possibly look after someone else when you so obviously need protection yourself?'

Serena looked at him mockingly. 'What, Lord Wintersett? "Taffeta phrases, silken terms" from you, of all people? You have no need to pay me pretty compliments, sir. I know you for what you are.'

'Do you, Serena? Do you? Then I must congratulate you, for I no longer know what that is myself. I know what I was in the past.'

A faint rose appeared in her cheeks. 'I must go,' she said. 'I have already been out here too long.'

'William was not so cowardly.'

'William was an invention, a dream. The reality is Serena, and Serena is bound by the conventions of society. I hear you have always avoided situations like this in the past, Lord Wintersett—indeed, that you have severely punished the poor ladies who have enticed you into them. Why do you wish to prolong this one?'

'You ask that? After our...tacit vow?'

The colour rose in Serena's cheeks, and she said hurriedly, 'I must return to the ballroom.'

'What if I refuse to let you go?' He took hold of her hand again.

She shook her head. 'Oh, no! Here in London you cannot blackmail me or force me to do your bidding— I have too much to lose.'

He tightened his grip and said softly, 'I think I could persuade you.'

'But you will not attempt to do so. It would not be

kind. And who knows? The great Lord Wintersett
might suffer a reverse. I might prove adamant!' She
took her hand away and moved towards the door. The
orchestra was striking up a waltz.

'Dance with me, then!' When she hesitated he swept
her into the ballroom and on to the floor. He put his
arm at her waist, and at her warning look he laughed
and said, 'Strict propriety, I swear, Serena!' Deco-
rously they circled the room, but there was that about
them which drew all eyes. The young bloods admired
Lord Wintersett's conquest, the young ladies envied
Serena for her daring capture, for the duration of the
evening anyway, of society's most eligible and most
dangerous bachelor. The matrons and chaperons whispered behind their fans and shook their heads.
Wintersett was beginning another of his flirts! It was a
pity that it should be quiet Miss Calvert. Perhaps her
success tonight had gone to her head.

But the two who were dancing were oblivious to all
this. They were lost in each other. James held Serena
with the lightest of touches, but they could not have
felt closer if he had embraced her. A curious feeling
of certainty mixed with a dangerous excitement ran
between them, surrounded them, isolated them from
the rest of the room. Watching their mutual absorp-
tion, society wondered and gossiped.

At the end of the dance Serena made to return to
her seat, but her partner refused to let her go. 'No!
Come to the supper-room—I want to give you champagne, Serena. I wish to discuss a promise.'

'A promise?' she echoed, flushing again.

'You would not listen to it in Surrey. You told me
to wait until we met in London. Now we have met,

and I will not wait any longer to claim what you must know is mine.'

'Aunt Serena!' Lucy's voice broke the spell. 'So this is where you are! You decided to dance after all?' Lucy looked curiously at Lord Wintersett.

'Lucy!' Serena was blushing in real earnest now. 'I. . .I. . .' She glanced at Lord Wintersett and took hold of herself. 'Lucy, I wish you to meet an. . .an acquaintance of mine, Lord Wintersett. Lucy is my niece, Lord Wintersett. And my charge,' she added with a warning in her voice.

Lucy's eyes were huge. 'Wintersett?' she asked. 'Lord Wintersett? But Aunt Serena——'

'Lucy——'

'What your aunt means to say, Miss Lucy, is that it does not do to believe all the stories you hear. Am I right?' James was enjoying himself. He had little doubt that this charming girl would discover in a very short time what sort of acquaintance he intended to have with her aunt, but was content to leave it for the moment. 'May I escort you both to the supper-room? We might discuss these stories over supper.'

Still looking slightly puzzled, Lucy allowed herself to be ushered to the other side of the ballroom. Here they were met by Michael Warnham.

'Lucy! Oh, good! You've found your aunt.' He looked curiously at Serena and Lord Wintersett, but decided to continue. 'Have you asked her yet? No?' He turned to Serena, with a charming smile. 'Isabella and some of the others are making up a party to go to Hampton Court tomorrow. We should like Lucy to come.' Lucy's expression made it clear how much she would like to go. 'Do say she may, Miss Calvert! My mother has agreed to act as chaperon.'

Serena was distracted as Lord Wintersett narrowed his eyes and turned his head swiftly towards the young man. She hesitated.

'Oh, Sasha, do say yes!' pleaded Lucy.

'*Sasha*!'

Serena smiled at Lord Wintersett's interruption. 'It's what Lucy calls me when we're alone,' she explained. 'A pet name from my own childhood. Very well, Lucy, my love. I'll see Lady Warnham later and arrange things with her. It's very kind of her.' She glanced at Mr Warnham and added, 'I suppose you wish to join Isabella now, Lucy? Perhaps Mr Warnham would escort you to her?' Lucy nodded, and Mr Warnham bowed and took her off.

'*Sasha*! That cannot be your name! But she called you Sasha. And he...the boy—he called you *Miss Calvert*! *Sasha Calvert*?'

Serena looked at Lord Wintersett in some concern. He was very pale, and he spoke jerkily.

'I had forgotten that we had not been formally introduced! How shocking!' smiled Serena. 'But if you don't like "Sasha", I am happy to answer to Serena. In fact, I prefer——'

'Why did you tell me your name was Serena?' he rapped out.

'Because that's what it is! Serena. But Lucy has called me Sasha since she was a baby.'

'Why did you not tell me this before?'

Serena looked at him as if he had suddenly become deranged. 'Why should I? My proper name is Serena. And you forget that until recently I was always "William" in Surrey.' She put a tentative hand on his arm. 'Are you not well, Lord Wintersett.'

'I am perfectly well, thank you,' he replied. As if to

bely this he put his hand to his head and ran it through his hair. 'Sasha Calvert,' he murmured. 'You're Sasha Calvert!' He looked down with distaste at her hand, resting on his arm. 'Your solicitude is excessive, I assure you,' he said coldly.

Serena flushed, then grew pale. 'Forgive me,' she said withdrawing the offending hand. A thought seemed to strike him.

'Where do you live, Sasha Calvert?'

Serena looked at him in amazement. He seemed to be speaking against his will, and his tone of voice was peremptory, even angry. He might have been able to speak to William like this, but not to Miss Calvert of Anse Chatelet! She replied stiffly, 'I fail to see why that should concern you, sir, but while in London I live in Dover Street. My home is in the West Indies.'

He turned away from her, and she thought she heard him say 'Oh, God!' but could not be sure.

Serena began to feel she was in some kind of nightmare. Though no one else was near enough to overhear their conversation, she could see that they were arousing a great deal of speculation. She said quietly, 'We are being observed, so it is difficult for me to speak. I am not sure what I have said or done to offend you, Lord Wintersett?' She paused a moment, looking up at his averted face with a plea in her eyes. When he remained silent she took a step back and said, 'Forgive me. I must have misunderstood your feelings. Or perhaps you are as capricious as your reputation would suggest. I will bother you no longer.'

He seemed to pull himself together at this, and turned again to face her. She was astonished at the change in him. His eyes were empty of feeling and his

face was like stone. He eyed her up and down with a
curl to his lips, then cast a glance round the room,
'You are right, Miss Calvert. We are being observed.'
He smiled and raised his voice as he drawled, 'No, it
is you must excuse me. I must admit I can hardly tear
myself away—especially after the idyll in the winter
garden, which you so. . .hopefully arranged. But, alas!
I must. However, you look so delightful that I am sure
there are many others here who would be only too
glad to take my place. Your servant, ma'am.' He
bowed and strode out of the room.

By exercising every ounce of self-control Serena
pulled herself together and kept her head high as she
walked back to the bench where Mrs Galveston and
Lady Warnham were sitting. She would not give the
assembled company the satisfaction of seeing the
extent of her shock or of watching her scuttle to some
convenient alcove or cloakroom to hide herself like a
hurt animal. When one of the Warnham sons offered
to fetch her some refreshment she accepted gratefully,
and took care to drink the champagne he brought
slowly and with appreciation. After a short while the
trembling in her limbs stopped, and she began to grow
very angry. Her pride would not have allowed her to
cut the evening short, but it was this anger which
helped her to endure it.

It was obvious that the massive snub Lord
Wintersett had delivered her so publicly was the chief
topic of conversation among the mothers and chaperons present, and though some of them regarded her
with sympathy there was a certain amount of head-
shaking and shrugging of shoulders. They all knew
that Lord Wintersett was a dangerous man to tangle
with, and, in the opinion of some, Miss Calvert had

been foolhardy in showing her feelings so openly.
They had all watched that waltz.

Criticism and sympathy were equally intolerable to
Serena, and, since she did not lack partners, she
escaped both by accepting every invitation to dance.
She dazzled them all. The diamonds in her ears glittered with no greater intensity than Serena herself,
but she could not have said afterwards who had
danced with her, or how long they had danced with
her, or what they talked about while they were dancing. At some time in the evening Lucy joined her,
obviously having heard some of the gossip, but Serena
said softly but fiercely, 'No, Lucy, not now. Tell me of
your outing tomorrow, tell me what you had for
supper, or what Mr Warnham was saying, or anything
you like, but do not, I pray you, mention. . .' She
stopped. She found it impossible to say Wintersett's
name.

The evening eventually came to an end and Serena
was at last able to escape to the haven of Dover
Street. She could not avoid Lucy's anxious questions,
but told her very little. She did not know herself what
had happened to cause Lord Wintersett to change so
rapidly, so how could she explain it to Lucy? After a
short while Lucy gave up asking questions and set
herself to restoring her aunt's spirits. For perhaps the
first time in their lives Lucy was the one who gave
comfort that night, and Serena was the one who
needed it.

Serena's behaviour in the next week did much to
re-establish her in the eyes of society. Mrs Galveston
had arrived in Dover Street the day after the ball and,
though she gave Serena a hard time herself—harder
than she realised—she also gave her some excellent

advice. After this Serena went about her usual visits and outings with composure, warding off all impertinent questions and comments by admitting, apparently frankly, that she had roused Lord Wintersett's anger and had had to pay for it. 'As a colonial,' she would say with a disarmingly rueful smile, 'I'm afraid I still have to learn what is done and what is not done. I think the gentleman in question——' she still could not say his name—'took my lack of formality for something more than I intended. Tell me, is he always so concei...er...so quick to assume that the ladies are in love with him?'

While there were still some who looked knowing when they heard this, most people were so impressed by Serena's quietly confident manner that they began to think that Lord Wintersett had indeed been too hard on a newcomer from abroad, that his well-known aversion to being pursued had in this instance misled him, and soon Serena was generally held to have been treated ungallantly. All the same, society looked forward with interest to see if there was to be another encounter between Lord Wintersett and Miss Calvert.

It was a week before this happened, and in the meantime Serena made a new acquaintance. Lord Ambourne's mother had returned earlier than expected from France, and had arrived in Rotherfield House the day after the Duchess of Stockhampton's ball. She called on Serena soon after that. When she was told that the Dowager Countess of Ambourne was in the carriage outside and wished to know if she were at home, Serena's heart sank. Of course she must receive her—it was very gratifying that the Countess should take the trouble to call. But another

Mrs Galveston was not a pleasing prospect, and this
high-born lady would be even worse, she was sure.
Serena was due for a surprise! John ushered in a tiny
figure in a pelisse and bonnet in the very latest mode,
who came forward saying in a charming French
accent, 'My dear Miss Calvert! How agreeable to meet
you! Forgive me for calling on you so early, but Lady
Pendomer's letter was written in such terms that I felt
I had to see the paragon she described as soon as
possible! And my son asked me to visit you, also.' She
surveyed Serena. 'But *alors*, you are much better than
I expected!'

Serena smiled her first genuine smile since the ball
as she indicated a chair and they sat down. 'It's very
kind of you to call, Lady Ambourne, but I'm afraid
Lady Pendomer is over-partial. I am no paragon.
Paragons are perfect, and I am far from that!'

'That is just what I meant! Perfection is very boring,
don't you agree? Now you must give me news of Lady
Pendomer, and then tell me about yourself. I wish to
know everything!' The Countess settled comfortably
in her chair, accepted some refreshment from a beaming Mrs Starkey, and proceeded to delight Serena for
the next half-hour. Though Lady Ambourne had the
indefinable air of a great lady, she was not at all
haughty or reserved. She talked freely of her son and
daughter-in-law, of whom she was clearly very fond,
and had Serena laughing at her descriptions of her
grandsons' antics. 'You will think me a doting grandmother, Miss Calvert—but how can I help it when the
children are so clever and so good? Well, perhaps not
"good" exactly—but so charmingly naughty!'

At the end of the visit the Countess asked Serena
to call on her soon in Rotherfield House. 'Bring Miss

Lucy Calvert with you—I am sorry not to have met her. Perdita and Edward will not be back from Normandy for a few weeks yet and I miss them very much, so you will be doing me a kindness. In fact, I should like to arrange some kind of evening party for you both, for it's time we had something to brighten up the family mansion—a barn of a place, Miss Calvert, but it does very well for balls and the like. Living in it is less agreeable.' She departed, leaving behind a faint breath of a perfume and a strange feeling of comfort. Though Serena had said nothing, of course, about Lord Wintersett, she had found the Countess warm and sympathetic. She would be a good listener if Serena ever needed one.

CHAPTER SEVEN

FOR a week after the Duchess's ball Lord Wintersett was not seen at any of the drums and assemblies held in the evenings, nor was he observed riding in the parks or walking in the gardens of London during the day. This surprised no one. It was said that he had recently been in the habit of disappearing to his estate in Surrey for days at a time. Though Serena secretly gave a wry smile at this, she was grateful for the respite. When she and Lord Wintersett next met she wanted to be in command of herself. Keeping composed in company in general was one thing. Coming face to face with a man she could have loved—for, lying awake in the hours of darkness, she had faced that fact—and a man who had treated her so inexplicably was quite another. However, they were both present in the Assembly Rooms exactly one week after the ball. Though Lucy was not there, having gone with Lady Warnham to another gathering, Serena stayed by Mrs Galveston, for she took care nowadays to behave with utmost circumspection.

He came in late with a lady on his arm, a ravishing blonde with a startlingly good figure. It was a pity, perhaps, that the lady was wearing pink, thought Serena critically; blondes should not wear pink. Nor was it perhaps in the best of taste to choose a dress which, in spite of its elaborate trimmings, so clearly revealed the lady's ample charms. Serena's own dress of pale blue zephyrine caught up over a slip of white sarsnet silk, which she had thought so pretty, suddenly seemed very tame.

'The devil!' exclaimed Mrs Galveston, startling Serena into turning round to her. 'Look at them! His lordship, looking as cool as you please, and Amelia Banagher. I thought that connection was finished some time ago, I must say.'

'Who is the lady, ma'am?'

'It is better for you not to know, Serena.' This was said with pursed lips. 'Indeed, if Miss Lucy were with us I should most certainly take you both home immediately.' Then, as her love of gossip got the better of her, she leant forward and said confidentially, 'Amelia Banagher comes of a highly respected Irish family. She married Lord Banagher when she was seventeen, but they haven't lived together for years, and her mode of life since has shocked everyone—though not quite enough to have her totally ostracised. Everyone knows that she was Wintersett's mistress last year, though they were discreet enough about it. They say she took it very hard when he discarded her. I wonder how she persuaded his lordship to bring her tonight? And how did she wheedle that magnificent necklace out of him?' The couple had been advancing up the room and both Serena and Mrs Galveston could now see them more clearly. 'He paid a fair penny for that, I dare say, if those rubies are real.'

The sight of Lord Wintersett had given Serena an unhappy pang, but now the anger which had never been far below the surface since the night of the ball began to burn again. 'They are real, and he did indeed pay a pretty penny, ma'am. I fancy you will recognise it when—if—they come any closer. The lady is wearing the Cardoman necklace.'

Mrs Galveston looked suitably shocked, and turned to Serena with an expression of sympathy. When she saw Serena's face her look changed to one of apprehension. Her young friend was flying flags of anger in her cheeks, and her eyes were glowing like those of a cat. 'I think we should leave now, Serena,' said Mrs Galveston, sounding nervous for the first time in years.

'I would not think of it, ma'am,' said Serena between her teeth. 'That would carry the flavour of retreat. And I am in no such frame of mind.'

It was too late in any case. Lord Wintersett was upon them and at his most urbane.

'Mrs Galveston, your servant, ma'am. I believe you know Lady Banagher?' Unsmiling, Mrs Galveston inclined her head by no more than a millimetre. Lord Wintersett turned to Serena. 'Amelia,' he said, without taking his eyes, which were glittering with malice, from Serena. 'May I present Miss Calvert of Anse Chatelet? Miss Cardoman Calvert.'

The two ladies exchanged what hardly passed for a curtsy. Lady Banagher raised an eyebrow. 'Cardoman? Isn't that the name——' She fingered the ruby hanging in the cleft of her breasts and gave Lord Wintersett a slow smile.

He took her fingers and kissed them lingeringly, then with a sideways look at Serena said, 'I believe it is called the Cardoman necklace, my dear. Miss Calvert, was it not at one time a valued possession of the Calvert family?'

'Hardly,' drawled Serena. 'It belonged to us, certainly, but the family has wanted to sell it for years.

Like so many other things, Lord Wintersett, its history is somewhat...tarnished.' With totally spurious concern she asked, 'Oh, dear, am I to understand you were the mysterious purchaser?'

Lady Banagher looked startled. 'But I thought it was a gift from a king? From King Charles?' She turned to her companion. 'You said——'

Serena swept on. 'King Charles had it made for his mistress, Lady Banagher. But there have always been so many of those, have there not? However, I think the necklace looks charming on you. Just right.' Mrs Galveston made a strangled sound and Lady Banagher at first looked uncertain, and then her brow clouded as she began to wonder whether Serena's compliment might not be all it seemed. It was clear that Lord Wintersett was in no doubt. His face, which had been somewhat pale, darkened, and he said curtly, 'Come, Amelia. It's time we danced. Mrs Galveston will forgive us. Miss Calvert.' He bowed and removed Amelia, who was still looking puzzled.

Mrs Galveston regarded Serena with admiration. 'Your great-aunt was always telling me what a spirited girl you were, Serena—I hope you will allow me to call you Serena?—but I must confess that when I first met you I was disappointed. But no more. I have never seen Lord Wintersett at such a loss. My felicitations. I think you may consider his unkind behaviour at the Duchess's ball well returned.'

Serena, still angry, said, 'I'm afraid it was ill done to involve Lady Banagher, however.' Mrs Galveston said something regrettable, which Serena ignored. Instead she continued, 'But you are wrong to think I was taking revenge for Lord Wintersett's behaviour at the ball, Mrs Galveston. That would have been better forgotten. I am convinced that for some reason which I cannot fathom Lord Wintersett means to injure me in any way he can. I believe he bought that necklace and put it on his mistress in order to bring the Calvert name into disrepute.'

'Oh, come, Serena. The necklace is too expensive a bauble to play with like that! It must be worth five thousand pounds at least! You must not let your imagination run away with you!'

But Serena remained unconvinced, and her suspicions were confirmed later in the evening. During one of the country dances she found herself partnered with her adversary—for that was how she now regarded him. She faced him across the set. He was pale again, and she saw now that he was thinner than he had been in Surrey. But his eyes were diamond-hard and his mouth set in ruthless lines. She remembered that she had once accused him of a lack of kindness. Now he looked. . .pitiless. They joined together to move up the room.

'I congratulate you on your rapier wit, Miss Calvert. But, for all your brave words, I think you did not enjoy seeing a necklace worn by your mother and grandmother round the neck of a harlot for all London to see,' he said.

'Conceited, mad, and no gentleman, either! Fie, fie, Lord Wintersett!' she replied mockingly. 'Have you forgotten that the lady is your partner for the evening, sir, when you call her such a name?' They swung away from each other, then as they returned she added, 'But you may hang the necklace round all such ladies in London for all I care; it makes little difference to me. My mother died when she was not much more than twenty, so I never knew her. As far as I am

aware she never wore the necklace.' She smiled
sweetly as they parted again, then said, as they came
back together to move up the set, 'So if your ambition
was to cause me chagrin, your ruse has failed. An
expensive mistake. Oh, but I was forgetting—the *rich*
Lord Wintersett does not consider such things.'

'By God, ma'am,' he said in a voice of suppressed
fury, 'if the necklace is to be worn by a harlot, then it
should be round your own neck!'

Serena was so shocked by the term he had used and
the very real animosity in his voice that she stumbled
and nearly fell. With relief she realised that they had
come to the end of the set and she could escape.

In bed that night she lay awake asking herself over
and over what had provoked that last remark. It had
not been idle abuse, she was sure. For some reason
Lord Wintersett regarded her as a Jezebel. But *why*?

James returned from the Assembly Rooms to Upper
Brook Street with his mind in a most unaccustomed
state of turmoil. He had planned the evening knowing
that Sasha Calvert would be at the Assembly Rooms
that night. He had relished the thought of Sasha's
humiliation when the world realised that the Calverts
were being forced to sell their most prized possessions.
How her Calvert family pride would resent seeing the
precious Cardoman necklace paraded before the
world on such an unworthy neck! For this he had
engaged the help of his former mistress, Amelia
Banagher, who had now become notorious for her
numerous affairs. She was always hopelessly in debt,
and a suggestion that her ex-lover might settle some
of her more pressing bills had been enough to persuade her to accompany him, and to wear the neck-

lace. Indeed, after the evening was over and James had escorted her back to her rooms, there had been an awkward moment when she had made it clear that she was ready to do more—for love. James was relieved that he had managed to extricate himself without offending her, for he had found the idea surprisingly repugnant. And, for all his planning, the evening had been a failure. He had no sense of triumph, felt no satisfaction.

He knew why. In spite of the discovery that Sasha and Serena were one and the same, he still felt a strange kinship with Serena. He had such a strong sixth sense about her that he was sure that his insults tonight and on other occasions had struck home. But only once had she lost her self-possession and revealed her distress—when she had stumbled in the country dance. And instead of being triumphant he was ashamed. His savage outburst to Serena during that dance had not been planned. It was the result of an unexpected surge of anger at her steady refusal to be daunted. Since his was a nature which needed to remain in command of himself as well as others, he was furious at this loss of control. And then, worse still, when she had nearly fallen he had experienced an overwhelming desire to catch her, to protect her. It was enough to drive a man mad!

He sat now in his library, looking at the necklace. Its huge cabochon rubies gleamed dully in the firelight—a pool of blood in his hands. He smiled reminiscently as he thought of Serena's reaction to the sight of the necklace. It was impossible not to admire her. Few women would have responded with such spirit and wit to his insults, his attempt to diminish her in the eyes of society. She had never allowed herself to be diminished. Far from becoming discredited, she had gained society's sympathy and admiration, including his own. But what was he thinking of? How the devil could he possibly admire Sasha Calvert?

In the days that followed James was no nearer to finding peace. The thought of Serena/Sasha was like a canker, a goad, which kept him awake at night, and unable to rest during the day. He hated Sasha for her treatment of Tony, and he hated Serena for being Sasha. He despised himself for being so confused, for wishing to punish Sasha, while taking pride in Serena when she frustrated his efforts.

He went back to Surrey, thinking that his determination to discredit Sasha Calvert would be strengthened if he had another talk with Alanna, if he reminded himself of the unhappiness the Calvert woman had caused his family. But in Surrey he found himself going for long rides on the Downs, taking Douce on to the ridge, where he was haunted by the memory of 'William', of their talks, their arguments, their shared laughter. He remembered with bitterness his fears that he would lose Serena in London. As he had. He was tormented by the two contrasting pictures—on the one hand Serena, a woman of intelligence and compassion with an integrity he had never questioned, and on the other Sasha, the destroyer, the wanton. And this visit to Surrey, far from strengthening his determination, seemed to be undermining it, for doubts began to creep into his mind. In his initial shock and blind anger at discovering that Serena and Sasha were one and the same he had not attempted to set one against the other—Serena's good against Sasha's evil. But was it *possible* for the Serena he had known to have done the things Sasha was said to have done on the island? Perhaps she had changed? Perhaps Tony's death had caused her to reform? She must have been very young...in fact, *very* young! He must talk to Alanna again. But he could not bring himself to mention Serena to Alanna—only Sasha.

'Sasha Calvert told me recently that her mother was only twenty when she died, Alanna. However I try, I cannot reconcile this with the age of her brothers. Surely Richard Calvert was older than Tony?'

'Yes. Yes, he was.' Alanna's voice was nervous. 'Did I not tell you? I thought I had. Lord Calvert was married twice. The Sasha woman was the daughter of the second marriage.'

'So how old was she when you were on the island?'

'Why are you asking me? What are you trying to do, James?'

'Merely to establish some facts. How old was she?'

'I don't know! What does it matter?' said Alanna petulantly. 'Old enough! Sixteen or seventeen, I think.'

'She once said she was now twenty-seven. That would make her fourteen.'

'Fourteen, fifteen, seventeen! Am I a mathematician? You've been spending too much time with Miss Calvert! I told you what would happen. She's such a liar, she will bewitch you as she bewitched Tony... Oh, Tony, Tony!' Alanna burst into loud sobs.

James waited until she was quieter, then said, 'Fourteen is not much more than a child, Alanna. I find it difficult to imagine Tony deserting you in favour of a child.'

'You don't know what they're like in the tropics, James!' Alanna said between further sobs. 'The

women mature at a ridiculously early age. Many of
the natives have children at thirteen or even less! And
she—Sasha—ran practically wild all over the island—
she must have had her morals from them.' She burst
out, 'Why are you asking these questions? I tell you
she never left him alone! Poor Tony had no chance.
Dear God, why do you remind me?'

Alanna was now very distressed. She clutched at
James, pleading, 'Get rid of her for me, James! Have
nothing more to do with her, but get her sent back to
where she belongs, I beg you!'

Disguising his distaste for her melodrama, James
said patiently, 'Be calm, Alanna. It takes time.'

With an exclamation of despair Alanna ran out of
the room, leaving James with the feeling that, if she
had enacted these tragedies thirteen years before, he
for one did not blame his brother for seeking consolation elsewhere. He told himself that women were
often temperamental when they were breeding—had
Alanna chased Tony into the arms of Sasha Calvert
by her own irrational behaviour? With an exclamation
of impatience he realised that even now he was seeking excuses for the unhappy business. Alanna was
probably right. Sasha Calvert had power to make a
man believe anything!

Before the incident in the Assembly Rooms, Serena
would have been content to go through the rest of the
season accepting that Lord Wintersett no longer
wished to continue their friendship, and learning to
live without it. She had reluctantly concluded that the
fact that she came from the Colonies, and her irregu-
lar conduct at the outset of their acquaintance—dressing as a boy and roaming the countryside—had caused

him to have second thoughts when they met in more
formal circumstances. The explanation was not completely satisfactory. The charm with which he had first
greeted her, his compliments in the winter garden—
these had seemed real enough. And that dance. . . Her
thoughts shied away from the dance. But his behaviour afterwards had been so extraordinarily cruel!
Then she heard more stories of Lord Wintersett's
summary dismissal of females who pursued him, his
heartlessness in other matters, too, and she finally
accepted his treatment of her as not untypical. What
she found impossible was to reconcile the man in
London with the man she had known in Surrey.

But now the situation had changed. That he or
anyone else should dare to insult her by calling her a
harlot was not to be borne! Not without some action
on her part. She had no male protector to call on—
the nearest approach to that was Lord Ambourne,
and not only was her claim on him too slight, but he
was also on the other side of the Channel. Besides,
she had no wish to create further scandal by calling
on an outsider for protection. However, the thought
of Lord Ambourne brought the Dowager Countess to
her mind. She would see if she could consult Lady
Ambourne.

Accordingly Serena took the Countess at her word
and called on her in Arlington Street. As Lady
Ambourne had said, Rotherfield House was imposing
rather than homelike, but Serena was led through the
huge state-rooms to the back of the house, where
there was a small garden-room. Here her hostess was
sitting on a comfortable sofa and she insisted that
Serena should sit by her side. They talked for a while,
but finally the Countess sat back and, putting her head

on one side, said, 'I have enjoyed our chat, Miss Calvert, but you shall now tell me what is exercising your mind. If I can be of any assistance to you, you have only to ask.' Serena looked amazed and the Countess laughed. 'You look just like my daughter-in-law!' she said. 'Perdita swears I have second sight. But it isn't so. It was obvious to me that you were not entirely happy when we last met. Today you are angry, too. What is it, child? Begin from the beginning.'

Serena found to her astonishment that she was telling Lady Ambourne everything—her restlessness in Surrey after the freedom of her life on St Just, her expeditions to the Downs disguised as a boy, and her meeting with Lord Wintersett. She took care not to mention his name for she had decided that no purpose could be served by revealing it. And she had, besides, this ridiculous inability to say it! Her voice, which had been soft and warm as she had talked of her relationship with the gentleman in Surrey, grew more agitated as she went on to describe the gentleman's behaviour since. She omitted to say anything about the necklace, but told her listener the substance of the insult during the country dance. 'I am at a loss to explain it, Lady Ambourne. The gentleman's animosity is real. But he called me. . .called me. . .'

Lady Ambourne said the word for her. 'A harlot.'

'And he has no reason to suppose that I am anything of the kind!' cried Serena angrily. 'Our relationship on the Downs was totally innocent—more that of a boy and his mentor. I just don't understand! What am I to do?'

Lady Ambourne sat in thought for a moment. Then she said gravely, 'It is obvious to me that there must be more behind Lord Wintersett's behaviour than you have told me.' When Serena gasped she added, 'Please do not misunderstand, Miss Calvert. I do not believe for a moment that you are wilfully hiding anything of substance from me.'

'It's not that,' said Serena faintly. 'How did you know I was talking of. . .' She exclaimed impatiently as she once again found herself unable to say his name.

The Countess smiled. 'My dear child, I have known London society these past thirty years or more.'

'I suppose everyone is talking about us.' Serena's voice was bitter.

'There is naturally some gossip, yes. But I have heard nothing of what you have told me this afternoon—of Surrey and so on. And on the whole, you know, opinion in general is in your favour—if that is any comfort. Lord Wintersett is not universally liked.'

'Do you know him?'

'I'm afraid he is a great friend of my son's. They were at school together.'

In some confusion Serena started to gather herself together. 'In that case, you must forgive me, Lady Ambourne. I am sorry to have caused you embarrassment. I. . .I must go.'

'What are you thinking of, child? Edward's friendship with Lord Wintersett does not mean that I am blind to that gentleman's faults—any more than I am blind to Edward's faults. In some ways they are very similar. Oh, yes. I assure you they are! They can both be completely ruthless when it suits them—and they can be cruel. But Edward has been more fortunate than James. He was surrounded in his youth by a loving family, and he now enjoys a very happy marriage. James, on the other hand, had a tyrant for a father, and his family circumstances since his father's death have been most unhappy.'

'Is there no one he loves?'

'There are, or were, two. One is his mother, whose devotion was divided between her husband and her younger son. I have always thought that it says much for the basic soundness of James's nature that the other person he loved was this same younger brother. But he is now dead.'

'What happened to him?'

'He died abroad some years ago at about the time James came into the title. His mother has never properly recovered from her double loss.'

'Do you like him, ma'am?'

'I think I do. Edward is a good judge of men, and though James is generally held to be coldhearted I think this is not really so. But it would certainly not be easy to find out. Of one thing I am certain. He is a just man.'

'Then why is he so cruel to me?'

'I do not know, but there must be some reason which he thinks justifies his behaviour. Are you sure, quite sure, you cannot think of anything?' Serena shook her head. 'No. Well, I shall do my best to find out. Will you allow me to make some discreet enquiries?'

Serena took her leave a little later, after arranging to call on the Countess again in three days' time.

When Serena called at Rotherfield House again three days later she found the Countess in an unusually grave mood.

'Miss Calvert, I think I have at least found a previ-

ous connection between your family and Lord
Wintersett. If you remember, I mentioned a younger
brother who died abroad some time ago.' She looked
penetratingly at Serena.

'Yes?' Serena was puzzled.

'I am somewhat surprised that you do not seem to
know that he died on St Just.'

'Oh, no! Forgive me, Lady Ambourne, but that
cannot be so. If it were true I would have known of it.
Nothing ever happened on St Just without my
knowledge!'

'His name was Tony,' Lady Ambourne continued.
'Tony Stannard.'

In a voice that was almost unrecognisable Serena
said, '*Tony Stannard* is—was—Lord Wintersett's
brother?' Lady Ambourne nodded. 'Oh, God!' Serena
buried her face in her hands.

There was a silence. Finally Serena lifted her head
and whispered, 'I had no notion. . .I simply did not
connect the two names.'

'That is obvious, my child. However, the link is as
yet slight. There is little in the fact that Mr Stannard
died on St Just to account for Lord Wintersett's
enmity.'

Serena drew a long shuddering sigh and said, 'What
have you learned of his death, Lady Ambourne? What
does London say?'

Lady Ambourne was still grave. 'It was reported
that he fell victim to a tropical disease.'

Serena got up and moved restlessly about the room.
'Tony Stannard! Poor, poor Tony! And a Wintersett!
Oh yes! I understand now.' She stopped in front of
the Countess, who was looking as if she had more to

say. 'What is it, Lady Ambourne? Why do you look like that?'

'There are rumours that the circumstances of Tony Stannard's death were not as reported.' Serena turned away, but the voice with its charming French accent continued relentlessly, 'Rumour says that the young man killed himself. No one seems to know why, however.'

Serena remained silent.

The Countess appeared to be choosing her words carefully as she said, 'You came to me for help and advice, Miss Calvert. I would not normally press you to reveal anything you do not wish, but it seems to me that the cause of Lord Wintersett's enmity must lie in his brother's death. You have already confided a great deal of your story. Do you feel able to tell me anything more? I think I have no need to assure you of my discretion.'

Serena thought for a moment. 'I cannot discuss Tony Stannard's death, Lady Ambourne—not even with you,' she said slowly. 'But if it will not weary you, I will tell you something of the events which led up to it. They might well go towards explaining Lord Wintersett's enmity, for they reflect little credit on the Calverts. Though I should have thought it would be directed rather towards my family than to me. . .'

'My memory is very accommodating. I shall remember only what I need to know in order to help you. I should be extremely surprised if there is anything to your detriment in the story.'

'There is one aspect of which I ashamed. But I will tell you, all the same.'

The Countess sent for some tea and told Purkiss that she was not to be disturbed for an hour. Serena

was soon launched into the unhappy story of the
Stannards' visit to St Just.

'My father had heard through a Cambridge friend
that Tony Stannard wished to study tropical plants, so
he invited the Stannards to St Just, and offered them
the hospitality of Anse Chatelet. Tony Stannard was
newly married when he came to stay. His wife,
Alanna, was quite young and very pretty—I think she
was Irish—and at first they seemed to be devoted to
each other. But after a while she started to complain—
she didn't like the heat, she didn't like the insects, she
was afraid of what the sun would do to her complexion. It wasn't what she had been used to, I suppose.
Perhaps even more, it wasn't what she had looked for
in marrying Tony Stannard. I gathered that the family
was quite rich, and she had hoped to play a leading
role in society.'

'It was natural, I suppose. A young girl, pretty,
married to a rich man. Surely she could reasonably
expect a fashionable life?'

Serena shook her head. 'I was still quite young at
the time, but even I could see that the study of plants
was Tony's life. He was a brilliant botanist, you know.
It was obvious that the fashionable world was not
for him. But Alanna Stannard was not really at all
interested in Tony's work, and she soon gave up
accompanying Tony on his expeditions into the rain
forest. I must confess I was secretly glad.'

'Why?' asked the Countess, opening her eyes wide.
'What had it to do with you?'

'I used to guide Tony on his expeditions. I knew the
island better than anyone. If Mrs Stannard came with
us we were constantly having to stop—to rest, to help
her across a stream, to clear a wider path. . . And we

had to carry all sorts of extra supplies—creams and
lotions, cushions and rugs, water, wine. We were
always having to stop for picnics. You can imagine
how impatient a child would get with all this.'

'So Alanna stayed at home?'

'Yes. She remained all day on the veranda, feeling,
no doubt, that she was being treated very ill. You will
observe,' said Serena with an apologetic smile, 'that I
was not particularly fond of the lady.'

'I had noticed,' said the Countess with a smile. 'But
tell me—now that you are older and have more understanding, do you not feel some sympathy for her?'

Serena thought for a moment, then said, 'I don't
know. What happened afterwards makes it impossible
to judge.'

'Pray continue.'

'First I need to digress a little, to give you some
background. What do you know of the West Indian
islands, Lady Ambourne?'

'Not very much. St Just is one of the smaller ones,
is that correct? As you know, Henry Pendomer is a
second or third cousin of Edward's, so all my knowledge comes from him. He's the Governor of St Just.
But doesn't he look after some other islands as well?'

'Yes. Sir Henry governs a number of the smaller
islands together. In fact, he only spends about four
months a year on St Just.'

'And?'

'Thirteen years ago, when the Stannards came to
stay at Anse Chatelet, my father was still strong and
active. The Calverts have lived on St Just since the
days before there was a Governor there at all, and
until very recently they have always regarded the
island and its people more or less as their own. The

islanders looked on my father as a sort of uncrowned king, and my. . .my. . .brother Richard regarded himself as the Crown Prince.' Serena was finding this more difficult than she had thought, but the steady, sympathetic gaze of the Countess encouraged her to carry on. 'We all loved Richard. We were dazzled by him. I was his shadow, his slave, always trying to ride as well as Richard, to shoot as well as Richard. . . I had no other friend, wanted no other companion.' She sighed. 'He was always causing trouble, yet he would charm his way out of it all. He had such an infectious smile—you would find yourself laughing when a minute before you had sworn you would never speak to him again. And women. . .they were fascinated by him. It's difficult to explain. . .'

'You have no need. I have met someone quite like him, Serena.'

Serena looked doubtful, but carried on. 'It ruined him. The adulation, the feeling that he could do anything. . .anything at all, the lack of any restraint. . . I think that if he had had to struggle for what he had, if there had been a war he could have fought in, a cause he believed in, he might have been saved. But there wasn't. And finally he was overtaken by his demons. . . Even my father rejected him in the end. . .' Her voice faded and she paused. Then she squared her shoulders and said in a clearer voice, 'I was telling you about the Stannards. About Alanna Stannard. A pretty, new face on St Just was just the sort of challenge Richard enjoyed. He was never satisfied until he had conquered, and Alanna Stannard was instantly an object of desire.'

'And she. . .?'

'I think you must know the answer to that, Lady

Ambourne. Mrs Stannard was lonely, bored, and feeling resentful towards her husband for his neglect of her. She spent long hours alone. Whenever Richard set out to charm anyone he was irresistible. In this case the end was inevitable, I suppose.'

'Was there no one to stop them, to talk to Alanna?'

'No one. The Pendomers had just left St Just for their tour of the other islands. By the time they returned it was all over.'

'And no one else? What about your father?'

'Until the final, dreadful end, my father could never see any wrong in Richard. And I was a child—I didn't even realise what was going on until father told me later, when he thought I was old enough. Apart from that, I was out most of the time with Tony Stannard. I knew the island and its inhabitants so well, you see. I knew where the interesting plants were.'

'Poor Alanna!'

'Why do you say that? Alanna at least returned alive to England. Richard and Tony are both dead.'

'But Alanna's baby was born prematurely, and the child is still an invalid even now. Alanna never sought the gaiety of London life, but has lived in retirement in Surrey, looking after her son, ever since she returned. But you say your brother Richard died, too?'

'He fell two hundred feet from a cliff path near Anse Chatelet. We found his body the next day on the rocks below.' Serena shut her eyes and when she opened them again they were full of anguish. 'I blame myself for his death,' she said in a whisper.

The Countess put a sympathetic hand out and would have spoken, but Serena continued, 'Did you ...did you say that Alanna had a child, Lady

Ambourne? After she came back from the island?'

'Of course. He is Wintersett's heir.'

'But——' Serena stopped abruptly. 'No. No matter.'
She got up again and looked out at the gardens. Then
she added bitterly, 'I wish I had never come to
England! If it were not for Lucy I would return to the
West Indies tomorrow!'

'Come, come, this is no way to talk!' The Countess
led her back to the sofa. 'We have now accounted for
Lord Wintersett's unfriendliness. It is, I suppose, natural that he should dislike the name of Calvert, but I
think I can talk him into a more reasonable frame of
mind. He might even call later this afternoon.'

Serena said slowly, 'I am not sure we have quite
accounted for it. What he called me was specific, not
a slur on my family as a whole.'

'Then he must explain himself,' said the Countess
briskly. 'Unless. . . No, he is surely not such a fool!
Can he believe perhaps you. . .er. . .consoled Tony for
his wife's disloyalty? You were with him a great deal,
were you not? No, no! It is too absurd!'

'Indeed it is, I think—even for him! I was fourteen
years old—a child! Probably even younger than most
girls of that age. I regarded Tony simply as a wonderful source of knowledge—no, of marvels. He was a
born teacher, and I was thirsty for anything he could
tell me about the plants and trees of my own home.'

'Of course, of course. There must be another
explanation.'

CHAPTER EIGHT

WHILE Serena's conversation with Lady Ambourne
was taking place Lord Wintersett was making his way
to Rotherfield House in response to an invitation from
the Countess. He had arrived in London two days
before and had found Lady Ambourne's note,
together with a letter from Bradpole requesting an
interview. The lawyer had arrived the next day with a
folder of documents and the news that the substitute
manager on Anse Chatelet had indeed defaulted on
the payments, and that the agent in Barbados had
foreclosed as ordered. 'I have the documents here.
They only require your lordship's signature.' He
spread some legal papers out on the table.
'Er. . .Norret, the manager, has pleaded that he was
unaware how important it was to get the quarterly
payment in on the exact day, and further, that
unfavourable winds and tropical storms delayed his
journey to Barbados. He is supported in his plea by
Lord Pendomer, the Governor of St Just. I am aware
that I risk your anger in saying this, Lord Wintersett,
but I will say it just the same. It can do you no credit
to foreclose on what is in effect a technicality. I hope
you will consider changing your instructions to the
agent, and restoring Anse Chatelet to its former own-
ers.' He waited, but James was deep in thought. The
lawyer sighed and continued, 'However, if you remain
obdurate, the documents are here.'

James was in a quandary. For years he had sought

421

possession of Anse Chatelet with the sole aim of evicting the Calverts. The estate was now his, if he insisted—but he could not quite bring himself to let the axe fall. He thanked Bradpole brusquely for his news, and told him to come back in a week for his decision. Bradpole's face, which had been very serious, lightened when he received this indication that his client might be reconsidering his course of action.

James was still pondering this question as he made his way to Rotherfield House. But as he drew nearer to Arlington Street he began to speculate on the reason for Lady Ambourne's invitation. Ned, he knew, was still in France, so it was not to meet him. Strange! He was however very willing to visit the Dowager Countess, for he had always found her a sympathetic and amusing hostess. He arrived promptly at the appointed hour and was received by Purkiss.

It was at this point that Purkiss, the Ambournes' elderly and experienced butler, made his worst mistake in all his years of service. The lapse occurred when the visitor presented himself at the door of Rotherfield House, gave Purkiss his hat and cane, and said easily, 'You needn't bother to announce me, Purkiss. Is Lady Ambourne in the garden-room? Right, I'll go through.'

Normally the butler would have frozen such informality on the spot, but Lord Wintersett had been a familiar figure in the house since he had first arrived in an Eton jacket many years before. Purkiss also knew that her ladyship was expecting him, and that she wished her two visitors to meet. It was true that she had told the butler when he had taken refreshments in earlier that she was not to be disturbed for an hour, but that had been almost an hour and a half before. So Purkiss allowed Lord Wintersett to carry on, without first making sure that her ladyship was ready for him. . .

James strode confidently through the state rooms, but went more slowly as he drew nearer to the garden room. He could hear voices—the Countess had a visitor, it seemed. He stopped short, astounded, when he realised that the voice was Serena's. What was the Countess up to? She had been in London for some time now—she must know something of the situation between Serena and himself! Was she trying to effect some sort of reconciliation, perhaps because of Ned's position in this? Was that why he had been invited?

Then he heard Serena say, 'It's true that I pursued Tony Stannard relentlesly. All over the island.' There was a smile in Serena's voice. 'I suppose I had a bad attack of hero worship! At first he didn't take much notice of me. I was just an importunate child, a nuisance! But then, as time went on, he learned to tolerate my company and even to enjoy it! In the end we became surprisingly close. I think you could even say that I loved him, after a fashion.'

James's first impulse was to turn on his heel and stride back the way he had come. His second was to continue into the garden room and demand to know why his brother was being discussed. He was on the point of doing this when he stopped abruptly. The Countess had just asked 'I suppose you were missing Richard's company?'

'I suppose it might have begun like that. But at one time Tony seemed as important to me as Richard.'

'You haven't yet told me why you felt responsible for his death?'

James found himself holding his breath. What would Serena say?

'It was what I said to him shortly before. . .before he d. . .died. I was in a rage—I've always had a hot temper and this time I was in a fury. I told him. . . I told him I despised him. That he'd be better dead.' Her voice dropped so that James had to lean forward to hear. 'And he was dead, very soon after that.' There was a silence. Then Serena said unevenly, 'Why did I say such things to him?'

There was a rustle of silks, and Lady Ambourne's voice was soft as she said, 'But you were little more than a child! How were you to know that your words would have such a catastrophic effect?'

'He no longer saw me as a child. What I said affected him mortally. He had heard my father telling him he had no future on the island or anywhere else, and he looked to me, sure that I would comfort him. We had been so close! But suddenly I felt I hated him and wanted him to know it. It is my belief that my rejection of him that night caused his death.'

'My dear! How can you blame yourself? You surely did not really wish him dead!'

'Lady Ambourne, please do not misunderstand me. I regretted his death and still regret it—the Calverts do not seem to have had a happy hour since that dreadful time. But even now I cannot feel that there was any other way out for him. I only wish that I had never uttered the words which drove him to it. I think they will be on my conscience forever!'

James turned and went back the way he had come. When he reached the entrance hall he gave Purkiss a message to deliver to Lady Ambourne, something about urgent business elsewhere. The message was confused, for his mind was on what he had just heard. Sasha Calvert was a self-confessed adulteress, a woman who had driven Tony to his death, and whose chief regret was that this had made the Calverts unhappy! That and her uneasy conscience! It was enough to remove any doubt about Anse Chatelet—and more! He sent for Mr Bradpole that night.

Alanna Stannard sat in the window of the drawing room and gazed out resentfully at the green lawns and flower-filled rosebeds of Wintersett Court. The London season was now at its height. How she would have loved to be part of that colourful parade! For thirteen weary years she had lived here in retirement, miles away from any kind of amusement. She had devoted her energies to looking after her son, with only a half-witted mother-in-law for company and an occasional visit from her formidable brother-in-law to enliven the monotony. She sighed. At first it had been easy, for it had seemed a suitable atonement for her sins. Then she had grown discontented. She still was, but now she was feeling more nervous with every day that passed.

For years she had lived with the lies she had told of her sojourn on St Just, and, though she had never been really happy, she had at least felt secure. Her word had never been doubted by her husband's family. Not only were the West Indies thousands of miles away—far enough to discourage casual communication—but it had been in the interests of both families to hide the truth as each had seen it. The Stannards had believed they were protecting Tony's memory

from the shame of betraying his pregnant wife, and
the Calverts had probably wished to protect their own
family from the scandal of Richard's seduction of a
guest. The facts surrounding Tony's death had therefore been well concealed by both families. All this had
worked to Alanna's benefit.

But now, with the advent of Sasha Calvert in
London, Alanna's world was suddenly threatened. She
was living on a precipice. She had done her best to
prevent any meeting between James and the Calvert
woman, but her efforts had failed. James had clearly
been talking to her in London, and had recently shown
signs of doubt, had even come down to Wintersett
Court to question Alanna further. Any day now he
might ask Sasha Calvert directly about the events on
St Just thirteen years before, and what would happen
then? Alanna shifted in her seat uneasily. Surely he
would take the word of his own sister-in-law, the
mother of his heir, against that of a Calvert? Of course
he would!

Alanna got up, fetched her hat and parasol, and
went outside. But though the sun was warm, she
shivered. What if James didn't take his sister-in-law's
word? Her old friend from Ireland, Amelia Banagher,
had told her how well society regarded Serena
Calvert, as she now called herself, in spite of James's
efforts to discredit her. Amelia, who had not enjoyed
the débâcle with the necklace, had also hinted that
James was more impressed than he admitted. How
stupid men were! These small tricks with necklaces
and suchlike were useless! Something outstanding was
needed, something to ruin Sasha Calvert once and for
all! Then no one would believe her, whatever she said,
and she would go back to her West Indian island and

be forgotten! Alanna already had a half-formed plan
in her head. It required a little more thought, for
failure would be disastrous, and then she would see
what could be done. But she would need help...
Alanna decided to write to Amelia.

While Alanna Stannard was plotting to do mischief to
Serena, Serena herself was doing her best to promote
Lucy's interests. She had never before put into words
her feeling of anguish and guilt about her brother's
death. Now, though Lord Wintersett's dislike was still
only half explained, she felt better for having unbur-
dened herself to the sympathetic ear of the Countess,
and felt ready to put her own problems aside for a
while and concentrate on Lucy. Michael Warnham
had become most particular in his attentions, and
Serena was taking pains to get to know him. He was
certainly an eligible candidate—twenty-three, heir to
a barony, and certain to inherit a large share of his
grandmother's considerable fortune. Isabella, his sister, was Lucy's great friend, and the Warnhams
appeared to approve of a possible match. Serena
found him pleasant and amusing, but she was not yet
certain that he had enough strength of character to
retain the respect of her high-spirited niece. If he had
not, it would be a sure recipe for an unhappy marriage. So for the moment Serena was keeping an open
mind. Lucy seemed to find much to admire in Mr
Warnham, and Serena was amused to see how willing
her niece was to defer to his judgement. There might
be more to this young man than she had thought!
   Her efforts on Lucy's behalf had led her into attending more balls, concerts and assemblies than she
would otherwise have wished. She had always

intended to keep in the background, leaving Lady
Warnham and Mrs Galveston to chaperon the two
girls. But in order to meet Michael Warnham, to
observe him in company with Lucy, she had to take
an active part in society. She was aware that Lord
Wintersett's eyes were frequently turned on her,
sometimes brooding, sometimes with an unaccounta-
ble gleam of satisfaction, but she never allowed herself
to be put off. Serena was proving to be a minor
success.

One evening, at a reception given by the French
Ambassador, Serena was delighted to see the
Countess of Ambourne approaching. The Countess
was accompanied by an extremely handsome man in
his thirties, dark-haired and grey-eyed.

'Ah, Serena!' she cried. 'I have such a pleasant
surprise for you! I wish you to meet my son Edward.'

Lord Ambourne smiled quizzically as he bowed.
'My mother has her own quaint way of putting things,
Miss Calvert. You must forgive her. The pleasant
surprise is mine, I assure you!'

Serena laughed and curtseyed. 'Lord Ambourne, I
would forgive your mother anything. She has been so
kind to me—as you have, too. I find your house in
Dover Street delightful.'

'The house belongs to my wife. I am pleased you
like it.'

'Then I must thank her. Is she with you?'

'She is in London, but not with us tonight. She was
a little tired after the journey.'

'I am sure Perdita would wish to meet you as soon
as possible, Serena. I shall arrange it,' said the
Countess. 'But have you yet spoken to the
Ambassador? Come, let me take you to him—he will

be intrigued to meet someone from the West Indies.
He has estates on Martinique, you know.'

'Ma'am,' protested Serena. 'His Excellency surely
has more important people to speak to tonight?'

'That shows you do not know him! Now me, I have
known him since we were children, and I assure you
he will always take time to talk to a beautiful woman.'
The two ladies, escorted by Lord Ambourne, made
their way through the crowded rooms into the
Ambassador's presence. His Excellency received the
Countess with cries of pleasure, and they talked rapidly in French for several minutes. Then he turned to
Lord Ambourne and asked most kindly after his family and his estate in Normandy. Finally he turned to
Serena, who was amused to find that the Countess
could perform rigorously correct introductions when
she chose.

'Miss Calvert,' said the Ambassador, 'I am
enchanted. Is it too much to hope that you will dance
with me? We could talk about Martinique and St
Just.'

Serena looked somewhat apprehensively at the
Countess, who nodded encouragingly. 'I am honoured,
Ambassador,' she replied with another curtsy.

The Ambassador proved to be an excellent dancer
and an amusing companion. Serena was enjoying herself enormously when halfway through the waltz an
aide came up to him and said something discreet. The
Ambassador pulled a face. 'Miss Calvert, I am desolate. Duty spoils my pleasure. But do not worry, I
shall leave you in good hands.' He looked round to
the gentleman who had been standing by them. 'Ah
yes! May I present the gentleman who has been
described to me as the best dancer in London, Miss

Calvert? Lord Wintersett! You are more fortunate that you deserve, milor'!' With a smile and a graceful bow the Ambassador was gone. Serena and James were left facing one another on the edge of the floor.

James bowed. His face was cold. 'Miss Calvert?'

'Please forgive me, Lord Wintersett,' said Serena, equally coldly. 'It was kind of the Ambassador to think I wanted to carry on dancing. But I find I am tired, and I must return to my companions. They will be looking for me——' She turned to go, but was held firmly.

'I think you do not understand, Miss Calvert. A request from an ambassador is the equivalent of a royal command. You must dance with me, however repugnant the idea is—to either of us.'

They set off in silence. For a while they circled the room carefully, avoiding anything but the slightest contact, but as time went on they each relaxed. They drew imperceptibly closer, James's hand more firmly at Serena's waist, Serena's hand resting more confidently on his shoulder. Serena shut her eyes. It was like the first time she had danced with this man—the same strange mixture of excitement and certainty, the same feeling of wordless communication. What James Stannard thought about her she could not begin to guess. But whatever it was, it had no effect on what she, deep down, had come to feel for him when they were in Surrey. It was astonishing, but nothing that had happened since had changed that. It seemed to have become part of the fabric of her being. Unwilling to continue with this melancholy train of thought, Serena opened her eyes. James was looking down at her with a bemused look in his eyes, as if he, too, was remembering their idyll.

Encouraged, Serena smiled, tentatively at first, then as his gaze softened she said hesitantly, 'Our friend William—Blake the poet, not Blake the boy from the hill—has words for this situation, I think. Will you listen?'

'What are they?' he said, still looking at her with a smile in his eyes. She began, ' "I was angry with my friend, I told my wrath——" ' But she was interrupted before she could go any further.

' "My wrath did end"?' The smile vanished. His face changed once more to that of an implacable enemy. His hand gripped hers cruelly as he said softly, 'I think not, Sasha! You do not escape so lightly, for all your wiles! And recalling our relationship in happier times will not help you, either. You deserve no privilege of friendship.'

'But *why* do I not deserve it? Why will you not discuss it with me?' In spite of herself her voice had risen.

'I suggest that you control yourself, Sasha Calvert. Unless you wish us to be the subject of yet more gossip? That would suit me better than it would you, I believe.'

The waltz came to an end, and the other dancers started to leave the floor. Serena began to follow them, but then stopped, turned to Lord Wintersett and said with determination, 'I *will* have it out with you! Here, if you will not find a more suitable place!'

He looked at her with a twisted smile on his face. 'Why is it that you can rouse my admiration, even though I know you for what you are? You are unique!' He took her arm and led her off the floor. 'Come!' he said, and opening the door of a small salon he ushered her into it. Serena just had time to see

Lady Ambourne's troubled gaze before Lord Wintersett shut the door. 'Now?'

Serena turned and faced him steadily. 'Lord Wintersett, I will not refer again to our "relationship in happier times". That period of my life shall be forgotten. I claim no "privilege of friendship", either—indeed, when we first met in London, and you behaved so...in such an ungentlemanly manner, I believed that my behaviour in Surrey had given you a disgust of me. I could not account for the sudden change in your conduct towards me in any other way! But there must be more to it. This antipathy, no, it is much more than that—this personal animosity puzzles and distresses me. I cannot account for it. I wish you to tell me its cause!'

'Bravely said! If a little disingenuous. You already know why.'

'You hold the Calverts responsible for your brother's death?'

'The other Calverts are all dead themselves. I hold you responsible, you alone, Miss Calvert.'

'But this is prejudiced nonsense! I loved Tony! I never meant him any harm!' When he turned away from her with an expression of disgust, she cried desperately, 'Help me to understand! They call you a just man—hard, but just. Why are you going to such lengths to punish *me*?'

'You do not yet know to what lengths I am prepared to go, Sasha Calvert!' The expression in his eyes as he turned back to face her was so malevolent that she took a step back.

'You hate me!' she whispered. 'I believe you really hate me. Oh, God! How could I be so deceived? To think I once imagined I could actually love you!'

'Love! I would sooner be loved by a loathsome toad! What could you possibly know about love? I've heard you talk of the kind of love you offer! A love that tells a desperate man that he is despised! A love that drives a man to his death!'

For a moment Serena was taken aback. The words were so familiar. Then it came to her. 'You were there! At Rotherfield House. You must have been eavesdropping! Eavesdropping on my conversation with Lady Ambourne. How dare you?' Serena was fast losing her temper. The thought that this man had listened unseen to the confession of her deepest, most painful feelings about her brother's death outraged her.

She lost control altogether when she heard him say, 'This moral stance sits ill on a harlot, Sasha!'

Something inside Serena exploded and she slapped Lord Wintersett with the full force of her arm behind the blow. He instantly grabbed her to him and kissed her hard. She tried to scream, but he held her mouth to his, so that she could hardly breathe. Her struggles to escape were futile, for his arms trapped her in an iron grasp. She felt sick. This kiss was worse, much worse than the first embrace on the hill, for though that had lacked any respect, this had not the slightest element of more tender feelings in it. Anger, a desire for revenge, a primitive lust, but no regard for her, not the slightest hint of any feeling for her as a person. When he finally released her she was so dizzy that she was unable to stand, and he had to hold her again to save her from falling. She stood rigidly, staring at him in horror, unable to hide her fear and revulsion. His face was white to the lips, a dazed look in his eyes.

'I. . .I. . .I don't know what to say, Serena. I don't know what came over me. . .'

She managed at last to move away from him, to walk to the door like a sleepwalker.

'Serena!' She stopped, but did not turn round. 'Serena, it was never my intention to attack you in that barbaric manner. I am sorry, deeply sorry.'

'I believe you,' Serena said harshly. 'You would rather kiss a loathsome toad, you said. But you k. . . kissed me just the same. Do you think that saying you are sorry can wipe it from my memory?' She put her hand on the doorknob.

He continued desperately, 'If you go out of the room now, looking as you do, the whole of London will be scandalised.'

Serena turned round then and looked at him ironically. 'Do you not think London should be scandalised at the punctilious Lord Wintersett behaving like a savage, a wild beast?'

'I am ashamed of my behaviour, Serena. I deserve your scorn and theirs. But even you must agree that I was provoked. Do you not think London would be equally scandalised at Miss Calvert using her fists like an untamed gipsy? No, wait! I am not concerned for myself in this instance. It is you I wish to spare. Wait a short while, please. Give yourself time to recover. You cannot wish to arouse the sort of comment I am sure would otherwise follow.'

She looked at him incredulously. He meant it! 'What are you at now, Lord Wintersett? I was under the impression that that was precisely what you wanted!'

'Not in this instance. This was no part of my plan. I. . .I do not know what came over me. I will say once again that I deeply regret what I did, and ask you to forgive me——'

He stopped as Lord Ambourne and his mother came into the room, leaving the door open. The Countess went quickly over to a door in the wall on the right and unlocked it. A maid entered. Then Lady Ambourne took Serena by the hand, and said in a slightly raised voice, 'Gracious, Serena, you look ill, child. How thoughtful of Lord Wintersett to bring you in here when you felt faint! I am sure Marie was a help until I managed to come. I am only sorry that Lord Wintersett's message did not reach me sooner. I have informed Mrs Galveston that I will take you home, and she will stay with Lucy and her friends. Thank you, Marie, you may help Miss Calvert to her feet.' She whispered, 'Forgive the French farce, Serena! It's the best I can do to prevent scandal. You have been closeted with Lord Wintersett for some minutes, and the tongues are wagging outside. We need not tell them that Marie has only just arrived! I've told her to swear she was here all the time.'

Lord Ambourne was giving his friend a long, straight look. As the little party made its way to Lady Ambourne's carriage he said coolly, 'Shall you be at home tomorrow evening, James? May I call on you? I think we have things to discuss.'

The next day was sunny, but there was a cool breeze which sent the remaining blossom on the trees in Green Park drifting over into the garden of Rotherfield House. The Ambourne family were sitting in the garden room. The window doors were wide open to let in the air, while those sitting on the pretty sofas and chairs were protected from the wind. The

younger Lady Ambourne was laughing up into her
husband's face as he spread a shawl over her knees.

'Stop, Edward!' she protested. 'I am not cold, not
in the slightest. Nor am I any longer tired! There is no
reason on earth why I should not visit Miss Calvert as
soon as I am respectably dressed! I wish to meet her!'

Serena heard this as she followed Purkiss through
to the garden-room and she thought what an attractive
picture they made. Lord Ambourne's dark head was
bent over the sofa on which his wife was lying, and
she was stretching her hand out towards him. The
expression on his face belied his next words.

'Perdita, I am already angry with you for coming
downstairs while I was out! Dr Parker expressly forbade it.'

'Pooh! You are tyrants, you and Dr Parker both,
and it will do neither of you any good to be pandered
to. Do you not agree, Mama?'

'Yes, but you know Edward will have his way,
Perdita. Except. . .'

'I knew it! What are you plotting?'

'I believe my plot is already here. The mountain has
come to Mahomet,' said the Dowager Countess, rising
with a hand stretched out in welcome to Serena. She
dismissed Purkiss with a nod and brought Serena
forward to her daughter-in-law's couch.

'My mother surpasses herself. The metaphor is not
even apt yet for Perdita. But now you may have the
pleasant surprise of meeting my wife, Miss Calvert,'
said the Earl with a grin. Serena looked down at a
woman of about her own age with eyes of the darkest
blue she had ever seen. The younger Lady Ambourne
was as beautiful as her lord was handsome, and
together they made a striking couple. It was easy to

see the reason for the Earl's concern, for Lady Ambourne was clearly in what was usually called an interesting condition.

'Surprise? What do you mean, Edward? The surprise—and the pleasure—are mine, Miss Calvert,' said Lady Ambourne, adding as her husband gave a laugh and even Serena smiled, 'What have I said? Why are they laughing, Mama?' When they explained, she said, 'Well, the thought may not have been original, but it is none the less true. Welcome, Miss Calvert. As you see, I find it a trifle difficult to get up at the moment——'

'You will not attempt to do so, Perdita,' said the Earl firmly, and when she looked rebellious he smiled and added, 'Please?'

'Then, Miss Calvert, you must sit down next to me and amuse me,' said Lady Ambourne. 'You see how I am beset with despots and conspirators. Now, I have a hundred things to ask you. You must tell me what you think of London, you must tell me about Miss Lucy and her début—I hear that Michael Warnham is growing most particular in his attentions, by the way— and you must tell me about Lady Pendomer and her family.'

The Dowager Countess left them together, and Lord Ambourne soon excused himself too. Serena spent a very pleasant half-hour at the end of which she could see that Lady Ambourne, in spite of her brave words to the contrary, was getting tired. She rose to go.

'I hope you will come again, soon,' said Lady Ambourne. 'We are not here in London for long. Edward has some affairs in London to see to, but we shall return to Ambourne as soon as he has finished. I

miss my children, and, though I wouldn't say so to
Edward, I must own that I find London tiring. But I
should like you to come again before I go.'

'You are very kind, Lady Ambourne. And so is
Lady Ambourne...er...the Countess...I mean your
mother-in-law.'

'Confusing, is it not. Well, the Ambournes do not
stand on ceremony when it is inconvenient to do so. I
think you had better call me Perdita. I notice Mama
calls you Serena, and I propose to do the same. We
may not have known each other in person for very
long, but Lady Pendomer's letters have made me feel
you are an old friend. Bring Lucy with you when you
next come. I should like her to talk to me about young
Mr Warnham, if she will. I am glad to hear you say
that you quite like his grandmother. I enjoy Mrs
Galveston myself, but there are many who find her a
tartar! Goodbye, Serena!'

Lord Ambourne appeared as Purkiss was ushering
Serena through the state-rooms. 'May I speak to you,
Miss Calvert?'

They went through to a study. Here the Earl gave
her a small glass of wine and saw her comfortably
seated.

'I hope you will not consider me impertinent, but I
am curious to know a little more of what happened
last night. Do you wish me to take the matter up with
Lord Wintersett?'

Serena grew pale. 'I...I think it is better forgotten,
Lord Ambourne. No harm came of it, I think, and...
and...' Once again she had this curious inability to
say Lord Wintersett's name. 'The gentleman had
already apologised to me before you came in.'

'For what?'

Serena pulled herself together. She raised her chin.
'It is kind of you to concern yourself, Lord Ambourne,
but I consider the matter settled. Lord. . .Lord W. . .
Wintersett embarrassed me, but, though I am
ashamed to admit it, I had provoked him.'

'You are sure that you are satisfied?'

'Yes. Quite sure.'

'I must confess I am relieved to hear you say so.
James is an old friend of mine, and I am not anxious
to pick a quarrel with him.'

'Oh, you must not think of it!' Serena cried. Then
after a pause she said, 'Lord Ambourne, you say you
are old friends. Has he ever spoken to you about his
brother?'

'Tony? Not a great deal. I never really knew him.
He was younger, of course, and rather a quiet person.
James used to talk a lot about Tony's work—he was
very proud of it. Tony was already making a name for
himself even before he left Cambridge, and we all
thought he was sure to go into academic life. He was
a bit of a monk at Cambridge and his marriage took
everyone by surprise, James most of all, I'd say. Why
do you ask?'

'What was. . .your friend's reaction to his brother's
death? Was he unbalanced by it?'

'What an odd question!' Lord Ambourne stared at
her, but though Serena grew pink she said nothing.
He shrugged his shoulders and went on, 'He was
certainly not unbalanced by it. I've never met any
man saner than James Stannard. But it did have a
strong effect on him, and he never mentioned Tony
afterwards.' He sat thinking for a moment. 'I suppose
he became more. . .inaccessible, though he was always
a bit cool, especially to anyone he didn't know. They

called him Frosty Jack at Eton, you know. He was
never so to me—we have been very good friends for
years.' He eyed her curiously. 'Why are you asking
me all this? Is there more to Tony Stannard's death
than the world knows? Did he in fact die of a fever?
Or is it true that he committed suicide?'

'I. . .I cannot tell you that. I was a child at the time.'
She began pulling on her gloves, and they both rose.
Then almost involuntarily she added forlornly. 'He
blames the Calverts for it all, and I suppose there's
some justification for that. But I find it strange that he
blames me in particular. I really don't know why.'

'Are you asking me to find out, Miss Calvert?'

Serena's thoughts raced. The idea was a tempting
one, but the two men had been friends for many
years. What if that friendship was destroyed because
of her? Lord Wintersett's apology the evening before
had seemed sincere—she doubted he would attempt
more tricks. Also, the season was more than half over,
and Lucy was now so well established in society that
Serena could reasonably take the less prominent role
that she had always wished for herself. If she could
avoid meeting Lord Wintersett for the short time left
he would forget her. Quite soon she would leave
England to return to the West Indies, and after that it
was most unlikely that they would ever meet again.
No, the mystery was better left alone.

She sighed and said, 'Thank you again, Lord
Ambourne. You are very kind. But I think not.
Instead, I shall try to avoid meeting your friend.
Goodbye.'

That evening over dinner Lord Ambourne asked his
ladies what they thought of Serena Calvert.

'She's a lovely woman, Edward. Not altogether in the usual manner...but those eyes! They are quite extraordinary—such a clear golden amber.'

'I would like an opinion on her character, Perdita, not her appearance. I can see her beauty for myself, and I agree with you. She is not completely to my taste—my preference is for sapphires, as you are no doubt aware—but very lovely.'

'She is unhappy, I think. Her face is sad in repose.'

'That is hardly surprising!' said the Dowager Countess. 'Serena's family history is far from being a happy one. She is quite alone in the world except for Lucy. And she has worked like a Trojan to keep the family estate going. Alicia Pendomer's letters have been so ecstatic on the subject of Serena's dedication to duty and other boring things that I was not at all looking forward to meeting her. But she is absolutely charming. I am quite baffled by James Stannard's behaviour—and very disappointed in him.'

'How can we judge, Mama? We hardly know anything of the matter. You tell me Serena Calvert is charming, but what value has that? She may even have been hardworking—but is she honest?'

Both ladies were quite clear on this point, and were incensed that Edward should think it necessary to ask.

After Perdita had gone to bed the Countess sought out her son. 'I don't want to worry Perdita with this matter, Edward, but I heard you tell James last night that you would like to see him.'

'Yes, I thought I would go in a few moments.'

'You wish to speak to him about his behaviour, I suppose? Are you and James about to fall out over this matter?'

'You may rest your mind, Mama. Miss Calvert has

said that she has no wish for me to take the matter further, so I am not about to challenge him, thank goodness. I'm glad she's so sensible. I cannot say I understand James's behaviour, but I shouldn't wish to lose his friendship over it. However, I think I would like him to be aware that Miss Calvert is a friend of the Pendomers and so entitled to some protection from me. I shall do it tactfully, so you need not look so worried. Do you know more than you have said about the affair?'

The Countess then related as much as she thought she could about the Stannards on St Just. It wasn't easy. She had given her word to Serena, so much of the story remained untold.

CHAPTER NINE

JAMES was not looking forward to this forthcoming meeting, any more than Lord Ambourne. He was not so rich in friends that he could afford to lose one, and Ned and his family had been very good friends indeed. During the dark days of his schooldays, when nothing James did ever pleased his father, when his mother treated him with indifference, and Wintersett Court was like a prison to him, a visit to Arlington Street or Ambourne had been like coming into light. Damn Sasha Calvert! Wherever he looked she was there, destroying everything he had ever valued.

When Lord Ambourne was announced the two men greeted one another cautiously, like fencers. But, to James's astonishment, it gradually became clear to him that Ned was not there to challenge or condemn. Unlikely though it was, Serena seemed not to have told Ned what had actually happened. It had been obvious the night before that his friend was willing to take on the role of protector, but Serena had apparently not desired him to do so. With a sigh of relief James produced a bottle of wine, and the two men sat down to chat more easily. One bottle led to another, until the candles were guttering in their sockets and the fire was almost dead. Ned asked idly, 'What *did* you do to Serena Calvert, old fellow?'

'She didn't tell you?'

'No, she said you'd apologised and that she had provoked you, and that she wished the matter to be forgotten. I'd give a lot to know what you did, though. It's my belief that Serena Calvert is a cool enough character, but she was certainly in a flutter last night.'

'I kissed her,' said James abruptly. 'And you're wrong about her being cool. She has a fiendish temper.' He fingered his jaw.

'Well,' said Edward, with a large gesture which betrayed how much wine the two friends had consumed. 'Well, the ladies often make a fuss about a kiss, but it can be a pleasant experience for all that. No harm done. She said so.'

'She said it had been a pleasant experience? I don't believe it.'

'Not that, no. But she said no harm had been done.'

'I wish I could believe that was true. I frightened her, Ned. And I'm ashamed of myself.' He burst out, 'That woman seems to bring out the worst in me. Sasha, I mean. Not Serena. No, not Serena.' He filled his glass and drank deep.

'You're foxed, James! Who's this Sasha woman?'

'She killed my brother.'

Edward sat up, reached for the bottle and poured some more wine into James's glass and some for himself. 'You're wrong, James, old fellow. Your brother killed himself, unless I'm much mistaken.'

'Who told you that?'

'Never mind. He did, didn't he?'

'Yes. Yes!' James got up and stood by the fire, kicking it with his boot. 'But *why* did he? You cannot imagine what it's like to live with that question, Ned. I don't suppose we shall ever know the answer now. I try to forget—I even succeed for a while, and then I go back to Surrey and see my mother and Tony's boy, and the question returns to plague me, together with the sense of waste, the bitter waste! You know what he was like, curse it! Why did he have to kill himself over a confounded woman?' James turned away from the fire and roamed restlessly about the room. 'He had his work—the Calverts couldn't have kept him out of it for long! God knows, the Wintersetts are a match for any damned colonials. And for Tony—Tony of all people—to do that to my mother. . . The devil take it! *Why*?'

'What makes you so sure that he killed himself over a woman?' asked Edward carefully.

'What else could it possibly be? Anyway, I have proof. I've even heard her admit it. Oh, for God's sake, let's leave it!' James looked moodily down at his glass and drank again.

Edward said slowly, 'I'll tell you something you might like to think over, James. A while back I almost made the biggest mistake of my life, just because I was too blind to see the truth. I could have lost Perdita because of it. Mind you don't fall into the same trap. Now tell me exactly what it is that you have against Serena Calvert?'

James stared at Edward and then he started laughing helplessly. 'Nothing at all, Ned, nothing at all!' Then he dropped down on his knees beside Edward, and whispered solemnly, 'But Sasha—now that's another question. Oh, what a surprise I have for her!' He slipped slowly down the side of the chair to lie in a heap on the floor.

Edward saw with regret that nothing more could be got from James that night. He called that gentleman's valet, and walked, somewhat unsteadily, back to Arlington Street.

The next morning Edward took one look at

Perdita's wan face, called Dr Parker, ascertained that
his wife would be able to withstand the relatively
short journey to Ambourne if it was taken in easy
stages, and declared that he and his wife would leave
London that afternoon. The Dowager regretted their
departure, but agreed with her son. Her daughter-in-
law smiled ruefully, wrote numerous notes, including
one to Serena, and then lay back thankfully in the
chaise and was carried away.

Thus it was that Lord Ambourne was unable to
pursue the mysterious question of Sasha Calvert and
the surprise in store for her. His overriding concern
for his wife caused all such thoughts to vanish from
his mind.

The following day James sat for most of the morning
gazing moodily into space. The meeting with Ned had
gone better than he had hoped. James was aware that,
had she wished, Serena could have caused a rift
between Ned and himself which would have been
difficult to heal. If Ned had heard the whole story of
James's behaviour at the French Ambassador's reception he would have been obliged to tackle his friend
about it. But Serena had not told him the whole story.
Why not? She had no reason to spare James. He had
insulted her, had attacked her, had even frightened
her. He frowned at the memory of the look in her
eyes when he had held her after that shameful kiss.
She was usually so dauntless, so spirited—the golden
eyes did not often hold such a look of fear, he was
sure. He got up impatiently. Why was he worrying?
For whatever reason, his friendship with Ned had
been preserved, and if all went well Sasha Calvert
would soon be out of Anse Chatelet and out of his

life. So would Serena. The thought did not make him feel any better.

James was relieved when a visitor in the form of Mr Bradpole came to distract him from his gloomy thoughts. But the damned lawyer brought with him the papers which completed Lord Wintersett's possession of Anse Chatelet. Neither gentleman felt particularly cordial. There was no comfortable chair for Mr Bradpole, no glass of Madeira, nor did the lawyer seem to wish it. Instead he gave the impression that he saw no cause for celebration.

'What do I do with these now?'

'The copies should be delivered to Miss Calvert, Lord Wintersett. Does your lordship wish me to retain the originals?'

'Of course. I'm not sure why you ask, Bradpole. Nor do I understand why you have brought the copies here instead of delivering them to Miss Calvert. You have her address.'

The lawyer said colourlessly, 'I thought your lordship might wish, even at this late stage, to reconsider your decision. Or, alternatively, you might wish to deliver them in person.'

'What the devil do you mean by that?'

'The acquisition of the Calvert estate has been an object with you for some time, Lord Wintersett. I believe the reason to have been personal rather than a matter of business. But if your lordship wishes me to deliver the papers I will, of course, do so.'

'Then do so, Bradpole' said Lord Wintersett curtly. 'Now, if you please—and damn your impudence!'

Mr Bradpole bowed and went out. James threw himself into a chair and wondered why the devil he was feeling so out of sorts. His head was aching, but

that could easily be accounted for by the amount of
wine he had drunk the night before. He had had
hangovers before now. It was not that. He smiled
sourly. Bradpole never gave up. 'Even at this late
stage'! Perhaps he should have ignored the lawyer's
implicit criticism and taken the papers round to Dover
Street himself? But truth to tell, he had been afraid.
After the scene at the French Ambassador's he could
well believe that Serena would refuse to see him
again. He got up and walked restlessly about the
room, reminding himself of the events on St Just,
holding them like a shield against the wave of desola-
tion which swept over him at this thought. After a
while he managed to subdue this ridiculous feeling
and sat down again to consider the lawyer's visit.
Serena would soon have the papers about Anse
Chatelet. How would she react to its loss? She would
probably be devastated, a thought which gave him
surprisingly little pleasure. This was Sasha's loss,
Sasha Calvert's loss, he reminded himself fiercely, but
it was no good. Thoughts of Serena were filling his
mind—regret for the pain he was causing her, a wish
that it had not been necessary. What the devil was
wrong with him? This was the culmination of years of
planning and waiting, and he should be feeling pleased
that they had borne fruit, not jaded and weary! The
trouble was that he seemed to be living in two worlds
at once, neither of them happy. He sat there brooding
for a while and then decided that a good dose of fresh
air would clear his head and possibly raise his spirits.
A ride in the park was called for.

On his return he found a note requesting him to
call on Miss Calvert in Dover Street at his earliest
convenience. He was astonished at the sudden feeling

of elation. The reason for her request mattered not at all. What was important was that Serena was at least prepared to face him again!

Serena was pacing up and down in the drawing-room of the house in Dover Street. The fateful papers lay where she had thrown them, scattered over the table in the window. Lucy sat wide-eyed and pale on the sofa.

'What does it mean, Sasha? We've always lived at Anse Chatelet; it's our home! He cannot take it from us! Can he?' Lucy's lip quivered as she spoke, and Serena stopped her pacing to take Lucy in her arms and attempt to comfort her.

'Don't cry, Lucy! Hush, my love! I'll get it back, I swear! Come, dry your eyes. He might come at any moment, and we must not let him see any weakness. He's a no-good——' Here Serena used some island patois which shocked Lucy out of tears and into laughter.

'Sasha! Whatever would Lady Pendomer say?'

Serena grinned at her niece. 'She wouldn't say anything, Lucy. She wouldn't know the words. I'm surprised you do!'

'I was brought up on the island, Sasha. You can't play with Joshua and the others without learning some of the things they say. How I miss Joshua and Betsy and the rest! Oh, Sasha, are we never going to see Anse Chatelet again?'

Lucy's mercurial spirits were descending once more. Serena said hastily, 'Of course we are! But Lucy, if you marry here in England, St Just would surely be less important to you than it has been till now. You like it in England, don't you?'

'Oh, yes, I love it! In fact, I'd miss Isabella and. . . and the others even more than I miss my friends on St Just. It's not that I don't love the people on Anse Chatelet, Sasha! I do, still! But. . .it's different here. Some of the people here are very important to me.' Serena looked quizzically at her niece, who blushed and added, 'I think I'd miss Isabella's brother most of all. He. . .he's fond of me, too, I think. But what would you do if he. . .if I. . .were to marry?' Serena saw that Lucy was thinking for the first time what marriage in England would entail, realising for the first time that it would mean parting from her beloved aunt. Lucy's face brightened. 'I know, Sasha! When I marry we can live in England together!'

Serena smiled wryly. Now was not the time to point out that she had no intention of living with her niece once Lucy was married. From the beginning Serena had made up her mind that she would see Lucy safely established, and then return to St Just to spend her energies on Anse Chatelet. Now, it seemed, this consolation was to be denied her. But she would not give up without a fight!

One result of this conversation was that Lucy was able to face the arrival of Lord Wintersett with composure. He came in dressed in impeccable linen under a dark green coat and riding breeches tucked into shining Hessians, his face impassive as usual. He gave a cool bow. Serena greeted him in an equally business-like fashion and said, 'You know my niece, I believe, Lord W. . . Wintersett.'

'I do indeed. Your servant, Miss Lucy.' Lucy got up, curtsied modestly and sat down again. He went on, 'Though I am surprised to see her present on this occasion. I thought it was to be a business meeting,

Miss Calvert. I assume you have had the papers concerning Anse Chatelet?' He took his glass and eyed the chaos on the table. 'Yes, I see you have.'

'It *is* a business meeting, Lord W...Wintersett,' Serena was glad that she could at least say his name, though she wondered impatiently why she couldn't say it without stumbling! 'The estate is Lucy's home, as well as my own. And you can hardly blame me for wishing for a companion in your presence.'

A faint red darkened Lord Wintersett's cheeks, but he drawled, '*Your* home, Miss Calvert? I think not.'

'That remains to be seen,' replied Serena swiftly. 'The manner in which you acquired my estates was doubtful, to say the least.'

'It was legal, Miss Calvert.'

'A minimal claim, I should have thought. Most men of honour would not have stooped to such measures. And though I am fully aware that an appeal to your sense of honour would be like asking a hyena to stop scavenging——' There was a gasp from Lucy, which she hastily suppressed. Serena ignored it and continued, 'I am persuaded that the courts might view an appeal with sympathy—especially as the Governor of St Just would support it.'

Lord Wintersett smiled mockingly, '"A hit", William, "a very palpable hit"!'

'Then may you be "justly killed with your own treachery"!' said Serena, her voice full of feeling. 'And we will omit further quotation, if you please. I enjoy that game only with my friends.'

'Well, then, my case might be destroyed, though I doubt it. But it will certainly not be destroyed by you! Believe me, your weapons are puny. Anse Chatelet is

mine by every law in the kingdom, and I defy anyone
to take it from me.'

'Of course! I had forgotten. The *wealthy* Lord W. . .
Wintersett can afford the best lawyers in England!'

'I haven't won Anse Chatelet with my wealth, Miss
Calvert, but by your own family's prodigality in the
past. If I hadn't taken up the mortgage, someone else
would have!'

'Pray do not attempt to defend yourself——'

'I am not,' said Lord Wintersett grimly, 'trying to
defend myself. I see no necessity to do so, not to a
Calvert. God's teeth, you squander a handsome and
profitable heritage and then come whining to me when
it is taken from you——'

Lucy jumped up and faced Lord Wintersett, her
cheeks scarlet.

'How dare you? How dare you talk to my aunt in
such a way? What do you know about it? Sasha has
worked hard and gone without for years—all to save
Anse Chatelet! She has never squandered a thing in
her life——'

'Except my brother's life.'

Lucy swept on, ignoring the interruption ' – and she
has something you will never have, not for all your
money. She has the love of everyone who knows her.
You can keep Anse Chatelet! Sasha will live with me
when I am married!'

His icy gaze swept Lucy's face. 'Married? That is
good news indeed, Miss Lucy. May I ask who the
fortunate young man is?'

A cold shiver went down Serena's spine at this
question. Lord Wintersett was a dangerous and vindictive man and he must not be allowed to threaten
Lucy's happiness. She put a hand on Lucy's arm. 'You

may not, sir. It is none of your business. Lucy, thank you for your defence, I am touched. I think Lord Wintersett's visit is almost over, so would you now leave us?'

Lucy looked doubtfully at them both, but Serena forced a smile and nodded her head, 'It's all right, Lucy, really! I wish you to go, please.' Lucy gave their visitor one of her best curtsies, every line of which conveyed disdain, and went out. When the door was shut once again Serena said urgently, 'She is young. And devoted to me. You must forgive her.' She was aware that she was pleading with him, but could not help herself. 'Her father was already a sick man when your brother and his wife were on St Just. He took no part in their affair. Do not. . .do not spoil her life.'

'You think I would harm a girl who can't have been more than five years old when my brother died?'

Serena said spiritedly, 'I could well be forgiven for thinking so! You have just annexed her home!'

'Not hers, Serena. Yours. I understand that Miss Lucy has a fortune of her own, and that you intend her to marry in England. Losing Anse Chatelet should mean nothing to her.'

'Nothing? Nothing! Why, you heartless, vindictive scorpion, how can you judge what a home means to a child. The feelings of love and comfort, the happy memories of childhood!'

He grew white and turned away from her. After a pause he said harshly, 'Lucy is fortunate if she has such happy memories of her home. But she is about to be married, she said, and she will soon forget the loss of Anse Chatelet when that happens. I repeat, I mean her no harm. You may believe me, Miss Calvert.'

Behind his words she sensed a feeling of unhappiness, of deep loneliness, and angry though she was it gave her pause. She said uncertainly, 'Though I have not experienced it, everyone says you are a just man. Hard, but just. It would not be just to punish Lucy.'

He said abruptly, 'If your niece marries in England, will you in fact live with her?'

Serena shook her head. 'No.'

'What will you do?'

'I had always intended to return to St Just in order to run Anse Chatelet. It was my ambition to carry on building it up again.' She looked up defiantly. 'It still is!'

'And if your appeal fails? As it will.'

'I. . .I might return to Surrey. But it would be hard, I admit. My aunt is elderly and set in her ways. . .'

'You might be forced to seek refuge with William!'

He seemed to regret the words as soon as they were spoken, as did Serena. They were both reminded of the companionship they had known and lost. He frowned, then seemed to come to a sudden decision. 'Miss Calvert, if you will promise to go back to St Just immediately I shall accept Sir Henry's word that the payment should have arrived on time and cancel the foreclosure. Anse Chatelet would be returned to you on the old terms. But you must leave England and not come back again, not ever.'

Serena was suddenly aflame again. '"You must not"! "You must promise"! Who the devil do you think you are, Lord Wintersett, to suggest that I should never visit Lucy in England—or even come for my own pleasure? I am a Calvert of Anse Chatelet, and would not be one of your pensioners—not for the world! If I cannot win my estates back with my own efforts, you may keep them! I am damned if I will accept your charity or your restrictions!'

He gave a reluctant smile. 'Forcefully, if not conventionally expressed. That temper of yours will dish you one of these days, Serena. You know, I find you an enigma. You would almost persuade me of your integrity, except that I have heard you condemned out of your own mouth.'

'Integrity? How could you possibly judge integrity? Where is the integrity in the low, cheating ruse you have employed to steal Anse Chatelet? And how can I have condemned myself out of my own mouth? I simply don't understand what you mean. Why did you say I had squandered your brother's life?'

'Because you drove him to his death, that's why!'

Serena looked at him blankly. '*I*? I drove him to his. . . But that is nonsense!'

' "I loved him", you said.'

'Yes, but——'

' "I pursued him relentlessly", you said.'

'Yes, but——'

' "I told him I despised him, that he'd be better dead", you said.'

'No! That I did not say! Not to Tony!'

'Then to whom?'

Serena was about to answer him, then she stopped short. Why should she betray Richard to this monster? 'I will not tell you,' she replied. 'But it was not to Tony.' He raised a sceptical eyebrow, but she ignored him. 'You are wrong about me, Lord Wintersett. I loved Tony, and I would never have willingly harmed him.'

He looked at her, confident of his case, scornful of

her attempt to plead her innocence. 'It had to be you,'
he said. 'There was no one else.'

Serena's eyes widened as the implication of what he
was saying hit her. 'I. . .I. . .' she stammered.

'Please continue!' he jeered. 'Tell me that Tony did
not kill himself! Or that if he did, it was not because
of a woman!'

'It was not because of me,' she said quietly. 'And
that is all I will say. You must believe what you will.
You have done your worst to the Calverts. It is now
time to forget. But I warn you, I will fight for Anse
Chatelet. And if you harm a hair of Lucy's head I will
cause you more anguish than you have yet known,
Lord Wintersett. Goodbye.'

When Alanna heard that Sasha Calvert had been
taken up by the Ambournes and was enjoying a
modest success in society, her fears for her own safety
reached breaking point. She had to rely more and
more on Amelia Banagher for her information—a not
altogether satisfactory source, for Amelia was no
longer received in the very best houses. Though James
had paid them frequent visits in the earlier part of the
year, he seemed now to have tired of the country and
was spending much more of his time in town. There
was a greater risk, therefore, that he would become
more friendly with the Calvert woman than was
healthy, and Alanna was in daily expectation of a visit
from an irate James demanding to know the truth
about St Just. She bestirred herself to complete her
plans.

It was towards the end of June and Alanna was
holding a council of war. To a casual eye this was a
tea-party in the garden, given by Mrs Stannard for

some Irish friends—a natural enough occasion. But the lady sitting gracefully by the sundial was one of the most notorious courtesans in London, and the distinguished-looking gentleman who had brought her was Fergus O'Keefe, an Irish soldier of fortune and a man of parts, all of them bad. Alanna was anxious to disgrace Sasha Calvert, and the other two were eager to get what money the rich Mrs Stannard would pay them to help her—though in the case of the lady there was a certain amount of personal ill-will as well. Amelia Banagher had not forgotten Serena's remarks at the Assembly Rooms.

'But how can you be sure that Sir John and Lady Taplow will be staying at the Black Lion, *acushla*?' asked Captain O'Keefe.

'Don't be stupid, Fergus! Do I not know where all of them have their favourite inns? Have I not seen the Taplows many a time at the Black Lion at Hoddesdon when they've been on their way back to London from Huntingdon? They haven't seen me, mind!' Amelia gave a rich laugh. 'They take good care not to. They might soil their disapproving eyes!'

'I dare swear you are seldom alone.' Captain O'Keefe accompanied this remark with a wink.

Amelia's laugh was scornful. 'Hardly! I've even been there with one of the Taplows' closest acquaintances. That was a lark! They almost twisted their heads off their necks in their efforts not to see either of us that time!'

'But Amelia, how will you see that word about Miss Calvert's fall from grace spreads through society? From what I've heard the Taplows are so upright that they don't believe in scandalmongering either, do they?'

'Alanna, pray stop worrying! I've set up an assignation myself in the same inn on the same night with Harry Birtles. He's the most notorious rattle in the town. I'll make sure he sees what he needs in order to make a juicy tale. It will get round, never fear. So with Harry to spread it, and the Taplows to confirm it, the plot can hardly fail. Be easy!'

'Very well. But I hope you are right. And the plot will only succeed if the rest goes well, too. Captain O'Keefe, what about your part?'

'Well I still think it would have been better for me to use my charm on the lady—it doesn't often fail, eh, Amelia? But you said not to try, so I've hit on the idea of hiring a coach and putting the Ambourne cipher on the panels for the night. Then I can have a message sent, supposedly from Lord Ambourne himself, asking her to visit him.'

'No, no! You must ask her to visit the Dowager, not Ambourne! She would never come out at night to meet him.'

The gallant captain pulled a face. 'She sounds a damned dull fish to me—I can't see much fun for myself in this business, and that's a fact!'

Alanna said coldly. 'You are not being paid to have fun, Captain O'Keefe. The woman is not to be harmed while she is in your power, do you hear? It's her reputation I wish to be damaged, nothing else.'

'You may rest easy, Alanna,' said Amelia. 'I'll make sure he behaves. We'll be together most of the night. He'll just appear when it's necessary in the morning.'

'What about Sir Harry? Won't you be occupied in. . .er. . .entertaining him?'

'Not if I slip a little something into his wine. He drinks like a fish. No, I can manage both of them.

Miss Calvert's virtue will be safe, if that's what
you want—though I think you're being a mite
overscrupulous.'

'I will not pay either of you if Miss Calvert is
harmed, Amelia.'

'Well that reminds me, Alanna, my dear,' said
Amelia. 'When will you pay us, and how much?'

'We agreed five hundred pounds——'

'Each?'

Alanna looked at the faces before her. They were
suddenly hard and watchful. She nodded. 'Each. I will
pay you each a hundred and fifty pounds beforehand,
a hundred and fifty immediately afterwards, and two
hundred when Sasha Calvert is finally disgraced. But
pray finish telling us what you plan to do, Captain
O'Keefe.'

'Once the lady has entered the coach she'll be taken
to the inn. The landlord has been primed—you did
say you'd pay expenses, didn't you, Mrs Stannard?'

'Reasonable expenses, yes. Afterwards.'

'Beforehand,' said the Captain softly.

'Very well. Carry on.'

'She'll not like being abducted, of course. Amelia
here will give her some womanly sympathy, and offer
the lady something to drink. Miss Calvert will be out
for the night after she drinks it.'

'You're sure you can gauge the dose accurately?'

'Mrs Stannard, once she has it in her, I could tell
you to the second when she'll wake up again! Was I
not once assistant to a doctor?'

Alanna looked doubtfully at Amelia, who nodded
reassuringly. 'It's all right, Alanna. I've known him do
that kind of thing before.'

Still looking doubtful, Alanna asked, 'And when she wakes up?'

'Before she wakes up,' Captain O'Keefe corrected her. 'When she's still half asleep, I'll make sure she's on display to the world through the open door of the bedchamber. If Amelia does what she's supposed to the world will include the Taplows and the chatty Sir Harry. By the time she wakes up properly her reputation will be like the seeds on this dandelion head.' He blew on the dandelion clock in his hand, and the seeds vanished on the wind.

After they had gone Alanna was uneasy. Necessity was driving her into this plot, but she did not enjoy the association with Fergus O'Keefe. He was charming enough, but she felt he could be dangerous. She must consider her plan a little more carefully, for she had a lot at stake. If O'Keefe did misbehave and the plot were discovered then nothing would save her, not even her relationship to the Wintersetts. The Ambournes would see to that, especially as they were to be involved, however indirectly.

Serena was busy during the next few days. She was disappointed that the younger Ambournes had returned so unexpectedly to the country, but was consoled when she found that the Countess was intending to stay on for some time. She sought the lady's advice on a suitable lawyer.

'Our family lawyer is Bradpole. He is very good, but I believe the Stannards use the firm as well. But Perdita had an excellent lawyer. Let me see...the name was Rambridge, I think. I shall send one of the men to make some enquiries at Lincoln's Inn tomorrow, Serena!'

Mr Rambridge called at Dover Street almost immediately. He was cautious on the question of Anse Chatelet, saying, 'The firm of Bradpole, Chalmers and Bradpole is highly respected, Miss Calvert. I would find it hard to believe that they would be involved in anything of a dubious nature.'

But after Serena had explained the circumstances, including the role played by Sir Henry Pendomer, the lawyer promised to look into it. Serena thanked him, gave him the papers and various addresses, and stressed how urgent the task was. At this he smiled and said, as all lawyers did, that one could not hurry the processes of the law, but then he became more human and assured her that he would not waste any time.

Serena also went down to Surrey to visit her great-aunt. Lady Spurston demanded to know the whole story, which was impossible. But Serena told her enough to rouse her indignation at the injustice, and she promised to give Serena all the help in her power.

Feeling she had done as much as she could for the moment Serena then devoted herself to Lucy's interests. It was now more important than ever that Lucy should be established, and though Serena still had private doubts about Michael Warnham she suppressed them. Lucy seemed to have made up her mind in his favour. She spent some time with the Warnhams, who were obviously pleased with their son's choice. Considering how modest Lucy's fortune was, this was a great compliment. They were a pleasant family, and Serena rather thought that her niece would be happy with them. She willingly agreed to allow Lucy to go down to Reigate with them for a few days. London was getting very hot and dusty, and Mrs

Galveston had expressed a wish to spend some time in the country.

Serena felt quite lonely when Lucy and the Warnhams had gone. The depression which was never very far away these days came down like a black cloud on her spirits. What if she did not succeed in her attempt to save Anse Chatelet? What would she do with her life? The prospect of living with Aunt Spurston was not an alluring one, and she suspected that her aunt would not view it with much joy either. After the death of her husband the old lady had become used to living alone. She had been willing to support her great-niece for a few months, but after Serena and Lucy had gone to London Lady Spurston had returned to her quiet life with relief.

Serena decided to try to forget her problems for the moment, and kept herself busy. Always with John, the footman, as her faithful follower, she paid calls, went shopping, buying small unnecessary things in order to cheer herself up, and visited the galleries and museums for which she had never till now seemed to have time. She went walking in the park, admiring the phaetons, the curricles and various other strange vehicles as they bowled along. The horses were beautiful. With a sigh she thought of Douce and Trask and the wonderful rides on the Downs.

'Good afternoon, Miss Calvert.' With a start she looked up. Douce's master had just drawn up in a dangerous looking high perch phaeton with a pair of extremely handsome greys.

'Sir,' Serena said coldly.

'You are alone? That is a rare phenomenon. Where is Miss Lucy?'

His tone was so affable that she regarded him with

suspicion. 'She is spending some days with friends,' she said as curtly as good manners would allow.

'Come, a drive round the park will do you good. John will help you up.'

'Thank you, but I would not dream of putting you to the trouble. . .'

'It's no trouble, Miss Calvert, I assure you. Are you afraid of the vehicle? There's no danger. John?'

John came forward, and before she quite knew what was happening Serena was high in the air on a narrow seat. With a word to John to wait where he was till they returned, Lord Wintersett drove off at a sedate trot. John was quite happy with the situation. Lord Wintersett was a friend of the Ambourne family, there could be no objection to him.

The two in the phaeton drove in silence for a minute or two. Serena was surprisingly at ease, and was enjoying the view of the park from her elevated position. She began to feel more cheerful. Suddenly Lord Wintersett spoke.

'Are you comfortable, Miss Calvert?'

'Thank you, yes,' she said stiffly. 'Why did you insist on taking me up? I find it very odd.'

'I hardly know myself,' he replied with a curious smile. 'I saw you standing there—you were looking as you did on your birthday, on. . .on the hill. Miserable. I suppose I wanted to cheer you up. Why, I cannot say!'

'I am perfectly happy! Your sympathy, if that is what it is, is misplaced, I assure you, Lord W. . .Wintersett.' She bit her lip in vexation. Curse that stammer! 'But perhaps your reason is less charitable? Perhaps you wished to taunt me, to find out if

I have changed my mind and am ready to accept your conditions?'

'I've withdrawn the offer,' he said. 'I've reconsidered, and have made other plans. But no, you misjudge me, Miss Calvert. I'm not here to talk about them. When will you manage to say my name without stuttering?'

'I don't know. But I'd prefer not to have to say it at all,' she replied. 'Pray set me down.'

'What, here? I'm afraid that is impossible. You must wait till we are back with John—London is a dangerous place to a lady on her own. By the way, that's a fetching little bonnet. It suits you.'

Serena was growing angry. She resented being forced to sit quietly while he said what he pleased. And she resented her enjoyment of this ride even more! 'I cannot imagine why you think I wish for your compliments. Do you enjoy having me in your power like this? Please take me back! Immediately!'

He smiled—a long, lazy, utterly charming smile. 'Well, you know, I rather do. But I shall take you back when you say my name again, Serena.'

'Will you release me if I do? And my name is Miss Calvert.'

'Only if you say it without stammering.'

'I have your word? Not that that serves any purpose.'

'You have my word.'

Serena took a deep breath. 'Then I wish that wealthy...witless...weaselly... Lord Wintersett would stop wearying me!'

He laughed. 'What a woeful whopper, woman! I beg your pardon—I should have said "Miss Calvert". That's better—you almost smiled! I think I'll surprise

you and keep my word. I have things to do. Good day
to you!'

He drew up by John with a flourish, saw her safely
on the ground, nodded and drove off, leaving Serena
completely mystified. What was Lord Wintersett up to
now? What were his mysterious plans? Whatever they
were, they seemed to have made him look more
favourably on her. For a moment he had almost been
the man she had known on the hills of Surrey.

CHAPTER TEN

SERENA had visited Lady Ambourne at Rotherfield House once or twice since the lawyer's visit. The Countess had seemed somewhat absent-minded, almost worried. So when Serena received a note from her that evening asking her to come immediately, and begging her to stay the night in Rotherfield House, she paused only long enough for Sheba to pack a small bag with necessities. Sheba was uneasy at letting her mistress go without her. She argued and wailed and prophesied doom until Serena became really annoyed. But Serena was determined to stick to what the note had asked. She could do no less for the friend who had been so kind to her.

The matter is urgent and confidential, Serena. If I could impose on your discretion, I should prefer you not to discuss this visit with anyone. You will, of course, have to tell Mrs Starkey you are spending the night with me, but say no more than that, I beg you. *Bring no one else.* Yours in haste, etc.

When she got to the door John was at her side, but she waved him away. 'Look, the Countess has even sent the carriage for me. Stay here, John.'

There was a maid in the carriage, but it was dark inside, and Serena couldn't see the woman's face. The groom helped her in and then they set off. Serena sat down and turned to the maid. 'What is it? What is wrong with the Coun——' Suddenly she was seized,

466

then two people swiftly gagged and blindfolded her.
One of her assailants was powerful and rough, and
when she at first tried to kick him he twisted her arm
behind her back and threatened to break it. The
woman, presumably the one who had pretended to be
a maid, helped to tie her bonds more firmly, but the
only voice she heard was that of a man.

The journey seemed endless. They were travelling
at a reckless pace, and she was thrown all over the
seat by the jolting of the carriage, unable to save
herself because of her bonds. She felt sick and faint—
the gag was uncomfortable and it was almost unbearably hot. She must in fact have fainted for a while, for
when she came to they were in the country, travelling
swiftly along a turnpike road. Turnpikes had toll
houses! She would listen for the next one. The keeper
would surely hear the commotion she would make.
But her captors had thought of that. As they
approached the gate Serena felt the man in the coach
pull her hood over her face and take her in his arms.
The coach stopped. The driver and the gatekeeper
exchanged a few pleasantries as the toll was paid.

'I shouldn't disturb the gentry inside, if I was you,'
said the coachman. 'They're 'avin' a rare old time in
there.'

Serena heard with despair how the tollkeeper
turned away and went back into the toll house.

The nightmare journey continued, but eventually
they pulled up. From the scents and the absolute quiet
Serena guessed they were deep in the country. Her
captor removed her gag, but not the blindfold. 'You
wish to make a call of nature? The maid will go with
you.' Serena hesitated but her need was urgent.
'Betty! Take Miss Calvert behind the bush. I'll whistle,

my dear, so you can hear that I'm keeping my distance.' He roared with laughter, but while Betty led Serena a little way off, he continued to whistle and talk loudly to the other men. Betty whispered hoarsely, 'Make haste! The Captain's a devil when he gets annoyed.'

'What does he want with me?' croaked Serena. Her throat was dry and her head ached abominably.

'Don't ask me! I do know it's not what you might think, though. Are you rich? Does 'e expect to get a ransom?'

Serena shook her head. 'If he does, he's in for a disappointment. Can. . .can you untie the blindfold? If I could only see. . .Betty, won't you help me escape? I have jewellery at home I could let you have. . .'

'It's more than my life's worth, miss! Come on!'

Back at the carriage Serena could hear Betty having an argument with the man she had called the Captain.

'Oh, go on, Captain! Let 'er 'ave a drink. She can 'ardly speak! Jest a little brandy won't do any 'arm! It's not 'uman to leave 'er to die of thirst. I could do wif one meself!'

'All right, all right. Not too much, mind!'

Betty returned. Serena could smell the brandy. The maid said, 'There y'are! One fer me, and one fer you. I've put a drop of water in it, 'cos I expect yer thirsty.' The cup was held to Serena's lips and she drank greedily. She heard the man say,

'Right! Off, my bonny fellows!' The last thing Serena remembered was being bundled into the coach again.

Serena opened her eyes slowly. The sun was slanting through the window. Was it evening or morning? She yawned. She was so sleepy. . . There was a horrible taste in her mouth, and her head felt thick. She wanted to close her eyes and sleep again but something told her that she must keep awake. Where was she? She tried hard to focus her eyes on the room. It was a bedchamber, but not her own. She looked down. She didn't remember undressing, but she was wearing her night shift. That maid. . .Serena had a dim memory of the maid helping her off with her clothes. Not very expertly. She tried to sit up. Her head! She must ignore it—she must get up. She would get up in a moment. . .

Suddenly the door burst open, and a tall man came in, leaving the door wide behind him. He was half dressed, his shirt undone and hanging outside his breeches. Serena struggled out of bed and tried to run to the door, but she could only manage a few steps before she staggered. There were people outside, staring in, and she opened her mouth, ready to scream to them, for help. But the man was too swift. He held out his arms as if he were expecting her to run into them, and then caught her tight to him, her face hard against his chest. She couldn't say anything, indeed she could hardly breathe.

'There, there, my darling,' he said loudly. 'I was only away a few minutes. See? I'm back already. Oh, Serena, my love! Have you missed me all these months? St Just was never like this, was it? There, there, Serena, be calm now!'

Serena's head was pounding. She tried to pull herself away, but his grip, in sharp contrast to his tender words, was cruelly tight. Her senses were swimming and she felt herself falling. From a great distance she heard him say, 'Wait, Serena! I'll carry you back to bed, shall I?' Then he shouted, 'What are you all staring at, damn you!'

The door was kicked shut and Serena was thrown on to the bed and held there, the man on top of her, his hand over her mouth. She was terrified. The man grinned, showing white teeth in a swarthy face. His eyes were black—he looked like the pictures of pirates she had seen in Jamaica. He whispered, 'I've done you no harm, and will do none, though the temptation is very strong, me darlin'. You're a charmin' little bundle, for all your prim outside! But if you say a word, I swear I'll lose my control. Understand? There isn't a soul in this inn that doesn't believe you're willing, so none will come in unless I invite them. Now, if you wish to come out of this safely, all you have to do is to drink this drop of cordial. You'll fall asleep and when you wake I'll be gone. No, don't shake your head. You're going to drink it whether you will or no, so better to do it without getting hurt.'

He stretched out, picked up a small glass, and put it to her lips. Most was spilled, but some of the bitter liquid passed through and was swallowed. It was enough to put her into a half-sleep. Some minutes later she heard him talking. There was someone else in the room.

'Stop your jangling, woman! None of your friends suspected, did they? How was I to know she'd come to as soon as that? However, all's well that ends well. My, but she's a brave one! It's a shame to do this to her, and that's a fact!' She heard them go out, and as the door was shut behind them she sank into unconsciousness.

When she next came to there was a chambermaid in the room, with a tray. It wasn't the girl from the night before. Serena's bag was on the chest by the bed, her clothes neatly folded beside it and on top was a note. The girl was looking at it. When she saw that Serena was watching her she blushed in confusion.

'Good morning, ma'am. I brought you breakfast.'

Serena sat up. 'Where am I?' she asked. The chambermaid burst into a volley of giggles.

'At the Black Lion, ma'am.'

'But where?'

'At Hoddesdon, ma'am. Shall I fetch your shawl?'

Serena looked down. She had been mistaken. The night shift was not one of hers. It was a diaphanous affair which revealed more than it concealed. She went scarlet. 'Please do,' she said curtly. 'Where is. . .'

'He's gone, ma'am. He left quite early. He left you the note, though.' She giggled again. Serena snatched up the note.

My love,
    You know I have to go, much as I hate to leave you. I'll arrange another meeting as soon as I can get away. Last night was even better than on St Just. All my love—A.

Serena had had enough. She told the chambermaid to leave her and got out of bed. There was a bowl and a pitcher of hot water on the washstand. She scrubbed herself till she felt sore and hastily dried and dressed herself. The effort exhausted her, and she sat down for a moment to rest and think. What was she to do? She must find out what had happened the night before; she must speak to the landlord. She went in search of him. He looked at her stolidly as she approached.

'Landlord, did you see me arrive last night?' Serena asked.

'No, ma'am, I think I must have been busy in the bar. Your room was booked a week or two ago, so I didn't bother too much.'

'Who carried the bags up?'

'I don't rightly know. I think you had your own people with you——'

'They were not my people! You must know! You're the landlord!'

'I'm sorry, ma'am. Last night was a busy one. We had a lot o' guests here. I can't remember seeing you arrive.' Serena turned away impatiently. Then she had another thought.

'Where are the ostlers? I'd like to see them, if you please.'

'Certainly, ma'am. Jem'll fetch 'em. Jem!'

But when the ostlers came they could tell her nothing. The coach had arrived, deposited three passengers, and then driven away. The maid had carried two small bags up. The gentleman had carried the lady, who had appeared to be asleep.

'The gentleman told us you were tired after the journey. Very thoughtful, 'e was. Very fond, like.'

'Be silent! He was not fond! I was drugged!'

'Yes, ma'am. As you say, ma'am.'

Their faces looked stupid and wooden. She would get nothing more out of them. Serena felt she would go mad. She returned to her room and sat down to think. There was a wall of silence in the inn concerning her captors of the night before. She was sure someone must know more, but who? And why had someone drugged her and brought her here to this inn, apparently only to put her in a large bedchamber for the night and then leave her? The sound of wheels caused her to run to the window and she saw a post-chaise turning into the yard. Serena watched as its passengers got out and stretched. The temptation to ask them for help was very strong. They were strangers, but surely they would understand? She had to get back to London. But as one of the travellers looked up at her window Serena hastily drew back. Perhaps it might be wise to consider her position. In view of the attitude of the innkeeper and his servants this was equivocal to say the least, and it might be prudent to avoid exposure, at least until she knew more.

There was a knock on the door. The landlord was there.

'Excuse me, ma'am. Were you thinking of travelling today, or do you wish to keep the room for another night? I need to know because of the chaise.'

'The chaise?' asked Serena blankly.

'Yes, ma'am. There's one booked in your name for today—Calvert, that's right, isn't it? For London. At least that's what's paid for.'

'Are you sure?'

The landlord looked as if he thought her weak in the head. Indeed, she almost felt it. He said patiently, 'A well-sprung chaise and four, together with coach-man and boys, hired for twenty miles, two guineas. I can show you the bill, if you wish.'

'Yes, I'd like to see that, if you please. Immediately.'

But the bill was unrevealing. It had been paid on the spot by the tall gentleman.

Further questioning of the landlord about the chaise produced nothing more than the conviction that this, at least, was above board. She would be safe to take it. But she was conscious of a touch of knowingness in the landlord's manner which went ill with his apparent stolidity. She became convinced that he knew more than he was acknowledging, and that he had probably been bribed.

'What is your name, landlord?'

'Samuel, ma'am. Samuel Cartwright.'

'Well, Mr Cartwright, I will take the chaise to London. It is clear I can do nothing more here. But, if you have taken part in this conspiracy, I warn you you may well lose more than you have gained by it.'

The landlord's expression did not change. 'I don't know what you mean, ma'am. I keep a respectable house here,' he said. 'In fact, begging your pardon, I'd rather your friend didn't book any more rooms at the Black Lion.'

Serena turned on her heel, and went out to the stable yard, where the chaise was waiting.

On any other occasion Serena could have enjoyed the journey back to London, for the countryside was pretty, and they passed through some places with famous names. But she pressed on, merely stopping once for a change of horses. The landlord of the Black Lion was a rogue, she was sure, but she dismissed him from her mind. The man behind him was more important. Her head still ached, and the drug had left an unpleasant taste in her mouth, but she ignored both of these and tried to concentrate on what her mysterious enemy was trying to achieve. Why Hoddesdon! Why the Black Lion, a coaching inn, and much in the public eye? If he had intended harm to her person he would have chosen a more out-of-the-

way spot. So, if she was right, he had not intended
harm to her person, he had merely intended her to
be noticed. She vaguely remembered the open door
to the bedchamber that morning. There had been
faces in the doorway, she had tried to reach them. He
must have left that door open deliberately! He had
wanted her to be seen, not just in the inn, but in the
bedchamber! With a blush she remembered the night-
gown—there was no doubt about the sort of rendez-
vous that garment was intended for! Serena's heart
sank as she saw the scheme for what it was. It was no
more or less than an effort to discredit her. And unless
she could prove otherwise, that was exactly what it
would do!

She walked in through the door of the Dover Street
house as the clocks were striking five. Mrs Starkey
was waiting for her with a smile, but her expression
changed when she saw Serena's face.

'Mercy me! What has happened, Miss Calvert?
You're ill!'

'No, no. Just a little tired. But I am hungry. Could
you bring some tea and a little bread and butter to
the small parlour, Mrs Starkey. I shall rest there for a
while. And would you tell Sheba I have returned,
please.'

She lay on the sofa in the small parlour and when
Sheba brought in the tea she asked her to close the
shutters. Sheba tried to persuade her mistress to go to
bed, but Serena's thoughts were too chaotic for sleep.
And they were leading her to one inevitable conclusion. As far as she knew, there was only one person
in London who wished her ill. One person who had
tried to bribe her to leave England. One person who
had told her just the day before that he had changed

his mind and had other plans. One person who had taken her off her guard by his pretended concern for her. She buried her face in her hands and let the bitter tears flow unchecked.

But Serena was too much of a fighter to give in to tears for long. After a while she dried her eyes, and considered what to do. It all depended on those people in the door. If they had not recognised her then all might not be lost, and a great deal was to be gained by saying nothing. Perhaps her captor had made a mistake in hiding her face against his chest so closely? She would wait to see. Lucy was returning tomorrow and they would be out most of the time. She would not alter her plans for the moment.

Serena went upstairs and changed her dress. Lady Pangbourne was giving a dinner party and had asked Serena to come with an old friend of her husband's. Serena must be ready for him. Sheba used her skills, which were now considerable, to disguise the ravages of the past two days, and when General Fanstock called, Serena was waiting in the drawing-room as cool, as composed and as beautiful as ever. They arrived at the Pangbourne house in Grafton Street at exactly ten o'clock. They were received graciously by Lady Pangbourne, and soon found themselves among what Lucy called 'The Pangbourne set', usually wrinkling her nose at the same time. It was true that the average age was high, and the average level of conversation worthy rather than scintillating, but Serena nevertheless enjoyed herself. She began to feel safer. Perhaps the people at the inn had either not recognised her or they did not belong to the very limited numbers which make up London society.

Halfway through the meal she found herself the

subject of a penetrating stare from an elderly dowager
some way up the table. She asked her partner who it
was. 'Hrrmph! Let me have a look. I think. . . Yes it's
Valeria Taplow, my dear. Charmin' woman. A bit of
a stickler, you know, but none the worse for that,
none the worse for that! John, her husband, is a very
nice fellow, too. Hrrmph! Great friends of mine.'

Serena was uneasy. That stare had not been one of
approval. But the evening passed without incident,
unless you would call it an incident that neither of
the Taplows had come over to speak to their old
friend.

Lucy arrived back the next day, glowing with happiness. She had had a wonderful week, with wonderful
weather. The Warnhams and Mrs Galveston were
wonderfully kind! Serena smiled in spite of her own
worries and waited. Eventually Lucy said hesitantly,
'Sasha?'

'Yes?'

'Sasha, you like Mr Warnham, don't you? Isabella's
brother.'

'I think he's charming.'

'If he. . .if he came to see you—to ask you if you
would let him pay me his addresses—you wouldn't say
no, would you?'

'Well. . .let me see. . .'

'Sasha!'

'Of course I wouldn't, you goose! You mean to tell
me that he hasn't already "paid his addresses"—or
some of them, anyway?'

Lucy blushed. 'Not exactly. But he wanted to talk
to you before we. . .before anything was made public.'

'He's a charming boy, Lucy. You are both
fortunate.'

'He's not a boy, you know, Sasha,' said Lucy
seriously. 'He's a man—the man for me.'

She was shortly to be proved right.

Lady Pangbourne's dinner party was followed the next
evening by a rout party with dancing given by the
Countess Carteret. Once again Serena was invited to
go with a friend of the family who had been waiting
for some time to escort the lovely Miss Calvert. Mr
Yardley was a lively bachelor and an excellent dancer,
and Serena was looking forward to her evening. She
was a little disappointed therefore that Mr Yardley
seemed to be somewhat subdued as he ushered Lucy,
Serena and Mr Warnham into the large ballroom in
Marchant House. Lucy was immediately taken off to
dance by Mr Warnham, but Serena's partner seemed
strangely reluctant. When Sir Harry Birtles came up
Mr Yardley willingly performed the introduction he
demanded, and then seemed to slide away.

'I hear you're a great sport, Miss Calvert,' said Sir
Harry with an engaging smile.

'I beg your pardon?'

'You know—the inn at Hoddesdon. I was there,
too. A great lark, what?'

Serena felt herself growing pale. 'I don't understand
you, Sir Harry. What do you mean?'

'Oh, come! I won't tell, you know. Soul of discretion, give you my word.'

Serena walked away without looking at him. She
went upstairs under the pretence of repairing her dress
and stayed there for as long as she dared. She must not
lose her head! After a while she was calmer and came
down again. Lucy and Mr Warnham came over from
the other side of the ballroom to join her. Lucy's face

was stormy. Before they arrived, however, a man, a
perfect stranger, came up behind Sasha and put his arm
round her waist. She turned swiftly and took a step
away from him. He smiled cynically and moved on, but
his friend, who seemed to have drunk more than was
good for him, lingered.

'Serena!' he whispered. 'What a lovely. . .lovely
name. Beautiful Serena! I could adore you.'

'Sir!' said Serena. But she did not have to say more.
Michael Warnham interposed himself in front of
Serena and said coldly, 'I think your friends are
waiting for you in the card room, Dauncy. Miss
Calvert is just leaving.'

'Come, Sasha,' whispered Lucy. 'Come quickly!'
Considerably shaken, Serena allowed herself to be
taken away, Mr Warnham in close attendance on them
both.

The short journey back to Dover Street was accomplished almost in silence. Lucy began to speak as soon
as they left Marchant House, but Mr Warnham put
his hand firmly over hers and said,

'Not yet, Lucy!'

'But——' She subsided when he shook his head at
her.

Serena was shivering. The plot appeared to have
succeeded all too well if the reaction of Mr Dauncy
and his friend was anything to go by. Now she was
forced to face the problem of what to do about it.
They reached the sanctuary of Dover Street, where
Mr Warnham suggested that they went into the small
parlour. Here he said gently, 'Now Lucy. Now you
may talk.'

'I know what you are going to say, Lucy,' said
Serena wearily. 'Let me spare you what must seem an

unpleasant task. London is buzzing with the story that
Serena Calvert is having a secret affair. That she was
seen in an inn outside London, having apparently
spent the night with her lover.'

Mr Warnham made an involuntary movement
towards Lucy, and Serena turned to him.

'Lucy and I have no secrets, and have never minced
our words in speaking to each other, Mr Warnham.
However, if I *were* guilty of the behaviour I have just
described, you may be assured that I would protect
my niece from any knowledge of it.'

Young Mr Warnham relaxed. 'I knew there must
be something wrong with the story. It isn't true.'

'There, I'm afraid, you are taking too simple a view.
It isn't true, and yet it is.' Lucy jumped up and ran
over to kneel by Serena.

'Sasha! Oh, Sasha, don't speak in riddles like this, I
can't bear it! I know you cannot have done anything
wrong; why can't we just deny the story, threaten to
go to the law. How can they say such things of you?'
Serena gently drew Lucy to the seat beside her.

'Because people who don't know me as you do,
Lucy, would find it difficult, if not impossible, to
believe that I am the victim of a very carefully laid
plot.'

'A plot!'

'Yes, Mr Warnham.' Serena went on to give the two
young people most of the details of what had happened the day before and at Hoddesdon that morning.
She finished up by saying, 'The conspirators were
particularly clever in that they saw to it that the story
would not only be spread—but believed, as well. I
know now for certain that Sir Harry Birtles saw me
there, and, unless I am mistaken, we will find that Sir

John and Lady Taplow were also present at the inn, and also saw me.'

Lucy flung her arms round Serena as if to shut out the dreadful picture her aunt had conjured up. But Mr Warnham was silent. Serena said sadly, 'It is an extraordinary tale, Mr Warnham, I agree. Hardly credible, indeed.'

At that he came over to sit on her other side.

'Miss Calvert, if I did not speak straight away, it was not, believe me, not in the slightest degree because I did not believe your account of what actually happened. I have known you for some time now, and Lucy has told me a great deal about you. To me, what you have told us is completely credible. No, I was thinking rather how one might best challenge the version going round London. Because you must! Your own good name, and Lucy's as well, are at stake.'

Serena turned swiftly to Lucy. 'Has anyone spoken to you. . .?'

Mr Warnham said grimly, 'No gentleman has approached Lucy, no. They would hardly dare while I am there to protect her. But. . .' He seemed embarrassed.

Lucy finished for him. 'The ladies are not always very kind, Sasha. I do not mean Lady Warnham—she is upset, of course, but she has been very sympathetic. She has suggested, however, that we—Michael and I—do not for the moment publish our engagement.' She looked defiantly at Mr Warnham. 'And I agreed with her.'

Serena looked towards the young man.

'I would publish it tomorrow, Miss Calvert, and so I told my mother,' said Michael Warnham. 'But Lucy is adamant. And perhaps she is right. It is better to postpone our own celebration until you are cleared, then we shall all rejoice together.' He got up, went to Lucy's side, and took her hands in his. 'You must not think that putting off the announcement of our engagement alters my determination to marry Lucy.' The two smiled at each other. Then he turned back to Serena. 'But, more immediately, I should like to help you in any way I can. Do you wish me to challenge Dauncy?'

'For heaven's sake, no!' cried Serena. 'You would soon find yourself challenging half the men in London! No, we must look for evidence to convince London society that it is wrong!'

'What about Sir Harry Birtles!' cried Lucy. 'Was he alone at the inn?'

'Most unlikely, I'd say.' Mr Warnham seemed to recollect himself. He turned to Lucy and suggested that she might like to leave her aunt and himself to discuss the matter. 'I dare say you will accuse me of being stuffy, Lucy, but you really shouldn't be involved in discussing Lord Harry's behaviour and similar matters. You can support your aunt in other ways.' Lucy looked mutinous, but he said firmly, 'I am not discussing this unsavoury business in your presence, Lucy.'

'Well, I shall go, but do not imagine I shall stop thinking about it. I wonder who Sir Harry was with?' With that she went, after hugging her aunt and giving Mr Warnham a slightly cool curtsy. Serena smiled.

'I see I have no need to worry about Lucy's future happiness, Mr Warnham. You will manage her very well. I cannot say how happy I am that you wish to marry.'

'Lucy is a darling,' he said simply. 'I think I am very

fortunate. But this is not solving your problem. You know, Lucy's question was an acute one. Your conspirators had to ensure that the necessary witnesses were there at the right place, and at the right time. The Taplows frequently travel to Huntingdon. It would be easy to find out when they would next be staying at the Black Lion. But Sir Harry. . . Who was Sir Harry's companion? You didn't see her, I suppose?' Serena shook her head. 'Would you like me to try to find out?'

'Can you do so?'

'Easily, I should imagine. Sir Harry is not noted for his discretion.'

'I would certainly like to know. And I think I will see Mr Rambridge—my lawyer. He is dealing with another matter for me, and may have some suggestions to make about this one. But now, Michael—you see, I regard you as one of the family—I would like to ask you to do something more for me.'

'Anything!'

'I wish you to make sure that Lucy and yourself are not seen in public with me for the moment.'

'Miss Calvert!'

'Lucy calls me Sasha. Could you? In private, of course.'

'I am honoured. Thank you. . .Sasha. But Lucy would never agree to desert you—nor would I.'

'I know that you wish to show society your regard and support, and I am touched. But it is better for Lucy's sake that she should be kept away from this scandal as much as possible—at least for the next day or two until I find out what I have to do. Will you do this? From what I have seen you are the person to persuade her.'

'Very well. But you must let me know if there is anything else I can do.'

'I will.' In spite of her weariness Serena smiled. 'I feel we have a man in the family again, Michael. It is very comforting.'

Mr Warnham left, wishing he had a white charger or an army or two to defend Miss Calvert. Keeping Lucy safe seemed a small thing compared with all Sasha's other problems.

What he did not realise was that Serena was at least as anxious to keep Michael himself out of danger. In his eagerness to defend her honour he might well find himself picking quarrels with gentlemen more experienced than he in the art of the duel. And it was for this same reason that she had not mentioned her suspicions of Lord Wintersett.

But she had not forgotten them either. Thus it was that the next morning found her demanding to see Lord Wintersett at his residence in Upper Brook Street. Percy was alone in the entrance hall at the time, and found it difficult to deal with this totally unorthodox occurrence. He was only saved by Lord Wintersett himself, who came out of the library and invited Miss Calvert to enter.

'How can I help you, Miss Calvert?' he asked when the door shut behind Percy.

'You know how you can help me! Withdraw this rumour about me that you have set round London!'

'I have heard the rumour, of course. I have had no part in spreading it.'

'You are too clever, and too cowardly for that,' said Serena, her lip curling in scorn. 'You, Lord Wintersett, stay in the background, merely pulling the strings for your puppets to hang me!'

Lord Wintersett looked down at the snuff box he was holding. His hand tightened, then relaxed. When he looked up again his voice was arctic. 'If a man had said that to me, Miss Calvert, I would have knocked his teeth down his throat—as an alternative to killing him.'

'I have no one to defend me, Lord Wintersett. It is easy for you to be brave with your threats.'

'What about your mysterious lover? Is he not a man?'

Serena looked at him with loathing. 'How can a creature such as you live with himself?' she asked, her voice quivering with feeling. 'You have ruined me, Lord Wintersett, and yet you still taunt me with the creatures of your own invention. You know I have no lover!'

'Is there no foundation for this rumour, then? You were not at. . .Hoddesdon, was it? You were not seen by the Taplows?'

'Why are you fencing like this with me? There is no one else here; why cannot you be open?'

'Tell me what you think I did.'

'I will not waste my breath on such an exercise. But I warn you, I intend to expose you, if it kills me! You may have bribed that landlord with all the wealth in England, but one way or another I shall rip your conspiracy wide open!' She went to the door.

'Serena!' He strode over to the door and put his hand on her shoulder. She wrenched herself free.

'Don't touch me!'

'Serena, what are you going to do?'

'Expose you for the villain you are!'

'And meanwhile?'

'Meanwhile I shall outface the scandalmongers and

the gossips. I shall carry on as if they did not exist. I will not give in to your blackmail!'

'Serena, society can be cruel; it isn't wise——'

'You may save your efforts to dissuade me, Lord Wintersett. I will not let you win.'

'Serena, what if I tell you that I had no part in any plot against you?' he asked rapidly.

'Who else wants me out of London?' Serena asked contemptuously. 'Who withdrew the offer of Anse Chatelet and told me that he had "other plans"?'

'But I only meant that I was going to St Just myself! I am leaving in two days' time.'

Serena whirled round. 'To St Just? You have wasted little time in your anxiety to review your new possession! I am sorry for the snakes on the island, for no viper, no fer-de-lance could rival your poison. Take care you don't bite one!' With that she pulled open the door and ran out.

CHAPTER ELEVEN

IT TOOK Serena some time to calm down, but then she went to see Mr Rambridge. He was not sanguine about the outcome of any action on the Anse Chatelet case, but promised to continue. When he heard the story of her abduction he was horrified. 'Why, Miss Calvert, I have known only one other case like it. What do you wish me to do? As you say, it would be impossible to scotch the rumours without first finding the villian behind the plot. Who wishes you so much ill?'

When Serena tentatively voiced her suspicions concerning Lord Wintersett Mr Rambridge was dismissive. 'All things are possible, I suppose, and a lawyer hears more than most. But that Lord Wintersett should stoop to such dealings I find it impossible to believe!'

'But I know of no one else who bears me any kind of grudge!' cried Serena. 'Mr Rambridge, I should like to hire a trustworthy fellow to investigate the inn for me. I found it impossible to get any information at all from the landlord and his tribe. Perhaps a trained investigator, and a man, might be more successful. Do you know of such a person?'

Mr Rambridge said he did, and if Miss Calvert wished he could present Mr Barnet to her in a very few minutes. 'He is just writing up the details of another case in the office next door. Can you wait? May I offer you a glass of Madeira or some other

refreshment?' Within a short time Serena had engaged
Mr Barnet, given the particulars of the inn and everything she could remember which might be of use,
rejected with scorn his suggestion that the Ambournes
might have had anything whatsoever to do with it, and
had taken her leave of both men. Mr Rambridge's last
words were, 'I am glad you did not tell Barnet of your
suspicions of your noble friend, Miss Calvert! I do not
acquit the gentleman of ruining a lady's reputation.
But that he should resort to such villainy to do so is
quite out of the question.'

That evening Serena went to a concert in
Northumberland House. She had taken a long time
deciding what to wear. The temptation to put on
a poppy-coloured India muslin dress was strong.
Equally strong was the desire to wear stark white or
discreet black. Each would make a statement to the
world—but all had their obvious disadvantages. In the
end she wore her topaz silk dress. Sheba brushed
Serena's hair until it gleamed like silk, then twisted it
into a knot high on her head. Aunt Spurston's diamonds glittered at her ears, throat and wrists, and the
amber-coloured silk of the dress reflected the tiger
gleam of her eyes. Lucy was spending the evening at
Lady Warnham's, so she was not there to give her
verdict on Serena's appearance. It was as well. She
would not have recognised her loving, impulsive aunt
in this creature of shining gold and ice.

Serena entered the great doors of Northumberland
House five minutes before the concert began and
started to walk up the wide staircase. Groups of
people were standing on the stairs chatting and view-
ing each new arrival. As Serena passed silence fell on

each group, and though the gentlemen eyed her, the ladies studiously avoided meeting her eye. Serena appeared not to notice. Her head held high, one hand holding the hem of her dress up, she mounted the stairs without haste, and without pause. The man standing at the top of the stairs looked down and thought he had never seen anything so graceful or so courageous.

'Cool customer, ain't she, Wintersett? Magnificent creature, though,' said a young buck standing nearby, eyeing Serena through his glass. Lord Wintersett gave him such a glacial stare that he vanished, and avoided the noble peer's company for the rest of the evening. As he remarked to one of his cronies, there was no sense in looking for trouble.

Serena reached the music room at last and took a seat near the front. She was studying her programme, so did not apparently notice that several ladies sitting near her got up and moved to a different part of the room. But a faint flush appeared on her pale cheeks. The silence that followed was broken by the rustle of silk and the voice of Lady Ambourne floating through the door.

'Serena, how pleasant to see you again! May I?' With a charming smile the Dowager Countess of Ambourne sat down next to Serena and proceeded to make light conversation until the music began.

In the interval it was even worse. The two ladies made their way to the supper-room, but, though the room was crowded, a space appeared round them wherever they stopped. There were smiles and greetings for Lady Ambourne, but no one offered to join them or to fetch anything for them. Lord Wintersett, watching from the other side, muttered a curse, and pushed his way through the crowd. 'Your servant, Lady Ambourne, Miss Calvert? May I get you some refreshment?' he asked with a low bow.

The Countess expressed her gratitude, adding, 'Is it not astonishing, Lord Wintersett, how very many underbred people come to these concerts nowadays? One might have thought that a love of music would encourage courtesy, but the opposite appears to be the case.' The Countess's voice was soft but penetrating. A number of faces round them grew slightly pink, and one or two people actually came up to join her. For a while Lady Ambourne and Serena were surrounded. When Lord Wintersett returned, carrying some glasses and a plate of delicacies, he had difficulty in reaching the Countess. Serena had somehow been edged to the outside of the group. But when Lord Wintersett presented her with a glass of champagne Serena looked at him expressionlessly, and emptied the glass into a potted palm next to her. Then she turned and left the room.

Lady Ambourne was drinking her chocolate in the garden room the next morning when Purkiss came in to ask if she would receive Lord Wintersett. The Countess was surprised. Only the most urgent business could excuse a call so early in the day. She told Purkiss to show Lord Wintersett in and to bring some more chocolate. Lord Wintersett, when he came, was dressed in riding clothes.

'Lady Ambourne, this is good of you. I apologise for disturbing you at this early hour.'

'Sit down, James, and share my chocolate.'

Since Lord Wintersett's good manners forbade him to say that he disliked chocolate intensely, it was as well that Purkiss brought him some ale—'As it's so warm, today, my lord.'

'Now, James, what is so important that you have to see me at this hour? I should think it is something to do with Miss Calvert?'

'Yes. She needs help.'

'Why are you concerned, James? I thought that you disliked her. Why do you want to help her now?'

'I don't know! That's the devil of it. Forgive me, Lady Ambourne, I shouldn't have said that.' He got up and went to the window. His back was towards her and his voice muffled as he said, 'I seem to be doing everything wrong! The trouble is that I don't know what to think or what to believe.'

The Countess looked at him with surprise. What had happened to self-sufficient, self-possessed Frosty Jack? She said thoughtfully, 'But you wish to help Serena all the same. Why do you not speak to Serena herself?'

'I. . . I cannot. She would accept nothing from me— not even a glass of champagne! Certainly not any kind of advice.' He came back and sat down. 'I'm doing what I can. In a few minutes I shall set off for Hoddesdon, to do a little investigating. My time is limited, however. I leave for Falmouth and the West Indies tomorrow night.'

The Countess's eyes widened. 'You're going to St Just?' James nodded. 'Then we must not lose any time. How do you wish me to help Miss Calvert? I would have done so in any case, you know.'

James came to sit opposite her, leaning forward in his chair. 'She's so obstinate, so fixed in her determination to defy society, and she will be badly hurt if she continues. You saw what happened last night.' He paused and looked down at his hands. 'She would not listen to anything I might say. Could you use your influence to persuade her to live quietly until this business is cleared up one way or the other?'

'I have already resolved on that. Indeed, I have been laying plans this very morning. But James, am I to understand that you believe her to be innocent?'

'Yes, I do! That is——'

'Is that your heart or your head speaking?'

'It certainly isn't my head. The evidence is almost overwhelming.'

'Good! Then it is your heart. Trust it. Are you in love with her?'

'At one time I thought I was,' James said sombrely.

'In Surrey?'

'She has told you about the time in Surrey?' The Countess nodded. 'I didn't know who she was, of course. Then when we came to London I found out she was a Calvert. Sasha Calvert. Since then my life has been in turmoil.'

'Why?'

'Tony died on St Just. What the world suspects, but does not know for certain, is that he killed himself. For years I. . .we have blamed Sasha Calvert for driving my brother into taking his own life.'

'What rubbish! She was only fourteen years old at the time!'

'I know that now. I had always believed her to be much older. But Alanna said. . . No, I will not repeat it.'

'Do you really believe that Serena was responsible for Tony's death, James? Knowing her, as you knew her in Surrey? Having observed her behaviour since she has been in London? Is there no alternative?'

There was a silence. Then James got up and said,
'That is what I am going to the West Indies to find
out. It's what I should have done years ago.' He gave
a wry smile. 'Serena believes I am going there to gloat
over my new acquisition.'

'Have you tried to explain?'

'She would not listen. She dislikes me too much. I
think I must go, Lady Ambourne. I have much to do
before tomorrow night.' He said with feeling, 'I wish I
did not have to leave England at this moment! Serena
needs someone to help her! But I must; my journey to
St Just cannot be delayed. I will be easier in my mind
if I know she has someone she can rely on. I thought
of writing to Ned, but I know he is anxious about
Perdita. Oh, forgive me again—I am so wrapped up
in my own concerns that I forget my manners! How is
Perdita?'

'We have been quite worried about her, but things
are better now. I think I can call on Edward if I need
him, James. Meanwhile I wish you *bonne chance* and
bon voyage. I will watch Serena's interests, never fear.'

'You believe in her, don't you, Lady Ambourne?'

'I have never doubted her for a minute.'

At Hoddesdon James soon got the landlord's measure, and with a judicious mixture of threats and promises of remuneration even persuaded him to talk of
the night in question. Mr Cartwright had, it appeared,
been asked—against suitable payment, of course—to
provide a particular room at the head of the first flight
of stairs. 'Best room in the house, that is.' He had
agreed to be blind when a certain chaise drove up, to
allow the passengers to see themselves to the room,
to keep his mouth shut if the lady asked any questions

in the morning, and to provide a chaise for her return
to London. Everything had been paid for with shining,
golden guineas by a man called the Captain. In answer
to further questions he said that Sir Harry Birtles had
stayed at the Black Lion more than once, always with
the same lady, but he didn't know the lady's name.
He thought it might be Aurelia, or Amelia—something like that. The Taplows—ah, they were a different sort, they were. Real aristocrats. They stayed
regular as clockwork every six weeks when they visited their daughter in Huntingdon. Everyone knew
that.

'Who arranged the matter of the rooms and so on?'

'The Captain. He came once beforehand to book
the room and have a chat, like.' To discuss terms,
thought James.

'Did he ask about Sir Harry and the rest? Or any
other guests? To find out when they would be staying
here?'

'I don't remember that he did. Not then. And apart
from the night he came with the lady that's the only
time I've seen him, before or since.' The landlord
hesitated. 'One o' the maids—she got the impression
the Captain knew Sir Harry's lady. But that don't
mean nothing. Sir Harry's lady is the sort who'd know
a lot o' gentlemen, if you know what I mean, sir.'

He gave James a vague description of the Captain
and Sir Harry's lady-friend, but more he would not,
or could not, say. James rather thought it was the
latter. He paid Mr Cartwright what he had promised
and asked to see the girl. Apart from giggles all he
could elicit from her was that Sir Harry had called the
lady 'Amelia' and that the 'Captain' had winked at
Amelia in the corridor, and then said something to

her. She too gave some sort of description of Amelia
and the Captain. James was about to leave when she
sidled up to him and whispered that she had something to sell him. She showed him a much handled
scrap of paper.

'It were in the bedroom, sir. The one at the top o'
the stairs. The lady left it behind. It were all she left,
too,' she added resentfully. 'That and a funny little
glass with nothin' in it. I threw it away.'

With growing distaste James read the note which
Serena had found by the bed when she had woken up
that morning.

> My love,
> You know I have to go, much as I hate to leave
> you. I'll arrange another meeting as soon as I can
> get away. Last night was even better than on St
> Just. All my love—A.

As he rode back to London James was debating
whether the note could be genuine. Who could tell? It
was all so uncertain! Some of what the landlord had
told him could support Serena's story. On the other
hand, much of it could be explained by the very
natural desire of a couple sharing an illicit bed to keep
themselves anonymous. But—this was perhaps the
biggest point in her favour—Serena hadn't been kept
anonymous. The presence of Harry Birtles at the inn
had made it certain that the whole of London now
knew of her 'affair'. Harry... Harry had been with
Amelia Banagher, he was sure. It might be worth
finding out which of them had set up that assignation.
He would call on Amelia when he got back to town.
He went over the note again. Who was 'A'? If it
wasn't genuine it was quite cleverly phrased. Not too

much—merely the suggestion that Serena had known the writer on St Just. Well, he would be there in a few short weeks and would learn a lot more about Sasha Calvert and her family.

Amelia Banagher was resting in her boudoir, a pretty little room of satin, lace and roses, when James came in. She received him with little cries of joy, and fussed over him for several minutes. But she had a fright when he said he had been to Hoddesdon that morning.

'I believe you spent the night there recently. With Harry Birtles.'

She started to be coy, but he cut through her protestations and said directly, 'Amelia, you and I have usually managed to be open with each other. I will pay your outstanding bills if you will tell me how it happened that you and Harry were at the Black Lion on that particular night.'

'I'm not sure why you wish to know, James. And at the moment I have no outstanding bills!'

His eyes narrowed. 'Now that I find most interesting. Indeed, it is quite extraordinary. No outstanding bills, eh? I think no further proof is needed, Amelia. Who bribed you?'

She was really frightened. Wintersett was not a man to play with. But nor was Fergus O'Keefe, and it wouldn't surprise her if what she and Fergus had done to Serena Calvert was criminal. Amelia decided to risk losing any influence she had ever had with Lord Wintersett in the interest of saving her skin.

'James, I have to confess I was angry with you for the way you and that woman treated me about the necklace,' she said, improvising rapidly. 'I wanted to pay you both back. I could see you were interested in her, and. . .and I wanted you to see how she was deceiving you.' Amelia got up and fetched a handkerchief. 'Would you like some wine, James? I'll send for some, shall I?'

'Thank you, but no, Amelia. Please continue with your story.'

'Well. . . I decided to arrange that Harry should witness her meeting with her gentleman friend at the Black Lion. Nothing more. I knew Harry would spread it round. He's from the West Indies, isn't he? Her friend, I mean.'

'You knew him?'

'Oh, no!'

'He appeared to know you. One of the maids saw you both.'

Amelia felt her cheeks grow pale again. Then she pulled herself together and murmured, 'A lot of gentlemen would like to know me, James. Many even exchange a word or two with me. It doesn't mean I know them.'

Amelia could see that James was not entirely convinced, but she was confident that her story would be difficult to disprove. Then he asked, 'What was he like—this gentleman from the West Indies?'

What should she say? If she described Fergus too well, James might track him down. 'I didn't notice him particularly. Fair, I think. Not too tall.'

After a while James left, and Amelia sank back with a sigh of relief.

The next day James returned to Rotherfield House. The Countess was surprised but pleased to see him

again. Once more he found her in the garden room,
with a letter in her hand.

'Come in, James. Come in and sit down. I've had
some pleasing news of Perdita. Edward says she is
much better. Quite her old self again.'

James expressed pleasure and the Countess sent for
some wine. Then she sat back in her chair and said,
'But now you shall tell me what you are here for. I
thought we had said our farewells? Have you been to
Hoddesdon? What did you find?'

James related to the Countess the result of his visit
to Hoddesdon, and his interview with Lady Banagher.
She grew grave immediately.

'A devilish conspiracy—I am not using the word
lightly, either.'

'I think Amelia Banagher was lying. Her description
of the man does not match what the people at the inn
told me in any respect—they said he was tall and very
dark. I am sure she knows him. Before I leave London
I must engage a reliable man to investigate further.'

'James, Rambridge was here today to enquire after
Perdita. He said that Serena had already engaged
someone—a very good man, he said. Would you like
me to pass your information to him?'

This was quickly decided on, and James promised
to let Lady Ambourne have what he had learned in
writing. 'But that is not really why I came, Lady
Ambourne. It occurred to me after I left you yesterday that the Warnhams might well be reconsidering
their approval of the match between their son and
Miss Lucy Calvert. That would be most unfortunate.'

The Countess looked at him pityingly. 'And you
think I have not thought of that? James, let me set
your mind at rest by telling you what I plan to do. I

shall persuade Serena, if I can, that she should retire
to the country for a while—until we have time to
establish the truth. I shall also suggest that I move
into the house in Dover Street—everyone knows that
I detest this place when I am alone—and that I
sponsor Miss Lucy myself. I think the standing of the
Dowager Countess of Ambourne is enough to silence
any possible criticism of Lucy Calvert, do you not
agree?'

James smiled for the first time. 'Lady Ambourne,
you are, as always, completely right!'

James had one last interview before he left. It was
with Serena, and was not planned. But he was irresis-
tibly drawn to Dover Street on his way to the
Gloucester coffee house, where he would pick up the
coach for Falmouth. She would not receive him at
first, but he eventually persuaded John to admit him.
She was alone except for a large negress.

'Shall I stay, Mis' Sasha?'

'No, it's all right, Sheba. Lord Wintersett will not
be here long.' The woman left, giving him a baleful
stare as she went.

'I'm leaving tonight, Serena. Have you. . .have you
any messages for the Pendomers?'

She smiled bitterly. 'What could I possibly tell
them? That I no longer own Anse Chatelet? That I
am disgraced and shunned by most of London
society? That Lucy's marriage is no longer so certain?'

'No. Though I think Miss Lucy's happiness is not in
danger. But I understand. Then I will bid you
goodbye.'

'You could not bid me anything more welcome!
Goodbye, Lord Wintersett. Enjoy your stay at Anse

Chatelet. I hope you are prepared to explain to our—
I beg your pardon, *your* people, why the Calverts have
finally abandoned them.'

'Serena, what will I find when I get there? Was
Tony's death an accident, after all? Is there another
explanation?'

There was silence while a variety of expressions
passed over her mobile features. A flash of temper, a
desire to speak, hesitation, doubt and finally sadness.
'I cannot tell you,' was all she said. 'You must judge
for yourself.' But her voice was gentle.

He moved closer. 'Will you be here when I return?'

'I don't know. I hope to see Lucy married but I am
not sure when that will be at the moment. After
that... I don't know.'

He drew her to him. She looked at him with troubled eyes, but made no effort to resist when he kissed
her, a long, sweet kiss. The kiss grew deeper, more
passionate until they were closely twined in each
other's arms, murmuring to each other and kissing
again and again. Serena broke free, but he pulled her
back to him, holding her tight, pressing her head to
his chest. He said into her hair, 'This business at
Hoddesdon—do you really think me so despicable?
That I would go to such lengths to ruin you, Serena?
After the time on the hill in Surrey—William, Trask
and Douce, and all those hours when we seemed to
share so much?'

'I don't know!' she cried, pulling away from him
again. 'I'm so confused. I've been told you were there
at the inn yesterday, giving money to the landlord.
But when you hold me as you did I cannot remember
that. One minute I think you're a devil, a monster,
and the next you hold me in your arms and I cannot

imagine wishing to be anywhere else! If you think we shared so much why did you treat me so badly? Oh, go to St Just and leave me alone, Lord W... Wintersett!'

'I thought you had mastered that stammer, Serena.'

'It is a weakness I despise, I assure you! It appeared after that first night in London. When you turned into someone I no longer knew... For a while I couldn't even say your name at all.'

'Then don't say it! Say James, instead! After all, I call you Serena—in private.'

'Serena and James—no, Lord W...my lord.'

'Never?'

'Perhaps. After your visit to St Just you may not wish to see me ever again.'

His face clouded. 'Will I hear of the Captain there? The man whose name begins with "A"?'

She looked blank. 'What are you talking about?' In silence James handed her the note he had bought from the maid. She glanced at it, then with a look of revulsion she threw it from her. She said in a strangled voice, 'For a moment I thought I had misjudged you, Lord W... Wintersett. I was even dolt enough to feel sorrow on your behalf! How glad I am that you have reminded me before you go of your true nature.' Serena's voice grew clearer. She said contemptuously, 'Did you enjoy kissing me so tenderly, arousing feelings I thought I had forgotten, while you knew all the while that this...this piece of filth was in your pocket, waiting to be produced? I acquit you of plotting to ruin me, Lord W... W... The devil take it! I will say it! Lord Wintersett! You were purchasing this note from the landlord in order to accuse me, not paying your bribe. But you are despicable, all the same. I have had enough of your tricks and postures. I never, never wish to see you again! And I wish you joy of your discoveries on St Just!'

She stormed out of the room, calling to John to see to Lord Wintersett.

The next day Serena and Lucy were sitting in the drawing-room of the house in Dover Street. It was a large, airy room furnished in shades of pale yellow and white, and the two ladies in their delicate muslins completed a very pretty picture. But it was evident that all was not well with them, for they were both pale and heavy-eyed. Serena had not slept at all. She had found it impossible to dismiss from her mind the vision of James Stannard travelling south-west to Falmouth. There was a long, tedious voyage ahead of him, and though he would find Anse Chatelet a worthy prize there would be little joy in it for him.

She had been haunted, too, by the events of the previous evening and the curious effect James Stannard had on her. She had told him that she never wanted to see him again, and she still meant it, yet the thought filled her with passionate regret. With a wry smile she recalled her conversation with Lady Pendomer before she had set out for England all those months ago.

'I wouldn't give up control of Anse Chatelet,' she had said. 'Not after all these years, unless I could find a husband I could trust to manage it better than I can myself. . .'

In Surrey, she had thought she had found such a man in Lord Wintersett, and the prospect had filled her with incredulous and humble delight. It was bitterly ironical that he should now be the man who had taken Anse Chatelet from her.

He would return, knowing how unjust he had been all these years. But it was too late. For all the feeling he had aroused in her the night before, it was too late. In London Lord Wintersett had been the cold-hearted manipulator everyone had talked of. The man on the hill had gone forever.

With a sigh Serena dismissed Lord Wintersett from her thoughts and turned them instead to Lucy. She was worried about the girl. It was so rare for her niece to be listless and silent—and these should be the happiest days of Lucy's life! But the shadow of society's reaction to her aunt was casting a shade over Lucy, too. Michael had been a constant caller, and the house was filled with his flowers, but even he had failed to lift Lucy's spirits. It was a relief when Lady Ambourne was announced and Serena got up to meet her, smiling in genuine welcome.

'Serena! How do you go on, my dear? And Lucy, too? I have come with all sorts of good news, a basket of fruit and fresh vegetables from Ambourne, and a suggestion.'

Serena sent for tea and they were soon comfortably settled.

'First, the good news. You must have seen how preoccupied I have been recently—so much that I fear I have neglected you. But, after worrying us all for a while, Perdita is now quite fit again. I had thought I should go down to Ambourne to be with her, but that is no longer necessary. I will remain in London a little longer.'

The two Calvert ladies both expressed their pleasure at this. The Countess continued, 'The fruit

and vegetables I have given to John to take to Mrs
Starkey. . .'

'And the suggestion?' smiled Serena.

'Ah, if I may, I should like first to discuss the
suggestion with you alone, Serena. Perhaps Lucy
could leave us for a while?' As Lucy jumped up to go
Lady Ambourne said, 'Don't go far away, child. This
concerns you, too.'

When Lucy had gone the Countess explained her
plan to Serena. 'What do you think, Serena? Perdita
would be pleased to welcome you to Ambourne.'

Serena hesitated. 'Thank you, Lady Ambourne, but
I do not wish to give society the impression that I
concede defeat. I have done nothing to earn their
censure. And I have hopes that Mr Barnet will come
up with something soon. . .'

'And if he does not? Oh, I know that James gave
him a great deal more to work with——'

'Lord W. . . Wintersett?'

'Did he not tell you?' asked the Countess, opening
her eyes wide in the full knowledge that James would
certainly not have told Serena anything. 'He learned
quite a lot in Hoddesdon. He is almost certain that
the woman with Sir Harry was that wretch Amelia
Banagher. Mr Barnet now has her under surveillance.
He is hoping that she will lead him to this Captain
fellow.'

'I see. . .'

'Do you, Serena? Do you really see?'

'What do you mean?'

'Why should James go to all this trouble to help
you? Going to Hoddesdon, undertaking this long journey to St Just——'

'Oh, no! He's going to St Just to look at his property.'

'Did he say so? I think you are wrong. I think he is going to find out what really happened on the island thirteen years ago. It will be a sad day for him when he does. Incidentally, why have you never told him about Richard and Alanna?'

'I wanted to last night when he came to see me, but it was for all the wrong reasons, Lady Ambourne. I was so angry with him that I wanted to hurt him, to tell him that his brother had died because of Alanna and Richard, not me. He might have refused to believe me, of course. He has refused to trust me so often before. But then I realised I couldn't. However heartlessly he has behaved towards me, I could not tell him this in anger, hoping to hurt him. Perhaps if things had been different. . .if we had still trusted one another, if I could have told him. . .in confidence and . . .love, I might have. But, feeling as I did about Anse Chatelet and his efforts to discredit me, how could I just blurt out to him that his brother had been betrayed by his wife, that his nephew, his heir, the only link with Tony left to him was perhaps not a Stannard at all, but part of the hated Calvert clan?'

'Many would have. As you said, to hurt him.'

'I could not.'

'And I will tell you why, Serena. I think you love him. As he loves you.'

'Lord Wintersett is not capable of the sort of love I am seeking, Lady Ambourne. And if he did once love me, in his fashion, then he will be cured of it by the time he gets back. I told him I never wanted to see him again.'

The Countess smiled and said briskly, 'I think you

are mistaken on both counts, Serena. But it is useless to talk about James for the moment. He must speak for himself when he returns. Now, about my plan. . .'

In the end Serena capitulated. 'But you would be doing so much for us, Lady Ambourne. I hardly know. . .'

The Countess leaned forward. 'The favour is not at all one-sided, believe me. Now that Edward and Perdita are settled I sometimes feel a little lonely—certainly in Rotherfield House! And I myself want to remain in London for the moment. Tell me, is Lucy in love with Michael Warnham? Does she wish to marry him?'

'Oh, yes! But——'

'But the Warnhams are worried, are they not? They are good, kindly people, but they have always been a touch over-conventional. You must let me help. Lucy deserves to be happy. She is a very pretty, well-behaved girl, and I guarantee that the Warnhams will accept her again once the world sees that she is sponsored by the Dowager Countess of Ambourne! Society will soon forget the scandal about Miss Calvert if Miss Calvert is not there to remind them of it. You may trust me, Serena. I know my world. And then, when the mystery is cleared up and your enemies are unmasked—as they certainly will be—you may return in triumph.'

After very little further persuasion Serena agreed to call Lucy in to see what she thought. She was afraid that Lucy might reject the offer out of hand, but she had underestimated the Countess. Within minutes all was settled, the only change in the plan being that Serena would not go to Ambourne, but back to Lady Spurston. She told the Countess and Lucy that she would not think of imposing on Perdita at this time, and there was enough sense in what she said for them to accept this. What she did not tell them was that, once with Lady Spurston, she fully intended to find her way to Wintersett Court. She had to see young Tony Stannard for herself! Almost the last thing Serena did in London was to arm herself with a map of Surrey from Hatchard's bookshop in Piccadilly.

The parting with Lucy was not easy, but both the Countess and Sheba assured Serena that her niece would be well cared for. Michael was also there to support Lucy, and Serena had every hope that their story would have a happy end. The Countess embraced her warmly and extracted from her a promise that she would visit Ambourne before long. Otherwise Serena left London without regret. Her hopes had been so high, the reality so painful. Lord Wintersett was now on the high seas, and she might never see him again. Perhaps it was as well.

CHAPTER TWELVE

SERENA gave Lady Spurston a limited account of her disastrous adventure, but it was enough to rouse all that lady's sympathy, especially when she heard that the Ambournes were championing her. She agreed that Serena's decision to retire to Surrey for a while had been a wise one.

'For you know, Serena, the season is three-quarters over. The world will soon have forgotten your story. And if you have retained the friendship of the Ambournes you will be able to return to London in time for next season.'

'Not,' said Serena with determination, 'not unless I am vindicated, Aunt Spurston. And perhaps not even then. Tell me, where can I find a new side-saddle?'

After some argument Lady Spurston had agreed that Serena could ride out as much as she liked as long as Tom, the stable lad, went with her. So Serena shook out her riding habit, learned, not without difficulty, to master the side-saddle again, and about a week after her arrival set off to find Wintersett Court.

Alanna had been burdened with a sense of doom ever since Lord Wintersett's lawyer had come down to Surrey and had announced that his client was off on urgent business in the West Indies. In three months—perhaps less if the winds were favourable—she would be unmasked. What was she to do? She was unable to sleep at night or rest during the day. She was irritable with the servants, and lost her temper more than once with her son. Day after day she walked the gardens, worrying over the problem. Should she go away—to her home in Ireland, perhaps? The thought was not a happy one. She did not relish living with her sister, looking after an elderly father.

But soon another worry was added to her burden. Fergus O'Keefe called, ostensibly to claim the last two instalments of his money, but making it clear that this was not to be his final visit.

'It's a fine house you live in, Alanna, my darlin'. I like callin' on you here, I do. I'll come again next week, shall I?'

She stammered, apologised, but gave in weakly when he said with a laugh, 'Now, don't be puttin' me off and me an old friend from Ireland. I'll leave you alone when I have me gaming house in Dublin, I promise you. But that costs a mint o'money, Alanna my love, a...mint...of...money. You wouldn't have a bit more put by now, would you? To help out an old friend. You might call it a security. A security! Now there's a thought!' He roared with laughter, but Alanna shivered and promised him another hundred pounds.

She did not delude herself that this visit would be the end of the story. In an effort to escape from the treadmill of her thoughts she walked the gardens till she was exhausted, but the fact was inescapable. In engaging Fergus O'Keefe she had put herself completely in his power.

Serena rode up the drive to Wintersett Court, and when she caught sight of a figure sitting on a bench under some trees she stopped, dismounted and gave the reins to her groom, who took the horse off to the stable yard. She walked over the grass towards the bench.

'Mrs Stannard?'

Alanna stood up. 'I'm afraid I don't. . .'

'You possibly do not recognise me. I was only fourteen when you last saw me.'

Alanna's eyes widened in horror. She jumped to her feet shrieking, 'Oh, no! You must go away from here! Get out, get out!'

'Please spare me the histrionics, Alanna!' Serena made no attempt to disguise her scorn. 'You must know by now that your brother-in-law is on his way to St Just, and that he will learn enough there to expose your lies for what they are.'

'Yes, but there may be a storm, or a shipwreck. . .' Alanna's voice died away. 'Why are you here?' she whispered at last.

'I have come to see the boy. And to ask you why you did it.'

'Did what?' asked Alanna warily.

'Why did you tell the Stannards that it was I who seduced Tony, not that it was Richard who seduced you?'

'What else could I have done?' cried Alanna passionately. 'The Stannards would never have given me shelter if they had known. . . Where else could I have gone? I thought it was safe enough—St Just was the other side of the Atlantic and I knew the Calverts would hush up Richard's part in the affair. The Stannards were desperate to have Tony's son with them. What else could I do?'

'Tell the truth.'

'Tell the truth? And what was that? That your

precious brother had rejected me, had laughed in my face when I told him I wanted him to marry me. Can you imagine what I felt when he told me he despised me? That he had no intention of marrying a damned tame bedmate, that he could have more thrills with the native girls in the village? That one bastard more or less made no difference to him, he had plenty.' Alanna was now hysterical. The successive shocks and lack of rest had been too much for her nerve. Serena tried to persuade her to sit down but she ignored her.

'He said that to me! Alanna Cashel! Not one of his native girls, but a Cashel of Kildone.' Alanna was striding up and down in front of the bench like a caged tiger. She had a handkerchief in her hand and was tearing it in shreds. 'He'd told a different tale when he'd been trying to get me into his bed. Oh, yes! I was mad for him, but I didn't let him see it. I held off till he swore he'd marry me if Tony were not in the way. So I let him love me... And then I found that the baby was coming...' Alanna sank down on to the grass. She was hardly conscious of an audience, but stared into space, reliving the past. She whispered, 'I went to Tony and told him I was going to leave him. He thought I didn't mean it. He refused to even discuss it. So I...so I...shot him.' She hid her face in her hands. Her voice was muffled as she sobbed, 'I got rid of Tony, but Richard didn't want me after all...'

'*You* shot Tony?'

Alanna was suddenly quiet. 'Did I say that? Oh, what does it matter?' she said wearily. 'There's no one else to hear and, anyway, no one can prove it now... I'll be gone soon and you're as good a confessor as any. Yes, I killed Tony Stannard. Everyone was so anxious to hush the whole matter up that no one

questioned that it was suicide. But I wish I hadn't
killed him!' She put her head back in her hands and
wept bitterly. Serena gazed at her in horror. This was
much worse that she had suspected.

Alanna looked up. 'I'm going away,' she whispered
brokenly. 'But I don't know what to do about
Anthony. He cannot travel. But how can I leave him
behind? What will happen to him?'

'He's Richard's son, you say?' Alanna nodded.
'Then he's my nephew and a Calvert, whatever his
birth certificate may say. I'll take care of him if the
Stannards won't. He'll be safe, Alanna.' Serena tried
to feel pity for this woman, but it was impossible. So
many lives wrecked through her wicked selfishness all
those years ago! Alanna looked up and caught the
expression of disgust on Serena's face.

'I've tried to atone. All these years I've stayed here,
hardly living. I have never been to London, never
travelled. All I have done for thirteen years is to act
as companion to Lady Wintersett, and to look after
my son——' She caught Serena's hands. 'You won't
tell him, will you? Anthony, I mean. You won't tell
him that I. . .that his mother. . .'

'No,' Serena disengaged herself. 'Alanna, you know
I cannot agree to keep silent if you stay here, don't
you?'

Alanna nodded. 'I shall be gone by next week, I
promise you.' She started to say something, hesitated,
then started again, 'There's something else I ought to
tell you. I was afraid you'd talk to James. So I. . . I. . .'
She stopped and looked at Serena uncertainly. Then
she said, 'No, I cannot. You will not help me if I tell
you.' She ran into the house as if she was being chased

by the hounds of hell. Serena stared after her. What had Alanna been going to say?

The next time Fergus O'Keefe called, Alanna was ready for him.

'I have no more money,' she said. 'But there are jewels—quite a lot. You can have nearly all of them. I'll just keep a few for myself.'

Captain O'Keefe's eyes gleamed. 'Where are they, Alanna, my soul?'

'They're in a safe place. You'll get them if you take me to Ireland with you. I could help you in your gaming club.'

'Now that is a surprise! It's not often that Fergus O'Keefe is taken unawares, but you've done it, my pretty one.' His eyes grew hard. 'I wonder why you're suddenly so fond of me, Alanna?'

She forced herself to laugh. 'I'm tired of living here, and that's the truth, Fergus O'Keefe! It's a bold man you are, and I've taken a fancy to see more of the world before I die—in your company.'

He looked at her appraisingly. 'Well, you've worn quite well; you might be an asset at that. It must be the good living you've had, but it won't be as easy a life with me, I warn you. What am I saying? Your jewels should make all the difference. A lot, you say?'

'The Wintersetts are rich—and generous. I've quite a few.'

'Where did you say they were?'

'I didn't. And I won't.'

Fergus paused. Then he smiled and said, 'Well I won't say I don't have a fancy for you, Alanna Stannard.'

'Alanna Cashel, Fergus. Alanna Cashel. Wait for

me at the end of the drive. I'll come in a short while—
we can hire a chaise at the next posting station. My
box is already there.'

With tears in her eyes Alanna went to her son's
room. He was asleep. She kissed him, and went to join
Fergus O'Keefe without a thought for anyone else or
a look back.

As for Fergus O'Keefe, he was happy to wait for a
while. He wasn't worried about the jewels—he'd find
them all sooner or later. He might even keep Alanna
Cashel for a time. She wasn't bad-looking, for her age.

Impatient as she was to see Richard's son, Serena
delayed her second visit to Wintersett Court until she
could be certain that Alanna had gone. For young
Tony's sake she was prepared to give Alanna a chance
to get away, but she did not wish to see her again. The
revelation that Tony's death had been murder, not
suicide, had filled her with horror. Nor did she believe
that the act had been the impulse of a moment such
as Alanna had described, for there must have been a
gun. Alanna must have kept a cool head afterwards,
too, for no one had ever questioned the cause of
death. Serena felt burdened with the knowledge.
Though she saw no sense in making it public after all
these years, the Stannards ought to know. But what
about the boy? She must do her utmost to keep it
from him. In the end she decided to wait. The facts of
Tony Stannard's death had remained secret for so
long that another month or two would not make any
difference.

Confirmation that Alanna had disappeared came in
the form of an advertisement in the *Gazette* for someone to act as companion to two invalids—a widow of

high birth, and a child confined to a wheelchair. The address given was Wintersett Court, Surrey.

Serena went straight to her aunt and showed her the advertisement. 'You must help me, Aunt Spurston. I want you to write me a reference for this post.'

'A reference, Serena? Whatever for? There is absolutely no reason for you to seek a post of any kind. Have you forgotten who you are?'

'No, Aunt Spurston, but if Anse Chatelet isn't returned to me then I am almost penniless, and shall have to find something to support me. And I wish to go to Wintersett Court.'

Lady Spurston was astonished, annoyed and finally angry, but she could not persuade Serena to change her mind. After a while she reluctantly agreed to provide a reference, but was outraged when she was asked to write it for a person called Prudence Trask.

'Now, that I will never do, for that would be deceit. Why can't you go under your own name, Serena?'

'Aunt Spurston, the Stannard family would never allow a Calvert to darken their doors.'

'All the more reason for not going there, I should have thought. What are you up to?'

Serena knelt down beside her great-aunt's chair. 'There is something I can do at Wintersett Court, I feel it in my bones—I know I can do more for this child than anyone else could. Don't ask me how I know, I just do. But if I go as Serena Calvert I will never get near him. Please help me! You have been more than kind to me here, but I know you secretly long for your peace and quiet again!'

Lady Spurston took a day to think it over, then agreed to write Prudence Trask a suitable reference.

'This is all against my better judgement, Serena, but
you are clearly set on it. And you have a way with
you, there's no question about that. I only hope you
can carry it off. But what will you do when Lord
Wintersett gets back?'

'I intend to be gone before that, but I can do a lot
in three months.'

Serena's interview with Lady Wintersett in the presence of a representative from the family lawyers was
a curious affair. Lady Wintersett looked ill, and said
nothing. The lawyer fussed and fiddled interminably.
Finally he said, 'Well, Miss er. . . Miss Trask, you
might have been suitable, but I am disappointed that
you appear to have had so little experience. Though
your reference is excellent, it is your only one. We
have had other, more experienced applicants. So
unfortunately. . .er. . .'

Lady Wintersett leaned forward and put her hand
on the lawyer's arm. She slowly nodded her head.

'You wish me to appoint Miss—er—Trask, Lady
Wintersett?'

Lady Wintersett nodded again.

'Very well. Miss Trask, I have decided that your
pleasant appearance and personality outweigh the
lack of experience. The position is an unusual one in
that you will be expected to oversee the running of
the house. Mrs Stannard dealt with all this until she
was er. . .called away. There is a steward, of course,
and a housekeeper. . .' He went into details of salary
and conditions of work, but Serena hardly heard him.
She was elated at having passed this hurdle, but she
was also puzzled. Lady Wintersett had appeared to
take no interest in the interview, so why had she

interfered? It was clear that before her intercession the lawyer had been about to refuse Serena the post.

The need for someone to take Mrs Stannard's place was so urgent that Serena was asked to start as soon as she could, and the weekend saw her installed in her own room in Lord Wintersett's country seat. She was occasionally overwhelmed at her temerity, but whenever she had doubts she thought of her nephew—sick and lonely in his darkened room. It had been explained to her that Mrs Stannard had been devoted to her son, but that she might have to be away for some time. The boy was already missing his mother, and he would need careful handling. Serena could hardly wait to meet him.

On the day after her arrival she was taken to Tony's room. Her heart was beating strangely as she entered, looked towards the bed, and saw the boy lying there. She had eyes for nothing else as she went over to him, and had to bite her lips to keep them from trembling. He was pale and thin, and had none of Richard's earthy robustness, but for all that Richard's eyes looked out at her from Richard's face—he was unmistakably her brother's child. The boy was staring at her. She saw now that he had been crying, and was trying to disguise the fact.

'You've come to take the place of mama,' he said. 'I don't want you.'

'I couldn't do that, Tony! I've just come to keep you company. It must be rather boring lying here on your own.'

His head turned, and Serena saw Lady Wintersett was sitting on the other side. She was regarding them closely. Serena got up in confusion and curtsied. 'Ma'am. . . Lady Wintersett, I'm sorry. I didn't see you

there.' Lady Wintersett smiled and shook her head.
She indicated that Serena should carry on.

'Tony, I knew your parents had been in the West
Indies, so I've brought you some pictures and books
about the islands. Would you like to see them?'

By exercising every ounce of self-control and
patience during the following days, Serena began
slowly, tediously slowly, to win the boy's confidence.
He was not a child. He was now nearly thirteen, at a
suspicious, temperamental age, but by concentrating
on interests outside the boy himself she was gaining
ground. Lady Wintersett's own physician, Dr
Galbraith, soon replaced Tony's former doctor and
Serena had a long talk with him about Tony's state—
the first of many. What he said gave her the courage
to throw open the huge windows in Tony's room and
let in some sunshine and fresh air. When Tony com-
plained that the draught from the open windows made
him cold, Serena was unsympathetic. 'That's because
you don't move! Come, let me help you into your
wheelchair, and you can throw your arms about a
little. No, harder than that!'

It was all uphill work, but Serena persevered. She
had never in her life shirked a challenge, and this one
was perhaps the most important of all. She made sure
that Tony did the exercises Dr Galbraith recom-
mended, rewarding the boy with treats when she saw
he was really trying. Lady Wintersett came to see her
grandson one day with a small puppy in her arms, and
Pandora, so-called 'because she was into everything',
quickly won his heart. He exerted himself more for
the puppy's sake than for anyone else.

'Look at her, Miss Trask! Quick, she's falling into
the chest—no, don't bother, I'll get her!' and he would

swing his wheelchair over to rescue the inquisitive puppy from whatever predicament she found herself in. He grew stronger with every day that passed, and seemed to miss his mother less as time went on—perhaps because his life was suddenly filled with so much that was new.

Serena told him stories about 'my brother Richard', who was always getting into scrapes—falling from trees, getting trapped in caves, doing all the things boys loved to hear, and it became a kind of continuous saga, where truth and fiction were mingled. She wheeled Tony out into the garden and they sat together on a bench under the trees and watched the birds and small animals at their work, while Pandora chased everything in sight, always with more optimism than success. Serena got the servants to seek out the bats and balls from the Stannard boys' childhood, and she improvised games with them on the lawn, games which often ended in laughter when Serena collapsed breathless on to the bench while a triumphant Pandora ran off with the ball or stick. Slowly she and Pandora together roused in the boy a desire to do more. He would stretch out for a ball thrown slightly wide and exclaim in frustration when he missed it, or he would watch Serena wistfully when she played with Pandora or rode one of the horses up to where he sat on the lawn. And all the time Lady Wintersett watched and occasionally, in fact quite often, smiled.

Serena was waiting for the moment when Tony would realise that he could do so much more if he could only walk. She had talked the matter over with Dr Galbraith, who had said that the child had started walking at the normal age, and had made good progress.

'Then the poor lad was ill—I forget what it was, measles or chicken pox or the like—and there were complications. After that Mrs Stannard treated him as such an invalid that he lost the will to use his limbs at all. I argued with her, of course, but she dismissed me and engaged another doctor. It is scandalous, Miss Trask, how much damage can be done by an overfond mother, all in the name of love!'

Tony's cheeks were getting quite sunburned. He grew daily more like his father, his tawny hair bleached by the sun, and his eyes, so like Serena's, sparkling with life. Then one day Serena threw the ball too high. Tony stretched up from the bench, realised he was not going to reach it, and stood up to catch it. He remained there looking down at the ball in his hands for a moment. 'Miss Trask?' he said uncertainly. Serena wanted to shout, to dance, to sing, but did none of these.

'Yes, Tony?' she said casually.

'I... I stood up!' As Tony said this he sat down suddenly on the bench behind him.

'So? What's so extraordinary about that? Some of us do it all the time.'

'But I don't!'

'You do! I've just seen you. Try again.' Serena's tone may have been casual, but all her being was concentrated on this boy. She watched his face as the desire to stand battled with his fear of failure. She strolled away, turned and threw the ball high a second time. 'Catch!'

Without thinking Tony stood again. He missed the ball, for in her excitement Serena had pitched it wide, but he grinned all over his face as he realised what he had done.

'Do you wish to try a step? I'll keep close by you.' Serena nodded encouragingly. Stiffly, awkwardly, Tony Stannard moved towards her, one step, two, three, then he almost fell. Swiftly she took his arm and helped him back to the bench. 'No more today,' she said firmly. 'Let's go back to the house. You must rest for a bit, and tomorrow there's something I want you to see.' As she put him back in the wheelchair she caught sight of Lady Wintersett in the large window overlooking the garden and impulsively waved to her. She was delighted to see Lady Wintersett lift a hand in response. That night a bottle of champagne appeared on the dinner table, quite without comment. The following morning she wheeled Tony round to the huge yard at the side of the house. Here she took him into a disused stable.

'What are we here for, Miss Trask? I want to go back to the bench! I want to stand again!'

'We shall go on to the lawn afterwards, Tony. I want you to meet someone here first. Parks has two inventions to show you. He's been waiting for you to be ready. Parks, this is Master Tony. Show him your puzzles.'

On the floor of the stable were two curious contraptions. One was a kind of wooden frame, a bit like a clothes horse but sturdier, and the other was a clumsy-looking saddle. Tony studied them carefully in silence.

'I think one might be to put on a horse,' he said slowly. 'But what are the things at the side for, Mr Parks?'

'To hold you, Master Tony. It's a special saddle to put on a pony.' Parks went out again and led in a broad-backed piebald pony. 'Like this one.'

Tony's eyes were wide with excitement. 'For me? I can ride? Now? Oh, Miss Trask!'

Serena laughed. 'Try the saddle,' she said. 'And then you can try the pony. If Parks is satisfied that you'll be safe you can ride round the yard. But first look at this.' She took the frame, held it in front of her and took some steps. Tony could now see that the frame took the weight of the body while allowing the legs to move. 'It's Parks's walking machine,' Serena said. 'I gave him the idea, and he made the design and constructed it. You must thank him for his trouble, Tony. He's spent a lot of time on it.'

Tony thanked Parks somewhat cursorily, for his eyes were on the pony. In a few minutes he was sitting on its back, well supported by the curious saddle. Parks examined it carefully and then led the pony out into the yard and they walked round it once in solemn procession. They did this several times, but when Parks gave Serena a significant look she said they must stop. Tony objected violently.

'I'm not tired, I'm not, I tell you!' But Serena was adamant.

'You'll have to go slowly, Tony. I want you to have some energy left for learning to use the frame. When you can walk properly on your own you'll be able to try riding on your own.'

That was the beginning of a time such as Tony had never known. Serena was hard put to it to restrain him from doing himself harm, so eager was he to be on the move all the time. The weeks passed and each day seemed to bring further improvement. The walking frame was used a lot at first but it gradually became unnecessary, and as Tony's muscles strengthened so the extra supports on the pony saddle were discarded. The boy fairly buzzed with happiness, and each evening as Lady Wintersett sat with him before he went to sleep he grew almost incoherent as he told her of his day.

It seemed to Serena that Lady Wintersett was less remote than she had been. She frequently joined them now out in the garden, and though she never said anything she was obviously taking an interest in their activities. Sometimes Serena was worried about the effect it might have on Lady Wintersett's recovery if she ever found out that Tony was not, in fact, her grandchild. She half hoped that it might never be necessary to tell her.

So high summer passed into early autumn. But though the mornings might be chilly the days remained warm and dry, and the gardens of Wintersett Court rang with the sound of boyish shouts and boyish laughter. Tony's tutor returned after the summer break, and it was decided that he should instruct Tony in the morning and late afternoon leaving the boy free to be outside during the main part of the day. Serena rode out with Tony regularly, always accompanied by a groom, but otherwise free to go where she wished. They rode far and wide, but Serena never took Tony up on the ridge. She felt no desire to see it again.

One afternoon in October they returned from their ride rather late. Tony was overdue for his lessons. They cantered into the stable yard, flushed and breathless, and were greeted by the sight of Douce waiting in the yard ready saddled, with a tall, bronzed gentleman standing next to her.

'I was just about to come in search of you,' he said.

'Uncle James!' shouted Tony, scrambling somewhat inelegantly off his horse. 'Look! I can ride!'

'So I see. My congratulations! Someone ought to teach you the finer points of the art—such as dismounting.'

Tony wasn't listening. He ran somewhat awkwardly to his uncle and said, 'I can walk, too!'

'It was worth coming four thousand miles just to hear that, Tony. How are you?' said James, smiling down at him. 'Though I think you have no need to tell me. Come inside, and tell me what you've been doing. Parks!'

'Yes, my lord?'

'See to the horses, would you. Come along, Tony! Miss Trask?'

CHAPTER THIRTEEN

ONCE inside the house Serena excused herself and started for the stairs.

'Miss Trask!' She stopped and slowly turned. Lord Wintersett smiled, presumably for the benefit of those around, for the smile did not reach his eyes. 'Where are you off to? I had hoped you would join us.'

'I. . . I have to change, Lord Wintersett. Lady Wintersett would not like me to appear as I am in the drawing-room.'

'Very well. I thought for a moment you might be attempting to avoid me. I shouldn't like that. . . Miss Trask.'

Serena put her chin up. 'I shall be down as soon as I can, my lord.' He nodded and followed his nephew. Serena continued on her way, but as she mounted the stairs her mind was on the scene in the stableyard. She was furious with herself for the sudden feeling of delight she had felt on seeing Lord Wintersett again. She had only just managed to stop herself from running to welcome him back with all her heart. What a fool she would have looked! His attitude towards her had been cool, almost unfriendly, and when she recalled her words to him before he had left for St Just she could hardly have expected otherwise. He looked well—the sea voyage had obviously suited him—but there were signs of stress and pain in the tanned face. It was no more than she had expected—not only had he been forced to relive the loss of his

brother, but he had also discovered that he had been
so wrong, so unjust all these years. For a man of his
temperament that must have been painful. Serena
pulled herself up short. Why was she feeling so sorry
for him? He was nothing to her! She must go away as
soon as she could, especially since his presence
seemed to have such a devastating effect on her. He
had appeared so unexpectedly that she had had no
time to escape, not even any time to prepare for this
meeting, to remind herself of all the things he had
said and done. Then she frowned and stopped where
she was. She suddenly realised that though Lord
Wintersett had looked coldly on her in the stableyard
he had not looked in the slightest degree surprised.
But how could he possibly have known she was living
at Wintersett Court under the name of Prudence
Trask? She shrugged her shoulders and continued on
her way.

Upstairs she had time to reflect on her position.
Whatever his feelings for Sasha Calvert were now that
he had discovered the truth, he must be furious to find
her installed in his home under a false name. And
what would Lady Wintersett think when 'Miss Trask'
was unmasked? Serena could not regret her subterfuge, for the time spent with Tony had been such a
joy to her and such an obvious benefit to Tony himself. But she had grown to like silent Lady Wintersett,
and was sorry that her employer was about to find
how her companion had deceived her. Perhaps her
son was telling her 'Miss Trask's' real name at this
very moment? Serena went downstairs again with
reluctance, not knowing what she was about to face.

When she entered the drawing-room she found
Lord Wintersett talking to Tony while his mother

looked on. A tray of tea and other refreshments was on the table by the sofa. It was a comfortable domestic scene, with no overtones of drama or untoward revelations.

'Ah! The worker of miracles herself. Come in, come in!' Lord Wintersett's tone was affable but patently false. Serena braced herself and walked forward, but as she sat down she was surprised to receive a warmly encouraging smile from Lady Wintersett.

'Tony has been describing your activities, Miss Trask,' Lord Wintersett began. 'I am astounded at his progress. Some of your machines sound most ingenious. Er. . .you perhaps have a gift for devices?'

Serena said calmly, 'You flatter me, my lord. Parks must have most of the credit for the machines.'

'But you designed them, Miss Trask!' cried Tony.

'Ah, a designer! That sounds more probable. But whatever you are, Miss Trask, you deserve our thanks.' Serena bowed her head. He went on, 'Though I could wish that you had taught young Tony here to dismount more gracefully. In the stableyard he reminded me of nothing so much as a sack of potatoes falling off a cart!'

Serena smiled at Tony's downcast face and said, 'But it isn't every day that his uncle returns from. . . where was it?'

'But, Miss Trask, you know! I told you Uncle James was in the West Indies. We've been studying the maps, Uncle James. I found St Just, and showed it to Miss Trask. It isn't very big, is it?'

With a sardonic look at Serena's pink cheeks Lord Wintersett said, 'Not big, but beautiful, Tony. And Anse Chatelet is a wonderful heritage. Now, it's time for you to be off. You have still to change, and I promised Mr Gimble that you wouldn't be too long. We shall have time tomorrow for more talk, but now you should go to your lessons.'

Tony objected, of course, but received little sympathy from his uncle. The boy gave Serena a resigned grin and left.

'Now, Miss... Trask. The improvement in your charge is incredible, and we owe you a debt of gratitude——' There was still the false note in Lord Wintersett's voice. Serena dared to interrupt.

'But now that you are back, Lord Wintersett, I dare swear you would prefer to choose a companion for your mother yourself. I was only engaged on a temporary basis. Much as I have enjoyed the work with Tony, I feel he hardly needs me any longer, and I shall understand if you wish me to go.' Her voice was matter-of-fact but her eyes pleaded with him not to expose her in front of his mother.

'The question is whether you yourself would rather go, Miss Trask—in the circumstances.'

'I would prefer Miss Trask to stay, James!'

The voice was Lady Wintersett's. Both Serena and James looked at her in astonishment, and James said, 'Wh...what was that, Mama?'

'I should like you to persuade Miss Trask to stay.' She smiled vaguely, got up, and before either of them had recovered enough to stop her she left the room, closing the door carefully behind her.

'Another miracle! Wintersett is full of them, it seems—since you have been with us!' Lord Wintersett turned back to Serena. 'But all the same,' he said grimly. 'All the same, Serena...'

'I know what you are going to say, and I agree with every word. It was deceitful, underhand, and a shame-

ful thing to have done. But I am not in the slightest
sorry! And now I shall go to pack my things.'

'You heard my mother. Those must be the first
words she has spoken for over ten years. She wants
you to stay.'

'It was very kind of Lady Wintersett to intercede
for me, but now you are back I would not be comfortable here. I am glad to have done what I have done
for your nephew——'

'*My* nephew? I think not. Or at least, only in name.'

Serena grew pale. 'You know?'

James got up and walked about the room. 'I think I
know most of it now. The days I spent on St Just were
very enlightening, though they did little for my self-
esteem. For a man who has always prided himself on
being fair-minded, I had been singularly blind. I suppose I understand why you couldn't tell me the truth
about Alanna. But why didn't you make any attempt
to warn me?'

'Would you have listened to me if I had?'

'Perhaps not. Perhaps it was right that I had to find
it all out for myself. I should have gone to St Just
years ago, of course. But at the time there was so
much else to be done— my father's death, my
mother's illness, Alanna and the baby. Disaster on
disaster.' He sat down beside her, his head bowed,
and though Serena knew he neither wanted nor
deserved her sympathy she put out her hand and
rested it on his arm. He took the hand in his, holding
it tightly. 'I thought so much about this on the voyage
home—how I would try to explain to you. . . And now
it seems so inadequate. . .' He got up suddenly and
walked away to look out of the window. 'It seems

idiotic now, of course, but Alanna's story rang so true that we accepted it without question.'

'Parts of it *were* true, but the characters were changed.'

'She substituted you for Richard and Tony for herself.' He turned round and asked, 'Did your father tell Richard to leave the island?'

'Yes.'

'Alanna was ingenious in her half-truths.'

'And desperate,' said Serena quietly. 'She may have betrayed your brother, but she had been equally badly betrayed by mine.'

'It's a sordid story, Serena, and I am ashamed for my part in it. I think I have most of it now. The last piece fell into place when the boy came into the stable yard this afternoon. I could have sworn it was William with you.'

'William?'

'Yes! William the Turbulent, William Blake, William Serena Calvert—call him what you like. The boy is the image of you, except for his hair.'

'Richard's hair was tawny, not dark like mine. My father used to call him his lion.' Serena drew a deep breath and said, 'Lord Wintersett——'

'You called me James a short while ago.'

'It was a mistake. What do you propose to do about Tony?'

'What the devil *can* I do?'

'There's your family to consider—if you had no sons yourself Richard's son would inherit the Wintersett title! That would be wrong.'

'Oh, there's no risk of that! It may interest you to know, Miss Trask, that I fully intend to have a wife and sons of my own in the near future!'

His arrogance irritated her and she said tartly, 'You can buy a wife, I suppose, with all that money you keep mentioning. But how can you be sure you'll have children, not to mention sons?'

He burst into unwilling laughter. 'You wretch, Serena! That's a possibility that had never occurred to me, I must admit!' He suddenly grew sober and said abruptly. 'I owe you an apology. . .much more than an apology. How can I possibly persuade you to forget the terrible things I have said and done to you? You swore the last time I saw you that you never wanted to see me again. I half thought you would run away when you saw me in the stable-yard, and I wouldn't have blamed you if you had.'

'You didn't appear very pleased to see me,' Serena said involuntarily. 'You didn't say anything except a haughty, ' "Come, Tony. . . Miss Trask!" '

'I assure you I was not feeling haughty in the slightest—what a dreadful word, Serena!—I was never more nervous in my life!'

'Nervous! You?'

'Yes, nervous. I was afraid that if I said anything at all out of the way you would disappear. So I was being very careful—both in the stable-yard and afterwards.'

'Why weren't you surprised?'

'Come, Serena! Don't insult my intelligence! Who else could Prudence Trask be? You forget, I knew by then that Tony was probably Richard's son. I guessed you would be with him. I remembered Prudence from a conversation on the hill. And of course I remembered Trask!'

'I am surprised you remembered so much.'

'I don't think I have forgotten anything about you from the day we met.' Serena tried to turn away, but he took her hands again and added quickly, 'But this is beside the point. I was asking you if you could forgive me—and unless you thought me a graceless monster you must have expected me to do so. Have you thought about your answer?'

'I have thought about it all the time you have been away. I saw the heartbreak Richard's actions had caused in your family, and I weighed that against the heartbreak and tribulations in my own. I think the balance is about equal, don't you?'

'But you are the one who has suffered, Serena. And you have been completely innocent throughout.'

'I wasn't alone in that. What about your mother? And young Tony? And Tony's. . .your brother? No, I think it's time to draw a line under the past.'

'You are more generous than I deserve.' He put her hands to his lips and kissed them. Serena snatched them back and moved away from him. She was very agitated. He got to his feet, grimaced and then said abruptly, 'I have had papers drawn up for the return of Anse Chatelet.'

'No! I. . . I don't want it back!'

He looked astonished. 'But I cannot keep it, Serena!'

'Anse Chatelet must go to Tony. You should keep it for him.'

He frowned. 'Are you sure?'

She said, 'Quite sure. Richard would have inherited Anse Chatelet if he had lived, and it should go to his child. But it will have to come as a gift from you. His name will always be Stannard, whatever his parentage. You will make sure he uses his inheritance wisely.'

'You would trust me to do this?'

'Yes. Yes, I would. You have always been described as a just man. You will do this. And now I must go.'

'No! Don't! You must stay! I have only just returned.'

'No, I must go, Lord Wintersett! I knew that you would ask me to forgive you. And I do. But I always intended to be gone from here before you returned.'

He saw she meant it. He spoke rapidly, jerkily. 'Serena, listen to me. I understand your feelings, believe me.'

She shook her head, saying, 'You cannot possibly understand what I feel! I don't even know myself.' She started to walk to the door.

James strode after her and stopped her. 'Wait, Serena! Please!' She looked at him coolly, clearly unwilling to linger. James could see that her mind was made up against him. He said rapidly, 'Let me try to explain.' He led her back into the middle of the room, where they stood facing one another. He took time to find the right words, and at length he said, 'At one time, on the hill, I think we were both very near to complete understanding. More complete than I have ever known with anyone else in my life. . . That friendship was very precious to me, Serena.'

'You destroyed it,' she said stonily.

'I know, I know! In my blind prejudice against the Calverts I destroyed it. But give me a chance to rebuild it! I could, I think, given time. Say you'll stay!'

She shook her head. 'You are not the man I knew on the hill. I could have loved him—no, I did love him. But you forget, I have known you in London. I have heard what they say about you——' He made a gesture of repudiation, but she raised her voice and went on, 'And I know it to be true! There is a hardness in you, a lack of pity, which I hate. I could never love such a man. I am. . .repelled.'

He grew white, and said almost angrily, 'There were times when you did not seem to hate me, Serena. Or will you accuse me of conceit for saying so?'

'I admit there's a strong attraction between us. And given the right circumstances such feelings can lead to love. But not with you. I do not trust you enough.'

'Serena!'

'Oh, I trust you to be fair with Anse Chatelet and Tony, and all the rest. But not with my heart, not with myself. You see, I too thought I had found my other self on the hill. It seemed like a miracle, an enchantment. More than I had ever dreamed of. . . And then . . .and then. . .' She could not continue but walked about the room in agitation. Finally she stopped and said decisively, 'No, I will not allow it to happen again. And if I stay here you will confuse me once more. I cannot stay. I will not!'

He saw that she was not to be moved by appeals to her feelings for him and switched his argument. 'What about Tony and my mother?'

'Tony will manage now. He needs the companionship of men, boys of his own age. . . Perhaps he ought to go to school. If Tony is to live on St Just it is important that he has the discipline that Richard never knew.'

'And my mother, Serena? She surely needs you as much as Tony. I think with you she could in time recover completely.' He saw that Serena was still unconvinced and went to take her hands in his again. When she stepped back he said desperately, 'Serena, I cannot coerce you into doing my bidding as I did on the hill. I know you too well to think of bribing you. I can only appeal to your reason, if nothing else. Without Anse Chatelet you have no real home. Stay here with my mother. I shall remain in London as much as I can; you will not have to see me very often.' He was pale under his tan, and his hands were trembling. For the first time Serena started to have doubts. Could she do as he suggested? Could she keep her unruly heart under control if she saw him only rarely? She was strongly tempted to stay, for she had grown fond of Lady Wintersett, and Tony would not be going to school immediately. And though Lady Spurston would give her a home, Serena knew that her great-aunt would really be happier without her. James was speaking again.

'I really will be in London, Serena. There is much to do there. I was so impatient to see Prudence Trask that I left it all.'

Serena looked at him without really seeing him. What should she do? How was she to decide?

'Serena?'

'Oh, forgive me! What did you say?'

'I said that I have to return to London soon. I must at least attempt to trace Alanna.'

'Is that wise?' Serena regretted this as soon as the words were said, but James clearly understood her.

'What is it that you are not saying—is it about Alanna? Do you believe, as I do, that she was behind the plot against you? Isn't that a good reason for finding her?'

Serena shook her head. 'Your sister-in-law couldn't afford to leave me free to tell the truth about St Just. I had to be discredited.'

'As you indeed were! Have you heard anything from Barnet?'

'He has traced the coach and I believe he has spoken to its driver from whom he had a description of the conspirators. But he has so far failed to trace Lady Banagher. I think Barnet is in Ireland at the moment.'

'Perhaps Alanna is there, too.'

Serena said urgently, 'Surely it's better to let her disappear! You cannot wish for the Stannard name to be dragged into this business.'

'I shall do my best to keep our name out of it, Serena, but if disgracing Alanna publicly is the only way to clear you then I shall do that, too.'

Serena looked at him with troubled eyes. Should she tell him now that Alanna had more to hide than a plot against Serena Calvert? If she did it might make him more determined than ever to find the woman who had killed his brother. And what would happen to her nephew then? She decided to remain silent for the moment. Instead she said, somewhat formally, 'I should thank you for your efforts on my behalf. It will mean a great deal to Lucy, too.'

'Have you seen her since you have been in Surrey?'

'We. . .we thought it better not. She writes once or twice a week. After Lady Ambourne took Lucy under her wing the Warnhams were willing for the engagement to be announced, but Lucy refused to consider marrying Michael before I. . .until my reputation was cleared.' She tried to smile. 'So your efforts are very necessary!'

'Not for yourself?'

'London does not seem so important down here. But yes, I should like to be vindicated, certainly.'

'Then why not stay? I promise not to weary you

with any more attempts to revive our...relationship,
Serena—and I will be off to London quite soon.'

She took a deep breath. 'Very well, Lord
Wintersett. I shall agree to stay here for the moment.
We shall see how we go on.'

Once more she was amazed at the transformation
of his whole personality as he smiled. He took her
face in his hands and held it while he kissed her
gently, saying as he did, 'To seal the bargain, Serena.
That's all.'

She almost changed her mind there and then. This
man was dangerous to her peace! This was a man who
could win her heart again. It would be as well for her
if this Lord Wintersett kept his distance!

James remained in Surrey for a little longer, but took
care not to take up too much of Serena's time. Lady
Wintersett began to speak more freely, and he spent
hours walking, driving and sitting in the drawing-room
with her. He gave Tony more of his attention than
ever before, too. He took the boy out riding, and
Serena found them one afternoon absorbed in the art
of looping the whip. She was sometimes persuaded to
go out with them, and the three of them roamed the
countryside in perfect harmony.

James and Serena met at dinner each evening, but
as it was always in the company of Lady Wintersett
Serena was forced to play her role of Miss Trask.
James watched with amusement 'Miss Trask's' efforts
to stay in character—her struggles to subdue her
natural liveliness and to disguise the air of authority
which was as much part of her as her golden eyes.
With each day that passed he grew more enchanted,
and had difficulty in stopping himself from trying to

spend every minute in her company. He constantly
reminded himself that he still had a very long way to
go before her confidence in him was restored, and that
he must exercise caution.

Each day he put off his return to London, though
affairs there were becoming increasingly urgent,
including the one project which was of paramount
importance to him—the clearing of Serena's name.
He told himself that it was wiser to leave Wintersett
before Serena realised how far their friendship had
progressed. She might well run away from him if she
saw how close they had become again, and he was
eager to keep her at Wintersett Court where he could
at least be sure of seeing her from time to time. But
still he lingered, unwilling to tear himself away.

In the end the matter was decided for him, when
Barnet sent a message that, after a long absence, Lady
Banagher was back in London. She had suddenly left
Dublin, where she had been staying with a certain
Captain Fergus O'Keefe and his lady, and had taken
the packet boat to Holyhead. Barnet was sure that her
destination was Portland Place. James left Surrey that
same day, promising Serena that he would soon have
the truth out of Amelia Banagher.

Serena was astonished at the dismay she felt when
James announced that he was returning to London.
She had grown to depend on his company, and she
suddenly became aware how much her opinion of him
had changed. Without forgetting for one moment how
hard he could be, here in his home she had seen
another side to his nature, had marvelled at his patient
gentleness in dealing with his mother and his apparently genuine interest in Tony. They had often sat

long over the evening meals in the evenings, and Serena had found that she was enjoying herself more than she could have imagined. It had sometimes been hard to remember that she was ostensibly an employee in the house, and more than once she had caught Lady Wintersett eyeing her with amused speculation as she listened to the wit and laughter in the conversation between her son and her companion.

So after James had left for London Serena felt lost and uneasy. The weather had turned wet and she wandered about the house restlessly, unable to settle to anything. She was gazing unhappily out of the drawing-room window when Lady Wintersett said quietly, 'You are missing my son, Miss Calvert?'

Serena turned round to deny this. 'Oh, no, Lady Wintersett! It's just that the rain... *What* did you call me?'

Lady Wintersett smiled. 'I think it's time we had a talk. Come and sit down.' She patted the sofa next to her and Serena meekly sat down. 'James has told me a great deal since he came back from St Just. You have been made very unhappy because of Alanna's lies, and I wish you to know that I am sorry. I blame myself.'

'But why?'

'I should not have accepted what she said so blindly. Indeed, I sensed that there was something wrong with her story, for though I spent hours with the child, I could never see my son in him. Then you came, and of course as soon as I saw you and young Tony together I knew why.'

'I suppose you are angry with me for deceiving you for so long. I... I had no wish to distress you, but it was the only way I could be close to my nephew. Can you forgive me, Lady Wintersett?'

'Easily, my dear. In any case, you have never deceived me, for I knew from the first that you were Serena Calvert. You see, I was walking in the shrubbery the day you spoke to Alanna—before you ever came here. I overheard your conversation.'

'You. . .heard? All of it?' Serena was suddenly afraid. 'Even. . .'

'Even that Alanna Cashel shot my son?' said Lady Wintersett with a note of bitterness in her voice. 'Yes.'

'And you haven't told anyone?'

'I wanted Alanna out of our lives forever, and was afraid of saying or doing anything which might prevent that. It is better so, much better, and I only pray that James will fail in his present attempts to find her.'

Serena looked at her thoughtfully. 'You don't wish to make Alanna pay for her crime?'

'What good would that do? It would not bring back the dead, and it might hurt the living beyond redress. Over the years I have grown to love Alanna's child, and I love him still, even though I now know he was never my true grandson. Indeed, we have come a long way in the last three months, Tony and I. And that is thanks to you.'

'What do you mean, Lady Wintersett?'

'I mean that you taught Tony that he must have the courage and determination to live a proper life. Watching you both has made me look at my own life and I have seen how much I have wasted! When I heard Tony's laughter about this house I wondered at my own silence. Each night when he tells me of his day and I see how eagerly he seizes hold of every minute I am ashamed of my past cowardice. And you have done this—for him and for me. I owe it all to you.'

'Lady Wintersett, please! Don't thank me. Whatever I have done has been willingly done out of love for Tony. I do not deserve your thanks. I have tried to deceive you. And I have taken the last link with your dead son from you.'

Lady Wintersett smiled. 'Strangely, I see more of my dead son's spirit in Tony now—now that I know he is not my son's child—than I ever could before.' She fell silent, then after a minute she went on, 'And far from taking my Tony away, you have given him back to me. I see that that surprises you, yet it is easily explained. Until you came and uncovered the truth I could never understand Tony's death. That he would reject his wife, his child and all of us here enough to take his own life was beyond my understanding. I simply couldn't bear the thought that I had failed him so badly, and it seemed easier not to face it, to escape from it into a sort of dream world of my own. Now I know that he didn't take his own life, and for the first time in thirteen years I am at peace. And I owe that to you, too.' She paused and then continued, 'I suppose some time young Tony will have to learn the truth of his parentage. I hear that he is to have Anse Chatelet?'

Serena said, 'It is his more than mine.'

Lady Wintersett smiled. 'It is as well. You will not need Anse Chatelet, Serena.'

Serena was about to ask her what she meant, when a servant came in with a letter for Lord Wintersett from a Mr Barnet.

'I know his lordship has already left, my lady, but

the letter is marked "Urgent". It is also addressed to
Miss Trask, should Lord Wintersett be absent.'

Serena excused herself and opened the letter, which
had obviously been written in haste. One paragraph
leapt to her eye.

Since writing my last report I have learned more.
First, Lady Banagher is no longer in Portland Place.
She has accompanied Captain O'Keefe to Horton
Wood House near Epsom Common. Second, further information from Ireland leads me to believe
that O'Keefe is the man we have been seeking in
connection with our case, but that he is also highly
dangerous. I must warn you that it would be foolhardy to approach him with anything less than
extreme caution. He left Dublin in order to escape
being arrested for murder. I shall give more information when I return from Liverpool, where I have
arranged to meet someone who knows more about
Captain O'Keefe. Meanwhile be very careful, I beg
you.

Serena sprang to her feet. 'Oh, no! Oh, my God!'

'What is it? What is the matter, Miss Calvert?' cried
Lady Wintersett.

'James is in the gravest danger! I must go to him at
once!'

'What are you saying? Why?'

'Read this note, Lady Wintersett! Barnet specifically warns us against O'Keefe, and James is almost
certainly already on his way to meeting him! He will
have failed to find the Banagher woman at Portland
Place, and I have no doubt that he will follow her to
Epsom. Lady Wintersett, you must forgive me. I must
warn him!'

Serena ran upstairs and rummaged at the bottom of her clothes press. Somewhere, carefully wrapped up, were the boy's clothes she had worn so often before, and she secretly thanked the touch of sentiment which had preserved them so that she could use them again now. Without any hesitation she changed into them, sought and found her pistol, and hurried downstairs. Lady Wintersett was so agitated that she ignored Serena's unconventional dress and urged her to waste no time. As Serena reached the door she called, 'Do take care, Miss Calvert. From what I hear, you could be in danger, too!'

She gave a shriek as Serena waved her pistol and replied grimly, 'Not while I have this, I assure you!' Then Serena hurried to the stables and, after a short consultation with Parks, who knew the area round Epsom well, she set off on Douce with that gentleman in close attendance.

It was a wild night, and heavy showers alternated with periods of brilliant moonlight as the rainclouds swept across the sky. Parks had produced a greatcoat for Serena and she was glad of it, but as they galloped through the night she noticed very little of the wind or rain. Her one thought was to get to the house in Epsom before James.

CHAPTER FOURTEEN

JAMES had arrived in London to find the Portland Place house closed and the knocker off the door. Cursing Barnet for his inaccurate information, he set off on a search round the clubs of London for news of Amelia Banagher, and at White's he met with success. Harry Birtles, who was more than a little the worse for wear, was holding forth on the frailty of women.

'Take the fair Amelia,' he said aggrieved. 'Nothing too good for her—ribbons, furbelows, flowers—even the odd bit of jewer. . .jewellery. What does she do?' He stared owlishly round.

'What did she do, old fellow?' asked James sympathetically, leading Sir Harry to a nearby table. 'Have some more wine.'

Sir Harry drowned his sorrows a little more and turned to clutch James's arm. He looked vaguely surprised to see whose arm it was. 'Wintersett? It's kind of you to listen, 'pon my word it is! But you know what she's like.'

'What has she done now?'

'Gone off! Portland Place shut, no servants, not a word to me! Only got back two days ago, too.' He looked cunning. 'But I know where she's gone, Winsh. . . Wintersett. She can't fool me!'

'Where's that?'

'Tyrrell's place at Epsom. God knows why! He's away in France, know f'r a fact.' Here Sir Harry almost lost his balance in an effort to whisper in

James's ear. 'It's my belief she's got someone down there. Why else go to a godforsaken place like Epsom? 'Cept for the Derby, and that's not run in the autumn, is it? She's with someone else, Wintre... Wintersett.' He looked melancholy, hiccuped and subsided quietly under the table. James left him there.

James returned to Upper Brook Street, deep in thought. Tyrrell was Amelia's cousin, and it was quite likely she would go to Horton Wood House if she wished to hide. But he had no means of knowing how long she would stay there—she might well decide to move on soon, tomorrow even. So, though it was late, he must attempt to see her that night. He quickly changed his clothes, wrote a note for Barnet, and set off on the old Brighton Road to Epsom.

He made good time in spite of the weather, for the road had a good surface, and he arrived at the door of Horton Wood House soon after seven. He had visited Tyrell with Amelia in the old days, and the manservant recognised him.

'I wish to see Lady Banagher on a matter of urgency, Parfitt. Please tell her I am here.' He was ushered into a small room off the hall and asked to wait. After a few minutes the manservant returned and showed James to a beautifully furnished salon on the upper floor. Lady Banagher was gracefully arranged on a sofa before the fire.

'James! How pleasant—and unexpected—to see you! I do believe you are looking handsomer than ever. Pray sit down. Have you dined?' Amelia looked relaxed, but her voice was pitched a little too high, and the hand holding the fan to shield her face from the fire was clenched.

'Thank you, but I haven't come to exchange civilised pleasantries, Amelia,' said James. 'I'm here to tell you that I now know all about Alanna's plot to discredit Serena Calvert. It was she who bribed you, was it not? You and Captain O'Keefe.'

The slender stick of the fan snapped, and Amelia turned white as she said with studied calm, 'I don't know what you're talking about, James. Why do you always think the worst of me?' With an effort she let her voice soften and she said with a pathetic look, 'It was not always so.'

'You may save your charms, Amelia. I know a great deal more than I did when I last saw you.' James paused. 'I know where the false Ambourne carriage came from, and the names of your hired accomplices. I even know what role you played—or should I say roles, *Betty*? And unless you do as I suggest all these details will soon be in the hands of the justices.'

'But that would ruin me!' she exclaimed, no longer able to hide her fear.

'As you attempted to ruin Miss Calvert. Yes. But I rather think in your case it might also mean prison.' Amelia burst into a shrill tirade, but James waited impassively till she paused for breath. 'Are you ready to listen to my suggestion?'

'What is it?' she asked sulkily.

'That you write a full confession, completely exonerating Miss Calvert, which will be sent to a number of prominent members of society, including Sir John and Lady Taplow, and Sir Harry Birtles. After they have read it, and you have confirmed it to them in person, I will help you to escape to Ireland or the Continent, whichever you prefer.'

'That sounds like a very fair offer, Amelia, me darlin'. But you'll keep my name out of it, if you please. It wouldn't be good for my health—or yours, either—if I was named in that document.' A tall, swarthy man came into the room. James regarded him coldly, ignoring Amelia's reply.

'Fergus O'Keefe?'

'So you know who I am already?' The Captain looked thoughtfully at Amelia. She shivered and said desperately,

'It wasn't me, Fergus! He knew before he arrived. I didn't tell him.'

O'Keefe turned his attention to James. 'I don't like anyone making free with my name, Lord Wintersett.'

'Why? Is it such an honourable one?' asked James, his lip curling in contempt. 'The name of a "gentleman" who accepts money to bring false disgrace to a lady? Of a brave soldier who makes war on women? Of a hero who goes to work on a defenceless gentlewoman, with no more than three or four accomplices? I assure you, I have no desire to make free with the name of a coward such as that. Once you have made amends to Miss Calvert I will willingly obliterate your name— and you—from my mind. They both disgust me.'

'James! Don't make him angry! Fergus!' said Amelia nervously. O'Keefe ignored her.

'You might regret those remarks, Wintersett,' he said softly.

'There isn't anyone here man enough to make me withdraw them, O'Keefe. Certainly not you!'

O'Keefe said slyly, 'I wouldn't get so positive about that, my lord! Wasn't I man enough now to persuade Miss Calvert to enjoy me company that night? Has she not told you how she begged for me favours? Didn't Sir John and his lady see her running to welcome me when I came back to her? A fine story that would make in the courts, would it not, now? And whether I was believed or not, the lady's name would be blemished forever, I'm thinking.'

James smiled grimly, and took a pistol out of his pocket. 'You have just signed your own death warrant, O'Keefe. I'll be damned if I let you tell that story in public. And I'll be damned if I let a cur like you go free!'

From his pocket he drew a second pistol, the twin of the first. O'Keefe eyed them and laughed.

'A duel, is it? Begorrah, it's ironic! A fine gentleman like you stooping to fight a duel with me. I'm honoured!'

'You shouldn't be, O'Keefe. It's the only way I can kill you and keep roughly within the law. Here, catch!'

O'Keefe caught the pistol and examined it. Then he walked a distance away, saying as he did so, 'But I might kill you, Lord Wintersett!'

'By all means try, fellow! Or is it only against women that you pit your strength?'

Just as O'Keefe turned with a snarl at James's last remark a door to the side burst open and a sorry-looking figure with wild hair and a torn gown ran into the room towards James crying, 'James, oh, thank God! James! Help me, please help me!'

But O'Keefe, beside himself with rage, had already fired without waiting for the count. The figure, caught right in the line of fire, staggered, tripped and fell.

'Alanna!' James ran to kneel down beside her, casting his pistol aside. He ripped off a piece of her petticoat and made a rough pad, placing it on the growing stain of Alanna's gown. 'Help me, Amelia!' he cried impatiently.

*   *   *

These were the words Serena heard as she came softly up the stairs, closely followed by Parks. The desperation in James's voice was unmistakable, and, grasping her pistol more firmly in her hand, she hurried towards the salon. A dreadful tableau greeted her eyes. Alanna Stannard was lying on the floor covered in blood, and James was kneeling beside her making desperate efforts to stem the flow. Amelia Banagher was nowhere to be seen. A movement to Serena's right caught her eye. The man who had abducted her was moving furtively in the direction of a pistol which was lying on the ground near James. He picked it up and sprang away.

'Now, my fine hero!' he said. 'Now we'll see who it is who dies, Lord Wintersett!' He raised the gun. James looked up, his face a mask.

'Alanna is dying,' he said. 'And you have killed her.'

O'Keefe spared a glance for the woman on the ground. Then he said brutally, 'Amelia's worth two of her.' He grinned. 'And she'll soon have company.'

James's gaze had passed beyond O'Keefe to where Serena was standing in the door, pistol in hand. Without any change of expression he said, 'Any company is more welcome than yours, O'Keefe. Even that of a loathsome toad.'

O'Keefe's finger tightened, and Serena fired her pistol. A howl of pain filled the air as O'Keefe staggered away down the room, his arm hanging limply at his side and blood dripping down from his hand. The duelling pistol lay harmlessly on the ground.

'Take charge of him, Parks, if you please,' said Serena briskly, as she picked up the pistol and handed it to her companion. Then she hurried over to kneel down beside James. Alanna looked ghastly. Her breathing was very faint, her pulse almost non-existent.

'James,' she whispered. 'I have...to tell...you. Confess... I killed... Tony. Shot...him.'

'Don't talk, Alanna. We'll get a surgeon to you soon.'

'No...time. Want you...to...forgive...me. Please.'

James bent his head and kissed Alanna's cheek. 'Of course, Alanna.'

'A life...for...a life, James.' Her voice died away then grew stronger. 'Anthony?'

'Will be safe with us, I promise you.' Alanna's eyes closed, then she opened them again and looked pleadingly at Serena. She was beyond saying anything.

Serena took her hand. 'Anthony will have Anse Chatelet, Alanna. It is his right. You and I, we both love Richard's son. I shall remember that and forget the rest.' A little smile passed over Alanna's face, and then there was nothing.

James got up slowly and then helped Serena to her feet. His face was drawn and tired, and in spite of her own exhaustion Serena had a passionate wish to hold him in her arms and comfort him. Instead she stood looking on as he gazed down at Alanna. Finally he spoke.

'"A life for a life", she said. All the questions, all the anguish, answered in one sentence. Poor Alanna, to have lived with that all these years! And in the end she saved my life,' he said sombrely. Then his gaze turned to Serena. 'And so did you.'

Serena felt like weeping, but she rallied herself and said crossly, 'I very nearly decided to let him shoot you. Did you have to refer to me as a loathsome toad?'

His face lightened and he smiled slightly. 'I thought that would spur you on. O'Keefe had no idea what a defenceless gentlewoman was capable of!' But in reply to Serena's look of puzzlement he only smiled again and then said, 'You must leave here straight away. I take it Parfitt let you in? I can deal with him, but it would not do for you to be discovered here by the surgeon, or anyone else. Parks comes from somewhere round here and he will find you a place to stay.' She was about to protest but he stopped her. 'I cannot come with you now, much as I would wish—I must deal with poor Alanna and the rest. What happened to O'Keefe?'

'Parks took him downstairs. I don't think I wounded him seriously, but perhaps I should go to see?'

'On no account! You must stay in the background. I shall find out how he is and let you know. Meanwhile come with me.'

They went slowly downstairs, and James saw Serena safely hidden in the room off the hall. He came back a few minutes later to tell her that Parfitt had brought in some of the stable lads to guard O'Keefe, though he hardly appeared to need it. He had lost a fair quantity of blood, and was half sitting, half lying on a settle in the kitchen with his eyes closed. One of the lads had bound his arm enough to halt the bleeding, and O'Keefe was now waiting for the surgeon and the parish constable, muttering about a boy in the doorway. Everyone was so shocked at Alanna's death that little attention was being paid to him. Amelia had disappeared, and some of the men had gone in search of her.

'I have told Parks to come here in a few minutes. He already knows where he will take you. You'll be safe with him, Serena.'

'What about you?'

'I shall do my best to clear up the mess here to my own satisfaction. With a slight blurring of detail I think I can satisfy the authorities, too. Thank God you're dressed in your boy's garb! Outside Parks and ourselves no one has the slightest idea who you are, so even if O'Keefe's mutterings do receive any attention the boy will never be found. Parks will take you back to Wintersett tomorrow, and I'll join you as soon as I can. You'll wait for me there?' He looked so anxious and so worn that once again she felt an urge to comfort him, and this time she did not resist it. She reached up and drew his head down to hers.

'I promise,' she said softly, and kissed him. He pulled her into his arms and returned the kiss, passionately and deeply, greedily even, as if he was trying to obliterate the memory of that scene in the salon. She made no attempt to resist, though he was holding her so tightly that it hurt. He was the first to pull away.

'I'm sorry,' he said. 'I'm sorry, Serena. Please, please forgive me. I don't know what came over me. Oh, God, I've said that before, haven't I? But it wasn't the same, I swear. Did I hurt you?'

'No,' she lied. 'And I do understand, James.' She smiled and caressed his cheek, and with a groan he drew her back into his arms, this time simply holding her and drawing comfort from the contact. Parks found them like this and cleared his throat. Reluctantly they moved apart.

'Sorry, my lord. But if anyone saw you they might get a bit of a shock—seeing as how Miss Calvert is still in her boy's clothes. Er...the surgeon is coming up the drive, my lord. He'll be here any minute.'

Recalled to his duties, James kissed Serena's hand and adjured Parks to take good care of her. Then he went out, and after a few minutes of waiting while the surgeon arrived and was taken upstairs Serena and Parks slipped away.

It was nearly a month before James managed to return to Wintersett for more than a night, though he sent daily messages to his mother and to Serena. The formalities of Alanna's death had to be completed, and after that James decided that she should be buried near her family home in Ireland. Her husband's grave was in the West Indies, and no one felt that there was a place for her in the Wintersett vault. James came down to collect Tony, and they made the melancholy journey to Ireland together. Serena visited Lucy and the Countess quite often during this period of waiting, but always returned to Wintersett after a few days. She heard from Lucy that Amelia Banagher had been caught and, though Amelia steadfastly denied having been present at Alanna Stannard's death, she had publicly confessed to helping in the plot against Miss Calvert. Perhaps to save her own skin, she swore that Fergus O'Keefe had in fact spent the night with her, only appearing in the early morning to play his role before Sir John and the others. Sir Harry rather shamefacedly agreed that he had fallen asleep early the night before, and had known nothing till the next morning. The news of Fergus O'Keefe's villainy had spread throughout a shocked London, and Serena's reputation was completely saved. Indeed, society eagerly welcomed her back, and the Warnhams were

anxious to discuss plans for Lucy's wedding. But
Serena had promised to be at Wintersett when James
returned, and she would keep that promise—they
must all be patient just a little longer. What kept her
awake at night was the question of what she would do
after that. James Stannard was gradually becoming
too important to her once again. She had decided
some time ago that she could not live with him. But
could she live without him? She took the coward's
way out and told herself that such questions would
have to be shelved until Lucy's future was finally
settled.

Eventually James and Tony came back to
Wintersett on a brilliantly cold day in November when
an early fall of snow covered the ground. Serena had
been for a walk, and they all arrived at the house
together. There was much exclaiming and embracing,
during which it seemed quite natural that James
should kiss Serena. Confused and laughing, Serena
broke away and said, 'Look at the view, all of you! To
you it may be commonplace, but to me it is incredible—I have never, ever, seen anything more
beautiful!'

'Have you not?' asked James, studying her flushed
face and glowing eyes. 'I believe I have, Serena.'

Lady Wintersett smiled and took Tony's arm. 'And
I believe Tony has grown as tall as I. Come, Tony! I
have so much to tell you, and I dare swear that
Pandora would like to indicate how much she has
missed you, too.' Her voice died away and Serena was
left alone with James.

'You are recovered from your experience at
Epsom? Unnecessary to ask—I can see you have.'
James's voice was studiously light as he led Serena

into the drawing-room. Here they walked to the window and gazed out at the dazzling scene. 'Serena——'

'James——'

They spoke together and apologised together, and both laughed. Serena said in a more natural tone, 'What were you about to say?'

'That I believe it is now truly over, Serena. The whole sad, ugly story. Alanna and my brother are both at rest——'

'And Richard.'

'And Richard, too. Young Tony Stannard will have his Calvert inheritance—perhaps if and when he learns the truth he might even wish to change his name, and Anse Chatelet would then have Calverts in charge again.'

'The name is not very important, James. I don't believe the Calverts deserve any special consideration.'

'There's one Calvert at least who deserves mine, Serena.'

Serena flushed again and said hurriedly, 'What else were you going to say? You hadn't finished, I think.'

James had been smiling at her confusion, but his face grew sober as he said, 'Fergus O'Keefe has been taken to Ireland, too. He's to be hanged for a murder he committed there.'

Serena shuddered, and James put an arm round her shoulders. 'It's no more than he deserves. I would have killed him if I had had the chance, you know that. Don't think of him, Serena. He's a villain. He would have tried to drag you down with him if he had come to trial in this country. As it is, Amelia has made a full confession and you have been completely vindicated. Did you know?'

'Yes, Lucy told me.' Serena moved away. 'And that brings me to what I want to say to you.'

'I can imagine what the substance of it is. But say it.'

'The Warnhams wish Michael's marriage to Lucy to take place quite soon now, and I must go back to Dover Street, James. There are so many things to discuss, so many arrangements to be made. I must go.' Serena's voice held a challenge, and James smiled.

'Pax! Pax, Serena! I have too much respect for my skin to fight you!' He grew serious again. 'I have had time to think recently. There is nothing like a funeral for concentrating the mind on what is important. I know now what I want, indeed I am not sure that I can live without it. But it will take time, and keeping you here against your better judgement will not help me to achieve it. It is no part of my plan to attempt to persuade you to neglect your other loyalties—they are more important than any I can claim at the moment, and you must feel able to go whenever you wish.'

Serena studied him. She hesitated, and then her cheeks grew slightly pink as she said, 'Not more important, James. More urgent.' He drew in his breath, but listened patiently as she went on, 'I cannot decide anything before Lucy is married. That is what I came to England to do, and I must do it.'

James smiled suddenly, that wonderfully warm, all-encompassing smile. 'Then you shall do it with my good will, and any help I can render. Come, Serena! We have work to do!'

Within a week Serena was re-installed in Dover Street. London was less full than it had been during the season, but there were enough members of that

small world known as London society in town to show
Miss Calvert their delight at her return. Invitations
were showered on her, and no concert or reception
seemed to be complete without Miss Calvert's presence. Serena smiled, talked, listened, and inwardly
laughed at the difference. Lucy and Michael had their
own celebrations but were also carried along in
Serena's wake and the Countess stayed a little longer
in London too. The whole world suddenly seemed to
be gloriously amusing to all of them. Though James
took care to be discreet in public, he was often to be
found at Dover Street, visiting the Countess it was
said. Serena found herself relying heavily on his advice
on matters connected with marriage settlements and
the like. In fact she found herself relying on him for
more than just advice—he was becoming far too
necessary to her altogether.

On the night of the reception held by the Warnhams
two days before the wedding the discerning would
have seen that Lord Wintersett was not himself.
Because the Countess had been called to Ambourne
and had been away for nearly a week, the frequency
of James's visits to Dover Street had been severely
curtailed. He had not seen Serena in private for
several days, and he found that he missed her company unbearably. Up till now he had managed to
maintain in public an air of cool indifference towards
her, limiting himself to the two dances permitted by
convention and never arousing comment from the
curious by paying her any undue attention. This had
been far from easy for, to his annoyance, he suffered
quite unreasonable pangs of jealousy. If the perfectly
harmless gentlemen who gathered round Serena
whenever she appeared—Mr Yardley, General

Fanstock and the like—could have read James's mind, they would have retired to their country estates immediately, glad to escape unscathed. But though James counted every dance they dared to dance with Serena, though he knew to a hair how many seconds they spent in her company, he had remained calm.

But tonight was different. He suddenly found he could no longer tolerate their monopoly of Serena's time, and just as she was on the point of accepting Mr Yardley as her partner for the waltz, James cut in ruthlessly and whirled her away towards the other end of the room before Mr Yardley had collected himself sufficiently to protest.

'That was quite shamelessly rude, Lord Wintersett!' exclaimed Serena.

'Miss Calvert,' said James through his teeth, 'I have watched you charm the heads off enough sheep-shanked dolts and idiots in the last few weeks to last me a lifetime. I intend to suffer no more.' With a flourish and a neat turn he guided Serena into a small conservatory off the Warnhams' ballroom.

'Oh, no!' Serena said with determination. 'I have been in a winter garden with you once before, Lord Wintersett, and I do not intend to repeat the exercise. You will kindly lead me back to the ballroom immediately!'

'Just a few moments of your company, Serena! I promise to behave with the utmost circumspection.'

'You will call me "Miss Calvert" in public, if you please. And forcing me into a private room, even to talk to me, is far from behaving with the "utmost circumspection"!' Serena was already moving back towards the ballroom, and James placed himself in front of her.

'A winter garden is not a private room, Ser—Miss Calvert.'

'Let me pass!' Serena was incensed, and tried to push him away. James laughed as he gathered her effortlessly into his arms, looked down at her flashing golden eyes and then kissed her. For a moment she resisted, then suddenly melted against him and for a moment he exulted in the feeling that once again flared up between them. But then she pulled away, exclaimed angrily, 'Utmost circumspection, indeed! I will not let you do this to me!' and slapped his face. The memory of what had happened once before on a similar occasion occurred to them both simultaneously. Serena's eyes widened and she stepped back. 'I didn't mean that, Lord W... Wintersett. Please—I didn't mean it!'

But the present situation was very different from the first, and James was amused rather than angry at the sudden change in Serena's manner. How could a man ever know what Serena Calvert would do next? Did she know herself? He started to laugh, and as she looked at him in amazement he laughed even more. Serena was offended and stalked out of the conservatory, head held high.

The Warnhams' guests were intrigued with the sight of Miss Calvert emerging flushed and angry from the winter garden closely followed by Lord Wintersett—whose appeals to her sense of humour were hampered by his inability to stop laughing. With real heroism, for Lord Wintersett's skills were famous, Mr Yardley hastened to offer Serena his protection.

'Don't tangle with her, Yardley! She doesn't need your help. Pistols or fists, she'd outclass you every time I assure you!' said James.

Since Mr Yardley took great exception to Lord Wintersett's levity, it was as well that Serena regained her temper in time to intervene.

'Thank you, Mr Yardley. But it would be better to ignore Lord Wintersett's poor attempt at humour. I cannot imagine what he means by it!' She looked coldly at James, daring him to explain.

James, recalled to himself, apologised with all the solemnity he could muster—an apology which was graciously accepted. Later that evening, when a set of country dances brought them face to face, James said with a glint in his eyes, 'All the same...Miss Calvert...you have given me a challenge tonight which I will not forget.'

'Pooh!' said Serena, secure in the knowledge that James would hardly demand satisfaction in public, and that there would be little opportunity for them to be private for some time. It took a great deal of determination on her part to stop herself from wondering how that might be arranged.

The Countess arrived back in Dover Street the following day in time for the last-minute preparations for the wedding. It had been agreed that the ceremony should be held in London, and that the celebrations afterwards should take place in Mrs Galveston's Portman Square mansion. All the Ambournes had naturally been invited, but the recent birth of the youngest Ambourne of all made it impossible for her parents to be present, though they had sent the kindest of messages and gifts.

The Countess spent a busy day but made time towards the end of it for a quiet, and private, talk with Serena. After rhapsodising over the new baby and talking very affectionately of Lucy the Countess suddenly said, 'And when are you and James announcing your engagement?'

Serena almost dropped her cup of chocolate in astonishment. 'I... I beg your pardon, Lady Ambourne?'

'It should not long be delayed, Serena. From what I have heard all London is speculating on what happened in the Warnhams' winter garden. They are saying, not without satisfaction I may tell you, that James has met his match at last.'

'But James—Lord Wintersett—has never mentioned marriage to me! And if he did I should probably refuse him.'

The Countess, who had been looking mischievous, grew serious at this. 'You cannot mean it? You and James are made for each other.'

'I doubt it. Lord Wintersett can be charming enough when he chooses, and I will even admit that a surprisingly strong attraction exists between us. But there is a want of humanity in him which I could not live with. I have told him so.'

'So he has broached the subject!'

'Only indirectly,' said Serena flushing uncomfortably.

'Serena, I have heard about your exploits in Epsom. They seem to have gone far beyond what anyone would expect, even of a friend. I wish you to look at me and tell me that you do not love James.'

Serena lifted her head defiantly and started to speak, but found she could not finish. In the end she was silent.

'You see? For better or worse you do love this monster. Now I want you to forget his past crimes and

listen to what I have to tell you of James Stannard.'
The Countess spoke impressively, and Serena's attention was caught, almost against her will.

'James is not an easy man, I know. He has little
patience with self-seekers, rogues or fools, and he
doesn't bother to hide his contempt for them. This has
made him unpopular in London, where there are
many such people. I know what they say, and so do
you.'

'I have experienced some of his contempt myself,
Lady Ambourne. Am I to believe that I am such a
person?'

'Serena, you are prevaricating. You know perfectly
well that the circumstances of your acquaintance with
James have been quite exceptional. And in fact
James's violent reaction to you and your family arose
from the deepest, most vulnerable part of his character—his love for his own family. For, in spite of the
fact that James was a lonely, unloved little boy, in
spite of the fact that his father treated him as a
milksop and a coward if he showed a mite of affection
or fear, in spite of being courted and flattered by half
of London solely for his wealth, James has remained
as true to those he loves as it is possible to be. It isn't
easy to know him—he is very wary of others—but
once he accepts you as a friend there is nothing he
will not do for you. And if he ever allowed himself to
fall in love—as I believe he finally has—then he would
be as anxious to please, and as vulnerable to hurt, as
anyone else. More so. Do not, I beg you, Serena,
reject such a man lightly. You would be throwing
away a chance of great happiness. Now that is
enough,' Lady Ambourne added with a sudden

change of tone. 'Tell me, where will Lucy live after she is married?'

They talked a little longer, but Serena was impatient to be gone. She knew she still had to see Lucy, and she wanted time to think.

Because of all the fuss of the wedding preparations, Serena had had little opportunity to have any real talk with her beloved niece. Though she knew it was unnecessary, she wanted a last reassurance that Lucy was happy with the thought of sharing her life with Michael Warnham and living in England. She need not have worried. Lucy had no doubts, was serenely certain that this was what she wanted.

'Everyone I love most will be here in England. How could I not be happy to live here?'

'Everyone?'

'Oh, Sasha, you need not pretend with me! I am young, but not stupid. Lord Wintersett may have returned Anse Chatelet to you, but you will never live there again.'

Serena wanted to say that Anse Chatelet was no longer hers, but for the moment that was Tony's secret, so she just asked, 'What makes you think so?'

'Sasha! You will be at Wintersett Court—everyone knows that! And, do you know, I like Lord Wintersett. He has been very kind to Michael and me.'

Serena tried in vain to disabuse Lucy's mind of the notion that Lord Wintersett meant anything to her.

'I know you, Sasha, and it has become clear to me during the past weeks that you are in love with Lord Wintersett. You cannot hide it from me, but don't worry, I won't say anything to anyone else—except perhaps Michael. It is plain for all the world to see that he is nutty about you.'

'Nutty!'

'Oh, forgive me—I meant to say that Lord Wintersett is more than a little enamoured of you. Oh, Sasha, I shall miss you! I shall be happy with Michael, I know, but I shall miss our fun together. Thank you, my dearest of aunts, for all the years we have had together. And I hope. . .no, I am sure that you will one day be as happy as I am. I cannot wait for tomorrow.'

They kissed each other and Serena left Lucy to her dreams. She herself had a more wakeful night. Everyone, it seemed, was conspiring to persuade her to look with favour on James Stannard. In the eyes of those closest to them they were apparently the perfect match. Serena wished she could believe they were right. Or that she could be sure they were wrong!

CHAPTER FIFTEEN

LUCY's wedding was the most joyous of occasions.
The weather was cold but brilliantly sunny, the guests
were cheerful, and the young couple radiant. The
marriage of the Warnham heir would always have
been an important event, but the Warnhams clearly
loved Lucy for her own sake, and the pleasure they
took in welcoming her into the family circle gave
Serena every reassurance she might have needed.
Long after the happy couple had left for a bridal tour
to the Continent the celebrations in Portman Square
continued. Lady Warnham, who was a great deal
cleverer than her loving mama imagined, had suggested that Lady Spurston might be persuaded to
come to London if Mrs Galveston invited her. As a
result of Lady Warnham's forethought, the two old
ladies spent a most pleasurable time before and after
the ceremony indulging in an orgy of gossip and
reminiscence and the rest of the party were left to
enjoy the feast and the music of the military band
provided by their hostesses.

Lady Ambourne was one of the first guests to leave.
She had come to Lucy's wedding, but was anxious to
return to Ambourne and her family. However, she
took time to have a word with Serena before she left.

'Lucy looked a dream in her bridal clothes, Serena.
She is destined to be happy, that one!' adding with a
roguish look, 'I shall look forward to seeing you in
yours! Oh, forgive me, my dear. I am an interfering

busybody—Perdita could tell you more of that. But I find it impossible not to interfere when I see people turning aside from happiness. Be kind to James; you will not regret it. And come to Ambourne soon!'

Serena started to look for her aunt. They were leaving London the following day to return to Surrey and she wanted to be sure that the old lady was not too tired. But Lady Spurston was having a nap in Mrs Galveston's private parlour, and Serena had not the heart to disturb her. Instead she wandered down to the library, glad to escape from the revellers and find a quiet place to rest herself. Her head was aching—and her heart.

James finally found her here. He came in, closing the doors carefully behind him, then stood watching her where she sat on the sofa.

'You look tired, Serena. Or sad. Are you thinking of Lucy?'

'Why should that make me sad?'

'I'm not suggesting for one moment that you have any doubts for her—no one who has seen her with Michael Warnham possibly could. But you two have been so close—it would be natural for you to feel a sense of loss.'

Serena's eyes filled with tears. Through all the preparations and fuss no one else had thought of this, not even Lucy herself. She looked down to hide her distress. James came over, cursing himself for a tactless fool, and sat down beside her. He took her hands in his. 'Serena, don't!' He swore as a teardrop fell on his hand, and pulled out his handkerchief. 'You've no idea what it does to me to see you cry—I didn't think you could. Here, let me wipe your cheeks. We can't have the legend of the indomitable Miss Calvert ruined.'

She looked up and smiled through her tears at this, but the sight of his face looking down at her so anxiously entirely overset her, and the tears fell faster than ever. He took her into his arms and cradled her, uttering words of comfort, till the sobs gradually faded and Serena regained her composure. She smiled apologetically and gently removed herself from his arms.

'Thank you,' she murmured. 'Forgive me.'

'For what?' he asked with a wry smile. 'For sharing your unhappiness with me? I count it a privilege. And it gives me hope you might agree one day to share more, much more than that. Oh, God, Serena, if only you knew how I regret the past! You say you have forgiven me, but the past lies between us like a serpent. If it were not for that I could now make you forget the loss of Lucy, and every other unhappiness. I know I could persuade your body to love me—you tell me that every time we kiss, so how could I not know it? But I want much more than that! I want your mind, your spirit, call it what you will. I once knew the enchantment of that communion, and I shall never forget it, nor cease to desire it.' His voice dropped as he said this, and Serena had to strain to hear. She turned towards him.

'James. . .' she said tentatively. 'James, it isn't the past which divides us. I've told you before, it's your lack of. . .' She stared at the man before her, and could not continue.

His face dissolved, as numbers of images flashed through her mind—James giving an unknown boy a ride to console him on his birthday, James in the park with no reason to trust or like Sasha Calvert, yet

sensing her loneliness and taking her for a drive,
James comforting the woman who had killed his
brother, looking on her with such sorrow as she lay
dying, James taking trouble to get to know Alanna's
son. The images increased—James teasing, James
laughing, James with his mother, James looking so
worried just minutes before—until finally all the
images melted and refocused into one, beloved, familiar face. She gazed at him in wonder, then she smiled
and her wonderful eyes glowed as she started to speak
again. 'James——'

The doors of the library opened and Mrs Galveston
came in with a flourish. 'Ah, Lord Wintersett,' she
began, 'There you are! Oh, forgive me, Serena, I
didn't see you at first. We are just about to set up a
whist table for the gentlemen. Would you like to play,
Lord Wintersett? And if you'll forgive me for saying
so, Serena, it isn't at all the thing for you to be in here
alone with Wintersett. This may be a wedding party,
but——'

'I'd be delighted to join you, Mrs Galveston,' said
James swiftly. 'Miss Calvert was saying she had the
headache, so I am sure she will be glad to be left in
peace. I will take my leave of you, Miss Calvert. Shall
I see you again before you return to Surrey?'

Under Mrs Galveston's watchful eye what could
Serena do but murmur regretfully that she was setting
off the next day? But as he reached the door she
asked idly, 'Are you intending to stay in London long,
Lord Wintersett?'

'I think not. I have been away from home rather a
lot recently and my mother will soon start complaining
that she never sees me.'

Serena hesitated and said, 'My young friend

William—I believe you know him?—has been asking after you. You might see him when you return to Surrey.'

The man standing by the graceful bay mare gazed over the countryside below. The brown and grey landscape was silvered with frost, but the afternoon sun was warm. He turned swiftly as he heard hoof-beats coming up the hill, and his heart leapt as he saw a woman with a laughing, glowing face riding to meet him. She came to a halt beside him and he held up his arms to help her dismount. But when she was on the ground his arms still encircled her.

'I half expected to see you dressed as a boy.'

'I was tempted, but I decided it was too dangerous. People might be shocked if they saw me as I am, but if I were dressed as William they would be infinitely more shocked. Besides, my groom is just below, at the bottom of the hill.'

'Very nearly respectability itself. But I thought it was William who wanted to speak to me?'

'No, James. I came as Serena, Sasha and William. All three of us have something to say to you, here on the hill where we first met.'

'What is it, my love, my torment and my very dearest friend?'

'We. . .' Serena hesitated, then she threw back her head proudly and said, 'I love you, James, and I trust you, completely, finally, for always.'

He gave a great shout of joy, and lifted her high in the air. The horses moved restlessly, and Serena said, laughing, 'Douce and Trask are shocked! Put me down, James, before they abandon such a disgraceful pair.'

James set her down and, still holding her hands in his, he said, 'Then I shall make us both honest again. Will you marry me, Serena? Will you give me, in William's words—the other William, of course, "Th'exchange of thy love's faithful vow for mine?"'

Serena smiled as she replied,

'"I gave thee mine before thou didst request it."'

James took her hands to his lips and kissing them he said slowly, 'I think Juliet had the best words after all.

> My bounty is as boundless as the sea,
> My love as deep; the more I give to thee,
> The more I have, for both are infinite.

Serena's eyes filled with happy tears as he added, 'If you will marry me, Serena, I swear I will love you and cherish you for the rest of our lives.'

'Yes! Oh, yes, James, please!' He kissed her again and again, muttering incoherently as he did, and Serena laughed and eagerly responded. After a while he took her to the edge of the hill and they stood looking down on the patchwork of fields below.

Serena said dreamily, 'It seems an age since we first met here on the hill. The first words you spoke to me were a quotation. It is fitting that we are quoting again now, though Romeo and Juliet were a sad pair of lovers in the end.'

'Quite. I can think of a much more appropriate play.'

'Which is that?'

'*The Taming of the Shrew*, of course!'

'James!' Serena turned in his arms in mock anger.

He quickly imprisoned her again, and when she protested he said, 'I have to protect myself against those fists of yours, Serena! But now that you are here. . .' James bent his head to her again.

Finally she murmured, 'There's one other thing. . .'

'What is it, my love?'

'If I promise to be a model wife the rest of the time would you, just once a year, take me for a week or so to some remote spot where I might be William again? To dress and ride like William?'

'You may have a fortnight,' said James largely. 'As long as you promise to become Serena again at nightfall?'

'Done! Now I should go back to tell Aunt Spurston of our engagement. Will you come with me? She will be delighted, I think.'

'I thought she disapproved of me?'

'And you so *enormously* wealthy, James?' said Serena opening her eyes wide.

'Devil! But that reminds me, my enchanting, loathsome toad,—you gave me a challenge a short while ago in London. Are you prepared to answer it now?'

'What challenge was that, my darling viper?' asked Serena laughing.

'Just this.' And, taking her gently into his arms, James proceeded to demonstrate how calm, how breathlessly exciting, how comfortable, and how dangerous a kiss in reply to a challenge could be.

To the surprise of no one, but to the delight of all who were close to them, Miss Calvert and Lord Wintersett were married very soon after. When Lucy returned to London she was often heard to complain that she saw a lot less of them than she might have expected, for they spent much of their time at Wintersett Court, and took their nephew several times to St Just—until the arrival of young Edward Anthony Stannard made that difficult. And once a year they disappeared for a fortnight. No one ever found out where.

MILLS & BOON®

*M*akes
any time
special

Enjoy a romantic novel from
Mills & Boon®

Presents™ *Enchanted*™ *Temptation*®

Historical Romance™ *Medical Romance*™

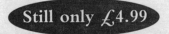